and his SONNY HAWKE *thrillers*

"If you look for the voice of authenticity in your books like I do, you'll swoon over Reavis Wortham. He's Texas true, and that's a fine thing to be."
—**C. J. Box**

"There's a term we use in the west, *the genuine article*, and those words fit Reavis Wortham to a Texas T."
—**Craig Johnson**

"Think: Elmore Leonard meets James Lee Burke."
—**Jeffery Deaver**

"The most riveting thriller all year!"
—**John Gilstrap**

"Wortham writes well in describing the forbidding landscape and the difficulties of those trying to survive in it, not easy even when people aren't trying to kill you. Readers who like action-packed thrillers that leave a lot of bodies should find *Hawke's War* to their liking."
—**PCA Mystery & Detective Fiction Reading List** on *Hawke's War*

"This elegant thriller that reads like a modern-day Western conjures memories of gunfighters of lore, a tradition Hawke proudly holds up while riding the ranges of Texas's Big Bend National Park . . . Wortham hits the bull's-eye dead center in this tale worthy of Louis L'Amour and James Lee Burke. Once of the best thrillers I've read this year, featuring emotional landscapes as sprawling as the physical ones."

—*The Providence Sunday Journal* on *Hawke's War*

"This is one of those books, settings, and characters that make you want to cheer for the U.S. of A. In addition, this is also a brand-new character to star in his own brand-new series, so there's a lot more of Hawke to go around. Add in humor, a great cast of characters, both good and bad, along with a terrific ending, and *Hawke's Prey* becomes a must-read for everybody."

—*Suspense Magazine* on *Hawke's Prey*

"An intuitive, creative synthesis of contemporary politics and policy into an original plot . . . Wortham writes excellent action sequences and knows how to ratchet tension. With pitch-perfect West-Texas flavor, Wortham paints a complex picture of Ballard, providing good backstories for his large cast of characters."

—*Lone Star Literary Life* on *Hawke's Prey*

Also by REAVIS ZANE WORTHAM

HAWKE'S TARGET

A SONNY HAWKE THRILLER

REAVIS Z. WORTHAM

PINNACLE BOOKS
Kensington Publishing Corp.
www.kensingtonbooks.com

PINNACLE BOOKS are published by

Kensington Publishing Corp.
119 West 40th Street
New York, NY 10018

All Kensington titles, imprints, and distributed lines are available at special quantity discounts for bulk purchases for sales promotions, premiums, fund-raising, educational, or institutional use. Special book excerpts or customized printings can also be created to fit specific needs. For details, write or phone the office of the Kensington sales manager: Kensington Publishing Corp., 119 West 40th Street, New York, NY 10018, attn: Sales Department; phone 1-800-221-2647.

This book is a work of fiction. Names, characters, businesses, organizations, places, events, and incidents either are the product of the author's imagination or are used fictitiously. Any resemblance to actual persons, living or dead, events, or locales is entirely coincidental.

ISBN-13: 978-0-7860-4180-0
ISBN-10: 0-7860-4180-3

First printing: July 2019

10 9 8 7 6 5 4 3 2 1

Printed in the United States of America

Electronic edition:

ISBN-13: 978-0-7860-4181-7 (e-book)
ISBN-10: 0-7860-4181-1 (e-book)

This one is for my cousins,

DERRYL FRANK JOHNS *and* GARY MAXFIELD.

Thanks to you guys from that tiny community of Chicota for your military service in Vietnam. Derryl, I still owe you for the time you once pulled me out of a ditch when a car ran me off the road—and Gary, I didn't take that lighter when I was ten, I found it on the road in front of your mama's house. Just wanted you to know.

Chapter 1

Dressed head to toe in Mossy Oak Brush camouflage, Alonzo Wadler settled onto the ground in the Coconino National Forest outside of Flagstaff, Arizona. Virtually invisible, he sat perfectly still with his back against a tall ponderosa pine, a position allowing a 180-degree view of the open forest.

As had become his recent habit when he was alone, Alonzo's mind went to his wife, Betty. They'd met in high school back in Gunn, Texas. There wasn't much to do in the tiny community tucked into the Southeast Texas piney woods back in the 1970s, only spitting distance of Louisiana, but their interests were virtually the same and they were inseparable. Once he graduated, they reluctantly moved into the family business for a steady income.

He smiled at the memory of her sweet smile and auburn hair.

The crack of a limb an hour later caused his heart to pound so loud he expected it to be heard by anything with ears. He tensed and willed his nerves to calm.

Index finger along the outside of the rifle's trigger guard, only his eyes moved to scan the landscape.

Several deep breaths later, a mature doe wandered into view, just off the wooded ridge stretching across his field of vision. The hunter wasn't happy with the mule deer's appearance, especially when she stopped and tested the air with her black nose. Not liking what she smelled, she gazed across a downed tree laying between them and seemed to meet his eyes.

Hearing a slight noise, her head swiveled toward the opposite direction. Alonzo took that moment to rest his left elbow on a bent knee and snug the .270's stock against his shoulder. He placed the Simmons' Aetec crosshairs an inch above her back.

She turned back and stomped her delicate hoof, hoping to startle whatever it was that worried her.

She stomped again and watched.

Go on, mama.

An experienced hunter since boyhood, he knew better than to move. Motion gives predators away. They know this and use it to their advantage when they're hunting. The now-familiar pain in his stomach broke his concentration. It was increasing in frequency and duration, but this time seemed to be nothing more than common acid indigestion. He wanted one of the pills in his pocket, but his reason for being there was too important, and he toughed it out.

The deer's soft brown eyes fixed on his pine tree, knowing something was there, watching. She stomped once again, and finally decided to trust her instincts. Stepping quickly off the trail, she disappeared into the forest with a flick of her tail. A second, younger doe trotted into view and was gone.

The man sighed. He'd been so focused on the first muley that he hadn't seen the second. His dad, Marshall, spoke from the past, his deep East Texas accent strong in Alonzo's memory.

"You weren't aware. Even if you're not looking directly at something, you'll catch it out of the corners of your eyes. It could be a bird flitting through the trees, or a rabbit hopping through the underbrush.

"When you see it, stay still. Don't turn your head. Everything that lives in the woods is watching, and you'll give yourself away. The rabbit looks for movement, and when it sees something, it freezes, because it knows whatever is out there is likely looking for dinner."

They hunted together in the East Texas pines when Alonzo was a sprout, and he recalled the terrible day that made him who he was. As everything else in his life, it was driven by his grandfather, Daddy Frank Wadler. That old man ruled the entire clan from the time they were born.

It happened on a squirrel hunt one frosty morning with his dad and Daddy Frank. They arrived in the Sabine River bottoms less than a mile from their farmhouse as the sun announced the day. Ten-year-old Alonzo never liked being around his granddad, even under the protection of Marshall.

Slipping quietly through woods thick with pine, pecan, and oak, Daddy Frank led the way with Marshall and Alonzo following closely. The drainage area that suited him overlooked a wide, leaf-covered slope leading down to the creek.

"Sit there, boy." Daddy Frank pointed at a red oak tree. His voice was low, authoritative. "A tree behind you breaks up your outline."

The boy met his dad's gaze. Marshall nodded, and they settled to the ground.

Without fail, Daddy Frank pulled out a plug of Days O Work chewing tobacco, end cut of course, and carved off a chunk with his razor-sharp knife. Tucking the chew into his cheek, gray with stubble even back then, he closed the blade, returned it to his pocket, and became still as the trunk itself.

Daddy Frank didn't even lean over to spit. He swallowed the tobacco juice when necessary, something even the most hardcore chewers couldn't do. He expected Alonzo to be just that still.

Dawn revealed the thick bottomlands. A squirrel scampered into view, jumping from limb. When the time was right, Marshall raised his little .22 semiautomatic rifle to aim with glacial speed, and one shot through the head brought the squirrel to the ground.

Daddy Frank always made it clear that the hunter was allowed only one round per squirrel.

"Shoot 'em through the head, son." Marshall leaned toward the boy's ear and spoke softly. "They'll fall dead and won't scare the others. You don't want it flopping around down there in the leaves."

Alonzo's voice was barely a whisper. "Don't the shot scare the others none?"

"Nope. I reckon rifle shots might sound like thunder, but it's usually movement that scares animals. The woods ain't quiet like books tell you. They're alive.

Limbs rub together, or break and fall. Deer step on sticks. Bodark fruit falls hard, and pecans and walnuts hit with a lighter sound. Trees fall sometimes, too, and make a racket when they tear the limbs off other trees on the way down. Things with four feet rustle through the leaves covering the ground. When you open your ears, you'll hear more than most folks realize."

On that morning so long ago, a fox squirrel scampered into range, and the headstrong boy ignored Daddy Frank and Marshall's lessons. He decided to try a shoulder shot with his .22, like when they hunted deer. At the time, the youngster was full of what the old men up at the Gunn store called "piss and vinegar." He figured he'd show both of them a thing or two about what he'd learned from *Outdoor Life* and *Field & Stream*.

Indecision at the last moment, and nerves, caused the boy's aim to waver. Alonzo missed badly with the open sights. The little body tumbled through a web of limbs on the way down, creating more disturbance than he thought possible. The dying squirrel finally caught itself by a hind foot in a thick tangle of vines, hanging upside down long enough for Alonzo to sneak a peek at Daddy Frank's angry face. The horrifying rattle reached their ears, and the boy worked the rifle bolt to finish it off.

"Nope." Daddy Frank's voice was low, but clear. "You had your chaince, Alonzo. One shot."

Alonzo's face flushed hot and tears filled the boy's eyes at the horrible damage he'd caused. "But it's *suffering*."

"That's right." The old man sitting twenty feet away

shifted to glare at the boy. "It's your own damn fault, because you didn't listen to your daddy."

The dying squirrel dangled by the claw on one toe, blood dripping from its nose. The pattering sound on the dry leaves below was clear as a bell in the still autumn air.

"Just this time? I won't do it again." He turned toward Marshall. "Please, Dad."

Marshall paused and threw a glance at *his* dad, who glared back. "No. Don't you let him do it, Marshall. Sit there and watch, and listen. You'll learn to mind after this."

Right then, Alonzo hated his grandfather. For five minutes that seemed an eternity the boy stifled great, shuddering sobs that would only get him into more trouble.

Men don't cry. Daddy Frank, the elder, made sure that no one in his family cried, or he'd give 'em something to cry about.

It was obvious they were teaching Alonzo a lesson, but one that hurt. The boy got mad and raised the rifle again to finish the squirrel's suffering and end the terrible ordeal.

"I said no, boy." Daddy Frank looked as if he were going to stand. It should have been Marshall's place to correct his son, but the old man held every family member in a vise grip. "You quit that cryin' or I'm gonna give you something to cry about."

Marshall raised a hand. "Dad, let me . . ."

"No! You ain't much tougher'n that little crybaby of yours. It's about time somebody got ahold of him to toughen that boy up." The harsh leader of the Wadler family had whipped every man who challenged his authority, and no child was going to disobey.

Alonzo looked at his dad for support, but Marshall wouldn't meet his eye.

The squirrel died moments later and released its hold, falling with a soft thump on the moist humus covering the ground. The woods quieted, until another fox squirrel scampered through the treetops and stopped only yards away to crack a pecan.

"Shoot." Marshall's soft voice barely carried. "Show him."

Alonzo's voice broke. "I can't." The tears trickling down his cheeks were frustrating, and the boy desperately wanted to wipe them away, but he knew the movement would give them away, once again bringing a reprimand. "I might miss again."

"Shoot, he said, and this time through the head." Daddy Frank spoke from right behind the boy, startling him. He'd moved without a sound. "Do it, or I'll slap your jaws into next week."

The boar squirrel stopped to test the air, offering a perfect profile target. A blue jay's call echoed through the woods.

Blinking his eyes clear, Alonzo took careful aim with the .22 rifle. When the squirrel's head disappeared behind the front sight, he squeezed the trigger, slowly, the way he'd been taught.

The little rifle cracked and the squirrel fell from the limb, dead long before it hit the ground. Only then did Alonzo wipe his eyes.

"Better'n the last shot." Daddy Frank grunted and shifted his chew. "Marshall, you get ahold of this prissy kid and teach him not to backtalk me, or I will, and then it'll be me and *you*."

Now, sitting directly on the ground almost dead center of a vast pine forest over a thousand miles from East Texas, Alonzo Wadler held a Remington .270. The traditional workhorse of deer hunters across the nation was loaded with 130-grain Hornady SST rounds.

Each morning for the past three days, Alonzo arrived in the dark, sat beneath the exact same tree, and waited above a trail leading to an old trapper's cabin a mile away. He'd scouted his prey's tracks on the first day and was confident he'd be by again. It was only a matter of time.

A pine cone fell from high above, and a tarantula wasp buzzed his head. Time passed slowly after that. Nothing wandered into view, and by noon his stomach pain had intensified to the point of watering his eyes. He closed them for a long moment, trying to decide if he wanted to call it a day.

When he opened them again, a bearded man stepped into view, returning down a trail he'd walked days earlier. The man shouldn't have been in Arizona at all. A California felon, he'd jumped bail and left the state.

Alonzo's nervousness vanished like water down a drain. The rifle rose almost of its own accord, and the sight picture through the scope jumped into focus. The hunter moved the barrel ever so slightly to the right and acquired first a head and then the shoulder, the only exposed parts in the thick brush.

The safety came off with the flick of his thumb. Two more steps, and the prey was in the open. Alonzo shifted the crosshairs to his chest and waited.

The scope's crosshairs moved to the second button down on the man's shirt.

Alonzo's finger gently tightened on the trigger. He never felt the trigger's break, but the rifle cracked. Despite the scope's jump, he saw a fine red mist explode behind the man's body as the SST round destroyed his heart and lungs.

Dead before he hit the ground, career criminal and convicted felon Nicholas Barbour fell where he stood.

One shot and another one down.

Alonzo shivered in relief, because he'd wanted this one so badly. "Payback, you son of a bitch! I wish to God I could kill you twice." A sob hitched in his chest and he choked it down.

Regaining control, he stood without ejecting the spent round and picked up the thin nylon ground tarp he'd been sitting on. Quickly rolling it into a ball, he stuffed it into the small daypack that had also served as a backrest through those long days of waiting. Slinging the rifle over his shoulder, he scanned the ground.

Two days of waiting, and the only sign he'd ever been there were a few scuffs that most people would miss. Instead of crossing the distance and kicking the man's face into a pulp like he'd fantasized a hundred times, Alonzo hurried in the opposite direction from the already cooling corpse.

The day was growing warm when Alonzo reached his four-door Dodge pickup parked on a lonely gravel road in the national forest. He unlocked the door, stripped off his camo clothing, and pitched everything into the back seat before starting the big diesel.

He chased down a pain pill with a swallow of water from a bottle in the console and shifted into gear.

Prissy boy, my ass.

Chapter 2

The eastbound desert highway west of Alpine, Texas, shimmered under a hot afternoon sun. I thumbed off the Dodge truck's cruise control at the sight of the blocked two-lane up ahead. The opening riffs of "Gimme Shelter" by the Rolling Stones was too loud at the slower speed, so I cranked the volume down a couple of notches and studied the backup of vehicles.

Over in the shotgun seat, my black Labrador retriever, Buster, perked up when the engine brake growled, slowing the dually. My cell phone rang. I would have ignored it, but it was Major Chase Parker, commander of the Texas Rangers Special Unit.

The clot of cars slowed me to a crawl and I pulled onto the shoulder to talk. "Yessir."

"I need you to meet me in your office. We have a little situation that's gonna be your baby." He spends a lot of time in my part of west Texas, though the Rangers' Division Headquarters is in Austin.

"I'm feeling fine, thanks."

He was silent on the other end. "Okay. I get it. How're you healing up?"

I'd gotten banged up during a little altercation not long before that like to've put me in an early grave, so I was once again riding a desk. "Thanks for asking. Like I said, fine. What's up?"

He sighed like he usually does when we talk. "We have some kind of vigilante crossing the country, executing people who've gotten off murder raps on technicalities, or felons who're out on pardons. It looks like he's gonna be here in Texas any day now, from what we've been seeing. This one's right up your alley."

"He send you a schedule?"

"You want to quit being a smartass?"

"I can try, but I ain't guaranteeing nothin'. You at the office now?"

"I'll be there at three o'clock."

I scanned the chanting crowd. "I'll do my best."

"Fine. See you then."

He hung up, and I dropped the phone into an empty cupholder mounted in the floorboard to study the cars overflowing from the Marfa Lights viewing area's parking lot. More vehicles lined both sides of the table-flat highway.

"Again?"

Buster turned his brown eyes toward my side of the cab and woofed.

"You're right. Ethan's gonna be right in the middle of this one, too. It looks bigger'n the last demonstration."

A few people were sitting in the viewing center's shade and smoking. They were a mix of our part of the world out there in far West Texas, white, brown, and

Native Americans. I figured they were there to protest the existence of the Trans-Pecos pipeline for the second time in a month.

Trying to be friendly, I raised two fingers from the steering wheel in a wave, because that's what Texans do, but no one lifted a hand in return. At least no one used a similar gesture to tell me I was number one.

Men and women in straw cowboy hats and a bright assortment of do-rag bandanas and wave caps watched with impassive faces as I pulled back on the highway and rolled through the corridor of vehicles. Once clear, I mashed on the foot-feed, knowing I'd find the drivers, and the action, less than two miles ahead.

I was right. The highway was completely blocked with protestors who had the light traffic choked down to a standstill. Half a dozen sheriff's department Police Interceptors, highway patrol cars, and trucks idled with their lights flashing both on the shoulder and in the pull-out at BranCo's pipeyard, an enclosure scraped clean of vegetation and full of pipe and equipment. A handful of pipeline workers watched from behind the safety of a brand-new chain-link fence.

I pulled onto the dusty shoulder and crept past the line of cars, crunching over rocks, sage, and low-growing cactus until I came to a tangle of highway patrol cars and other vehicles belonging to television and news crews. There was an open space between clumps of prickly pear and yuccas. I steered onto the hardpan and stopped at a knot of people milling in the bright sunshine between the highway and a bobwire fence that ended at the pipeyard.

Buster rose to follow me out of the truck. "Stay. I'm gonna leave this AC going for you, but don't get over here and lock the doors on me."

He woofed an answer and sat back down to stare out the windshield. He'd locked me out a year earlier when I left the big dummy in the truck cab with the motor running. Annoyed that he couldn't go, Buster pawed at the driver-side armrest and hit the electronic lock. After my runnin' buddy, Sheriff Ethan Armstrong, finally showed up with a Slim Jim to pop the lock, I took the spare key from the fob and kept it in my pocket from there on out.

Even with so many people around, I wasn't worried about leaving the truck running. Nobody was going to get inside with those white fangs of his showing.

Once outside I was blistered by angry looks from the trapped locals, vacationers in their automobiles, and the protestors between them and the yard gate. A dozen or so activists turned at the slam of the truck door and stood shoulder to shoulder with the intention of blocking my way.

Knowing better'n to show any emotion to the angry collection of anti-pipeline marchers, I locked eyes with a Native American demonstrator in a blue bandana. He looked to be ten years younger than my age and sixty pounds heavier. Ignoring the man's ALL LAND IS SACRED poster, I headed directly toward Big Boy, maintaining a steady pace.

His glare held solid until I was close enough for him to recognize the *cinco peso* Ranger badge on my shirt. Big Boy's eyes flicked up to my new straw Cattleman hat, then down to the hand tooled double-rig belt holding the 1911 Colt .45 semiautomatic.

I was banking on the Texas Ranger reputation to work its magic, and when I was close, he waved a turkey wing fan in my direction. "You *Rangers* think you're something."

"We just represent the law."

"*Your* law is allowing this!" A young woman spat in the dirt beside my black Lucchese boot. She held a sign saying, SAVE OUR LAND! "It isn't *our* law."

"I don't like this pipeline any more than y'all, but I have my job to do, just like you." I waved a hand toward a local news crew filming the protest. "They got what you wanted. Let's just do it without any real trouble and everybody get in out of this heat, how 'bout that?"

Big Boy took my measure for a beat before stepping back to let me pass. I nodded my thanks. "Much obliged."

I kept walking, ignoring a barrage of comments thrown at my back, and hoping none of those folks were violent. I couldn't hold my own right then because I hadn't fully healed up from a bullet wound on my side.

There was more rattling and yelling behind me, but it was for the benefit of the camera that swept in our direction. A cluster of officers gathered around half a dozen demonstrators who'd chained themselves to the pipeyard's access gates.

Looking cool and collected, Presidio County Sheriff Ethan Armstrong knelt on one knee, talking to a female protestor. Gathered in a semicircle around them, the demonstrators of varied races in bandanas, feathers, and matching T-shirts were all waving signs, flags, and Indian totems. Seeing me, Ethan rose and tilted his Stetson back. "Howdy, Sonny. Somebody call you?"

Despite his calm voice and demeanor, I saw the fire in my high school friend's eyes. "Nope. I's headed to Alpine when I came up on this little demonstration." I scanned the ring of shouting protestors. "Most of these folks are strangers."

"Might near everyone." Ethan leaned in close so I could hear over the noise. "I sent Malone for some bolt cutters and then I'll clear this bunch out."

"You taking any of 'em to jail?" I didn't see anyone in cuffs.

"Not yet. I'm gonna get these dummies loose from this gate and give 'em a chance to leave on their own. If they don't, *then* I'll cuff 'em up."

The crowd was there protesting the new pipeline going through our county and under the Rio Grande, a hundred miles away. In a way I was kinda with them. The pipeline was an eyesore, and those cleared dirt highways through the desert brush were custom-made for illegal immigrants and drug smugglers to travel north from the Rio Grande, to disappear into the American fabric. They usually followed landmarks along dry creek beds and arroyos, power lines, and even railroad tracks, but the easement made it faster and easier.

One of the BranCo construction crews still working on the pipeline called in when a red Chevy Avalanche following a temporary access road drove by bigger'n Dallas. Border agents arrived in minutes and made a bust that was on the national news that night. Five hundred pounds of grass packed in the Chevy had a street value of over a million dollars, and it was the first time we'd caught drug runners using the new "superhighway" over the buried pipeline.

I took a good long look around us. The mixed group waited on the shoulder and in the highway to see what would happen next. A couple of the deputies were urging them to clear the road while the drivers caught in the protest were getting increasingly irritated.

Ethan held a hand up to a shouting demonstrator who shook a sign. DEFEND THE SACRED! "Hold your horses, bud. We're gonna be here for a while yet." He turned back to me. "You look like you're feeling better."

I rolled my shoulders in answer. "Better. Still a little stiff. I'll be on the desk until the Major turns me back out."

"You're doing a lot of that lately. You're the only Ranger I know who spends more time off duty than on. Maybe you need to stay out of trouble."

"Well, I'm trying. I've been out of circulation for a while, but then again, when I'm on, it's intense."

He chuckled and scanned the crowd, which hadn't stopped chanting from the moment I arrived, "Stop the lies, water is life, stop the lies, water is life!" That one was about the threat of oil leaks and the pipeline's potential to contaminate the water table. Water is precious anywhere, but in the arid high desert north of Texas's Big Bend National Park, its value is even higher.

I studied the crowd that was growing angrier by the minute. "How long ago did you send for the bolt cutters?"

Ethan shrugged. "Half an hour."

"I have a pair in the truck."

His eyes lit up. "Good. We can have 'em loose by the time Malone gets back." He whistled through his teeth and waved the highway patrol officers back to the gates. I went to the truck. The crowd around us parted like water around a rock as I cut through the pack. A DPS helicopter clattered overhead, circling the blockade.

Like I figured, no one had bothered the truck, and Buster was looking cool as a cucumber sitting there behind the wheel in air-conditioned comfort. He was keeping an eye on two young men leaning against a nearby car parked half on and off the shoulder. I knew if they so much as stuck a finger inside the truck, they'd draw back a nub.

They'd already figured that out for themselves.

I was reaching for the back passenger door handle when I looked over the bed and past the young men's vehicles to see a silver four-door Ford F-150 caught in the traffic jam. The windows in the back seat were blacked out, but I had a good view of the passenger's distinctive profile through his open window. He looked familiar, and I ran through my mental files, trying to remember where I'd seen him. It took a moment to recollect he'd been on a wanted poster I'd seen only a couple of hours earlier.

We don't get the old-fashioned paper posters mailed to us anymore, but Ethan's secretary always prints those that come through email and pins them to the bulletin board in the sheriff's office. I also get them through email from the FBI and other entities, as well as from Major Chase Parker.

The driver saw me looking in his direction and his head snapped back so fast I almost heard his eyeballs click. The passenger with a nose that looked to have been flattened with a shovel raised his right hand as if to adjust his cap, keeping it against his cheek way too long.

A name popped into my head. Miguel Torrez. Wanted for armed robbery, drug trafficking, and assault with a deadly weapon. I suspected the driver to be Eric Navarro, his cousin, whose résumé was much longer.

"Buster, you have the truck."

I swiveled to find Ethan, but he'd knelt back down to speak with one of the people chained to the gate, and I couldn't see him. The rest of the deputies were turned away from me, and I couldn't catch anyone's eye. Luck was on my side. Navarro had stopped close to a Nissan coupe in front and couldn't back up because of a jacked-up white Chevy pickup right on his back bumper.

Or so I thought.

Torrez said something to his cousin behind the wheel, then swung back around to see if I was paying any attention. My eyes were still on the truck, and that's all it took. Navarro snapped something to Torrez, who reached down for what I assumed to be a weapon. Navarro shifted into reverse and slammed against the Chevy truck with the lift kit. The distinctive thump and crunch of collapsing metal floated over the crowd as the Ford's tailgate caved in under the Chevy's high bumper.

There was no subtlety at that point. "Ethan!"

The people nearest me quit chanting. Their silence spread like ripples across the crowd, and nearly every head there focused on the apparent accident. Navarro dropped his truck into gear and hit the gas, crunching the Nissan coupe's back bumper and shoving it into a sedan in front.

He jammed the Ford back into reverse to make a three-point turn. I was fifty yards closer than any of the other lawmen who were rushing to converge on the scene. From those circling in the helicopter, it must have looked like filings drawn to a blue Ford magnet.

I drew my .45, the smooth Lexan-covered Sweetheart grips familiar in my hand.

The entire situation was a nightmare. Too many cars, too many civilians, and a possibly armed felon who didn't care about anyone but himself. That *possibly* armed qualification evaporated when Torrez stuck his arm through the open window and swung an old-school Mac 11 subcompact machine pistol in my direction.

My stomach dropped. "Everybody down!"

He squeezed the trigger, streaming a burst of .380-caliber rounds in my direction. At the same time, Navarro spun the wheel to U-turn into the open lane and escape back the way they came. He stomped the gas, burning rubber and white-smoking the tires. The truck jerked forward when the Goodyears shrieked on the concrete.

I zigzagged between the parked cars as the truck's rear end slewed when Navarro dodged a car parked on the shoulder. Centrifugal force jerked Torrez's arm and widened the arc of spraying bullets. Hot lead punched holes in half a dozen vehicles between me and the escaping felons, spiderwebbing windshields and side windows. People dropped like wheat before a scythe.

A deputy opened up with his service weapon at the same time Navarro centered the truck in the westbound lane to get gone. The distinctive gunshots hammered the air, crisp as hammer blows. A second pistol joined in, doubling the volume.

I raced around the tail end of the white Chevy pickup, close enough to see Navarro behind the wheel, swinging a pistol around in my direction with his right hand. He fired three times over his left bicep as the truck accelerated.

My .45 came up, the sight picture lining up on his ear. Planting my feet, I fired three fast times. Two of the three missed, but the third caught him at the tip of his shoulder. He dropped the pistol and slumped forward. The angle was such that I no longer had a clear target, so the next best thing to do was empty the magazine into his left front tire. It exploded with a dull pop, wrenching the wheel from Navarro's suddenly limp hand at the same time Deputy Frank Malone roared up in his cruiser in the open lane and slammed into the Ford head-on.

Navarro disappeared into the expanding airbag in an instant.

At that point, lawmen appeared from between the logjam of idling cars. With nothing but empty desert on the opposite side of the Ford truck, they weren't worried about collateral damage and opened up with a fusillade.

Muscle memory took over, and I thumbed the magazine release on my Colt, slapped in a fresh one, and raced toward Malone's steaming car. At the same time, the passenger door on the truck popped open, and Torrez tumbled out on the opposite side, taking cover behind their now well-ventilated pickup. He stuck the machine pistol over the bed and held the trigger down, spraying rounds in still another random arc that kept both innocents and lawmen scrambling for cover.

The passenger door to Malone's cruiser creaked open, and he crawled across the front seat to roll onto the hot pavement with a pump shotgun in his hands. Once outside, he crabbed toward the rear of his cruiser to keep it between him and Torrez. "What'n *hell!!!??*"

I ducked down behind the car and joined him at the rear. "Bad guys."

His face was red from the deployed airbag in his cruiser. "No shit!"

"Driver's dead, I think. There's another one."

Gunfire rose.

Malone flicked off the shotgun's safety. "I saw him just before we hit."

I pointed toward the passenger side of the wrecked truck. "He might pop up over here."

"Hope he does."

Staying low, we duckwalked behind the steaming cruiser, and I peeked up through the back glass. Thinking himself protected by the pickup's open passenger door, Torrez was changing magazines beside the truck's right front fender.

I waved for Malone to follow. "Move now!"

Struggling to insert a fresh magazine in the little machine pistol, Torrez was intent on the weapon and didn't see us closing in. There wasn't any shouting from us to throw up his hands or surrender. We got the angle and stopped the threat when Malone's 12-gauge joined in with my .45. Hit with a full load of Number 4 Buck and the rounds I threw in, Torrez dropped to the hot, sandy shoulder and was still.

I rose and saw Navarro slumped over the steering wheel. One look at his dull eyes told me he was forever out of the picture, too. "Clear!"

Ethan and the deputies eased around the truck, not really taking my word for it, but I didn't blame 'em. I watched Ethan kick the Mac 11 out of the dead man's reach. Through my gunfire-damaged ears, the sound of screams and crying filled the silence. The helicopter circled overhead, adding to the chaos, and I realized my side was on fire.

Holstering the pistol, I felt around to see if I was shot again, but it was only the half-healed wound that had woken up.

Shaking his head, Ethan joined us beside the wrecked cruiser. "What'n hell was that all about?"

"There was paper out on those two this morning and they saw I'd made 'em. You're gonna have to speak up a little, though. My ears are ringing to beat the band."

A DPS State Trooper opened the truck's back door and whistled. "Good goddlemighty! Y'all take a look in here!" He waved to the other officers. "I bet there's a million bucks in cash back here."

"Drug money, I bet." Taking his Stetson off, Ethan wiped the sweat from his forehead with a trembling hand. "Looks like you're back on the desk again, and I think I'm gonna recommend that Major Parker keeps you there for the rest of the year."

"Can I count on you for that?"

Chapter 3

Daddy Frank Wadler leaned over the back of his pickup bed, scratching a three-day growth of chin stubble and talking with his oldest son Jimmy Don and Sheriff Buck Henderson. Surrounded by tall East Texas pine trees, they were parked on a remote black-top road in Jasper County, in the old-time tradition of country friends. "Let me get this straight, them two Mexicans got themselves killed out there in the Big Bend and lost my money?"

Sheriff Henderson's Police Interceptor was parked on the shoulder behind the pickups, as if he'd pulled them over. His lights were off. "I told you it was a bad idea to hire outside contractors."

The old man, who was in good shape for his early eighties, grimaced in disgust. "What happened?"

"They made the delivery in Arizona like they were supposed to, but got caught in some kind of protest outside of Alpine."

"What the hell were they doing in Alpine?" Daddy Frank's eyes blazed. Fingers laced and forearms resting on the bed of his white truck, Jimmy Don stared at the ground under his feet.

"One of 'em must've got the idea to get off the interstate and run the back roads." Buck adjusted his straw hat. "Frankly, it kind of makes sense, unless they had an idea to head for Mexico and take the money, which they might have been doing. I sure as hell never trusted 'em in the first place.

"Anyway, we'll never know. From the report I read, somebody recognized one of 'em and they lost their damned minds and opened up with automatic weapons. They should have turned around and gone back the other way and nobody would have known, but they got themselves killed. Now here's what I think. You need to quit with these experiments and go back to how we've done it for years."

The old man's eyes flashed. "That ended when that damned BranCo oil company showed up, them and their damned pipeline. Things have to change around here whether we want it to or not."

Buck waved at the thick pines around them. "Hell, they offered you enough money for the easement. I don't see how a cut through the woods can cause trouble. It'll be cash in your pocket."

"Sixty thousand dollars ain't shit, and it's my land."

"They'll take it under eminent domain if they want to."

"That's what they said."

"So, take the money."

"No. I don't stand aside for no man, and I damned sure ain't steppin' aside for that damned BranCo bunch."

"Dad, I don't see what it'd hurt." Jimmy Don scratched under his gimme cap and reset it higher on his forehead.

"All we'll need to do is move the storage containers deeper in the woods. We can have that done long before they start cutting the easement."

"Well, for one thing, I don't want no easement through our place. You know as well as I do they'll clear off a road that we don't have no control over. That means company people'll be driving through here any time they want. We can't have that."

"They'll mind their own business."

"Like hell they will, son. Didn't you see where that line'll be laid? It's too close to the fertilizer barn for one thing, and the truth is I don't want no feds this close to the business."

"Ask them for more money, then, it it'll make you feel better, and then buy off the crews who come through here. They'll look the other way if they see anything. Hell, put them on the payroll and they'll be double happy."

"No, I ain't paying for my own land over'n over again."

Buck lit a smoke. "There's nothing you can do about it. They've already cut all the way up to your line from the north, and I found out last week they've closed a deal with the Simpsons just south of the Morris land. That means it's just you and that Morris, and I heard they're about to take the deal for more'n sixty thousand. BranCo's coming through here come hell or high water, and you need to make the deal and figure a way around 'em."

"Oh, I've got an idea all right. I'm gonna shut this whole damn project down and make 'em move the line west of us."

"That makes sense, since the Sabine's too close to the east." Jimmy Don laced his fingers. "But how you gonna do that?"

"Alonzo's bringing me back a present from California, along with my money. Plastic explosive."

The sheriff's eyes widened. "What are you gonna do with *that*?"

"I'm . . . we're gonna blow their damned pipeline up in half a dozen places, along with that Beaumont refinery BranCo owns. They might force their way through here, but they're gonna pay for it in more ways than one."

"What makes you think you can get away with it."

"Because I'm the meanest sonofabitch in East Texas, that's why."

Chapter 4

A week after the shoot-out between me and the two fugitives out on Highway 67, Major Chase Parker sat in an antique wooden chair on the opposite side of the coffee table in my living room. Legs crossed and his Stetson hanging from the toe of his boot, my lanky supervisor studied the black-and-white photos of my ancestors on the opposite wall.

"I swear, I never saw a Ranger who spent more time on the desk than you."

"People keep telling me that. It's not like I *want* to be there."

He raised an eyebrow. "You gonna offer me a beer?"

I didn't have a chance to answer before my wife Kelly came around the kitchen island and crossed into our recently converted, open-concept living room. We agreed on most of the renovation and subsequent decorations, including whitewashing the original shiplap revealed when we took down the sheetrock, but I held the line on the oversize words, letters, and cotton bolls that were all the rage.

She handed him an ice-cold Coors, the original yellowbelly. "You want lime with that?"

He grinned at my petite bride. She may be small in stature, but she sure fills a room when she walks in. "No ma'am. This isn't a Corona, and thanks for that, by the way, because I never liked those skunky Mexican beers."

The screen door opened, and my dad pushed through with a paper bag full of groceries in each arm. He saw the Major and grunted. "Well looky here, another real-life Texas Ranger."

It was funny hearing it come from him, a retired Ranger who's damn near as famous as Joaquin Jackson. He passed one of the bags to Kelly. "You're spoiling these boys. Neither one's worth it."

The screen door opened again, and in came Mr. Beck Tillman, waddling like a duck from the missing big toes he'd lost in Korea. Though the old war veteran looked to be on his last skinny legs, he was still as tough as boot leather.

Major Parker's eyes flicked to the pair and then to me. "The bus from the old folks' home just pull up?"

Dad laughed and took off his hat, now that his hands were free. "All right. We deserve that. Howdy, Major."

"Mr. Herman. Mr. Beck."

Mr. Tillman put his hat on the coffee table, crown-side down, and settled onto the couch with a grunt. "We interrupting anything?"

The suddenly full living room was silent while the Major took a long swallow of beer. "Naw, I just came by to check on Sonny and talk to him about an assignment. He missed our last meeting because of that little altercation out at BranCo."

He had my interest. I'd been sitting around too long. "Tell me more."

Arms full of groceries, Kelly headed for the kitchen. "I'll get y'all a beer, too, Dad."

"Much obliged," Mr. Tillman said.

Major Parker plowed ahead. "I need to get you busy and away from anything in this part of the world that can shoot. I was thinking of assigning you to investigate a couple sexual-harassment claims against elected officials, now that the governor's gotten approval from the legislature."

The Major watched my reaction. In the past, those kinds of allegations by folks in office, and that included judges and lawmakers at the capitol, were investigated in-house, in the legislature, then reported to the Senate and House leadership. The governor's idea was to guarantee that claims were taken seriously and charges filed when the Rangers found reason to make arrests. I must have looked like I'd swallowed something bad, because his eyes glinted, and I knew he'd been pulling my leg.

"I wouldn't do that even to you, Sonny. There's a case I want you in on. It fits this new position I made for you. When we talked on the phone last week, I mentioned we're tracking an individual who's executing known felons who've gotten off on technicalities."

"Vigilante?"

"Yep, and we don't have any idea who he is, but we're finding his work. The first person he killed was a paroled felon named George Crawford out in California. Our guy put an end to his career by sticking a knife in his heart in a parking garage."

Dad chuckled. "That you know of."

The Major frowned. "Huh?"

"You *think* he was the first."

"Good point, Mr. Herman." A flicker of a smile crossed the Major's creased face. He's like all of us in the law-enforcement brotherhood, and the way it used to be when people revered older folks with a lifetime of experience to draw on. "We're *thinking* the first one was Crawford. Second guy, we think, was Nicholas Barbour. He'd been in and out of institutions most of his teens and diagnosed as delusional."

Dad opened his mouth to ask a question, and I cut him off. "How so?"

The Major turned back to me. "He tried to break into the governor's house out in California to make him pay for what he said the governor had done to him. Then he was in and out of jail for five years before he completely lost it and killed an entire family. Institutionalized again for five years, they let him out on early parole, and he got drunk and ran over a woman, killing her.

"Barbour was released on bond, and they found him wearing a bullet hole in the Coconino National Forest out of Flagstaff. He shouldn't have been out of the state, but then again, he'd already proven himself untrustworthy."

Now that Dad was retired, he didn't believe in being politically correct. "Sounds to me like your vigilante did us all a favor."

Mr. Tillman grunted an agreement.

The Major raised that eyebrow again. It was one of the few ways he ever expressed emotions. "Some people say so."

The Old Man leaned forward to ask another question, but the Major stopped him. "We figured out they were connected after another felon who should have been in jail in New Mexico was murdered. Same thing. A lifetime of crime, out of prison when he should have been serving life, and then found dead in a car in a Walmart parking lot with his brains leaking out of a twenty-two-caliber-size hole behind his left ear."

"If it's the same guy, then he's coming thisa way." The Old Man took a beer from Kelly and grinned his thanks. She handed Mr. Tillman another and went back to put away groceries. She's usually not that kind of Susie Homemaker. My bride's the strongest, most intelligent woman I've ever known, but she loved the Old Man and Mr. Beck and would do anything for 'em.

"That's what we think. No one had any idea they were connected at first. Local law enforcement was working on individual cases until he killed *another* released felon up in Amarillo and a sharp detective there remembered something he'd read a few days earlier about the murder in New Mexico. He started putting the pieces together and contacted the FBI because the guy's crossing state lines. They called us."

"What happened in the panhandle?"

"Guy named Shanquille Clay Gibson murdered a college girl at West Texas A&M in Canyon. They arrested Gibson because of a video that showed him talking to her in a Subway restaurant that night. Detectives in Canyon held him and continued to question the guy for several hours even after he said he wanted a lawyer. Apparently, he's diabetic and started to break down because he didn't have his meds, and finally confessed. They searched his house, found the victim's underwear and a scarf containing both their DNA. They also found more than a dozen pairs of other panties that they've since tied to past murders, but the whole thing was thrown out when the judge determined that the evidence was tainted fruit."

When a case is dismissed on a technicality in the criminal-justice system, it often means that a court has determined that the evidence sought to be used against the defendant was obtained in violation of his constitutional rights. It was obvious that the Canyon detectives should have stopped their interrogation when Gibson asked for a lawyer, so anything they found after that was what the legal system calls "fruit from a poisonous tree."

I watched the expression on Dad's face. He'd left the Rangers years earlier when he and every other lawman in the state failed to find the man who'd killed my mother. I knew what he was thinking, that if he'd arrested Mom's murderer, he couldn't have stood it if the guy had gotten off.

"Where'd they find Gibson's body?"

Major Parker nodded. "Laying between two cars in the side parking lot of an adult club in Amarillo called The Bare Den out on Loop 335. It was a twenty-two to the back of the head again."

"So he's finished there, according to his past kills, and is headed somewhere else."

"Yep." The Major tilted his beer. "Now the question is which way did he go. We have no idea."

I pictured a map in my head, thinking of the main roads and interstates radiating from Amarillo. "If he takes 40 or goes north, he'll be out of the state already, in Oklahoma or even Kansas."

"That's a possibility, but he could be headed deeper into the state. Even if he's already in Oklahoma or somewhere else, I need you to look into this."

He was asking a lot. There were already nineteen Rangers in Company C up there. Though we're all one family, those guys were going to wonder why a Ranger from Company E was sent to dig around in their territory.

It was bound to happen at some point, though, because the Major put me in a new position not long before as a "roamer." The idea was to send me out for specific assignments wherever I was needed in the state. Governor Randal Bridges and Ranger Division Chief Jeff Harrison had signed off on it, giving me more autonomy in decision making than the other Rangers. We hadn't advertised it much, and this assignment was the one to break in the idea.

Within that framework, I was allowed to form a ghostlike Shadow Response Team, or SRT. There was already an SRT within the Ranger organization that's easily found on the internet when you look up Texas Rangers, but mine consisted of only two people outside of our organization, Yolanda Rodriguez and Perry Hale.

"Fine. If it'll get me out of this town and off the desk for a while, I'll do it."

"I knew you'd agree." The Major finished his beer

and placed the empty bottle on a stone coaster. "Even though our vigilante is taking bad guys off the street, he's causing more work for us. You guys go track this one down and put him in jail."

Mr. Tillman put his bottle on the small table beside the cushioned chair. "I got to go pee." Lifting himself with both hands on the arms, he grunted to his feet. "But I'll tell y'all one thing. I believe if I's y'all, I'd find this feller and give him a medal for doing what ought to've already been done."

Chapter 5

The sun was low in the panhandle sky by the time Alonzo pulled into the parking space in front of his fifth-wheel trailer in the Murphy Springs campground not far out of Amarillo. Unlocking the door, he waved at a fellow camper and climbed the metal steps and inside the Crossroads Cruiser.

"Honey, I'm back. Just stay there. You don't have to get up right now. I'll fix us some supper when I get finished."

After opening the windows for ventilation, he settled at the dining table, opened his toolbox, and completely cleaned a little .22 pistol. "I'll start some supper in a little bit. We're leaving in the morning, hon."

He listened for an answer and nodded his head. "That's right. We have a couple more stops to make before we get home, and then you can rest all you want, and I can, too."

The sun was down by the time he finished cleaning the semiautomatic pistol. The sky was awash in yellows and pinks that darkened with the loss of light when he went back outside to build a fire in the metal ring. He hoisted his glass of Glenlivet as a wave to an elderly woman walking her dog down the campground's asphalt road.

She waved back. "Hello, Alonzo." She pulled at the leg of her baggy shorts and paused as her schnauzer watered a wooden site number. "We're leaving in the morning."

"We are, too."

"I didn't get to meet your wife. I'm sorry she's not feeling well."

"Betty's doing better today. She'll be fine by the time we get home."

"Safe travels." The woman moved on without looking back, watching the little dog look for another object to squirt.

Alonzo settled into an aluminum chair under the camper's awning to stare into coals. He wondered if he should feel anything for shooting Gibson outside the Amarillo strip club or the guys in California, or Arizona . . . or New Mexico.

Remorse?

Guilt?

Fear?

Not a damn thing. All that had been beaten out of him years ago by Daddy Frank.

That's what they get for letting these people out to roam the streets.

He winced as a lance of pain shot through his stomach, much more intense than the one in the woods. He dug a prescription bottle from his pants pocket, shook a pill into his palm, and washed it down with a swallow of scotch. The spasm passed soon enough, and he took another sip of good single-malt whisky. The light was gone by the time Alonzo finished a third drink.

The clouds lowered even more. The pleasant yellow glow from the camper's lights spilled outside, creating a dim island in the darkness. He finished the drink and went inside to meet up with one last pour.

Afterward, he carefully slipped into bed beside Betty as a strong south wind arrived and rocked the trailer. He lay there with his back to her still body, waiting for the pill to take effect, and thought back over the past few weeks. The country was going to hell, Alonzo was dying, and there was nothing left for him any longer.

Wrapped in almost total darkness, he studied on his recent delivery from a lifetime of submersion in the Wadler family philosophy and moonshine business established back in the 1950s. Daddy Frank decided there was more money in the drug trade and switched to marijuana in the '60s, and finally cocaine in the late '70s.

No matter what they did, the old man would never be satisfied with the amount of drugs they moved across state lines and came up with the idea to increase the delivery of his products when he noticed how many people were hauling campers these days.

Snowbirds moved in great herds of white fiberglass twice a year. Once in the autumn when the cold north wind pushed them from the northern states down to the

Texas Gulf Coast. After spending most of the winter in the state's comfortable climate, the warm south winds started the migration back to their homes.

Years earlier, those moving east to west on I-10 interested him more. The family patriarch began making big money on that interstate during the cocaine boom. Now everything including illegal prescription pills such as hydrocodone and Xanax moved through the southern tier of states in a river of delivery vehicles. In the last twenty years, the drug pipeline serviced by major waterways in Texas, Louisiana, Alabama, and Mississippi received injections of even more illegal drugs destined for Florida and the Southwest.

Daddy Frank's new idea to utilize RVs was based on a vision he had about a muddy river flowing across the country, one full of great white hailstones floating without impediment. He and the Preacher discussed it the next day when they were driving to Beaumont. The old man passed a truck pulled over by the highway patrol and noticed a camping trailer that barely slowed in the next lane.

The fresh image of white hailstones floating on a river's surface came to mind at the same time they passed the bright, shiny camper, and the new delivery system was born.

Alonzo snorted in the darkness and then stilled, afraid he'd disturb Betty lying beside him. No matter how well their plan came together, it would do nothing to bring his life back to normal. He'd get home soon, with half a million in cash from the drug delivery hidden under the bed along with the Semtex plastic explosives, and Daddy Frank would still be in charge.

He had a little surprise for Daddy Frank, who had wrecked his already unstable life with his *new* delivery plan.

Alonzo didn't believe in Daddy Frank's idea any longer. He was done with everyone, and all because of a drunk felon named Nicholas Barbour.

Chapter 6

I glanced around at the bare West Texas landscape on my way to Amarillo. Folks who've never driven that part of I-27 have a hard time visualizing the Big Empty. Our state is so large, we don't describe distances between cities and towns in terms of miles, but how many hours it takes to get somewhere.

The only things in sight were scattered ranch houses and barns, an occasional silo, and bobwire fences. Even the trees were few and far between, unless they were planted around houses for a windbreak and shade, and the only other things above ground level were the overpasses from crossing highways.

Oh, and a lot of sky.

Thirty minutes later I'd been thinking so hard about the vigilante that I was surprised when Amarillo suddenly appeared. Getting my head back into city driving, I pulled into the parking lot of the Amarillo sheriff's office a few minutes later. A strong south wind almost took my hat when I stepped out of the truck. A Texas flag cracked under the Stars and Stripes in the strong wind that most of those living in the panhandle would consider a breeze.

There was one night about twenty years ago when I was staying at a motel in Amarillo and the steady wind was so strong at eleven that night the flagpole actually leaned to the north, pulled by flags stretched so tight they looked to be starched.

A dusty ranch pickup pulled in front of the sheriff's office and stopped not far away. The wind brought me the grassy odor of fresh cow shit from the tires and undercarriage, or maybe it came from the cab, tracked in by the local cowboy with his faded jeans stuck in the tops of his boots. The sun-creased rancher climbed out at the same time, tugging his stained hat down in the wind, nodded in my direction, and stomped inside.

I was almost to the courthouse steps when a fireplug of a sheriff himself came through those same doors, tugging his hat down. "You must be Sonny Hawke. I'm Andy Cates."

"That's me." I shook hands with the sheriff, stepping to the side for a deputy to pass. "Looks like y'all're busy."

"Always. Folks can't seem to learn to behave."

"They suffer the same failings down in the Big Bend. Anything new?"

"While you were on the way up here, your Major Parker sent me a report about two more murders in Albuquerque, New Mexico, most likely committed by this vigilante. One, a felon by the name of Rodolfo Felipe Delgado, was convicted of manslaughter and got a plea agreement to several felonies and was released from jail on his own recognizance when he agreed to enter a drug-treatment program he never attended.

"Someone reported a foul smell coming from a gray trailer house surrounded by a chain-link fence in the Mountain View neighborhood of South Valley. When the police arrived on the 10-54 possible dead body code, they found the trailer baking in a bare dirt yard. Delgado's corpse was lying on the couch with most of his brains dried on the wall beside him. There was no weapon nearby, so they ruled out suicide.

"The second murder victim was Judge Debra Palmer, who had released Delgado under the speedy trial umbrella recently established by the New Mexico Supreme Court. The houses in the Los Ranchos de Albuquerque neighborhood were the nicest places in the area. Her husband found the judge floating in her swimming pool after he came home that night. Shot once in the back of the head."

I turned to get the wind more to my back. "This old boy's been busy."

"Sounds like it. We have a BOLO out on him, but it's like looking for a needle in a haystack. No description of him or his vehicle."

"Or her."

Sheriff Cates raised an eyebrow. "Good point, but I can't recall ever hearing of a female vigilante."

"These days, I expect anything."

The glass doors opened and a sullen young man stumbled outside, propelled by a push from the rancher, who I assumed was the boy's daddy. He grabbed the youngster's collar and jerked him to a halt in front of us. "Beau, you apologize to the sheriff and to that man there for what you done."

Beau looked to be around eighteen and half-terrified of us. "Ssss . . . sorry. I won't do it no more."

The rancher's gray eyes were full of fire. "And say it to that Ranger. You're lucky it wasn't *him* that drug you in."

I met the kid's watery eyes. His chin trembled. "Sorry, sir. Didn't mean no harm."

"It wasn't me who brought you in."

"No, I 'magine he'd-a shot you." The rancher took a deep calming breath. "Now, get in the truck. I'm gonna work your ass off stringing wire for the next week." He reset his wide-brimmed sweat-stained hat, nodded in my direction. "He's gonna learn his lesson before I'm done with him." Shaking his head, he followed the young man to the truck.

Sheriff Cates and I watched them pull onto the street. I grinned. "What'd the kid do?"

He chuckled. "Nothin' worse'n I ever did when I was his age. Him and friend got into their daddy's whiskey last night and put a stuffed rattlesnake in an Origins bag and took it out to the Silver Spur café to have some fun. They set the bag down beside a car in the parking lot and went inside to see what would happen.

"Some silver-haired woman saw it on her way in and picked up the bag like it was hers. Halfway through supper she just couldn't stand it anymore. She had to see what she'd scored in the parking lot. She put the bag in her lap and peeked inside. Apparently a stuffed snake-in-a-sack looks just like a live one."

We laughed as the pickup pulled out on the street.

"Witnesses say it looked like she was hit with ten thousand volts of electricity. She jumped up and fell back onto another table in a drop-dead faint, then they say she rolled off on the floor, her foundation garments made public and her head dribbling like a loose basketball for a minute before the bag closed."

"That doesn't seem like an arrest offense."

"Wouldn't have been, but things unraveled even more when paramedics showed up and strapped her on the gurney. They put the bag and her purse by her feet at the same time she came back around. It set her off again." He pointed in the direction of the disappearing truck. "Genius there said he was her son and jumped in the ambulance to ride with her."

"So?"

"So, halfway to the hospital he got sick from the whiskey. That's when the ambulance called it in and pulled over. My boys brought him in, and his daddy made him spend the night in jail before he came to take him home."

"I'd be willing to bet you won't see him in here no more."

We chuckled, and the sheriff hung his thumbs in his gunbelt. "Ain't that the truth? We're gonna keep a lookout for this vigilante you're after, but I wish I had more for you. What are you gonna do while you're here?"

"Go over to the Big Texan, get a steak, and then check into the motel there to wait and see what happens next."

He sighed. "I'm afraid that's *all* we can do right now."

"Something'll break, and when it does, I'll be close by and ready."

Chapter 7

The morning was cloudy and cold underneath the big panhandle sky. Alonzo sat in the doorway under the camper's awning, surveying the empty panorama that was Llano Estecado, an arid and virtually treeless plateau near the Texas/New Mexico border. Seventy miles to the west, Billy the Kid allegedly slept under a slab of concrete, in an iron cage resembling a nineteenth-century jail cell, and surrounded by a low adobe wall.

Most of the campsites in the stark, barren campground were empty except for a distant silver Airstream camper parked in the shade of a mature cottonwood tree. Despite the fact that Alonzo had taken the last campsite at the end of the park's lead-gray asphalt road, a cheerful elderly couple walked past his site with their fuzzy little white yapper. It tried to pee on everything they passed, even after it had exhausted its limited supply of urine, and spent most of its time standing on three legs, straining.

Just back from the drugstore, Alonzo exchanged friendly waves and sipped a hot cup of cowboy coffee.

A yearling doe picked her way through the sage and clump-grass-dotted landscape. A disposable cell phone buzzed in his shirt pocket. He punched the answer button. "What."

His Uncle Jimmy Don chuckled from over six hundred fifty miles to the east, in Gunn, Texas. "Most folks usually say 'howdy.' It sounds better."

For once the cancer in Alonzo's stomach was quiet, and he didn't want anything to wake the snarling badger up again. He scratched fingers through thinning hair and took a long, deep breath to remain calm. "You at work?"

"That's all I do these days. People always need lumber, and I don't think the saw at this damn mill ever quits singing." Most every member of the family held jobs to keep up the pretense of social acceptability. Those paychecks didn't hold a candle to what they were making in the family business. "Where're you?"

Alonzo closed his eyes and envisioned the Big Thicket sawmill where he'd worked as a kid. He could almost hear the blade's whine as experienced mill workers sliced fragrant lumber out of the long, stripped pine trunks, or "strip logs," that came in all day on the East Texas log trucks. Daddy Frank owned the sawmill that was one more entity in his diversification portfolio.

Bracketed by the winding, muddy Sabine River to the east, and the equally gritty Trinity River to the west, the Big Thicket was once more than 3.5 million acres of woods so dense in places that little sunlight reached the ground. The earliest pioneers who first settled there in the early 1800s were a hard breed who either preferred the solitude of the woods or grew to love the refuge where they could live their lives as they pleased without interference from outside entities.

Those people back then evolved their own customs and way of life that was passed down for generations in a land where a man could get lost simply by stepping off the road. Swamps, cottonmouth moccasins, panthers, endless game trails, bayous, wild hogs armed with razor-sharp tusks, swarms of mosquitoes, and unexplored land all served to prevent most casual intrusions.

The Thicket, as most East Texans called it, was a good hideout for displaced Indian tribes at first, then for those who wanted to become scarce for a while, getting away from the rules and restrictions put upon them by society. Still hemmed in by thick tangles of vines intertwined with myrtle and yaupons, a barrier that kept most people out.

Jimmy Don didn't get to know everything, and Alonzo always played his cards close to the vest. He told a lie. "Caprock Canyon State Park, drinking coffee, and watching old people walk their dogs." No one gets everything they ask, and he didn't want anyone to know exactly where he was. "I think I might start a new career as the Outdoor Fashion Police. People in their seventies shouldn't wear shorts with long white socks. It ain't pretty."

"Wish I had your job. I reckon you finished what we sent you out there to do. We ain't heard from you in over a week, and Daddy Frank's getting antsy. I guess you delivered the product."

Alonzo's stomach burned at the mention of the forty kilos of cocaine he'd delivered to a distributor in California, making him wonder how many pills he had left in the bottle. He didn't figure he'd run out before getting back to Gunn, and after that, it wouldn't matter. "I dropped it off and got the cash, just like I was supposed to."

"Any trouble?"

A pause. "No."

"Good to hear. I kinda got worried that something went wrong. We expected you to be back by now."

"Me, too. Betty's been sick and I haven't been up to snuff myself. We're taking our time."

Jimmy Don was silent for a long time. Just when Alonzo thought his phone had dropped the signal, his uncle's voice came through clear and loud. "Taking your *time*? Now? Daddy Frank's about to bust a gut waiting to hear from you, and you know how he is. You have something to tell me? I heard there might have been trouble."

The badger in Alonzo's stomach woke up and started tearing at his guts. That was just like his family, knowing everything there was to know about him. "What'd you hear?"

"Got a call from California. A detective working a case and needed to talk to you."

"A case 'bout what?"

"That's what *we* want to know."

"I don't have no answer to that. Me and Betty're on the way."

"Son, you should have already been here."

"I'm trying to fit in and drive the speed limit. I don't want to get pulled over with all that cash in here. I suspect a drug dog would still smell what we hauled, and I don't want to take the chance."

Alonzo and Betty were the initial test run, joining the thousands of other vacationers and retirees driving the roads and staying for a night or two in low-cost national forests, state and national park sites, or private campgrounds.

"Well, you need to hie on back here or we're both gonna answer to Daddy Frank."

Alonzo remained silent, thinking about the man he despised.

"Is there something else you need to tell us?"

"Nothin' right now."

Jimmy Don snorted. "We were thinkin' you may have triggered somebody's alarm bells somewhere along the way, and that's why you're being so slow. Any idea how that coulda happened? Maybe when you bought the cheese?"

He was giving Alonzo a way out, if something was really wrong. Daddy Frank, the meanest man in Southeast Texas, scared everyone but Jimmy Don, the old man's elder son. If Alonzo was dragging his feet because he suspected someone was following, Daddy Frank would completely understand and move Alonzo's stock in the family to a much higher level.

"Come on, Jimmy Don. Let me do my job." Despite the badger clawing at his guts, Alonzo couldn't up and tell Jimmy Don the truth, that he'd lost his spirit. To do so would be a death sentence, and even though he was dying a little more each day, he had business to attend to before settling in for the long sleep. "Y'all just hold your water. I'll be there soon enough."

A Buick LaCrosse sedan cruised slowly past and parked near the park's stucco restroom building. Alonzo kept his eye on the car until the doors opened and an elderly couple creaked their way out of the car and into the restroom.

"Well, hurry up and get home. He needs the cash for that big delivery from Colombia and that cheese, though I think he's out of his damned mind wanting to use that shit to stop the pipeline from coming through. You can make it in a day and a half. Those South American boys don't like to wait, you know."

"Fine." Alonzo thought fast and a lie formed. "The tires on this rig are wearing faster'n they should, so I'm gonna have to keep it around sixty the rest of the way. I don't want to have a blowout and risk having the highway patrol stop to help. I have a new set waiting on us in Comanche. Then I can book it the rest of the way in. I have reservations at the Evening Star RV Park there tomorrow night."

"Sounds like a plan. Get it done, and we'll see you when you get here."

"Sure." Alonzo thumbed the phone off and slipped it into his shirt pocket. Flinging the cold dregs of his coffee onto the bare sand, he rose and went inside. He set the cup on the dining table by a plastic CVS bag full of cosmetics.

"Hey girl. That was Jimmy Don." He paused, waiting for a response that didn't come. "Well, anyway, I got you some different cover-up that's closer to your skin tone. It might be a *little* darker'n what you've been buying, but I think it'll work."

He unwrapped a Glade Plugin and replaced the old one in the outlet over the kitchen counter. "This says it smells like cashmere. Didn't know cashmere *had* a smell." Alonzo carried another into the fifth-wheel camper's upper bedroom, where it was needed the most. "We're leaving in the morning. I have a couple more stops to make before we get back home. I don't care *what* Daddy Frank wants, I'm takin' my time."

Chapter 8

In Gunn, Jimmy Don punched off the burner phone and thought about pitching it into the smoking burn barrel beside them in the timber yard. "Something's wrong."

Standing in the middle of an odd dichotomy, a wide, barren graveyard full of stripped timber stacked as far as the eye could see, the yard was surrounded by the thick piney woods of the Big Thicket. Skinny paved roads radiated outward in half a dozen directions, winding through the thick green forest to clear-cut leases where not a tree stood upright.

Log trucks crawled back and forth on those roads, hauling stacks of pine logs that sometimes hung ten feet beyond the end of the long, forty-five-foot trailers. There in the mill yard, they were stacked like behemoth toothpicks until their time came to meet the giant saws.

Willy Henderson, Sheriff Buck Henderson's second cousin, circled the barrel to get out of the smoke. Taking off his gimme cap, he pulled a strand of long dark hair into line with the rest of his greasy mop and re-placed it. A jagged white scar ran from his forehead, across a dead eye as white as a marble, and down his cheek, where it ended at the corner of his mouth—the result of a steel cable that snapped when he was a log-ger. "Why do you say that?"

"Because of the way Alonzo sounded, and the things he said. I know for a fact that Betty's dead. I got a call at the house from the funeral home in California. Alonzo wrote a check to 'em and didn't sign it. They weren't mad about it, more like they're used to people making mistakes in times like that. I made out like I was him and gave 'em a credit card number to pay for the embalming and casket."

"She's dead? How'd . . ." Willy's mouth opened and closed like a fish. He switched to another train of thought. "They believed you?"

"They believed in the money that came through. Them people that deal with the dead don't care who pays, as long as they get what's owed 'em. I told 'em I didn't remember the day she died because it was all a fog for me, and the lady out there was more'n helpful. She told me Alonzo buried her out there, but I can't understand why he didn't let us know, or why he won't admit she's gone."

"I 'magine he's all tore up." Willy sat back down. "That woman expired him. What'd she die from?"

"Didn't ask, and I think the word you want is 'in-spired,' she *inspired* him. Remember, I was supposed to be Alonzo on the phone, but then I Googled her name and it came up on one of them small-town police beat reports that little papers do. She was killed out there in California when some drunk ran her down in a crosswalk, murdered by a feller with a long list of convictions. He kept getting out over and over again . . ."

"That sounds like some of our kinfolk and half the guys on Daddy Frank's payroll."

"Sure does, but anyway, this was one bad dude." Jimmy Don grunted. "He bonded out, again, and I got that from the detective I talked to. And now I'm wondering if Alonzo didn't settle with him on his own. That could be why he's running so far behind schedule. You know how he is."

Willy absently stroked his beard and stared with his one good eye into the fire, watching the crispy red embers pulse in the heat. "That's what our people'd do."

"Yeah, but he don't need to be doing that right *now*. He could've waited until we got done in a couple of weeks, and one or two of us woulda gone back out there with him."

"So what happens now?"

Jimmy Don studied the stacks of stripped pine logs. Brass nozzles sent streams of water into the air, raining moisture onto the timber so it wouldn't dry out and crack or split before they were ready to process. It also kept beetles from causing damage.

"We keep on keeping on with the plan to pick up the delivery that's sitting on that ship out on the Intracoastal right now. Personally, I'm more interested in hearing how easy it was to move the product in the camping trailer." He looked around to be sure no one was within earshot. "If it works, we can move that shipment in a week. That's money, son!"

Willy bit his lip. "Well, don't count your chickens

before they're gathered. And you ought not talk like
that right out in the open. I wouldn't put it past Daddy
Frank to have somebody else working here that we
don't know. You never can tell who's listenin'."

"That's eggs."

"Huh?

"You said count your chickens before they're gathered. You meant count your chickens before they're
hatched."

Willy shrugged. "Whatever. We're still making
good money on the thing we've been doing all my life.
I still think we need to quit diddlin' with a good thing.
We expanse this operation even more, and not even the
sheriff can cover for us."

"Don't let Daddy Frank hear you say that, and the
word is 'expand.'"

"Whatever."

Chapter 9

Had anything been tall enough, the late evening shadows would have stretched across the two-lane. As it was, there was little on the edge of Dimmitt, Texas, that stood more than twenty feet. Most of the scrub around the dying plains town of less than four thousand people an hour south of Amarillo was sage, cedar, and a few scattered houses.

Alonzo steered the fifth-wheel rig into a barren pull-through site in Archie's RV Park on the southern edge of town. A feedlot provided the thick odor of decomposing cow manure and urine.

Alonzo didn't mind the aroma one little bit for reasons of his own.

He positioned the trailer on the gravel pad, killed the engine, and had the landing gear down in only minutes. The tiny RV park had only two dozen sites, and four of them were occupied by dusty trailers that had been there for months.

He had the trailer set up and was inside thirty minutes later. The Spring Fresh plug-ins weren't doing their job, but the smell of the feedlot helped. Cattle always drew flies, and they swarmed thick against the trailer's screen door. Two or three got in every time he went in or out, and that caused problems with Betty.

Once inside, Alonzo washed two pills down with a glass of water and picked up a flyswatter. He killed two in the kitchen and scraped them onto the floor, where they mixed with the dried carcasses of their kinfolk. There were still plenty of cosmetics on the counter that he hadn't taken out of a plastic bag. He collected a handful and carried them along with the flyswatter into the master bedroom in the raised front section of the trailer. He cranked the air-conditioning up to reduce the odor and remove as much moisture as possible from the air.

A bluebottle fly buzzed the bed and lit on the mirrored closet door. The swatter whistled through the air, leaving a dark smear on the glass.

He sat on his side of the bed. "Honey, I'm gonna freshen you up some before I go out." He waved at still another fly that buzzed her head, which was the only thing not covered by the sheets and blanket. "Your hair still looks good, but I think you need a touch-up."

He opened a jar of flesh-toned cream and applied it to her cold cheeks. He couldn't bear the inevitable process of decomposition that was taking a toll despite the embalming process. He'd smeared her lipstick that night he pulled her out of the casket and hadn't been able to correct it to his satisfaction. By that time he was careless and almost exhausted from both the physical labor of digging up the grave and the emotional toll it took to complete the job.

"I have a guy to visit here in town, and then we're heading out in the morning. We both need to get home. The boys are waiting for what we have down in storage." He finished with the dark makeup, wiped his hands on a stained towel, and unscrewed the brush on a container of mascara. He'd brushed her face with his elbow during the night and needed to repair the damage.

"I'm getting' pretty good at this, you know." He chuckled and ran the tiny brush through her eyebrow "I watched you enough to know how to do it."

Finished, he leaned back to study his work. "I know you wouldn't like what I'm doing, but that's okay. A man has to do certain things, and this is my calling; besides, I don't have that much longer to make amends anyway." He doubled over in a wash of pain. "I just wish I didn't hurt so bad. It'd make this a lot easier."

He paused as if listening to her response. "I 'magine you'd have trouble seeing the difference between what me and the family do, and these criminals we're sending to Hell, but there's a clear difference. We supply a product, or that's all we did before Daddy Frank lost his damn mind.

"It's *him* that put us here, and if that sonofabitch Barbour that ran over you'd been in the pen where he belonged, then I'd still have you." He wiped at his overflowing eyes. "What we do for a living ain't that bad. People want it. They pay for it. None of us ever saw anything wrong with providing something people ask for."

He wiped at the tears that welled in his eyes. "It's all right, though. I'll be with you directly, probably faster than I ever imagined. But before we get back home, there's a few more who needs killin', but I'm runnin' out of steam."

He rose, gathered the cosmetics into a flowered makeup bag, and zipped it shut. He paused, taking in the shape of her body under the covers and thinking about the man with a rap sheet as long as his arm who'd killed her the night he was meeting with the men who paid them for the cocaine he'd hauled from East Texas.

Guilt had overwhelmed him that night in the emergency room when he'd arrived too late. The sheet covering her face was too much, and he collapsed on the floor, knowing he'd trade all the cash in the truck and everything he had to get her back.

If only.

If.

If he'd been there to take her to the convenience store she never would have left the trailer. Supper was cold on the stove when he got back around midnight. An empty box of black pepper was sitting on the Corian island. Knowing how much he enjoyed pepper, she'd decided to walk the three blocks to the grocery store while he was trading money for Semtex plastic explosives on a San Francisco dock. He hadn't taken her with him, because he didn't want to put his sweet wife in danger.

Not putting her in danger got her killed.

Alonzo snorted at the irony and tucked the blanket tightly around her still form. "This next one'll pay, honey. We'll save the state some money." Finished, Alonzo returned to the dining area. He slapped another fly on the table and picked up his iPad. Punching it alive, he re-read a news item on the screen.

KVII in Amarillo reported 40-year-old Eric Lang was convicted three times in the 2010 death of Terry Moore in a capital murder-for-hire charge.

Each conviction was appealed, which resulted in the awarding of new trials due to various legal technicalities such as improper documentation, failure to maintain a proper chain of possession of evidence, contradictory evidence, and juror misconduct.

Lang's case was retried a third time for a lesser included charge of felony murder. His defense team appealed the offering of felony murder after the conviction, citing felony murder and not a proper lesser included charge for capital murder.

The Texas Court of Criminal Appeals agreed. They set aside the conviction and vacated the sentence; however the Court was legally unable to grant a new trial for capital murder.

The judge then granted Lang's motion to acquit on the capital murder-for-hire charge, ensuring that he could not stand trial for capital murder again. He was released from jail in January. In an interview with KVII, Lang again stated his position.

"I told you I was innocent. *The justice system did its job and now I'm going home to Dimmitt and resume my life.*"

"Well, yes and no." Alonzo typed Lang's name into a directory search engine that brought up the man's home address and landline phone number. "You're here in Dimmitt all right, but the resumption of your life is about to end. Like I said, you just *think* you got off."

The sun was going down when he steered the truck onto Lang's street at the outer edge of town.

Chapter 10

Jimmy Don Wadler and half a dozen friends and relatives were gathered in a ring of light around the tractor-rim firepit eight miles outside of Gunn, Texas. A thick line of pines fifty yards across the freshly mown lawn sparkled with the flashes from hundreds of lightning bugs. Crickets called from the aromatic damp grass and a chorus of tree frogs serenaded the evening. A great horned owl's hoots filled the still air.

The gray frame house sitting on ten acres of mixed hardwoods and pine had been in the Wadler family for three generations. The back porch mirrored the front, except for the rust-stained freezer filled with venison, ducks, and wild pig, and a rusting refrigerator full of beer.

The men ringing the firepit lounged in a variety of seats ranging from aluminum lawn chairs to cast-off dining chairs to one old cane-bottom antique that kept settling into the soft ground.

In a canvas folding chair, Jimmy Don Wadler waved at an annoying mosquito, sipped from a bottle of beer. "We got troubles with Alonzo."

His eyes flicked toward the house and dark gravel road beyond. No one could drive up without being noticed, but you never could tell when a government man would come creepy crawling up through the woods with one of them parabolic microphones.

"They should have been back here a week ago. I know we told 'em to take their time and act like all them other people dragging trailers around the country and wasting money just to look at scenery, but now I'm worried. Betty's dead, and he didn't call *one* of us. I'm afraid he's gone off the deep end."

The announcement wasn't news. They'd all heard about her death and wrote it off as an inevitable part of life.

Willy Henderson adjusted his seat in the old-school aluminum chair and belched. Because of his blind eye, he turned his head like a chicken to see Jimmy Don on the left. "That ain't good. I told you to let one of *us* go. Just drive out there and come straight back. Hauling that much cocaine in a camper don't make no sense. I coulda done it."

"Yeah you did, and you'd've probably got caught." Jimmy Don's eyes roamed down Willy's overweight frame, camouflage gimme cap, thick brown beard hanging to his chest, to his Mossy Oak camo shirt, faded jeans and the worn-out hunting shoes on his feet. He avoided looking at the man's one white, dead eye that almost glowed in the firelight.

Willy proved himself to Jimmy Don and the family years earlier by shooting Daniel Fredericks behind the ear and dumping the body in the Sabine. Daddy Frank had enough of that meth-head family cooking their shit two miles from his house. It was too close to his own operation, so he'd asked Daniel, the dad, to move or quit. Daniel ordered him off the property and threatened to shoot Daddy Frank if he ever came around again, telling them what to do like he had the right.

Daddy Frank ordered Willy to set the meth house on fire, to make his point. In response, Fredericks moved a faded, dented house trailer in front of the pile of ashes that was once their home and started his lab back up again.

On the old man's new orders, Willy waited one morning out behind the trailer until Daniel Fredericks stepped out back to pee into the ashes. Willy knocked him in the head with a baseball bat, threw the semiconscious man into the bed of his pickup, and drove down to the Sabine bottoms, not far from what they called the fertilizer barn.

The body never surfaced, probably eaten by the gators drawn by such treats in the past. The remainder of the Fredericks family got the message and moved away.

"You guys need to understand that the cops are looking for folks like us out there, dressed like you." Jimmy Don plucked the beer bottle from the holder between his index and middle fingers, took a swallow, and replaced it.

"It's them damn meth-heads down in the bottoms that's bringing all the troubles." Mike Dillman laid it off on the tweakers who occupied the bottom rung of the drug-using public. He fished a fresh beer from a brown Yeti cooler with a rattle of ice. "Calling attention to country folks just tryin' to get by."

Clifford Raye burst out laughing, flipping his rattail braid out from under his collar. He scratched a mosquito bite on the back of his ear with a hand that was missing the little finger from a logging accident. He'd moved from logging trees to working at the sawmill, a place he considered safer. "That's funny for you to say. It's your mama's side of the family that's cooking that shit back up on Blackwater Bayou."

Mike ducked his head at the truth, licking his buckteeth that tended to dry out against his lips, and lit a fresh cigarette. "Yeah, and I don't have nothin' to do with any of 'em. I tried to get 'em to stop, but hell, they make ten times more money a day making crystal than any of 'em *ever* made workin' for the Walmart in town."

"They'll get caught pretty soon." Sammy Saxton smoothed the lush mustache growing like melting wax down to his jawline. He worked at the BranCo refinery northeast of Houston one hundred miles from Gunn, Texas. "They oughta go to making whiskey like God intended before they get crossways with Daddy Frank. At least that's a product we don't move much of no more."

Everyone laughed, all except for two men sitting with their backs to the creek bottom. One, a rawboned Pentecostal preacher currently going by the name of Curry Holmes, listened silently with large, soft hands resting on his knees. With a worn Bible balanced on one skinny thigh, he was the only one not drinking beer.

The other man slouched in an aluminum chair with a cowboy hat pulled down low over his eyes so that the only visible feature was his thick brush-pile mustache over a white chin. A badge pinned above his pocket reflected the firelight.

Sheriff Buck Henderson was in some way related to every one of the men around the fire, and especially closer to Willy. New move-ins laughed when they thought of how nearly everyone in the county was kinfolk, so intertwined by blood that they even had double cousins. The newcomers figured out pretty quick not to talk about anyone, because the conversation would surely reach the wrong ears through the homegrown grapevine that was East Texas behind the Pine Curtain.

Jimmy Don noticed how quiet Buck had become. He waved a lacy gallinipper out of his face and watched the Newton County sheriff light a fresh cigarette from the short butt held in fingers callused from decades of minor burns.

"Look, we're getting close to moving an ass-load of product, and we need Alonzo to get back with that money." Jimmy Don was starting to get frustrated at the direction the conversation was turning. Daddy Frank was the man in charge, and Jimmy Don was second. "We need that cash and all of us need a payday."

"You're right about that." Holding the beer with three fingers, Buck drained the bottle and dropped it onto the grass. "Y'all haven't give me a payday in a month, and I have overhead. Willy, fish me out another'n."

Willy opened the cooler between him and Mike and pulled out a dripping Coors yellowboy. He lofted it to Buck, who twisted off the cap, tilted it so the foam wouldn't get on his jeans, and pitched the cap into the fire.

Jimmy Don hawked and spat. "What overhead?"

"I need to grease a few skids to keep the road open in both counties." The sheriff in Newton County, he also had expenses over in nearby Jasper County. "There's a couple of ol' boys in the highway patrol who'll look the other way ever' now and then. There's also some . . . contractors who come in handy to do a little enforcement work, too, when we need 'em, if you get my drift. I want to make sure that road from Beaumont stays clear. I don't want my boys to get crossways with anybody not on the payroll. You know what'll have to happen then."

"Hallelujah!" Preacher Holmes's soft voice carried across the yard. "And when the Lord thy God shall deliver them before thee; thou shalt smite them, *and* utterly destroy them; thou shalt make no covenant with them, nor show mercy unto them."

"Deuteronomy." Sheriff Henderson nodded, squinting around the smoke from the cigarette hanging from his lips. The sheriff drew deep, the cherry glowing red in the darkness. He blew smoke from his nose in a long dragon exhalation without taking the cigarette from his mouth. "I got a problem with this pipeline idea of Daddy Frank's. I can sweep a lot of things under the rug, but if he starts blowing up oil pipelines and a refinery, then it's gonna get bigger'n me. His camper plan'll work, especially with this shipment coming in, but we need to talk him out of using that plastic explosive Alonzo's carrying. He does that, and it's gonna put us under a microscope."

"Well, he's mad," Willy said.

Buck smoothed his mustache. "And that's what's gonna get us in trouble."

Daddy Frank Wadler was the family elder and well-known as the self-avowed meanest man in Newton County, where Gunn was located. His vision called the

Plan came the night he took his most recent bride, an eighteen-year-old black-haired Cajun gal from over in Acadiana Parish named Shi'Ann LeBleu. It was borne in the throes of their wedding night when the Viagra he took reacted with his advanced cardiac disease, sending him into a mild heart attack resulting in a brief glimpse of the white light at the end of the tunnel.

When responding paramedics shocked him back into this world, Daddy Frank called the clan together in his hospital room and recounted what he'd seen when doctors said he'd died and from there the Camper Plan came into being.

"Where's the old man tonight?"

Jimmy Don adjusted his seat. "He's across the line in Beauregard Parish with Boone. Scooter got outta line and traded some of our guns to that coonass Thibideaux gang to support his damned habit. Daddy'n'em went over to settle up."

Well-known to Louisiana law enforcement, the Thibideaux family had moved from New Orleans after Hurricane Katrina in 2005. They had long history of shipping crystal meth up and down I-10. Within the last couple of years, they'd shifted their operation to include meth cooked up in trailers and shacks hidden in the woods and swamps on the western side of the state, near DeRidder. They were far too close to the Wadler operation.

At the mention of Boone's name, Willy flinched. "Boone's a creepy sonofabitch." He swallowed. "Scooter didn't give 'em the *converted* rifles, did he?"

"He damn sure did, and I don't want the ATF sniffin' around here wondering where them Thibideauxs got fully automatic weapons." Sheriff Henderson's voice, thick and gravelly from a four-pack-a-day habit, ended the conversation. "That river ain't a wall between us, there's a bridge, and we ain't that far away."

"I doubt they'll come lookin'." Jimmy Don tilted the bottle and drained half. By daylight Scooter was going to be looking at an eternity in a shallow grave, if Daddy Frank was in a good mood, or as gator shit if he wasn't. "Boone's gettin' good at what he's doing."

Boone was the most cold-blooded killer any of them had ever heard of. Daddy Frank first saw the slender, completely hairless man with abnormally long skinny fingers sitting in front of a prefab metal gas station over in Honey Island. Daddy Frank said he first noticed Boone because of the man's spiderweb tattoo over the entirety of his skull and covering one eye and cheek. A bloodred spider virtually pulsed on the back of his head.

His arms were covered in scars, and one ran across his throat from ear to ear as if someone had tried to cut it and failed.

It was Boone's dead expression that won the old man over. Daddy Frank made small talk, and Boone's facial features never changed. He didn't crack a smile or build a frown. The only way Daddy Frank knew the man was interested in their evolving conversation that eventually included wet work that needed to be done was when Boone finally met his gaze without blinking and nodded, once.

Boone had one look that served all his emotions, a completely blank expression. His lips were a thin line except when he spoke. It was terrifying to think that he completely lacked common emotions, and that proved the truth when Daddy Frank finally found what he'd suspected.

As far as they knew, Boone's one true talent was violence.

The man was like that spider tattooed on the back of his head. He seemed to be completely removed from anything around him until Daddy Frank gave him an order, which he carried out without question.

Once Daddy Frank understood what he had, he settled Boone in a small shack in the woods at the back of another property in the Sabine River bottoms and provided the strange skinny man with whatever he wanted. That proved simple, because all Boone needed was food and books, both of which he consumed voraciously.

"Here's what the old man said." Jimmy Don drained his beer. "One of y'all to go out and meet Alonzo at the Evening Star RV Park in Comanche. Tell him Daddy Frank said to let you pull the trailer back here. Hearing it came from him, that should light a fire under the slow sonofabitch. You can make it in a day, and then we can get that off our list."

Willy raised his hand to volunteer, and Jimmy Don shook his head. "Nope. Hell, I'd pull you over if I was the law, just to see what you'd been up to." They chuckled and Jimmy Don finished his beer. "Mike, you have enough time built up out there at the refinery you can get off easier'n the rest of us."

He nodded.

"Oh, and Boone's going with you."

Silence dropped like a wet wool blanket on the group at the mention of the man's name.

Mike swallowed. "Uh, Jimmy Don . . ."

"Daddy Frank said."

"I'd just as soon take a sack of live cottonmouths in the cab with me as to ride out there with that freak."

"I know it." The crunch of tires on gravel reached them, and Jimmy Don stopped talking.

Headlights flickered through the trees as a vehicle approached. A whip-poor-will took the night song's lead as an unfamiliar late-model sedan came into view two hundred yards away, then slowed when it neared the house and parked on the side.

Sheriff Buck Henderson pushed himself upright and strolled toward a thick cedar growing in the open yard. They'd all visited it at least once that night to pee. He stepped behind the thick bush and waited there with one hand on the butt of his holstered Glock as the driver killed the car's engine beside the other pickups.

The porch light snapped on, bathing the trucks in a pool of yellow light. The blinds were still open, and through the single-pane windows, they could see Marshall Wadler, Jimmy Don's other brother, in his wheelchair inches away from a new sixty-inch flat-panel TV.

The strange sedan's driver emerged and stopped halfway between his car and the house. Jimmy Don relaxed when he saw his twenty-year-old son, Tanner. He'd named the boy after the little fighter in the movie *The Bad News Bears*. Unfortunately, his son turned out to be more of a sensitive, tearful young man who hadn't measured up to either name, his first, or last.

The back door to the house opened and Tanner's very young and pregnant wife, Donine, rushed out with a squeal of excitement and threw her arms around him. She flipped a glowing cigarette butt into the yard. "You bought a new car!" She pronounced it *cawr*.

"It's a lease, but it's ours."

"It's a Taurus!"

"Sure is. You can't beat a Ford. They gave me a good deal and I was like, sure."

"Let's take 'er for a spin!"

Tanner released Donine. "In a minute. I need to talk to Daddy, and then we'll go."

Jimmy Don drained the bottle. "A *car*, and a lease, too. That boy ain't got the sense God give a goose."

"Ain't that the truth?" Mike had been leaning forward, as if that would help him see the unfamiliar car better. "Hey, Jimmy Don. What if Alonzo don't want to let us take over and drive his rig home?"

Jimmy Don met Mike's eyes across the fire. "Make him."

Chapter 11

It was daylight at the Big Texan motel when I threw my bag into the Dodge's back seat. My phone rang. "Hello."

"Sonny Hawke? This is Sheriff Cates here in Amarillo. Got some news for you."

I swallowed the last of the in-room coffee that tasted slightly of mildew and dropped the paper cup into the holder. "Shoot."

"They're working a murder down in Dimmitt that fits your man to a T, except it's off the Interstate. Small highways. So his MO is the same for murder but not for travel."

I grinned at the contradiction. "I was just guessing that he'd travel down I-40. It looks like he's decided to go a different way."

"Looks that way to me. Call Sheriff Davis in Dimmitt." He gave me a phone number and the directions to a parolee's house at the edge of town. "He'll be waiting there for you."

"Thanks. I'm on my way."

It wasn't long before I was on State Highway 60. The divided four-lane ran straight south through the wide-open Caprock country. Retracing my route went against my grain, and I couldn't help but regret that I hadn't decided to stop in the small town sixty miles south of Amarillo. I wanted to slap my forehead.

The guy was maddening. After Albuquerque, he'd decided to take less-traveled roads. There were a couple of problems with that, in my opinion. Killing folks in larger cities like Amarillo gave you an easier way out, with folks less likely to recognize you as a visitor. It gave me the notion that he didn't care if anyone saw him now. Less caution meant he might become even more volatile.

A couple of miles passed while I studied on that idea, and then it hit me. He wasn't from a city. Maybe he was more comfortable in small towns because that's where he grew up. My tires ate up the miles as my mind wandered. If you were on the road, what did you need?

Hotels or motels. Cafés or restaurants. No one would remember seeing strangers there. Convenience stores and gas stations. The same anonymity. Was he traveling on the cheap or spending big bucks? How would we find him? Was there some common denominator in these towns that he might need, but on a smaller scale?

I was rolling at the posted seventy-five miles an hour and caught up with an RV cruising twenty miles under the speed limit. The road was clear so I blew around him like he was sitting still. The gray-haired driver waved as I passed.

Texas friendly.

I picked up my cell phone and called Yolanda Rodriguez, my go-to gal when it comes to computers or shooting things up. Apparently there was a cell tower close by. Sometimes service can be spotty out in the Big Empty. She answered on the first ring. "Yessir."

"This guy's changing his MO."

"Good morning to you, too. Perry Hale, you want to tell Sonny good morning, too?"

I heard his voice through the speaker. "Mornin', boss."

My SRT couple was already up and running. "Oh. I was just driving and thinking."

"I get it." The lilt in Yolanda's voice told me she was kidding, but I felt bad because I'd done the same thing to the Major a few days earlier. "What's up?"

"Well, good morning." She had me derailed, and I had to think. "It looks like this guy I was telling y'all about before I left is off the interstates now. I got a call from the sheriff in Amarillo, who said our target might have killed a parolee named Eric Lang down in Dimmitt. Since he's off our original pattern, see what you can find out about other recent murders in the area within the last couple of days. And while you're at it, see how many fairly recent parolees are scattered around the state."

"That's a big job."

"I know it, but I've been driving and thinking."

The girl was a champ. "I'll see what we can come up with. I'll call when I know something. Perry Hale, tell Sonny bye."

"Bye!"

I sighed. "I get it. You two keep your minds on the job."

Perry Hale's voice came in loud and clear. "We can, now."

"Hush!" I heard a smack and knew Yolanda had pasted him one. "I'll let you know."

We hung up and I followed Highway 385 to Dimmitt. Though most of the little panhandle town was dying on the vine, the usual small-town businesses like the café, drugstore, antique shops, and ironically, a downtown real estate office were still alive. The local hospital seemed to be managing well, and there were several highway patrol cars parked in front of the DPS station. An appliance store, the obligatory True Value hardware store, and a Dollar General said the tough bantam-size agricultural town just might survive the hard times and prosper again.

I'd given Sheriff Davis a courtesy call before leaving the Amarillo city limits. He was used to working with the Ranger Dan Bills assigned to Company C who lived in Hereford, about twenty miles away.

The cigar-chomping sheriff wearing khakis and a tan shirt was waiting on me in the front yard hemmed in with yellow crime-scene tape. Another strip was fixed across the front door of a typical ranch-style house built in the 1960s. He waved as I drifted off Highway 385 and into the drive.

"You look like a Ranger. Cameron Davis." He stuck out his hand as I climbed out of the truck.

"Good to meet you, Sheriff Davis. Sonny Hawke."

"I figured you'd be interested in this one. Got a parolee here, Eric Lang. He was murdered last night."

"Where'd you find him?"

Davis tilted his straw hat back and pointed with the

cigar between two fingers. "Half in and out of the door right there. I expected Dan Bills to be here with you."

And right off the bat I was in dangerous territory. "Well, Dan's out of pocket, and I'm investigating similar murders, so here I am. What do you think happened?"

"I don't *think*. I *know* what happened. Somebody knocked on the door and shot Lang three times when he answered. Killed him graveyard dead and then drove off like nobody's business."

I looked the two-lane up highway and down. Whoever'd pulled in had no way of hiding his vehicle in the long, bare driveway. "Witnesses?"

"Lang's mama. Said she heard the knock and the shots."

"Didn't see the shooter?"

"It takes Miss Abigail a while to get out of her chair. One of them electric lift jobs that stands her up, but the gears move slow. Hell, even if she did get a look at the guy, her cataracts are so bad I doubt she'd have seen much more'n a shape."

"So this loser was living with his mama?"

"Yep. Fits the profile, don't it? He never got off the tit, just moved in and lived off her Social Security check and a little retirement her old man left her. She never believed that sorry outfit did any of the things he was accused of."

"Did anybody unroll his rap sheet for her?"

"Not that I know of, but it wouldn't have mattered. She didn't *care*." He chewed on his cigar. "She started covering for him when he was a kid and got in trouble in school. Always said, 'Not my boy, my Eric wouldn't do something like that.'"

"You sound like you heard her."

"Knew her all my life, and him, too. Went to school with the sonofabitch."

"I've heard *that* story a hundred times."

"Yep, and you'll hear it a hundred more."

"She have anything else to say?"

"Well, her eyesight's gone, but not her hearing. Said the killer sentenced Lang like an old-timey judge, said, 'This is for the crimes and murders you've committed.'"

"That's a pretty long speech for the victim to stand there and listen to."

"Said it after he shot, while Eric was breathing his last."

"Hum."

"Said the killer had a diesel. Heard it through the open door when he drove away."

"She sure?"

"The old gal was raised on a farm and only moved to this house when her husband died back in ninety. She can probably tell what make of truck it was from the sound."

"What happened then?"

"Said she saw Lang laying in the door and dialed the operator."

"Not 911?"

Sheriff Davis removed his cigar and spat onto the sparse, dry grass. "Said she was so rattled she couldn't remember the phone number for 911."

We laughed together.

The sheriff stuck the cigar stub back in the corner of his mouth and adjusted it with his tongue. "The truth is, whoever shot Lang did ever'body a favor. We were already looking at him for some burglaries that started about the same time he got back, and if I's a bettin' man, I'd say he had something to do with starting up a new business here selling crystal meth and that's caused a little . . . tension . . . with the Smith family who lives just across the county line."

"Who're they?"

"About the sorriest bunch of no'count sonsabitches you ever saw. I'm thinking they might've had something to do with this killin', if it wasn't your guy, and here's a little interesting tidbit. The sheriff over in Swisher County has a hunch the Smiths were working with a couple of guys *you* know of."

"Who's that?"

"Do Miguel Torrez and Eric Navarro ring a bell?"

A cold chill went down my spine. "Those are the guys I tangled with back outside of Alpine."

"That's right. There's a little drug pipeline running from down in your part of the world in Big Bend, through here and up to Amarillo where it catches I-40 east and west. Sheriff Guzman over in Swisher County says those boy's names popped up last week when he took one of the Smith boys in for possession. It wasn't enough to hold him but for overnight, but when I told him you were on the way out today it rang his bell. Anyway, I'm fixin' to head over there right now to meet him 'n talk about this shooting. You can come along if you're still interested in what happened down your way, and then you can mark this one off your list of people your traveler's after."

"The Traveler. That fits him."

An eighteen-wheeler passed with a clatter when his Jake brake engaged. Out of habit I glanced up at the same time a pickup passed in the opposite direction pulling a silver Airstream.

"Um humm. I'll go with you." My cell phone rang. "Give me a minute, will you?" I walked back to my truck. Another Jake brake slowed an eighteen-wheeler as it approached the town limits, the engine throttling down loud enough to make it hard for me to hear. I stuck a forefinger in my opposite ear, at the same time wondering how anybody could stand living on such a loud highway. "Hello."

"Got a minute?" It was Yolanda.

"Sure."

"I did an internet search for people in West Texas who've been released from murder charges on technicalities. You'd be surprised at how many felons get off because of paperwork, or because a judge is feeling generous that day. There's a lot more than your guy there, Eric Lang."

"None of this is surprising at this point."

"Well, I narrowed it down from where you are, say to Quanah then south to Del Rio, and this Dimmitt guy popped up with a few more. Since you said the killer might be headed east. I looked on Google Maps and plotted some of the names. There are three within a day's drive if you don't get a lead on his whereabouts. I guess he got away as usual."

"Yep. Nobody saw him, just heard his voice. But at least we're on his track. Now we need to trail this guy. Where else do you have felons he might be interested in?"

"Wichita Falls, Comanche, and Del Rio."

My heart sank as a mental map appeared stretching from the Rio Grande on the southern border up to the Red River dividing Texas from Oklahoma. "Pretty big spread."

"Well anyway, if the guy isn't headed toward let's say Dallas or Ft. Worth on 287, then he may be going somewhere else? Like Austin or Houston. He might be looking to stay off the main drags."

I listened to her supposes and watched one of those big campers they call a "diesel-pusher" pass. An itch in the back of my mind was driving me crazy, and I felt like the answer to everything was right there but I couldn't get a good hold on it. "That kind of fits with what I called you about driving over here. He might be staying away from big cities for some reason, and picking his way through these little burgs now."

Something tickled the back of my brain again, and the memory of passing the fifth-wheel camper an hour earlier popped up in some strange connection. I'd long ago learned to trust my instincts. My subconscious was working on a problem that I didn't even know existed.

Yolanda's voice brought me back. "Right. I think I need to dig a little deeper and see what's behind him, like that detective back in Arizona did. Maybe put together a list of people who recently got off on technicalities, then work backward from their victims' names."

"Dang, girl. You said you didn't have a law-enforcement background."

"I read."

"Good for you. Me and the sheriff are headed out to

talk to some folks. They may be able to help. If it don't pan out, I'm heading for where you said, Comanche."

I heard Perry Hale on the other end. She either had the volume on her phone turned up or she'd put me on speaker. "You sure decided fast."

"Call it a gut feeling. I don't think he's headed for any of the borders."

Chapter 12

Sunrise in Bouregard Parish began with high, pink clouds reflecting the morning's glow over the cypress trees lining the banks of LaBeouf Bayou. Fog rose from the low places where cool night air settled onto the warmer water. A graceful gray and blue great heron flapped ten feet above the muddy surface, its wingspan nearly six feet from tip to tip.

A house perched on stilts located not far from an S-curve on the bayou that ultimately flowed into the Sabine was still dark. In the shadows where the light hadn't yet penetrated, a splash like a gator slapping its tail startled a raccoon that was washing its breakfast on the bank.

Two shapes moved down a two-track dirt driveway leading from the unpainted house with the windows open for any breeze. It began a mile back where the drive intersected the crumbling blacktop lane the locals wishfully called a road.

The shapes materialized into two men walking down the bare parallel tracks, the bottoms of their pants wet from overhanging grass. A doe feeding on the fresh grass at the edge of the woods snorted and bounded away at their approach.

Wearing a floppy crusher hat, Daddy Frank moved with surprising ease for a man in his early eighties. A worn pump shotgun rested over his shoulder. He paused and pointed a crooked finger at the quiet house.

In the other skinny lane beside him, the creature named Boone seemed to glide above the sand in a loose-jointed stride. He wore an oversized shirt, cargo shorts, and kayaking sandals. His dead eyes locked in on the house, then scanned back to his master. Nodding without expression, the bald, tattooed man stepped off the track and through the knee-high blazing star and cone-flower grass to disappear into the woods as silently as the doe.

Daddy Frank remained rooted in place, enjoying the morning light. He couldn't see the bayou through the rising fog, but the sound of a bass exploding on a bug made him smile. Several whistlers rocketed overhead. The wind over their wings made the ducks sound like tiny jets.

He scratched the gray bristle on his cheek and spoke to himself in a voice barely above a whisper. "Maybe this is what Heaven's like."

The sun finally crested the cypress and pine trees, sending bolts of brightness onto the house and the yard, the light reflecting off the windshields of three jacked-up trucks. Many parts of the track blazed with light, but Daddy Frank waited in the dense shade of a thick cypress.

Soft bumps from a disturbance in the house reached his ears and he tilted his head to listen. A shriek cut off as if someone inside had thrown a switch and then more, louder bumps followed. Table legs stuttered across a wooden floor. A startled male voice yelled, the sound dying as fast as it came through rusting window screens.

Hard, flat reports from a firearm ended with a body crashing through the screen door. A man wearing only jeans rounded the porch and rushed empty-handed down the long stairs to the ground. Daddy Frank noted the terrified look on his face as he charged down the track to escape whatever was loose in the house.

Daddy Frank knew exactly what it was and remained perfectly still.

The frightened man gasped for air, and repeatedly glanced back over his shoulder as if the Devil himself was on his heels. The flight instinct absorbed everything that was human and the panicked meth-head raced away from Death with the tunnel-vision blindness only terrified quarry can know.

Only when Scooter was within shotgun range did the old man shoulder the 12-gauge and pull the trigger as if he were rabbit hunting. The man may have seen the movement in the shade, but it was too late. His chest absorbed a load of double-ought buck in a pattern the size of a hubcap.

Scooter's sharp, "Oh!" erupted in a gush of blood, and he fell onto his face, kicked once, and lay still as his heart pumped blood from nine .33-caliber holes.

Seconds later, Boone stepped out of the silent house with a bloody straight razor in one hand and a wet dishrag in the other. Looking as if he'd just enjoyed a fresh shave that peaceful morning, he cleaned the razor with care. Finished, he wiped his face, arms, and bare legs before pitching the rag back through the punched-out screen. He bobbed his head and took the wooden stairs with the smooth motions of a panther, strolling down the drive as if he was in a park. Behind him, smoke boiled from an open window.

When he reached Scooter's body, Boone lowered his head like a scolded dog. "I'm sorry, Daddy."

"There's nothing to be sorry about. That's why I was standing here."

His skin was moist. Boone wiped his nose with one palm and studied the wetness as if looking for something that might be alive. "But what if he hadn't run this way?"

"He did, though." Daddy Frank pointed back at the house. "The guns? They in there?"

"Nossir."

"Well, that cain't be helped. Both of them Thibideaux coonasses we're after in there?"

"Yes."

"They done for?"

"Yes."

"Good."

Daddy Frank remained in the same place, dim in the shade. "Scooter was good and loyal until he wasn't. We cain't leave him here, but I don't want him burned like them others. He's still family."

Boone waited, his face revealing nothing.

Daddy Frank drew a long breath through his nose. "You think that was a gator we heard splash a little while ago?"

"Probably."

"All right then. Take 'im up a ways and dump 'im in the bayou. Don't leave no tracks. Weigh him down out there."

"They might drag it."

"Ain't nobody gonna get out here for a few days."
Daddy Frank waved his hand. "By that time they won't
bring up much."

"Dental records." A light flickered in Boone's eyes,
the only appearance of life he ever offered.

"There is that." Daddy Frank paused, thinking. "I
hate to do it, but he brought all this on himself. Knock
'em out."

"May I have them?"

"For a while. But then we're gonna bury 'em in the
family plot."

"All of them?"

"You can keep one, and slice off his finger pads, just
in case."

The sun was high by the time they were back in
Daddy Frank's blue and white two-toned 1986 Ford
pickup. He pulled out of a cut in the trees and onto the
blacktop. Boone lay on the bench seat, his bald head
on Daddy Frank's leg. The old man drove with his left
hand on the wheel, absently stroking the spiderweb tattoo on the younger man's skull, the same way he used
to stroke his duck dog.

His eyes closed in ecstasy, Boone relaxed. "Daddy?"
"Hum?"

"I'm sorry he got out of the house. It wasn't your
place to end it. That was my job, and I failed."

"No you didn't. It wasn't but a pull of the trigger."
"Daddy?"
"Hum?"
"Thank you for the tooth."

The rough blacktop intersected the highway. Daddy

Frank steered onto the smooth concrete and accelerated. He spread his fingers along the blue lines of Boone's spiderweb. "You're welcome."

He patted Boone's cheek and reached for the satellite phone on his dash. With that settled, there was much to do before Friday's delivery.

And it was time for that crybaby Tanner to man up.

Chapter 13

Tanner Wadler drove his leased Taurus to work as the sun topped the pines, a frown creasing his brow. He was the only immediate family member who wasn't excited about the upcoming Plan. If he didn't know any better, he'd bet that another family's blood ran through his veins. Once he even told Donine that he went through the family Bible when he was in high school to see if he'd been adopted.

While the rest of the Wadlers were black haired and dark complected, Tanner was a redhead. His white skin burned and peeled in the humid summertime, while his other relatives darkened to the warm color of stained mahogany.

He turned down the radio, pulled into the employee parking lot, and killed the engine beside his friends' vehicles. The car blazed like a wet cherry beside the muddy trucks and SUVs parked in rows. As always, Tanner was the last one to arrive, but his foreman, Bo, was Tanner's best friend, who understood that Donine's pregnancy had been hard.

Tanner sat in his car with the windows down, breathing Beaumont's petrochemical odors that soaked into his sinuses. Sometimes he felt as though he could smell nothing but fumes from the refineries for days at a time.

He slapped a round container of Copenhagen against his thumb to pack the grind, then twisted off the silver cap, sniffing the fresh wintergreen to chase the sulfur away. Packing a pinch under his bottom lip, he tucked the can into his back pocket and closed his eyes as the rush of nicotine reached his brain.

Tanner spit a dark stream into a plastic Dr Pepper bottle he kept in the console. His cell phone rang. It was Jimmy Don. "Hey, Daddy."

"You workin' yet?"

"Naw, just pulled in. What's up?"

"Call me back."

"Yessir." Tanner hung up and opened the console. He plucked a burner phone from the empty console and dialed a number he'd memorized.

Jimmy Don immediately answered his own burner. "Good. Listen, I don't trust these others with this part, so here's what I want you to do. There's a couple of feds in Jasper. Get with Willy and y'all go make 'em disappear."

A cold chill went down Tanner's spine. "What kind of feds?"

"DEA, I guess. Maybe AFT if they got wind of the old man's dumbass plastic explosive idea. What difference does it make?"

"A lot. How do you like, know they're agents, and if they're here for us?"

"They've been snooping around, asking questions."

"It could be anybody."

"They're federal agents for sure. They checked into the Holiday Inn, went by the sheriff's office in Jasper, then came over here to Newton County and talked to Buck, and that's worryin' the old man."

"But, Dad."

"This ain't all my idea. It came from Daddy Frank this morning. We gotta move faster than we expected. He called y'alls names to do it."

Tanner shivered. He was as afraid of that old man as he was of a bear. When he was a kid and when Daddy Frank wasn't around, stories about the old man made the rounds and were sometimes used to frighten misbehaving children, warning that if they didn't straighten up and fly right, Daddy Frank was gonna come get 'em.

One story he knew for the truth. Once two strangers came out to the house late one night with pistols in hand. Competitors in the drug trade nearly fifteen years earlier, they met Daddy Frank in front of the barn and shot him three times in the stomach. The tough old man staggered backward, shirt becoming slick with blood, and pulled the ever-present .38 from his back pocket. Two shots in each man dropped them to the ground, and one each to the forehead anchored them for sure.

He sat down on a bench beside the barn door and waited for his relatives to come running from the house. Holding his stomach with both hands, he ordered the two bodies to be disposed of in the nearby bayou where the gators would finish the job. Only then would he get in the car and go to the hospital where he wove a story about a highway shooting that no one believed, but what the hell, he was kin to the sheriff even back then, so the issue was dropped.

Tanner rubbed his suddenly greasy forehead with shaking fingers. "Daddy, I done told you I'd do everything else, but I can't make myself be part of killing people nose to nose. How 'bout I help out pulling a camper? You know I can drive fast. Hell, I'll go set the charges on that pipeline if that's what you want. How about that?"

Jimmy Don sounded as if Tanner'd suggested they go fishing. "No, you do what you're told. 'Cause you don't look like the rest of us, I believe you can get close to those guys without 'em knowing what's happening. Get out there and watch for a little bit. You'll get a chance at some point, even if you have to knock on the door."

"Then what?"

Jimmy Don sighed in frustration. "Then take 'em somewhere out of town and make 'em disappear. Damn, son, this ain't *rocket* science."

"You want me to shoot them my ownself?" His mind raced, trying to think of a way out. "Willy's done that kind of work before. I'll back him up."

"No, Daddy Frank says it's time for you to start taking more action in the family business. That's how he got me ready to take over when the time comes."

"That old man's too mean to die, and I 'magine you're not gonna be taking over for years."

"No matter. He said to send Willy with you, and he's still running things around here, but you do the trigger work so's it's done right."

"Donine's getting pretty close to her due date. I don't think I should . . ."

"She'll domino just fine whether you're there or

not. She can get her mama to take her to the hospital, but I doubt it'll happen tonight. Now you do what I *say*."

Already numb with fear and dread, Tanner knew better than to argue. He felt a glimmer of hope. "Well, I don't have nothin' to use. I can't just go carrying rifles around town without people noticing. Willy has some, but I bet he won't want me using them."

"Go by the house when you get off. There'll be two revolvers in a bucket out by the shed."

Tanner's stomach sank. "Revolvers? Dad, if they're federal agents, they'll likely have us outgunned. You know they're carrying Glocks or something."

"I know it don't make much difference if you catch 'em with their britches down. It'll only take two shots." Jimmy Don's voice softened. He was a master of manipulation and had worked the boy his entire life. "The Old Man wants to know this is done tonight when he gets home. He wants to see us at the house after you're finished."

Tanner shivered, both from the thought of facing the Old Man and what he was told to do. He tried to stay as far away from his hard-faced granddaddy as possible. "Daddy Frank's back?"

"Yep. Now, do what I told you, unless you want to explain to him and Boone why you ain't interested in helping."

Chapter 14

I followed Sheriff Cameron Davis from Castro County to a farm road between Tulia and Dimmitt. It wasn't long before we splashed through a mud puddle bisecting the drive, then rattled across a train track before pulling up to a tiny white co-op office fifty yards from a peeling white grain silo.

Pumpjacks, sometimes called nodding donkeys or thirsty birds, rocked slowly in the scrub-covered pasture out back, their horse-like heads pushing and pulling sucker rods, pumping oil from the ground at a lazy, almost hypnotic pace.

Manuel Guzman, the Swisher County Sheriff, and two deputies were already waiting beside their cars in the dirt parking lot with a highway patrol officer in a "Texas tan" uniform.

I detrucked into the steady south wind I hate with a passion and ground my teeth, wondering how anyone could live in a place where it blows twenty and thirty miles an hour from that direction and the next day at the same velocity from the north. I asked a grizzled old farmer at an Amarillo gas station when I was about twenty-five how he stood it, and he studied on the question while his gas tank filled.

"Well, son, it's pretty aggravatin' for the first fifty years or so, then you learn to tolerate it."

The youngest of the deputies brightened up when he saw my badge and gunbelt. His starstruck eyes locked on my .45's Sweetheart grips, and I hoped he wouldn't make a big deal of it. I checked his name tag. Deputy Rivera had that puppy-dog look of excitement you see in freshman officers who want nothing more than the next adrenaline rush. I made sure to shake Rivera's hand after Sheriff Guzman, holding on for a heartbeat longer to look into the man's eager face and settle him down.

Sheriff Guzman looked as dried out from the wind and sun as a piece of beef jerky. He introduced the other two officers. "Deputy Acevedo and Officer Friedman." Guzman nodded his straw hat toward the east and unconsciously adjusted his blue tie. "The house is about a mile that way. This is nothing more than a knock and talk, but these Smith boys are crazy as shithouse rats." He smoothed his salt-and-pepper mustache as if deciding what to say next. "Three brothers, Mark, Gary, and Patrick. They were as nuts as their daddy before they started sampling the crap they're selling, but now they're worse."

Sheriff Davis chewed the unlit cigar stub in the corner of his mouth. "There's no tellin' who's there, so take it easy. Me'n Manuel just want to ask a few questions, and he'll take the lead since this is his county. Y'all are here to make 'em think and behave themselves."

Deputy Rivera inclined his head in my direction.

Rivera started in my direction, but I held up a hand to stop him. "Does anyone in there say that you have to take them or smoke weed?"

She nodded again, but it was almost imperceptible. "I'm fine."

A rote, repeated answer. "No you're not. I know these guys are bad dudes. You're not anybody's girlfriend. Where you from?"

She shrugged. "Not far away."

"Name the town, quick."

"It's, uh, Wichita Falls."

"What air force base is there?"

Her eyes dropped. "I don't know."

"Honey." My tone went softer. "Where're you from?"

For the first time, she tilted her head up to meet my gaze. "Oklahoma City."

I took that one. It came quick and another piece fell into place. A minor alone in a trailer with someone she wasn't related to is another warning sign. Now we had state lines involved. "I'm going to ask you a question that might make you uncomfortable, but I need to know. Ready?"

Wrinkling her smooth forehead, she nodded.

"Here it is, and I want the truth. I'm not going to ask you anything personal for the moment, but I need to know the answer to this really odd question. Do they make . . . movies in there? I bet there's a room full of light stands and lights, and cameras."

Her eyes widened and filled.

Sheriff Guzman was talking to Gary in a low voice, but the creep's attention was on us.

"You've been in some of them. Men come and go, and you're expected to entertain them, right?"

A tear formed and spilled down her cheek.

She nodded.

"Tell me the truth. Do you need help?"

A whisper. "Yes."

That one word was all I needed. I took her elbow as a rage built in my chest. I choked it down. "Come with me." We walked to my truck and I opened the door. "You're not under arrest, but I need you to empty your pockets. Do you have anything in them?" Her shorts were pretty-well painted on, and I didn't think she had anything on her, but she nodded. I knew it couldn't be a weapon or I'd have already seen the outline, but needles or a razor blade were a distinct possibility.

I held out my hand and she plucked something from her back pocket with two fingers. She dropped a strip of condoms in my palm and I had to drop my filters back in place real fast.

Over her shoulder, and past the truck, I saw Gary's eyes darken.

"That's what I thought."

Sheriff Davis shifted closer to the fender of his car. The three officers drew closer, talking amongst themselves.

"Get in the truck and stay here until I come get you out."

"He has a gun."

I nodded. "Where is it?"

"Behind his back."

Shit.

"Okay. Wait here."

I closed the door and started toward the trailer. Things had been calm up to that point, but with a gun in play, it could all go sideways pretty quick. Flashes of red burst inside my eyes, and it was all I could do not to charge up there and beat that little weasel into a greasy spot on the dried boards, despite the threat of a weapon.

Gary saw me coming and apparently recognized the Look on my face the twins tell me about. His eyes locked on me, even though Sheriff Guzman was still talking. I was halfway there when something changed in the man.

I called his name as if to ask him a question. "Gary!" Sometimes a person's name will snap them out of whatever they're thinking of doing.

It didn't work.

Chapter 15

Trouble happens fast. Gary'd faced us the entire time and the reason was the semiauto pistol stuck in the small of his back. He snatched it out of his waistband, shoved the muzzle into Sheriff Guzman's stomach before anyone could react, and pulled the trigger.

Guzman *oof*ed at the bullet's impact, grabbed for the pistol with his left hand, preventing the slide from completing the action from loading another round. His knees buckled, but he held on like a snapping turtle and stumbled backward, pulling Gary with him. The sheriff drew his Glock and stuck it into Gary's stomach. Off balance, Guzman pulled the trigger over and over at the same time he went through the warped rail, dragging the surprised child molester with him.

They landed with a hard thump on the packed ground at the same time the world exploded. Automatic weapons opened up from two different directions. Other men who I took to be Smith brothers had probably slipped out the back door as soon as we pulled up and waited to see what would happen.

Caught in a crossfire from the cedars at both ends of the trailer house, highway patrol officer Wayne Friedman and the other deputy Juan Acevedo dropped in their tracks. Lead sprayed across the enclosed yard. The sound was deafening. Sheriff Davis twisted and dropped out of sight as he threw himself around the front of the car.

Halfway across the open space between my truck and Sheriff Guzman's cruiser, I would have spun and taken cover behind the Dodge's block, but Karen was in there. Instead of drawing fire against her, I sprinted for the cruiser and flinched when an overturned fifty-five-gallon trash barrel between me and the gunman on my left vibrated with the impact of several rounds. It was enough to divert the bullets that whirred so close they sounded like angry wasps.

The other bad guys' fire was concentrated at first on the cluster of lawmen standing twenty yards away, giving me just enough time to snatch the big .45 from its holster and drop down against the cruiser's left front wheel. It wasn't much, but it had to do.

Sheriff Davis's pistol cracked twice. "Get down!"

I didn't see him and figured the poor guy was on the ground trying to crawl under the car. There was no telling if he was offering me advice or talking to someone else.

At his shout, the nearest gunman to my side shifted his aim back in my direction. A line of holes erupted across the hood, seeking me out and punching through the sheet metal with the flat sound of hammers on metal. Davis fired again, and it sounded like he was under the front end of his cruiser. I heard dragging sounds and grunts from his position.

Muzzle blasts through the tender green vegetation to my left gave the gunman's position away. I still couldn't see him, but there was no doubt where he was shooting from. I violated the Old Man's cardinal rule of hunting and the cardinal rule of shooting. The Colt rose in my vision and I lined the sights up on the muzzle blasts and deliberately squeezed the trigger one, two, three . . . four times at an unseen target. The limbs shuddered, and the firing stopped from that weapon.

Now you might be rolling your eyes at that, thinking that just like in Hollywood movies, a guy can shoot fifty times with a machine gun and miss every time while the good guy with a pistol shoots once or twice and kills the man. But the truth is that most people who use fully automatic weapons aren't familiar with them. It's hard to hold an automatic rifle still. The barrel tends to wave around, and rise up and to the right.

I'd spent enough time on the range for muscle memory to kick in. I'd leveled the pistol and squeezed off the shots with what the Old Man calls deliberation. It worked.

Now that I was out of the second gunman's line of sight, I peeked around the front of the cruiser. Deputy Acevedo's leg was shattered and blood poured from a wound in his neck and side where the rounds missed his vest, but the tough highway patrol officer wasn't out of the fight. Dragging himself with one elbow and shooting with the other hand, Acevedo used his good leg to push himself toward the closest protection, the trailer.

The deadly machine gun hidden on my right chattered again as the bad guy held the trigger down. One round impacted Acevedo's good leg. Another caught his shoe on that same destroyed leg and twisted that foot into an impossible angle. The officer shrieked like a panther and collapsed.

Small bursts of sand stitched from Acevedo's body toward Friedman, who was also down and trying to roll over. Sheriff Davis fired again. The only one of our guys I couldn't locate was Deputy Rivera, who was nowhere to be seen. With the car between me and the other gunman, I crabbed around the front and looked under the cruiser.

The automatic weapon went silent. Probably changing magazines. In the silence, I heard Sheriff Guzman groan.

He and Gary had been still so long I thought they were both dead. I crept to the front of the sedan, keeping it between me and the other guy. "Guzman! I can't get to you. Use your feet. Push yourself under the deck."

Another stitch of bullets threw sand and gravel in small fountains, forcing me back to cover.

I heard Guzman dig in to crawl at the same moment Gary came alive. Even with three holes in his stomach, the dirty little creep rolled onto his side and fired twice into Guzman's back from less than three feet away. Two quick shots hammered the enclosure and Gary snapped forward and then fell back.

I couldn't see where those shots came from. Dropping to my stomach, I found Sheriff Davis was almost under his car, using both empty hands to pull himself along the ground, and I couldn't understand why the gunman hadn't yet zeroed in on him. I peeked again and realized Davis was partially protected by a rusted-out wheelbarrow and a washing machine half-buried in old ashes and twisted metal.

That was where Rivera had taken cover. He'd figured out the angle to keep the trash between him and the gunman, and was belly-crawling toward me like someone out of that old TV show, *Combat*.

He got aholt of Davis's collar, and I raised up and shot the Colt dry to keep the shooter's head down as Rivera backed around the cruiser, dragging Sheriff Davis. The unseen rifle chattered again, stitching the side of the sedan. They collapsed beside me, and we ducked at the insane volume of noise. Though the gun was a hundred feet away, I swear I could feel the pressure wave of the shots.

The cruiser vibrated from the impacts of round after round. It seemed as if the shooter was trying to shoot us through the car. We were against the front wheel, keeping it and the engine block between us and the deadly rifle.

I saw blood on Rivera's shirt. Sheriff Davis lay still, though he was breathing. "You hit bad?"

Another line of stitches chopped at the car. One slug punched through to our side, causing us to flinch, though it was obviously too late.

"Yeah." Rivera slapped a fresh magazine into the handle of his Beretta M-9.

"Stay with me. Throw some more rounds in that direction so he'll duck his head. I bet he's ready to reload."

"You better hurry. I'm bleedin' out and losing my strength."

"Moving."

"Go!" Rivera stuck his hand up and fired three times to get the guy's head down, then still shooting, he raised on one knee and shot across the hood. The big 9mm pistol blasts came so fast they were a continuous roll of thunder until the seventeen-round magazine ran dry. I sprinted away from the car in the opposite direction from the shooter. It seemed to take forever to cross the open yard, but the deputy's fire kept the bad guy from shooting for the moment.

Thank you, Lord, for double-stack magazines.

I reached the safe cover of the cedars and plowed through without slowing. Soft, green limbs slapped my face as I bulled through the limber branches, losing my hat in the process. Holding my left arm in front of my face, I kept pumping my legs until I stumbled out the other side. It felt surreal when the wind slapped my clothes as I broke through in a seemingly different world.

I nearly stumbled over a body lying half in and out of the windbreak.

Two large exit wounds in his back proved I'd used enough gun. I figured him to be one of the brothers, and the guy was as gone as you can get, with a fist-sized hole in his head. The lower half of his body was still in the cedars and it looked as if despite his wound, he'd tried to walk out. An M-16 lay near to hand, shattered by one of my bullets.

I rushed past, around the outside corner and peeked down the line of cedars growing behind the trailer. To my left, there was nothing but open fields and irrigation equipment spraying water onto a crop I couldn't identify. Other than the house place beside me and half a dozen more rocking pumpjacks, I couldn't see anything but plowed ground.

A pistol barked again. The shooter answered with a long burst and then everything went quiet except for the wind bending the tops of the cedars. I stepped around a big piñon, which served to define the corner, and crept down the windbreak, listening. The back of the trailer was on my right. The shooter was somewhere around the next corner, and I hoped he didn't know I was coming.

Man, I wished I had Perry Hale and Yolanda with me. Those guys knew what to do in a firefight, and the only idea I had was to keep moving.

The pistol fired twice more, answered by a short burst from the automatic weapon.

Good. Rivera was keeping the guy busy. Maybe our orchestration had worked after all, and he didn't know I was coming.

Three-quarters down the line of cedars, I heard the distinctive rattle of a magazine change as the shooter reloaded. I didn't like that one damned bit. I'd been hoping he would be at the end of a mag by the time I located him. Then I'd be up against a few shots instead of what had sounded like full thirty-round magazines.

"Hey!" It was Rivera's voice quavering voice. "I'm hurt bad and out of ammo. I'm the only one left. You go your way, and let me drive out of here."

Good boy.

"No way, asshole."

The shooter's answer was low, as if he were talking to himself, but it gave me what I needed. I was at that last corner by then, about to round the east side. The stiff south wind blew the tops of the cedars overhead, and thrashed the limbs on the outside of the trees around the corner. There was another piñon pine there, and I knelt beside it to listen.

The guy couldn't be more than twenty yards away, judging by where the bullets had been coming from, and the soft answer. I've shot enough deer to know good and well he'd have to be in the windbreak, almost inside the enclosure so he could make clean shots, but not be seen.

Evergreens and pines don't drop leaves, so there were no worries about my footsteps giving me away. I crept around a few pine cones lying on the outside edge of the windbreak and knelt to listen. Wind soughed though the greenery. An eighteen-wheeler passed on the highway, followed by the hiss of cars and a truck pulling a camper.

The sound rose and fell as they passed, and once again my mind went to that place where it separates itself from what's happening, good or bad, and allows words to pop up that do me no good. The Doppler effect. That's the rising and falling sound of a car passing.

Great. Unless I wrote that in the action report to the Major . . . if I lived that long, it might be one of the last things I remembered. I caught the disappearing camper from the corner of my eye and wished I was going camping somewhere instead of sneaking up on a guy with an automatic weapon. The moving limbs were distracting, making it almost impossible to see inside the windbreak.

I focused on what was ahead so my mind wouldn't dredge up any more useless words right at that moment.

A dove flapped into the cedars from over my shoulder and barely lit before something spooked it. With a flutter and peeping cry, it fought clear of the branches and shot over the empty field until it disappeared into the distance.

Dammit! If I'd been paying attention, the two doves that spooked just before Gary opened the door would have told us those two guys were leaving out the back. But at least now I knew where the shooter was.

The guy wasn't taking any chances. I got the idea he wasn't buying Rivera's story about being out of ammo, and if I'd been *him*, I'd be looking for *me*. That's what I figured he was doing.

A particularly stout gust of wind slapped the cedars, making them moan and rustle. An open gap in the soft limbs, probably made by some animal, gave me access to the interior of the man-made grove. Pistol held at what today's range masters are calling compressed-ready, meaning it was chest-high and in position for up-close and personal action. I took two steps into the trees and saw a shirtless guy on one knee with his back to me.

Why are all these guys always running around without shirts?

Another ridiculous thought. This one from my daughter Mary, who once said while watching the television show *Cops*, "If they aren't wearing a shirt, they're guilty."

I started to shoot him and get it over with, but knew that once an investigation was launched, they'd have my hide for the entry holes in his back. Seems you have to give the bad guys time to turn around and give up these days. I drew a bead at the hinge of a pair of wings tattooed on his spine, took a deep breath, and half let it out.

"Hey."

He stiffened and whirled. The minute I saw the side of his face and the rifle come around, all discussion was over. He was three-quarters of the way around when I shot him just under his arm in the left side of his chest.

At the same time, a steady, deliberate string of shots rang out, sounding like someone practicing on a firing range. The bad guy'd raised up into a gap in the cedars. The first three or four rounds caught him solid, but as he fell, Rivera kept pulling the trigger on that Beretta.

And now the bad guy wasn't soaking up the shots heading straight for me.

I threw myself to the side as rounds cracked past way closer than I liked. Lead either punched through the soft wood of the cedars or glanced off the sides and whirred away with an evil buzz.

Rivera was bound and determined to use every round in that magazine. I flattened out on the ground, and by the time his pistol was empty, the only sound was the wind in the cedars.

Chapter 16

Roads chop up the vast majority of the East Texas landscape into a patchwork quilt of highways, pastures, and cropland. Greenbelt forests spread for hundreds of miles through this landscape like arteries consisting of meandering courses of rivers, creeks, ravines, washes, and swamps linking farms to communities to towns to cities.

The humid air was thick and fragrant from freshly mown lawns and grassy bar ditches full of muddy water, decaying leaves, and crawdads. As the day died, Tanner Wadler drove with one hand on the wheel of his leased Taurus sedan, elbow hanging out of the open window. He and Willy left the calm, quiet country behind and merged into the light traffic on the edge of Jasper, a country town only twenty minutes from Gunn. Pink and orange clouds diffused the sky, painting a colorful backlight over the western edge of the small East Texas town.

As they drew closer to the cluster of businesses on the main drag, those comforting country smells were overwhelmed by woodsmoke from barbecue restaurants, old grease from three fried-chicken takeouts built within spitting distance of each other, and exhaust fumes left behind by a car that hadn't been inspected since God was a kid.

"I don't like this one damned bit." Steering with one hand, Tanner squirted a brown stream into the quarterfull Dr Pepper bottle. "I've never killed anybody before."

Willy shrugged and adjusted the seat belt across his chest. His dead eye was on Tanner's side, forcing him to completely turn his head to see the young man. "It's the easiest thing in the world to do. Just point and pull the trigger."

"I knew about one. You've done others?"

"When Daddy Frank gave the order."

"I didn't know that."

"You don't know a lot of things."

"I'm already so nervous I'm liable to blow my own foot off. How about we tell Dad these guys were gone when we got to the hotel? We can say we waited as long as we could, but they never came back."

"He'll know better." Willy smoothed his beard. Tanner noticed the man's hands were steady as a rock. "Even if he *does* believe you, he'll just send us back tomorrow. I don't want to get crossways with your granddaddy, neither."

A light at the next intersection turned red, and the flow of cars and pickups rolled to a stop. Tanner touched the revolver tucked under his shirt. His was a thirty-year-old Colt Python with a three-inch barrel, deep blue and so cared-for it looked brand new. Most likely stolen in a home burglary, it was loaded with heavy .357 rounds that would be devastating at close range.

An egg-shaped sedan in the lane on Willy's side vibrated the air with the heavy bass beat of rap music coming from enormous aftermarket speakers mounted in the trunk. All the windows were down and four young black men bobbed their heads to the beat.

Tanner unconsciously plucked the bottle from the holder and held it, ready to spit again. "Who are these guys we're supposed to take out anyway?"

Willy took a worn snub-nose .38 out of the right front pocket of his bib overalls. "Don't make no difference. Daddy Frank says they're against us and to take 'em out."

Tanner waved a hand at the cars. "Hell, half these folks are against us."

"And the other half are on our side. These sons-abitches right here ain't though." Willy turned toward the car beside them, his elbow hanging out the window, the thirty-eight in his hand, but hidden from the other car. "Hey, turn that shit down!"

The muscular driver in a white T-shirt that was blinding against his thick bicep stuck his hand out the window and flipped Willy the bird. "Kiss my ass, you white motherf . . ."

The man's voice trailed off when Willy turned his entire head toward the car. The scar, the dead eye, and the .38 scratching an itch in his beard ended the young man's train of thought.

"Oh, shit!"

The passenger behind the driver leaned as far back

into the seat to provide as small a target as possible. "Turn it down, man."

Unconcerned by what was happening only three feet away, Tanner kept talking as the music from the other car dropped in volume. He'd heard Willy argue with other drivers before. "I doubt that. If they were, they'd be working with us already. Most of these people don't know anything about what's going on in this country in the first place."

The light changed, and Tanner accelerated with the flow of traffic. The sedan fell behind as Willy put the .38 back in his pocket and hooked his elbow out of the window. "I hate that rap shit. It's so loud you can go tone death in a New York minute."

"Tone deaf."

"Huh?"

"It's pronounced tone deaf, not death."

Willy shrugged. "You know what I mean."

His unusually clipped voice made Tanner reconsider correcting Willy about his speech, but he'd always mispronounced words and garbled old sayings enough they all looked forward to what he'd come up with next.

"Find us some decent country music. This fancy thing *does* have a radio, don't it?"

Tanner squeezed a button on the steering wheel with his thumb and "Florida Georgia Line" came through the speakers scattered around the car. "That ain't anything *like* country. Hang on." He pressed again and George Strait picked up where the pseudo country band left off. "You know we could make things worse if these men really are feds."

Willy shrugged. "We're gonna do what Daddy Frank told us. You don't want to cross the old man, then you'd have to deal with Boone."

Tanner shrugged. "I'm not sure he's as bad as y'all make out. You know he reads a lot. I saw him one day not too long ago waiting for Daddy Frank in his car, and Boone was reading Nietzsche."

"Is that one of them Indian guys who writes westerns?"

"No. He was a German philosopher who had a huge influence on Western philosophy. Not westerns, for chrissake."

"Well, I don't know nothin' about all that. I didn't go to college."

"Well, neither did I, but . . ."

"But all that highfalutin kind of talk don't mean nothin' when it comes to staying alive in this world, and you don't go thinkin' Boone's like you just because he reads. Hell, he's mean as a snake and crazy as a shithouse rat. I suspect you'll do what Daddy Frank says and when he says it."

"Yeah, well, he ain't always right."

Willy rode without responding.

"I've never killed nobody. The only thing I've ever shot is deer and dove."

"Don't make no difference. Daddy Frank says to get rid of 'em, and we're gonna do it." He spat out the window in disgust and wiped some dribble off his beard. "They're right. It's time for you to man up."

Chapter 17

Alonzo Wadler sat in his camper's doorway, sipping a cup of hot coffee and staring into the live oak and mesquite trees shading the long gravel sites in the Evening Star RV Park outside of Comanche, Texas. A light breeze washed over his camp smelling of hot dust and coming rain.

Dark clouds built in the northwest, freshening the breeze even more. Lightning fractured the leading edge of the storm, and the distant boom of thunder finally arrived. Alonzo tried to remember how many seconds you were supposed to count between the flash and boom to determine how far away the storm was, but finally gave up.

Comanche was his next-to-last stop to deal with still another criminal who'd manipulated the justice system. Like the rest of his family, Alonzo hated meth dealers and despised those who bought from them. How could anyone smoke something made from chemicals from under the kitchen sink? He shook his head in disgust and worked on a plan to take Michael Earl Livingston from the face of the earth.

His coffee was cold when an elderly man walking a white poodle passed his campsite. The man stepped over to the picnic table and held out a steel Yeti mug. "Thought you might like a little local treat. They have a new coffeehouse here that roasts and grinds its own beans."

Alonzo rose from his position in the door and joined the stranger beside the grease-stained wooden picnic table to get farther from the trailer. He couldn't trust the air fresheners and perfume to completely cover the smell that was getting stronger as the humidity increased. "Sounds good to me."

The man sat a squatty steel Yeti across the picnic table and stepped over the bench seat to settle in for a visit. He held up a second mug. "This is what they call their Signature Blend. It'll chase away the dampness."

Alonzo took the opposite side and raised his in thanks. "I like good coffee."

"It's better than that Starbucks crap everyone is drinking these days." He stuck out a hand. "Name's Jefferson, John Jefferson."

"I'm Alonzo."

They sat in silence for a few moments, enjoying the morning. Jefferson smacked his lips and wiped at a fine layer of dust covering the table. He saluted the coming storm. "That's gonna drive us inside in a little bit. I told Mama that if you were like me, you love the outdoors and hate to be trapped inside by the rain."

The man's reference to his wife as Mama was pure East Texas. "You're right about that."

"You a cop?"

Alonzo was surprised at the sudden change in conversation, and the old man's estimation. "A lot of people get that idea."

"You look like a cop. I pride myself on recognizing lawmen."

"I guess you were in law enforcement?"

"Naw. Bum leg wouldn't let me pass the physical. I retired from the railroad. You don't see many men camping by themselves this way."

Alonzo almost smiled. The old guy was desperate to find out who he was. Some people are naturally nosy, and the harmless questions came from a man who liked company and conversation. Alonzo grew up around men like that, who hung around their tiny community general store, sitting on benches and shooting the breeze with the local Spit and Whittle club. He'd grown up on their stories and conversations, when he could get away from Daddy Frank for a little while.

"I'm retired, too." He jerked his head toward the trailer. "Wife died a while back, and this was my escape."

Jefferson's eyes radiated sympathy. "I understand. Just had to get away. I'd be like that if I lost Mama."

Instead of answering, Alonzo sipped at the coffee and wishing it was the chicory he'd grown up with.

"My wife saw you pull in last night. You set that rig up in no time flat."

The Gladys Kravitz kind of neighbors even live in campgrounds. Alonzo smiled again, thinking of Jefferson's wife peering through the windows of their Silver Stream and screeching at her husband. "John! Look how fast he set up."

Have to keep that in mind.

Jefferson kept talking. "We're from Dallas. Here for spring turkey season. I have a lease about three miles away, but it don't have no electricity or water. Mama don't rough it no more'n this, so we stay here. The weather's been just right, and the toms are gobbling by daylight. I didn't have any luck yesterday, but I ran across a guy who did pretty good. I'm going out before first light in the morning. You want to join me?"

The question surprised Alonzo. "Well, that sounds like a great idea, but I'm gonna be leaving first thing in the morning. We're heading home."

"We? I didn't know you had anyone with you."

A cold chill went down Alonzo's back, and he wanted to slam a fist into the side of his own skull. The realization that he'd screwed up woke the badger in his stomach with a vengeance. He fought the urge to double over and vomit the coffee that was suddenly bitter in his throat. "I don't. I'm still used to saying we, meaning my wife, who's gone."

"I understand." Jefferson slapped the table. "Well, that storm's gonna get here pretty soon and I need to get my awning in before the wind picks up. Finish your coffee and just leave the mug settin' here. I'll have to walk the dog in a little bit, and I'll get it then."

"Good to meet you, and thanks for the coffee."

He left, and Alonzo sat there feeling pretty good until he remembered the phone call he'd received that morning from Mike Dillman. Once again Daddy Frank was dictating his life even from over three hundred miles away, sending Mike to meet him and pick up the trailer and the cash.

That wasn't the way Alonzo worked, and the longer he'd been away from Gunn, and the more time that passed since Betty died, the more he'd decided to separate himself from the Family. Losing her had taken the wind from his sails and he couldn't be a part of it any longer.

He just wished he hadn't told Mike where he was camped, but the badger had been gnawing on his guts for a full hour, and the pills hadn't yet taken effect. At the same time he was so rattled by the sudden call that he'd told them more than he wanted.

At least he hadn't said he was alone. Those kinds of drastic events could cause Daddy Frank to react in ways he didn't even want to think about.

Chapter 18

There hadn't been much rain west of Abilene, and the colorless landscape of ranches and grassland looked as baked as the desert. I rolled through barren, flat country with little shade. Even the cattle were somewhere else. Most of the time the only movement I saw was dead grass blowing across the highway and one pumpjack idly bobbing up and down.

Every now and then I'd pass an abandoned house and barn. It was odd that the trees the ranchers had planted for shade were usually dead also, as if giving up themselves after the owners had surrendered. The windmills that had drawn water for decades no longer pumped, the blades often missing, dented, or shot to pieces.

In Texas, the cities are booming while most of the western part of the state was drying up and blowing away.

The blinding, late-evening sun behind me hung halfway to the horizon. Despite my sunglasses, I had to tilt the rearview mirror to the "nighttime" setting just to see. I was empty as the land around me, and tired, drained of both energy and emotion.

Rolling down the highway, my mind shifted into neutral and I thought about the report I'd written by hand when Ranger Bills arrived at the scene of the shoot-out. It was late in the day by the time the bodies were taken away and the crime scene at the trailer was clear, though I knew that another investigative team would be out there at dawn. I wouldn't leave until I felt that Dan was satisfied with my story.

Lieutenant Bills was one of the twenty Rangers assigned to Company C that encompasses everything from the Texas panhandle up against Oklahoma, down to Plains and Yoakum County on the New Mexico border, east to the small Texas town of Bowie in Montague County and unfortunately, all the way down to Central Texas and Comanche, where I was headed.

Dan Bills lives in Hereford, only twenty miles away from Dimmitt. He'd been on his way back from somewheres else and was out to the scene less than an hour after it happened. Knowing there was another Ranger involved, he came out both as a fellow officer and as part of the investigation in his region. That's part of what we do, conduct criminal and special investigations and assist local law-enforcement officials. I could tell from the look on his face that he didn't appreciate having me digging around in his part of the state.

Despite being out in the middle of nowhere, my cell phone rang, reminding me that you never know where you have service. It was clamped into a holder blocking the center AC vent. I turned down the radio and punched the screen with a forefinger. "Howdy, Major."

Commander Major Chase Parker's voice boomed from the speaker. "Sonny, what'n hell happened up there in Dimmitt?"

I knew better than to be a smartass right at that moment. "More than any of us expected." I outlined the events from the time I met Sheriff Davis until Patrol Officer Rivera ended the shoot-out only seconds before passing out.

"You hurt?"

"Not physically." I held the steering wheel steady with both hands as an eighteen-wheeler passed me doing more than eighty miles an hour. The truck's backdraft raised grit that peppered the windshield like dry sleet when he pulled back into the lane.

My Dodge shuddered. "The thing of it is that they had nothing to do with Lang's death. They were just local punks who should have already been serving life sentences down in Huntsville. It was a dead end for me . . . sorry, I shouldn't have said it like that."

"You saved that little gal. They might have missed her in there, and no telling what could have happened to her."

"Yeah, and it cost them their lives."

"They knew the job, and would have been there anyway. Those brothers were human traffickers. Don't go second guessing yourself."

My eyes burned, probably from all the crap kicked up by the south wind. The weather guessers were predicting a late cold front that would surely bring rain stretching from Wichita Falls in the north central part of the state, all the way down past San Angelo before sweeping southeastward toward Louisiana and the Gulf. "You calling me back to the office?"

"Thought about it, but no. Putting you back on the desk won't make any difference now."

"I stepped on some toes while I was there. How'd Dan Bills take it? I know what he told me, but I'm sure he had more to say when y'all were talking."

"He's mad enough to chew nails." Major Parker's voice wasn't accusatory, just matter-of-fact. "Said he should have been investigating a local shooting involving local law-enforcement officers instead of having a Ranger from another company drop by unannounced and then leave once he showed up."

"I didn't leave that fast. He worked me over pretty good with questions. I wrote up a report and hung around as long as I thought I should."

"Well, I was on the phone for a good long while and had to tell him about your new assignment. He finally cooled down and admitted that he liked the idea of this new concept, but he says you still shoulda checked in with him when you got to his region."

My face flushed. "You're right. I intended to, but didn't get over there, or call." I considered telling Major Parker that I figured he'd already done so, since I was out breaking new ground for him, and in my opinion, he should have been running some sort of interference for us all. Bringing it up would sound like whining, though, and I ain't like that. "I told him I'm on the way to Comanche. He wanted to call ahead and tell Enrique Elizondo to meet me."

"He's a good man. One of the best rangers in Company C."

"Yep, but I'm supposed to be doing this on my own.

I don't have any intention of pulling him into any of this."

I didn't want to tell anyone about Perry Hale and Yolanda, neither. The Major knew of course, but they were my idea and supposed to stay in the shadows, so to speak.

A truck pulling a fifth-wheel camper went around me faster than any rig should be moving. It was one of the big ones damn near forty feet long. Even though my truck's pretty good size, it felt like a locomotive was rolling a yard away. Right on his tail was an eighteen-wheeler bearing down like a giant blue whale.

There was that tickle again on the edge of my consciousness. What was it that triggered a memory I needed?

I backed off the accelerator. The big rig was next to get past and I flashed my headlights to tell him he was far enough ahead to pull back into my lane. The driver immediately clicked his turn indicator and moved over, using his flashers to tell me thanks. A few seconds later he pulled around the fifth-wheel.

Major Parker's voice cut through my thoughts. "You still there?"

I snapped back to the real world. "Yessir. Must have lost the signal for a second."

"Where are you?"

"Between Dimmitt and Comanche."

"Why there?"

"No solid reason, except that I have a hunch our vigilante's headed east."

"So you think you're just gonna drive to the middle of the state and wait?"

"Like I said, following a hunch."

"Fine then. Call me as soon as you know something."

He hung up without saying good-bye like he always does. I punched the phone off only seconds before it rang again. This time it was my wife, Kelly. I plucked it off the bracket and answered. "I was gonna call you when you got home."

"I bet. Where are you?"

"People keep asking me that."

"What's that mean?"

"Nothing. I needed to call you, though. The first thing I have to tell you is I'm fine."

She took a deep breath. "Uh oh."

I told her about the shoot-out as I passed pastures full of mesquite and cedar, scattered ranches, and turnouts to gates blocking two-lane tracks that vanished in the distance. She didn't say a word until I finished.

"You need to come home for a while."

"Why's that?"

"Because it's gonna hit you at some point, and I think I need to be with you when it happens."

"I'll be a while yet, if it does. Besides, I'm in the middle of tracking this guy down and haven't had much time to think."

"Look, buddy, I know what it's like driving those highways. You think more when you're behind the wheel and it's just you and the road."

She knew me better than anyone else. Folks don't realize Texas highways go on forever. It takes all day to travel the width of the state from El Paso to Texarkana, and part of that's at 85 miles per hour. The best part is that once you get west of I-35, a line reaching from Dallas–Fort Worth to Austin and San Antonio, the highways open up and you can set the cruise, lean back, and let your mind wander.

I'm bad about that. I can start out at one place and all of a sudden realize I have no idea where I am, or where I've been. I can blink and a half hour later wonder if I've gone through a town at all.

"Well, right now, more than anything else, I'm thinking about where this guy I'm after might be headed." Holding the steering wheel with my left hand, saw a spot on my thumbnail. Scratching at it with the forefinger on that same hand, I realized it was a speck of dried blood. It flaked off, and I fought a shudder.

Kelly's voice snapped me back. "What happened to that little girl?"

There it was again, my bride worrying about kids other than our own. That's one of the things that made her a fine teacher and the best person I've ever known.

"Karen's fine. She was in my truck the whole time. She finally fessed up that she was sixteen and a runaway. She has family on the way to pick her up right now. She'll be home before long."

"She's gonna need counseling."

"That's the truth." I knew where Kelly was headed with that line of reasoning, and that's another reason I love her so much, even though she sometimes drives me nuts trying to be mother to the whole world. "And a doctor, I imagine. I know what you're thinking, and we're not bringing her to our house. She has a family in Oklahoma. They'll take care of her."

The empty two-lane road snaked through the arid ranchland, much of the color washed out from the recent hard winter. The grass was coming back, but slowly. Fence posts flashed past, and I realized I was driving way too fast, taking the curves with enough speed that the dually strained to slip off the road. The highway rose and fell in swales, unusual for that part of the country. I let off the gas and relaxed my one-handed white-knuckle grip on the steering wheel.

"They've done an *outstanding* job so far." Her voice dripped sarcasm.

"Easy, girl. We don't know her story or her parents' story, either. Kids run away. You know as well as I do that girls her age are nothing more than hormone factories. You do the best you can and pray they get out the other side of adolescence in one piece."

"Well, it sounds like she's not an adolescent anymore. In years, yes, but in life experiences, she's probably as old as we are."

"That's what makes you such a good teacher and mom. But we're not adopting this damaged girl. She'll be fine. How're *our* kids?"

"They're fine. Mary has a new boyfriend, and Jerry's complaining there's nothing to do when he gets home from school." She paused. "He's in trouble at school again for that temper of his."

A quick temper was one of those things he'd inherited from my side of the family. Over the years, I'd learned to control it for the most part, but not the other little curse I'd given him, being impetuous.

I pictured the twins. Jerry flopped on the couch with the TV remote in his hand, and Mary on the phone, either talking or deeply involved with whatever new social-media platform the kids were using at the time. "Have him mow the yard."

"Yes, master. I need to tell you something else . . ." Her voice disappeared as the phone dropped the call when the road dipped into a low place and out of cell-tower range.

I pitched the phone onto the dash and gripped the wheel. It frustrated me that I'd lost the signal, and my spirits sank even further. A lump formed in my throat from feeling sorry for myself, and I had to swallow a couple of times. Once again my hands were white knuckling the steering wheel, and I had to consciously relax.

As I crossed a low-water bridge and crested the next rise, a feral cat darted out from a clump of tall grass growing under a downed mesquite laying over a fence and streaked toward the other side of the road. It was almost under the right front tire before I even saw the tabby, and there was nothing I could do to miss it.

I'd long ago taught the kids not to kill themselves trying to miss an animal on the road. My children's lives were worth much more. The same went for me and Kelly. I felt the slight thump under the dually's back wheels. A quick glance at the results in my passenger-side mirror told me there was nothing I could do for the poor animal. I glanced around, but there were no houses anywhere within sight. It wasn't anyone's pet.

A sudden tightness in my chest rose like a volcano, and my eyes filled with tears. I needed to tell my wife I loved her, and for her to tell the kids for me, but the damned cell service dropped. I started to pull off to the side, but the shoulder there was almost nonexistent.

It was only a cat. Probably one someone had tired of and dumped.

A lump rose once again in my throat, and I swallowed.

Karen was only a young girl caught in a cruel world and forced into human slavery right here in the United States. My twins were close to the same age, and the thought of Mary in the hands of men like those back at the trailer brought my stomach into my throat. And it wasn't only girls they preyed on. Boys were subjected to the same perversions from those who live just beneath the surface of civilized society.

My eyes burned.

The dead lawmen outside of Dimmitt left behind wives, children, and families.

My chin quivered, and I clamped down.

I'd killed men again, and honestly thought I was tough enough that it wouldn't bother me anymore. At least that's what I told the therapist the department insisted that I see after my shoot-out in Mexico a few months earlier.

An empty roadside park shaded by spreading live oak trees beckoned, and I pulled over and killed the engine and cried like a baby while the hard-south winds rocked the truck.

It was only a damned cat.

Chapter 19

Tanner and Willy waited outside the Holiday Inn Express in Jasper as the sun settled below the treetops. As far as their small community of Gunn was concerned, Jasper, at 7,500 people, was a big town. Families in Gunn usually drove to town for groceries at least once a week, or to eat out, for a movie, or to visit the doctor.

Gunn itself was nothing more than a hamburger stand, a feedstore, gas station, a couple of small antique stores struggling to survive in crumbling buildings built during the Depression, and an automotive repair shop that also sold flatbed and cattle trailers.

Tanner's nerves were tight as fiddle strings even though nothing was happening. They watched from the parking lot of the local farm supply store selling everything from deer stands to clothing. Tanner parked near stacks of corral panels, galvanized water troughs, and pallets of barbed wire and steel fence posts.

More cautious than his dad or Daddy Frank, Tanner had no interest in going into the hotel and knocking on their targets' door. The youngest of the clan, he was more in tune with technology and well aware that cameras recorded daily life even there.

They were taking a risk just sitting in the parking lot, but he'd scanned the area and noted that the supply store only had a couple of cameras pointed toward the entrance. Had it been a chain store like Tractor Supply, the company would have been more concerned about the nighttime theft of the farm and ranch items stacked in the lot year-round.

Tanner was also on edge from the south wind gusting up to forty miles an hour, bringing even more Gulf moisture to the region ahead of the coming cold front. "I've about had it with this wind."

"At least it keeps the skeeters away."

"It keeps me in when it blows like this."

"It won't last." Willy smoothed his beard. "Weatherman says it'll turn out of the north here in a little bit. It's coming up a cloud, and I bet it's gonna be a toad strainer."

"That's toad strangler."

"Well, I can't announce some words right."

Tanner started to correct him again, but he was secretly afraid that Willy would really take offense. The seemingly mild-mannered and quiet man who appeared somewhat simple could turn to violence on a dime. "Well, when it comes out of the northwest, it'll blow just as hard and I hate that, too."

"Bitch bitch bitch. You'll be complaining there's not enough breeze come July."

"At least all this'll be over by then."

Willy drew a deep breath. "Yeah, and things'll be different. We'll be some rich sumbitches!"

"How can you say that? All we're gonna do is put more product on the roads and increase our chances of getting caught. We need to go back to the old ways where we made good money and weren't interested in getting rich."

Tired of the conversation, Tanner was about to change the subject when the two men they were looking for stepped through the glass doors of the Holiday Inn Express and walked to their dark Chevrolet sedan.

Tanner started the car's engine, frustrated that the headlights came on automatically. "There they are."

Willy straightened in his seat as the Chevrolet pulled out of the parking lot and onto the street. Tanner waited until he could put a couple of vehicles between them and dropped in behind the car. The agents drove as if they had a specific destination in mind, headed south.

The sky darkened, and lighted signs flickered on in a wash of neon and halogen glare. High clouds took on orange, yellow, and pink highlights. The traffic signal caught them, and on the yellow caution arrow, the agents turned onto rural Highway 190, going like they were headed for Louisiana. Tanner stayed well behind and was glad he did when the agents suddenly pulled into a left-turn lane five miles from town and made a sharp U-turn.

"Shit. They're going to the Swamp."

Willy rubbed his stomach at the name of the local restaurant specializing in crawfish boils and seafood. "Sounds good to me. You think it's to eat?"

"Don't see any other reason right now. I doubt they're going in there at this time of the day to question somebody."

"I could use some fried catfish. It'll be dark when they come out. It'll be perfect."

Tanner made the same 180-degree turn and pulled

into the half-full dirt parking lot. The sprawling restaurant tucked into the piney woods lining both sides of the divided four-lane highway was the only business within miles. The Swamp's blue and red neon sign glowed against the cotton-candy pink and orange sky.

The agents drove past the entrance and around to the side, parking near the woods and away from the others. Tanner pulled in between two pickups, positioning his car to see the entrance in his rearview mirror. They waited for several minutes after the agents entered, to be sure they were seated before he and Willy went inside.

The aromas of crawfish spices and fried foods enveloped them as soon as they walked into the loud restaurant. Green was the predominant color on the walls, the counter, and the murals depicting life on the bayou. Posters featuring any movie filmed in a swamp or deep piney woods helped set the backwater tone.

Tanner pointed at an empty booth on the right when the hostess in a white shirt and jeans gathered two plastic menus together. "Can we have that one?"

She glanced over her shoulder and shrugged. "Sure."

They slid onto the vinyl seats within clear view of the entrance and settled in to wait.

Unlike when they arrived, the dark parking lot was completely full by the time Tanner and Willy stepped back outside. A line of hungry customers stretched out the door and dissolved into a crowd waiting under the porte cochere for their names to be called over the PA. Families, couples and groups of young people drank beer and talked on benches under the overhang. More customers gathered in familiar groups between the vehicles parked closest to the entrance, smoking and waiting for their turn in the popular restaurant.

The twenty-foot Swamp sign featuring a happy green alligator on one side and a crawdad on the other cast a glow onto the underside of low clouds that had thickened overhead. A line of headlights from cars and pickups waited on the road's shoulder to turn into the packed lot. More vehicles prowled the ragged rows, looking for a parking place.

Willy slipped both hands into the pockets of his overalls. "This place is a goddamn gold mine. We need to open one ourselves."

"This is called a legitimate business, and it takes work, seven days a week, and you probably don't want that."

"Don't matter none. I's just popping off." Willy burped, full of fried fish. Tanner had barely touched his two fillets, instead listlessly dipping his fries into a puddle of catsup from time to time. Not wanting to waste the food, Willy had eaten his, too. He glanced upward at the heavy clouds. "Bottom's about to fall out."

Instead of getting into Tanner's sedan, they leaned against the front bumper. Both loaded their bottom lips with Copenhagen and spat. The wintergreen flavor rose in the damp night air. No one noticed, assuming they were just two more people waiting for a table. The moist night air held the scent of fried food, grease, cigar smoke, and the damp loam from the woods surrounding the restaurant.

June bugs buzzed through the darkness, throwing themselves with soft crunchy thuds against everything and anything solid. As they waited, Tanner became more and more nervous. His hands twitched of their own accord with the enormity of what they were about to do. "If they come out and we miss them, and they leave in the morning, then everything'll be all right."

"Except we'll have to tell the old man what happened, and I ain't fixin' to do that just because you're acting like a little ol' titty-baby." Willy leaned over and spat. "There ain't no way I'm gonna get Boone sicced on my ass." He straightened. "Here they come. Get ready."

"Get ready for what? You don't think we're gonna do it here, do you? Look, I changed my mind, let's get away from all these people . . ."

Willy watched the unsuspecting men thread their way through the crowd and toward their car parked near the rear of the building. Unlike the other customers, they wore slacks, light shirts, and sport jackets, obviously not locals. One was Asian, the other could have been a move-in from Brooklyn.

Lit only by a string of patio lights under the restaurant's eaves, and some spillover from the lights on the back of the wooden building, the men were easy to spot moving down the uneven row. To Tanner, the scene took on an unreal tone in reflected light from windshields, chrome, and in many cases, freshly washed and waxed paint jobs.

Around the corner, a woman laughed, her voice light and full of life.

Deep in conversation, the agents didn't notice the men leaning against the Taurus the next row over. Willy snapped his fingers softly. "Hot dayum, do I have an idea that's gonna save your sissy ass."

"What's that?"

"Come with me and do the same thing I do."

"Here? Now? With all these people around?" Tanner hesitated, wanting to simply get in the car and drive away, but when Willy glanced back over his shoulder to see if he was following, Tanner fell back into the life-long pattern of doing what he was told.

The agents' Chevrolet was parked only ten feet from the tall pines. The restaurant's lights spilled only a few feet into the woods before the trunks absorbed the glow and dissolved into darkness. Willy caught up to the men, who finally noticed they weren't alone.

The shortest of the two, the agent with Asian features, glanced up from the cell phone that glowed in his hand. Logy from full stomachs, the strangers had no idea they were in danger until Willy came up behind the muscular driver with Italian features who was fumbling in his pocket for the keys.

Willy stopped only steps behind the two strangers, just before they split up to get in. The driver's eyes went flat at the sight of the .38 in Willy's hand, pointed at his middle.

The second agent squinted as his eyes slowly adjusted from the bright screen on his phone to the two locals beside them. "Hey, be careful with that thing."

Willy kept the pistol low and out of sight. "You boys be cool and keep your hands where we can see 'em."

The agents froze, eyes flicking back and forth between Willy and Tanner. Sensing the younger man was more easily addressed, the one with Asian eyes turned his attention to Tanner. "What's this?"

The sight of Tanner's dark blue Colt Python ended further discussion. Tanner was sure the man could see he was terrified. "Keep your hands where we can see them." He glanced over his shoulder to make sure no one was watching.

Willy quickly circled the driver. "I know you boys have guns. Take 'em out and put 'em on the ground right now. Do it slow and use your fingertips."

"What makes you think we have guns?"

"Hell, this is Texas. Everybody has a gun. Do what we say, give us your billfolds, and we're gone. Fast and simple."

The driver with the high and tight haircut raised an eyebrow. "Robbery. Fine then. You can have what you want." Their eyes met across the top of the car, but they removed their weapons with the tips of their fingers. As one they bent down and laid the weapons on the gravel lot.

Willy nodded, keeping his voice low. "Yep, we're gonna get what we want all right, but we're not doing it here. See them woods right there? We're fixin' to talk in 'em where people cain't see. Y'all turn around and we'll follow. Keep them hands down at your sides, and when we get inside the trees, you'll give us your money and keys and we'll be gone."

The agents exchanged glances and nodded as one. High and Tight turned toward the trees behind the restaurant. "Fine then. Let's get this over with."

Tanner again risked a glance across the tops of the parked cars and toward the highway. No one was paying them any attention. The man with Asian eyes joined the other man, who led the way into the woods with Willy behind.

Nerves jangling like fire alarm bells, Tanner followed slightly to the side, with the Python held low against his leg. Their footsteps were silent on the thick carpet of pine needles. With his suddenly heightened senses, Tanner felt the scent of the trees was stronger than ever before. The smell mixed with damp vegetation and the cloying, sickish sweet odor of a dead animal rotting nearby made his stomach roll, and he swallowed several times to keep from puking.

They entered the woods defined by the lights, and mere steps later, all four were engulfed in the gloom. The straight trunks lining the open parking lot threw long shadows that merged into darkness that grew impenetrable a hundred yards later.

Willy stopped where there was still enough light to see. "All right. That's far enough."

High and Tight stopped and turned toward the pair of silhouettes. "What now?"

Tanner spoke, startled that his voice was hoarse and cracked. "Names."

The Asian frowned. "Names? I thought this was robbery. I'm Ricky Kwan, and he's Tom Fontana."

"What are you two doing here?" Tanner's voice squeaked high from nerves. He cleared his throat. "Who are you with?"

"The railroad." Fontana spread his hands. "We're railroad agents. What is this?"

"Don't matter what they say." Willy interrupted.

Tanner held up his free hand. "Hang on a sec. Do you two know who we are?"

Fontana snorted. "Why would we know the names of common thieves like you two?"

"Then why are you here?"

Kwan tilted his head. "Why are you interested in *that*? I thought you just wanted our money."

Tanner shifted from foot to foot. "There's something else going on here. I don't understand."

Fontana spread his hands. "Look, we don't know what you guys have going, but like he said, we're railroad agents, looking into a shipment of Saltillo tiles coming up from Mexico that don't match up with the weight of the manifest."

"That don't make no sense." Willy was getting impatient. "You're investigating tiles that don't weigh the same as you *expect*? That's bullshit."

"No, really, it was red-flagged by customs." Fontana's tone became almost conversational. "The train car we're investigating is supposed to contain tiles made down in Monterrey. They've been shipping to a warehouse in Shreveport, and the weight doesn't match up with the order.

"That kind of thing rings our alarm bells, so the guys down on the border think there's something fishy with the shipment, that maybe the Mexicans are cutting corners on production and shipping subpar tiles. We've been taking turns with another team of agents staked out to see if anyone comes around the car."

"That's bullshit." Tanner frowned. He was never good at thinking fast on his feet, and all this talk about weight and tiles was confusing. The only thing he understood was the family business and the fact that they were in over their heads. "You think there's drugs in there. Maybe cocaine?"

The agents exchanged glances. "We hadn't thought of that."

Tanner's head spun even more. The Wadlers were experts in shipping, and they'd never used such a method to move drugs. He wondered if this was some kind of double-cross between Daddy Frank and a competitor. "Then why would you be here if it's in a warehouse across the line?"

Kwan licked his lips. "It's on a siding right now, just outside of town. Been there for four days. Look, guys, we don't know what's going on with you, but right now we don't *care* what *you're* doing, if it doesn't have anything to do with the railroad."

"This is bullshit." Willy stepped forward. "Tanner. Get it done."

Tanner hesitated. The veins in his forehead pulsed. His scalp tightened. He felt his own eyes widen. "Wait. Let me think." Was the old man *testing* him? Nothing rang true, and his head spun. He had no business dealing with these men. Tanner never aspired to be anything more than a simple cog in the family business. This whole thing was beyond his experience and desire.

Behind Willy and Tanner, an older couple walked to their car parked near the agents' sedan, gravel crunching under their shoes. Willy angled himself to see both their victims and the parking lot. "Tanner, their story's bullshit."

"No, it's not." Tanner lowered the Python. "People can't make stuff up like this, not this quick. It has to be true."

Kwan drew a deep breath. "You're right. We're leaving in the morning. The boxcar is scheduled to be picked up at seven. Then we're gone with it."

Tanner saw a way out. "Let 'em go. Like I said, we can say we missed 'em."

"No." Willy thumb-cocked the pistol.

Fontana's eyes widened. "Hey, wait. What is this? Please believe us."

"I do." Tanner stepped back, hearing car doors slam behind them. Laughter floated on air that smelled of fried food. "We're letting you go. You, Chinaman. If you're railroad agents, you have handcuffs. I want to see you take yours out with two fingers. Use your left hand."

"Do it slow." Willy swung the muzzle of his pistol back and forth.

Tanner watched Kwan slowly take a pair of cuffs from behind his belt. Then Tanner flicked his pistol toward Fontana. "You, too. Then y'all put 'em on one wrist."

"Here, you do it." Kwan pitched his cuffs toward Tanner. They floated toward him, the steel glittering in the light.

A pistol appeared in Fontana's hand. Willy pulled the trigger. The muzzle flash was like a flashbulb. Trees absorbed part of the flat report. Fontana grunted and folded, dropping onto a carpet of pine needles like an abandoned puppet.

Tanner started at the suddenness of the shot. "Oh."

A semiautomatic appeared in Kwan's hand as fast as a magician flicks his fingers and a card appears. Willy swung his revolver and shot again, catching Kwan in the left side of his chest. The second flash stopped the action like a strobe.

The wounded man shrieked and twisted. His compact semiautomatic pistol fired twice as he staggered back. One of the rounds whined off a tree behind Tanner with a low wobbling sound.

Two more shots hammered the still woods, and then a following string of muzzle flashes startled Tanner and froze the moments, bathing the woods in brief, stark light. It was a full second before he realized they'd come from *his* pistol.

Kwan fell onto the carpet of pine needles and stilled. Willy fired twice more into Fontana's body. Anchor shots.

Heart pounding, Tanner glanced over his shoulder like a high school student at a schoolyard dustup, looking for the principal to arrive. He was startled when Willy grabbed his arm and pulled. "Come with me!"

Numb, he allowed himself to be pulled through pines, running parallel to the back of the restaurant and matching Willy's stride through the trees. Aided by the light from the restaurant, they stayed in the woods. Tanner stayed close to Willy, who slipped effortlessly around the thick trunks as if he were following a trail. Moving like deer, they stayed out of sight and pushed through the thin understory brush to the opposite side of the restaurant.

Willy paused just beyond the circle of light and studied the parking lot. "It's clear." He noticed the Python still in Tanner's hand. "Hide that!"

The stunned young man looked down, surprised to see it in his hand. He tucked it under his shirt, into the small of his back. It was uncomfortably hot against his spine.

Unintelligible shouts from several people reached them. After a moment, more shouts from different voices joined in. Tanner forced himself to breathe slowly as they stepped into the clearing and threaded their way through the cars and trucks to re-emerge in front of the restaurant.

This time the thick odor of fried food was almost too much for Tanner's already rolling stomach, and he gagged. Much of the crowd had surged toward the commotion originating from the dark trees. Willy shoved him forward and they emerged from the darkness to join the remaining crowd of confused customers milling in place.

Gasps and questions filled the air.

"What was that?"

"Somebody's shot."

"I think it's a fight."

"There's been a killin'."

Ignoring the inane questions, Tanner and Willy stopped beside a group of customers who stayed far away from potential drama or danger. Tanner was sure the people around him could see the hot pistol under his shirt and would start pointing fingers at him at any moment, screaming, "Murderer!"

The Swamp's manager pushed through the front door. "I had Henry call the sheriff's department. They're on the way."

A heavy woman waved her thick arm. "Chuck, they say there's two people dead over yonder."

"What happened?"

"I didn't see it."

The manager, named Chuck, turned to the crowd. "What happ'ned?" He recognized a face in the crowd. "J.T., you know?"

The redheaded farmer shook his head.

"Anybody know what's going on out here?"

The question was addressed to no one in particular, but for some reason that Tanner couldn't control, he pointed and answered. "I heard somebody say they heard shootin' back over there." He held the finger out much too long and realized he was standing there like a statue. He lowered his arm, refusing to look at those around him, and examined his fingers as if expecting to see gunpowder residue. "I don't know anything else."

The manager ducked around the edge of the building. "What's going on out here?"

Willy cleared his throat and turned to Tanner. "You ready to go?"

The simple question snapped Tanner back into the real world. "If you are."

Their conversation, common to the area, was so mundane no one even gave them a thought. Feeling as if he were carrying fifty-pound feed sacks on his shoulders, Tanner walked to his unremarkable Ford and joined the flow of customers who wanted nothing to do with backwoods shootings or the police who would soon arrive with questions for everyone.

Chapter 20

The morning sun made its way through the back window of Mike Dillman's GMC pickup as they shot down the highway thirty minutes west of Waco. Boone rode shotgun.

Mike was far from comfortable around the strange, hairless man who'd been virtually silent since they left. A man of few words, Boone slept until the sun came up.

They were entering the arid central part of the state covered in scrub, sage, and mesquite that had taken over much of the ranchland on either side of the highway. Long shadows from live oak trees stretched across rocky creeks. Growing without impediment, the oaks spread their limbs wide, sometimes so far that their weight caused them to touch the ground.

Mike's nerves were getting the best of him, and he decided to initiate a conversation to break the silence. "I hate this part of the country."

Head bowed over a book, Boone didn't reply.

Mike pointed "There's a turkey. Did you see it?"

Boone finally looked up from the book in his lap. "No."

"Yeah, a big gobbler. Wonder what he was doing out in this wind. Game usually settles in when it's blowing this hard 'cause the limbs are moving and they can't see or hear anything that's trying to eat 'em."

"I wouldn't know."

Mike glanced up at the gray morning sky. Irritable because he had no business driving to Comanche, he was also on edge with Boone in the truck because he felt he could have handled this himself.

For the first time since he'd known Boone, the strange man offered an interesting comment. "I used to live out here."

Startled by the revelations, Mike cut his eyes toward Boone's shaved head and that spiderweb tattoo that creeped everyone out. "Never expected you to be from this part of the country."

"My parents lived just out of Waco when I was ten." Boone closed the book he'd been reading, using his finger to mark his place in *The Art of War*. "They were Branch Davidians, followers of David Koresh. Some claim he was Jesus Christ, the Messiah who'd returned, but Preacher Holmes says that's not true." He looked at Mike. "Hallelujah."

Mike shivered at the joyless interjection. He couldn't tell if Boone was being sarcastic or was in the throes of the message. "I've never heard you talk this much."

"None of you ever really talked to me before."

They rode for more than a mile in silence. Mike tapped a cigarette loose and lipped it from a crumpled pack. He was reaching for a lighter when Boone spoke.

"Open your window if you're going to smoke that."

While Mike thumbed the switch to lower the window, Boone remained perfectly still, as he had since he marked his place in the book. It was his way.

Now steering with both hands, Mike mulled that statement over in his mind. "I thought everybody died when Koresh burned that Mt. Carmel place to the ground."

"David burned them up."

"That's not what I heard on television."

"The reporters weren't in there. I was, at least until David made me leave a few days before he lit it."

"Just you? What about your parents?"

"They were incinerated. He forced them to send me away. He didn't like the way I questioned his declarations and faith. He pronounced me the spawn of Satan. I was banished."

The GMC plowed a hole in the wind, following the curving highway that alternately led through pastures, then around low, mesquite- and cedar-covered mesas. They passed a cedar cutter's house surrounded by stacks of trimmed and split posts. The home-grown business looked almost serene under the heavy clouds but would feel like a blast furnace in the summer when the temperatures reached as high as 110 in the shade.

"How old were you?"

"Ten when they made me leave."

"Wait a minute, that happened in nineteen what?"

"Nineteen ninety-three."

"So you're how old, thirty-three?"

"You weren't good in math, were you? I'm thirty-five."

"You don't look it."

"That's because I don't have any frown lines or worry lines."

Mike had other questions, but was afraid to voice them.

"Just like I'm not worried about killing Alonzo. You know that's why I'm here, don't you?"

A cold knot formed in Mike's stomach. "Nobody told me that."

"Because you're the driver."

"I don't want Alonzo hurt."

"Don't care. Daddy said."

Mike could feel the bald man staring at him. "He's Daddy Frank's grandson."

"It don't pay to cross the old man."

"Look. Were you planning to use that razor of yours?"

"Of course."

"Then would you let me do it? Let me shoot him and make it fast. It ain't right for you to cut him. He don't deserve that."

"None of us deserve our end."

"So would you let me do it?"

"As long as he's dead, Daddy won't care."

Trying to get the deed off his mind, Mike needed to change the conversation. "Good. Let me ask you this. What happened to make you get those tattoos?"

"That's none of your business."

Mike cut his eyes, expecting to see something that would tell him that Boone was pulling his leg at the same time the strange man, with the cold eyes of a diamondback, opened his mouth to emit an expressionless guttural laugh at his own joke. "I'm just kidding."

Bile rose in Mike's throat, and the smoke suddenly tasted like the ashes it produced. Feeling like a mouse dropped into a snake tank, Mike couldn't wait to get into Alonzo's truck so he could get away from that lunatic.

Chapter 21

Parked alone in front of Dan's Burger Stand in Jasper, Tanner waited for his breakfast sandwich to arrive. He scrolled through a long list of phone numbers in his cell phone and made a call. It rang three times before his uncle answered.

"Hello."

"Uncle Alonzo. This is Tanner."

The voice on the other end went flat. "What's wrong?"

His eyes burned and the young man struggled not to cry. "Uh, look, like we know Aunt Betty died and you're in some kind of trouble. I don't want anything to happen to you, so you better not come back. Where are you?"

"In Comanche. What happened?"

"A lot, and I'm afraid there's more on the way. There was some federal agents here and now they're dead. Daddy Frank's like, gone out of his mind and he's thinking there are more following you all the way back here to the porch."

The line was silent and Tanner waited. A mockingbird went through its repertoire of calls. A carload of high school kids pulled under the overhang beside his sedan, their radio up loud with modern country music.

Tanner turned up the air-conditioning and rolled up all the windows. "You still there?"

"Thinking."

"'Bout what?"

"About him blowing those oil lines and the refinery. I bet if I can get him to be where one of those charges are set, I can blow that old bastard straight to hell."

"It'd be the best thing that could happen, but Boone's always watching."

"I'll make sure he's there with him. Ain't that a kick?"

Tanner's scalp tingled. With Daddy Frank gone, it'd be clear sailing for him and Shi'Ann. They'd been slipping around for way too long. It would give them the opportunity they'd been waiting for to run off.

His chest swelled with elation. Uncle Alonzo would punch the old man's ticket, and he'd get out of the trap he'd fallen into. "Will you really do it?"

"He sure as hell deserves it. You want to help?"

Heart pounding, Tanner held the phone tight against his ear and watched the carhop come toward him with his breakfast. "You want me to help kill Daddy Frank?"

"I might need you to help set it up. That's all."

"Uncle Alonzo, what're you doing, really?"

"Son, they're releasing felons left and right, and they're getting back on the streets, killin' and robbin' and rapin'. . . ." His voice choked. "That's what happened to my Betty, and I'm gonna make 'em all pay. I started with a guy in California while I was looking for the one who ran her down, then I got him in Arizona. I intend to send as many to hell as I can."

"You can't do that."

"Ever'body's gonna pay for what they've done, even our sorry-assed kinfolk. All 'cept you."

Tanner waited as the carhop hung a tray on the outside of his window. He passed her a ten-dollar bill and waved away the change. The girl near his age flashed him a wide grin and paused. She clicked the point out on a pen and wrote her phone number on the receipt. Handing it to him, she winked and walked away, twitching her rear to keep his attention until she got inside. Tanner swallowed and returned to the conversation. "Not Daddy! You ought not blow up the refinery, neither. Knocking out the pipeline in a couple of places is one thing, and I can do that seeing's how they can just plow through your land, but there are innocent people in the refinery."

"Fine then. I'm gonna call and have the whole damn family meet me out at the fertilizer barn when I get there. Gonna tell 'em I got more money for the delivery than they expected and we can divvy it up right then and there, like it's Christmas.

"Ol' Buck Henderson and Preacher'll be there, too. The greedy bastards'll all come a-runnin'. It'll be a clean sweep, all except for you and your gal Donine. Y'all back me up to get 'em out there, then get gone so you won't be around when it all goes up."

"The only way that plan will work is if you set it off while you're there." Tanner heard the rattle of pills in a plastic bottle and wondered what kind of drugs Uncle Alonzo was taking. "They won't let you leave once you get home. You know that."

He took the cardboard cup of hot coffee off the tray

with trembling fingers and spilled it on his jeans when he tried to open it with one hand.

The sound of ice tinkling in a glass and a deep, horse-like gulp told Tanner his uncle had washed the pills down, and it probably wasn't iced coffee.

"That's the idea, son. I'll clean my soul at the same time I wipe this miserable family off the planet. I'll go straight to Heaven at the same time."

"That's, like, insane. I don't want you to die, Uncle Alonzo."

"We're all gonna die at some point, and I'm talking about getting some payback for Betty, and me, and you, son. You're the only one worth a damn in this family. You have a chance to make something of yourself. With the old man gone and the Business shut down, you can get free and start a new life with Donine. I'm gonna stop and put the money I have here into a bank deposit box under your name and mail you the information and the key. That way you can take a little bit out of it at a time and the government won't know. Go to college and make something of yourself. Which one do you use?"

"Tanner told her."

"It'll be in there tomorrow morning. I'll drive into town right now. I imagine this burg has a branch."

"Well, thanks."

"I'll call Jimmy Don and tell him to get ever'body together in the fertilizer barn to divvy up all this money. You let me know when they're all together in there. You got that?"

Tanner had to set the coffee cup into the holder on the console at the mention of his dad, Jimmy Don. In his mind, the idea of taking out the whole family didn't include *him*. "Yessir."

"The same thing I'm telling 'em, that I have a truck-load of cash, like I said. Now get everything in place, 'cause I'm-a comin'."

Tanner hung up, both elated and terrified. He didn't want to be part of killing his family, even though he hated them all. He didn't want the blood of innocent people at the refinery on his hands. His heart pounded with the idea of both his Dad and Daddy Frank dying, no matter how much he hated them.

But even with the thought of all that money in his hands, he couldn't stomach Alonzo's plan.

He was so confused.

Chapter 22

It was only five hours from Dimmit to Comanche, Texas, but I was so wrung out that I stopped at the first place I came to after crossing I-27 and took a room. Not a destination hot spot for tourists, the little 1950s-era American Inn motel in Floydada was just what I needed.

It had a bed and a shower.

The next morning I pulled up beside the Fleming Oak on the Comanche town square. That old town near the geographic center of the state was bigger than it looked on a map. I'd been there as a kid with the Old Man, who wanted to show me the ancient live oak tree. Dad loved the story of ten-year-old Martin Fleming and *his* dad, who used the tree growing in the middle of a grove in 1853 as cover when a band of Comanches attacked their campsite.

They survived, and a settlement sprung up on the site. Named after the warring band who claimed the territory as their own, Comanche grew around the tree that remained untouched for decades. When the town council decided it was in the way in 1911, since it was on the town square, they ordered it cut down to pave the area in front of the courthouse. The boy, by then an old man known as Uncle Martin, showed up with a shotgun to protect the oak that once saved his life.

My dad felt it was a glowing story of Texas pride, and made sure I saw the tree for myself. The town hadn't changed much since I was a teenager, though unlike many small Texas towns, Comanche wasn't dying, but maintaining a tenuous hold on life.

The morning air was already getting warm, but the sky was heavy and dark. The radio said the weather was about to change. The phone rang. It was Yolanda.

"I told you never to call me at this number."

"Funny guy. You in Comanche yet?"

"Yep. What do you have?"

She became all business. "The guy you need to check on there is forty-six-year-old Dewane Mundy, who was sentenced to more than three hundred years for child sex crimes and was freed from prison less than a month ago. He was convicted of molesting at least eight boys and girls."

"Then how'd he get out?"

"He appealed, saying pretrial delays violated the state's speedy trial statutes. In February, the Texas Court of Appeals agreed, throwing out the conviction and ruling he couldn't be retried. The D.A. there in Brownwood County appealed, but the state Supreme Court decided not to take up the case. They upheld the court's ruling." Yolanda finished up. "I'm not an attorney, so that's all I have."

I returned a rancher's wave as he passed in a dirty white pickup. "All right. I'll call you in a little bit." I strolled across the parking lot to the courthouse. The sheriff wasn't in, but a hatless deputy was sitting behind a desk, drinking coffee from a stained cup reading WEAKLEY-WATSON HARDWARE, BROWNWOOD, TEXAS.

I nodded good morning. "One of my favorite hardware stores."

The deputy almost blew coffee through his nose when he saw me. I guess they don't see many Rangers in Comanche. "What?"

I pointed. "Your cup. I have one like it at home, says '36th Annual TOWA Dove Hunt, Weakley-Watson.' Got it from a friend who's an outdoor writer."

He still didn't know what I was talking about, but he sat the cup on a stack of papers. Spilled coffee soaked in to form a ring. "I hope that's not a formal report."

"Huh?" The deputy glanced down at the paper. "Shit!" He snatched the cup up by the handle, spilling even more on the top page. He held it aloft with one hand and looked for something to blot the paper.

"Here." I took his cup so he wouldn't destroy any more official reports.

The deputy snatched tissues from a Kleenex box and dabbed at what hadn't soaked in. Seeing the coffee was steaming hot, I took a sip, and that unnerved the poor guy even more. I figured it was time to help him. "I'm Sonny Hawke."

"Uh, yessir. How can I help you, Ranger?"

"Sheriff in?"

"Nossir." He dabbed at the page some more and finally decided he might oughta stand up. "He'll be in directly. I think he's across the street at the café on the corner. I'm filling in for Helen here, she's our dispatcher."

"Well, a deputy oughta make a pretty good recep-

tionist, too. Sounds like I should have gone for breakfast first then."

"Here he comes now."

The office door opened behind me, and I turned to
see an old boy I'd run into a couple of times over the
years. His wide smile showed a mouthful of white
teeth. "Sonny!"

I saluted him with the confiscated coffee. "Howdy, G."

His attention flicked from the cup, to the deputy, then
back to me. "I see Daryl here loaned you my mug."

I kinda felt bad about calling him a receptionist. To
make up for taking his coffee, I got him off the hook
for using the sheriff's mug. "I picked it up myself." It
wasn't a lie.

He raised an eyebrow. "Come on in my office."

I followed him inside a cramped room containing a
metal desk, metal filing cabinet, and an extremely uncomfortable looking chair. A stained Mr. Coffee on a
small table by the window looked as if it'd been there
for years. The pot was half full, and there were no
other cups in evidence.

"You want this back?"

He opened a desk drawer and took out a mate to the
one in my hand. "Nope. I keep that old one out for Junior
out there. He likes the handle and uses it when he thinks
I'm gonna be late. I'm surprised he let you have it."

"I didn't ask." I took another sip, decided it was getting too cool, and added more from the pot.

"You didn't drive all the way out here for coffee."

"Nope. I'm chasing a guy."

"Who is he?" Gomez filled his own cup and sat
down in his chair.

I leaned against the file cabinet. "Don't know."

When he raised his eyebrows, I told him the whole story, including the events in Dimmit the day before. "Damn, son."

Knowing exactly what he meant, I fought a heave in my stomach. "Ain't that the truth? This guy's twisting us in knots. There's a chance he's here looking for an individual named Dewane Mundy."

"I know *that* sonofabitch. His mama shoulda drowned him when he was born."

"Well, she didn't, and I think this vigilante's gonna try to do the job for her."

"So what do you want to do?"

"I'd like to stake his house out."

Gomez bit his lip in thought. "No can do. He lives out on the edge of town, and there's no way we can put a car out there that won't be seen."

I sipped the coffee as he clicked on a radio station playing big band music. I grinned at his choice of music. He grinned back. "Reminds me of when things were different and in my mind, more honorable. Besides, it keeps me calm."

"I'm more of a Dwight Yoakum kinda guy myself. Any other ideas then?"

"How about waiting *in* the house with him?"

"Naw, I don't want to associate with the man." I was sure he'd buck and snort at the idea of having a lawman in his house. But the more I thought about it, the more I liked the idea of going in and snowballing the guy to get what we needed.

His desk phone rang. Instead of answering, he called through the half-open door. "Take a message."

Deputy Daryl appeared in the door a minute later. "You have to talk to this one right now." Gomez raised his eyebrows in question. Daryl threw me a look and tilted his head in my direction. "You might want to put it on speaker."

It was a three-way glance-fest for a minute before the sheriff leaned forward and punched the blinking phone. "This is Sheriff Gomez. Who's this?"

"Uh, I, uh, need to tell you something."

We heard a woman's voice, soft in the background and then it was gone.

"Go ahead."

"Uh, I have an uncle who I think is there in your town with a load of plastic explosive."

Disgusted, Gomez learned forward to hang up. "Look kid, there's laws against prank calling."

"This ain't no prank. It's Semtex." He paused. "And there's maybe four hundred pounds of the stuff, I imagine."

That was way too much detail for a prank call. Four hundred pounds of plastic explosive was impossible, but the specific name raised the hair on my neck.

The sheriff tightened, and I stepped closer to make sure I didn't miss anything. Gomez picked up a pen and flicked a blank pad closer to hand. I waved it off and plucked a little notepad out of my pocket.

"Okay, I'm listening. What's he doing with it, and where is he?"

"I don't know where he is for sure." Wind noise told us the caller was outside.

"Okay, you're sure he's here in Comanche."

"Yessir."

"How do you know?"

"He just told me on the phone."

"Does he live here?"

"Nossir."

We traded raised eyebrows.

"Where *does* he live?"

"Why, here."

Gomez's brow wrinkled in irritation. "Where's here?"

"I can't tell you that. I don't want to go to prison, 'cause you're gonna find out a lot more when you get there, and I wanna stay out of it. Can't you like, just go pick him up and leave the rest of my family out of it?"

We exchanged glances at the strange request. "You won't go to jail for telling me about this. We'll keep it confidential."

"Uh, yeah, right. I know how the government is."

Deputy Daryl was still standing there. Gomez scribbled a note telling him to call the phone company and have them trace the contact. He disappeared into the outer office and a second later I heard him talking with someone. Gomez returned to the caller. "Okay, son, what's your uncle's name."

He cleared his throat, a "tell" when someone is lying and needs a moment to think. "John Wadler."

Gomez wrote it down.

"What's he going to do with this plastic explosive?"

There was silence on the other end. "Y'all let informants go, don't you?"

His answer was instantaneous. "Sure do."

"No matter what they done?"

Our eyes met again. "The law allows us some flexibility to work with people who give us information regarding dangerous individuals or crimes that are about to be committed."

I almost grinned at his vague answer straight from the book.

"They'll kill me if they find out. Can me and Don . . . my wife like, go into that witness protection program?"

"That's above my pay grade, son. You're talking about the Federal Witness Program, but I'm sure the FBI'll have to be called in on this, or the ATF. They'll work with you. If this is the truth, and your story pans out, I'm sure they'll take all that into consideration. But you're getting' way ahead of yourself here. Where you calling from?"

"Don't matter." The silence that followed those two words lasted so long I was thinking the call had dropped. "Uh, Uncle Lon . . . Bill, he's gonna use it to kill a lot of folks."

"Here in *Comanche*?"

"No, somewhere's else."

It was obvious the young man on the other end of the line was scared to death, and lying at the same time. He couldn't remember which first name he'd given us, but there was something about the story that rang true.

"Okay, you said *some* people. How many?"

He cleared his voice. "There's a bunch of 'em, my whole family, and they ain't the best in the world, but I don't want to be involved no more."

"Look, I know this is scary, but I'm going to need a lot more information than just this. How about you start from the beginning and give me all the details so we can get to work on it. How much explosive are we really talking about?"

"Four hundred pounds, like I said."

Gomez leaned forward and laced his fingers on the

desk. "Son, only the military has that much plastic, I'd think."

"Them and now my uncle."

"Look, you need to quit beatin' around the bush and tell me what you know."

"I'm not ready to say. I need to get some people out of there first. Just see if you can find him."

Gomez's face reddened, and I could tell he was doing all he could not to blow up at the kid. I was thinking he was a kid, and these days for me that stretches from age fifteen to thirty, and in some cases even more.

"But you gave me his name, John, then Bill Wadler. Give me his *real* first name and an address in your town and I can make a few calls."

"No. Don't call nobody." His voice was full of panic. "Look, let me get a couple of people out of town, and I'll call you back with everything you need. Maybe you'll already have him by then, right there in your town. How's that? You stop him and then we can work out a deal, but I have to be gone outta here before I give you the rest of the family or they'll come after me."

Gomez wrote "family" on his pad.

Sounds came through the receiver making me think the caller was ginning around, maybe pacing back and forth while he talked, or fooling around with something. He could have been driving, though state law had changed and people weren't supposed to drive and talk on a handheld device.

"Look, kid. That's not going to happen until you tell me who and where he is." Still wearing his straw hat, Gomez tilted it back on his head. "There's a helluva lot more than you're letting on. Son, no matter what you're guilty of, this kind of info can go a long way in helping us with the law when the time comes."

"My family's like, insane. I helped 'em do something . . . it wasn't my idea, but I had a part, but I don't want to do no more. Look, if you'll just go pick him up I can get out of here and call you back with everything you want to know."

The sheriff's voice snapped like gunfire. "You're not listening to me! I can't pick the man up if I don't have a name, description, and *location*!"

The boy on the other end must have turned, because the wind blowing across the phone made it almost impossible to hear. I imagined his hand shaking as it held it to his ear. I leaned in. "Look, son. This is Texas Ranger Sonny Hawke. I just happened to be here on something else. You know our jurisdiction covers the entire state, don't you? Tell me what you know, what you've done, and *I'll* handle it."

He didn't sound much older than my own twins, and I thought about what they'd be like, carrying the guilt that seemed to rest on this young man's shoulders. Gomez was about to say something else when the kid answered.

"They made me kill"—the wind snatched words that we needed—"agent . . ."

Gomez recognized it, too. "Son, you need to get out of the wind. I'm having trouble hearing you.

I glanced out of Gomez's window. The stiff wind carried a Styrofoam cup across the parking lot, and I wondered how far away the kid was. When the wind picks up in Texas, it can blow from Beaumont to Laredo. With a cold front arriving, it was a sure bet that the wind would pick up in advance of the leading edge of cool air, and that meant he could have been calling from anywhere along that line.

Was he right there in Comanche?

The rushing sound quit and a door slammed. A radio suddenly blared to life before the caller turned it down, and he was distracted for a moment. It took a second to realize he'd started a vehicle. "All right. Is that better?"

We listened as static filled the line and the young man's voice became garbled. He was traveling, because we heard the familiar electronic Space Invaders sound as the call came close to dropping.

"You still there?"

"Right here, I still don't understand what you said earlier." Gomez clicked his pen several times, thinking. "I need more specifics about the people you say were killed. I need the other names."

The Space Invaders noise rose up and there it was again, issues with technology. In the old days the call on a landline would have likely been clear as a bell, and there wouldn't have been issues with cells.

The answer was lost before he came back on. "He's pulling a . . ." More static. "I'll call back when I can. I got to think on this a little more."

"Son, we don't have much time to work here if what you say is true."

". . . ain't . . . a lot of things, but I'm not a liar . . . fine then . . . gun . . ."

"Guns? I'd expect as much." Gomez was writing as fast as a secretary taking shorthand. "What kind of guns and I for sure need to know where you are and . . ."

"No . . . guns . . . gun . . . gonna drive his truck . . . barnnnnn"—space invaders again—"set it off . . . already dead, I think . . ."

We were both straining forward as if that would help the reception. He was gone, and Gomez stared at the phone, as if it was his receiver's fault the conversation had ended. "Well, hell."

I realized I'd been holding my breath. A clap of thunder made us both jump after talking about explosives. Gomez gave a little chuckle and sat back.

"You think that's real?"

I was wondering that, too. "Well, it sounded real, but it might be some kid playing hooky from school, looking to liven things up a little."

"I wouldn't put it past the kid being *in* the school." Gomez clicked his pen some more, and I saw it was probably a nervous habit. "I had a dumbass call in a bomb threat from the lunchroom, telling me the place was going to blow up. He hung up when I asked what they were serving in the lunch line."

We were silent for a minute. Gomez tapped his pad with the end of the pen. "So, do you want in on this one?"

"It's interesting, but I already have an assignment. I'd never get anywhere if I followed every rabbit that popped up."

"I know what you mean. I'm gonna do a little digging here and see what I can find out."

"I'm gonna go across the street and have breakfast." I tilted my head toward the window. Thunder rumbled again at the same time lightning flashed. "And then decide what to do about my vigilante. Who knows, I might just do what you said and wait there in the house with that feller Mundy."

"But there's no promise that your guy's gonna show up."

"None at all. I'm doing all this on a hunch based on a theory from a friend of mine who's good with computers and thinking outside the box. It was her idea he was coming this way and maybe making a stop here in town."

Gomez stared at the scribbles on his pad. "Well, order the steak and eggs, but stay away from the hash browns. They're not the shredded kind."

"Good to know." Rain spotted the window. I set his Weakley Watson cup on the desk. "Thanks for the coffee. I better get going. I'll holler at you in a little while."

"Sounds good." He returned to his notes, and I headed out into a splatter of rain as thunderstorms shifted the wind into a new direction.

Chapter 23

It kept acting like it wanted to rain on the streets of Comanche. Sprinkles wet the concrete, just enough to send a little runoff around the front tires of the cars and trucks parked in front of the Rockin' R Café. I was in the booth by the front window, sipping coffee after finishing a plate full of eggs over easy and medium-rare steak.

Lightning cracked, and the windows vibrated. Some of the western motif artwork on the walls rattled. I was half-expecting a bolt to hit the old Fleming oak. Instead, one struck the satellite dish on top of the courthouse in a shower of sparks, plunging the entire place into darkness. The lights in the café flickered, then steadied.

I slipped the cell phone from my pocket and thumbed it alive. The signal was strong, so I typed in a few key words to do a little searching on my own. I'm not completely inept with those things.

There'd been something bothering me that I couldn't put my finger on, and when I heard the kid talking to

Gomez on the phone, it came back. He said something that triggered it awake again.

Another thunderclap rattled the window, and nervous laughter from other customers scattered around the ranch-style café filled the room.

The dark-haired waitress, who'd probably been the town homecoming queen twenty years earlier, came around with a coffeepot. "You want some more?"

I pushed the mug toward her with one finger. "Yeah, better had."

She refilled the mug and hung around for a minute, interested in the grips on the .45 in my holster. "I have a Glock."

I gave her a smile. I've been working on my "aggravated but trying to be nice" expression. "It's a good gun."

She pointed. "Do you know your pistol's cocked?"

"That's the way you carry a forty-five."

"That's a forty-five?"

"It is." I knew what was coming next. I raised my right arm a little. "They call them Sweetheart grips. My granddaddy put them on there during the war."

During World War II, GIs found a use for a new product called Plexiglas. It was used for windows in planes and on vehicles, but when they discovered how easy it was to work, they created a new form of trench art by removing the standard wooden grips on their sidearms and replacing them with the transparent material.

As in the case of the Colt M1911 on my hip, servicemen placed a picture of a pinup girl or their sweetheart underneath the right-hand side, giving them the name of Sweetheart grips. The other side often remained clear in order to see how many rounds were in the magazine, but revolvers had them on both sides.

"That's my grandmother holding my dad."

"Well, I was gonna ask you."

"I knew you were. They're unusual all right."

Rain slashed against the window. Her eyes drifted over me for several seconds. She cocked a hip. "You need anything else?"

"Not right now."

She drifted off to the next table occupied by two young men and a woman who yelped each time lightning cracked. My refilled mug was scalding hot. "Goddle-mighty!"

I tilted the mug, spilled coffee into the saucer and picked it up with the fingertips of both hands and sipped. "That's better."

The waitress came back by. "Granddad used to cool his that way in their kitchen when I was a kid. I haven't seen anyone saucer coffee in here for some time."

I gave her a wink. "They don't know me here, and I doubt I'll be back anytime soon so's they remember me."

She winked back and I tried not to watch her walk back to the counter.

I paused. "Agents." I plucked the little pad out of my pocket and flipped a couple of pages. That kid mentioned agents, and before that, he said they made him do something.

I drummed my fingers on the table. Another thought I couldn't get a handle on. I took the pen from my shirt pocket and wrote.

Agents. My Old Man. Trucks. Kill. Gun.

I kept having thoughts that I couldn't get ahold of or

how they connected. I studied my notes. He said they, whoever they are, made him do something he didn't want to do, and specifically said the word, kill.

I Googled the words Texas, killed, murdered, agents.

"Well, look what popped up."

It was a story filed by the *Jasper Newsboy* about two DEA agents who'd been murdered in a robbery outside of a local restaurant the night before.

Thinking about the story, I watched light traffic pass outside. A diesel truck pulling an Airstream camper passed. The hair rose on the back of my neck.

Wind blew another light sprinkle of water onto the elevated sidewalk, wetting the hundred-year-old iron hitching rings anchored in the concrete. They were probably still used from time to time when the locals rode their horses through town just for the fun of it. It's not uncommon to see that in rural Texas, but I've also seen youngsters ride their horses up to the McDonald's in Amarillo.

"Good lord."

That'd been rattling around in my head ever since I was in the panhandle. I didn't know what it was, but there was some connection that had to do with eighteen-wheelers and campers. Then when I was with Sheriff Davis, it popped up again. I'd been noticing them out of the corners of my eyes, like the Old Man told me to do when we were huntin'. He always said to pay attention to everything around me.

I thought for a second.

Eighteen-wheelers and campers.

It kept coming up, over and over again. In that gun-fight yesterday, the same thing. Big rigs and RVs. And now the kid said his uncle was in Comanche with the explosives, but not wherever he actually lives. What better way to haul four hundred pounds of anything without anyone suspecting, than in a camper?

I tapped the pad with my pen, thinking. Putting together those pieces broke the dike that prevented me from recalling the ideas that had been teetering on the edge of my consciousness.

I called Yolanda, because she answered her phone better than Perry Hale. She answered on the fifth ring. "Hey boss."

"The boy with you?"

I could hear the smile in her voice. "He's right here."

"I figured. Look I'm putting some things together. I think our bad guy's heading for somewhere in East or Southeast Texas." I told her about the phone call that came into Sheriff Gomez's office and my suppositions. "The kid sounded scared to death and he used fake names, but I think the surname might be real, and it's unusual. I've never heard Wadler before."

"Me neither. I can find out more than you'd imagine."

"I bet you can. Run that through whatever you subscribe to and see if anything pops up."

"Will do. I'll call you back."

I hung up and glanced out the window. It was even darker than before, except when lightning fractured the clouds. I caught the waitress's eye and she came over, smiling from ear to ear when she reached the table.

"You need some more coffee already, or something else?"

"What's the nicest campground close to town?"

She cocked a hip and looked confused. "Why, that'd be the Evening Star Campground."

"Which way?"

She pointed. "Just a ways."

"That's all I needed to know." I gave her a couple of tens and slid out of the seat. "Keep the change."

"Sure will! Come back if you want anything else."

With that worrisome offer tucked away, I headed out for the Evening Star.

Chapter 24

By eleven in the morning, gray clouds hung heavy and low over the East Texas pines behind the Wadler house. The wind picked up with even more force in response to a line of building thunderstorms rolling in from the west, sometimes gusting to thirty mph. The forecast was for the storm to intensify as the cooler, drier air clashed with the moist Gulf air.

A dozen grackles winged over the house, heading for cover. A woodpecker hammered somewhere out of sight, seemingly unconcerned by the weather.

"Let me get this straight." Jimmy Don Wadler prowled his backyard in fury. "Daddy Frank told you to deal with those two agents and your idea was to shoot 'em behind the busiest restaurant in the *county*!"

Tanner swallowed. Willy stared at his camouflage hunting boots. It was almost too much, and Tanner wanted to bolt, but he couldn't leave without Shi'Ann and was supposed to meet her later that evening.

"Dad, we had 'em, but then we found out those guys weren't here to investigate *us*. They're railroad agents staked out and waiting on a car that didn't weigh in right. And I was like . . ." He raised his hands palm up. "And they said yeah, we're railroad agents and we're here for that and I was like, really? You didn't want us to get involved in *that*, did you?"

"They ain't railroad agents. They were *feds*!" Jimmy Don's face was beet red with rage.

"That's not what they told us." Tears welled. Frustrated, Tanner wiped them away with one hand.

"You two beat anything I've ever seen." Jimmy Don stopped pacing and threw up his hands in frustration. He pointed a finger at Willy, who stared at his feet in misery. "Why didn't *you* do what you were told? You're the oldest. Haven't you learned nothin'? I told y'all to make those guys *disappear*." He gestured with both hands to simulate explosion. "That way it would take a few days for things to start happening, and we'd know what to do."

Before Willy could answer, Tanner cut in. "It's not his fault. One of 'em pulled a pistol, and we didn't have no choice." Tanner squared his shoulders. "I had to make a decision right then and there, and I did. You're the one who's always telling me to man up."

Sheriff Buck Henderson spoke from the shadows on the porch. He'd leaned his cane-bottom chair back on two legs against the house. "Yeah, and now we're in a mess. I got called in on this after you two stupid idiots went home and crawled into bed last night."

Tanner and Willy were standing beside two lawn chairs, but both knew it'd be a bad idea to sit down while Jimmy Don stomped a trail in the grass.

Willy looked miserable. "Can't you steer it away from us, cuz?"

"It ain't that simple. It's not just me working on this

case. I had to make it look good and assign a couple of deputies to investigate, and here's the hard truth. There's already half a dozen DEA agents in town to investigate the murder. Yeah, I said half a dozen, because that's who you shot and left laying right there instead of makin' 'em disappear like you was told. I'm gonna be talking with all six of 'em in a little while, but further-more and all that, one of them sonsabitches you put holes in ain't dead."

The yard fell silent, as if even the birds were stunned by the news.

Jimmy Don stopped pacing. "What?"

"Yeah, one named Fontana was dead at the scene, but the other one, Agent Kwan, is still alive. He's in the hospital. Y'all couldn't even *shoot 'em* right. He came around long enough to give a damned good description of you two. You done screwed the pooch, boy."

Tanner took a deep breath to calm himself. How could anyone survive six point-blank rounds from a .357 Magnum?

Jimmy Don ran a hand through his short gray hair. "Why didn't one of you tell me last night? Instead of coming and explaining what happened, y'all just dis-appeared. Donine called *me* to see where you were when you wouldn't answer your phone. She thought y'all were in a bar ditch somewhere. I thought them agents'd killed both of you."

Tanner shrugged and didn't answer for several heartbeats. "It shook me up so bad I didn't want to go home and wake her up."

"Let me remind you, there's another phone in your car that you're supposed to answer, because it's *me* on the other end of the line. Boy, I thought I made it clear to you that phone's one you don't ignore. So where'n hell were you?"

"Driving, for a while."

"You just drove around with what you thought was a murder weapon in your car. You still have it?"

Face numb with fear, Tanner pointed at his car. "It's under the seat."

Jimmy Don spat off to the side in disgust as Buck's chair thumped down on the boards at the news. He walked down the steps and crossed the yard to Tanner's Taurus. The wind almost took his hat, and he set it tighter on his head. Buck used a handkerchief to open the door and knelt inside, standing moments later with the Python in the handkerchief.

Watching the sheriff lay the blue-black pistol on his cruiser's hood, Jimmy Don's voice quieted. "What the hell, Willy? Why didn't you call me?"

Willy absently fingered the thick scar under his dead eye. "It didn't cross my mind." He turned toward Tanner, his face lined with worry. "I thought you was gonna tell him when you come home."

At a loss for words, and even more terrified now that Willy had thrown him under the bus, Tanner could do nothing but spread his hands in explanation.

Buck opened his trunk and took out a pair of white cotton gloves, came back around, and opened the pistol's cylinder. "Been fired six times." He squinted at the fat cartridges. "All Magnum rounds."

Tanner swallowed.

Jimmy Don spun back to his son. "The doctors told Buck they took one .38 from Kwan's chest. You missed with all six shots. Did you even try to *hit* those guys, or did you just shoot to make it look like you were trying to kill 'em?"

Tanner couldn't have been more shocked by his dad's accusation that he intentionally let Willy do the killing.

"Jimmy Don," Willy said. "They was close. It was dark, and them guys come out with hideout guns after we disarmed 'em."

"But *you* hit 'em both."

"I was closer."

"How come?"

Tanner and Willy went silent.

Jimmy Don ignored Willy, turning his attention once more to Tanner. "So you screwed up, didn't shoot a thing but the air and a tree or two, then screwed up again by disappearing and driving around with the gun in your car while I tried to call you."

Tanner saw a ray of hope. "Well, even if I'd got pulled over, the gun won't match the bullets."

"You know what's wrong with you, boy?"

The "boy" ignited a rage in the young man that washed over good sense. He saw himself almost out of there, free and clear with Shi'Ann while the laws closed in and took everyone else to jail. Oppressed and fearful for most of his life, the comment cut him free. Tanner squared his shoulders. "You know, I've been wondering exactly what my problem's been for years. Why don't you tell me?"

Jimmy Don's own frustration and fury boiled over. He slapped Tanner, rocking him back. With a rage bordering on insanity, he followed the slap with a left cross that caught his son full on the jaw. Tanner stumbled back, and then Jimmy Don was on him, throwing punches into his only son's face as if he were trying to kill him.

Powered by arms worked iron hard by a lifetime of physical labor, each blow landed with the force of a lead pipe. Already knocked almost senseless, Tanner staggered as the world spun into a blur, fighting to stay conscious. After the first punch, his face went numb, and he didn't feel the others as much. The idea of fighting back against his dad never crossed his mind. Hands up to ward off the blows, he fell back as Jimmy Don pressed in, face twisted in rage.

Ears ringing and eyes flashing, the blows split his lips, but it was as if his whole face was full of Novocain. Tanner finally tripped and his knees buckled. He held up a hand, a feeble attempt to stop the onslaught.

Any other time Jimmy Don would have followed someone to the ground and finished them there. That's what the old man taught him. Continue the attack until the opponent was dead or, at the very least, rendered unconscious. But despite his fury and Tanner's failure, the young man was still his son. He stepped back, breathing hard as the barely conscious twenty-year-old rolled onto his side, spitting blood.

A gasp from the porch broke the moment. "Stop it!" Donine rushed down the stairs as fast as her huge belly would allow and ran to Tanner. She knelt, crying. "He don't deserve this!"

Jimmy Don rubbed his knuckles and backed up a step. "Can you hear me, boy?"

Groaning, Tanner nodded and struggled to sit up.

"Good. You're my son, and I love you, but you cain't fail me now. I know there's more to this story than you told me, from beginning to end." He pointed. "You're lyin' to me about something. Willy here's gonna tell me all he knows, and then I'm gonna decide what to do about this. You hear me?"

"Yeah." Tanner spit out a tooth along with a mouthful of blood. "But I done told you the truth."

"I'm gonna get it all from him, so you cough up the rest. Where was you when I was callin'?"

Tanner felt his broken nose with trembling fingers. His whole life was literally on the line at that moment. He inhaled, gagging on the mix of blood and mucus from the beating.

"I went down and parked on the river and fell asleep behind the wheel." An ocean of emotions rose and he choked down a sob of pain and embarrassment at what had happened in front of his wife and the other two men. "All that business took so much out of me I felt like I was in a coma. I didn't hear nothin'."

"Whereabouts on the river?" Jimmy Don wasn't finished, not by a long shot. The 510-mile Sabine River snaked through the pine forests of East Texas before it emptied into the bayou country near the Gulf Coast. Wide, deep, muddy, and unpredictable in rainy weather, there were thousands of access points, from deer trails to sand bars to shacks built with cast-off materials and inhabited by people hiding from Life itself. "Where'd you go?"

Tanner swallowed. He hadn't expected to be questioned so much. His thoughts were fuzzy. "Under the old iron bridge where we used to fish."

Decades of locals driving the old dirt road to the abandoned railroad bridge and parking on the bank kept the area clear enough that some folks launched flat-bottom boats from the shallow bank. Teenagers often went parking there, hidden by the piney woods, and more than one baby was conceived in the darkness overlooking the river, including Tanner's own. In the summertime, it wasn't unusual for people to camp in the open space in good weather.

Jimmy Don stared at his son. "So what do you think I'm gonna do with you two?"

"I know what *I'm* gonna do." Buck pitched the .357 to Willy, who caught it and held the pistol like it was a dead possum. "First off, get rid of this. What went with *your* pistol?"

Willy slipped the empty revolver into the front pocket of his overalls and reached for a can of Copenhagen in the other and slapped it against his palm. "In my trailer."

"Anyone see you there?"

"Naw."

"Good." Buck stripped off the cotton gloves. "Take and carry that pistol home with you and throw 'em both in the bayou somewhere. I'm not too worried about that one, but it was your gun that killed Fontana and wounded that Korean."

Willy forced a grin. "I thought he was Chinese. I can't tell none of them Celestials apart."

The sheriff grunted. "Willy, you sure have a way with words." He pointed at the young man lying on the ground with his head in Donine's lap. "Did you ride out here with Tanner?"

"Yeah."

"Get in the car. I'll carry you back. These two need

to talk, and Tanner, I suggest you straighten up and fly right before some housewife calls to tell me where you were." The look he gave Donine was explanation enough.

"You going to meet with them agents?" Jimmy Don turned his back on the young couple.

"Yep. I'll see how they're handling things and point 'em the other way." He nodded at Willy getting into the front seat of his car.

Eyes dead, Jimmy Don nodded back.

Buck opened his door and paused with one hand on the top and a foot resting on the floorboard. "But Jimmy Don, you better get a handle on this one. We're too close to blowing this whole thing, and I don't intend to go to Huntsville. If I's you, I'd put everything on hold until all these agents are gone."

"Cain't do it. We got a buy on Friday. Big one we can't back out on, because them folks we're dealing with're meaner than we are. Daddy Frank said."

"Well, then don't set no charges on that pipeline. Just leave it alone for right now."

"Daddy Frank . . ."

"Yeah, I know. Daddy Frank said." Buck slammed the cruiser's door, dropped behind the wheel, and spun the tires as he left.

It was silent in the yard except for the wind whistling around the eaves and soughing in the trees. A blue jay cried in the woods. Jimmy Don turned back to his bloody boy and the daughter-in-law holding him in her arms. "Son, I gotta tell Daddy Frank about what happened. I can't keep you on the sugar tit with this one."

Beaten and semiconscious, Tanner felt the bottom

fall out of his stomach. "Is he gonna be here for sure today?"

"He'll call before long. Right now he's worried that the feds are on to Alonzo, too. That dumb-ass brother of mine could be leading them right to us, and that can't happen. You need to understand something though, son. I'll explain what you told me as best I can, but if he tells me to do something, I'm gonna have to do it. It'll be me on his side of the line, and you on th' other'n. If he wants Boone to settle up with you when he gets back, I cain't do nothing, even though you're family. You understand what I'm saying?"

Unable to answer and suddenly more alone than any other time in his life, despite Donine's presence, Tanner nodded and wiped blood from his face.

"All right, then. Is there anything else you need to tell me?"

"Nossir."

Jimmy Don studied the couple. "What a pair."

Tanner laid back in his wife's lap, his head against their unborn baby, and cried over not only the pain, but the shackles that held him right there where he was.

He couldn't tell them Daddy Frank's young wife Shi'Ann LeBleu had phoned him right after they left the supposedly dead agents behind the Swamp and told Tanner that the Old Man and Preacher Curry Holmes were gone to Beaumont to seal a deal on an incoming shipment that originated in Colombia.

It was the best news he'd heard in days, giving them the whole of last night to themselves. The things she knew how to do released all the fear and tension from Tanner's encounter with the two agents.

The thought of her lying naked on top of the sheets as he called the Comanche sheriff that morning didn't help him now. He was on his own, and right then decided to be completely finished with the family and the Business.

By tomorrow the both of them would be shed of Newton County, Texas.

Chapter 25

Northwest of the Comanche campground, an angry line of roiling clouds heralding the cold front had finally arrived. With a rush of chilly air, the grass and sage that had been leaning toward the north reversed direction. A light shower passed through, signaling what was to come.

Thunder vibrated the air and made the few glass dishes in the trailer's cabinets rattle. Back from town and the bank, Alonzo finished rolling the canopy back in, anticipating the storm. He'd mailed the paperwork, some cash, and the safety deposit box key to Tanner. That'd be a kick when the kid unlocked the bank box for the first time.

Two cardboard boxes that once contained copy paper but were now full of wrapped hundred-dollar bills rested on the back floorboard. A bin full of Semtex plastic explosive was strapped into the passenger seat, lest it jostle the little surprise he had in there.

He slid the aluminum lawn chair into the cargo hold and settled down to sit in the doorway. From the time he was a boy Alonzo enjoyed storms, and despite the pain in his gut and the love of his life now lying cold and still in the back seat of his truck, he was looking forward to the change in the weather.

He felt better now that he'd decided to drive straight through the day to meet the family in the fertilizer barn. The time crunch played hell with his extermination plan to put a few more felons in the ground before he got home, but hey, if he could take out just one more before sending his grandfather to hell, Life would be fulfilled, what there was left of it.

If.

If was the problem. *If* he ate all of his pain pills before he got there, they'd numb the badger in his stomach enough to finish the job. *If* the old man was where he needed to be, it was the perfect solution that would work out well for Tanner, Donine, and their unborn baby.

But now he saw a problem heading his direction, set to unravel everything. Alonzo learned the hard way a long time ago to trust his instincts by watching Daddy Frank reign over the Wadler family and most of the people living in Newton County.

So when a pickup drove down the state park's blacktop road and he recognized the man riding alone in the cab, the hair prickled on the back of his neck. Something was wrong.

The truck almost passed, but at the last minute Mike Dillman saw Alonzo sitting in the trailer's doorway. He pulled off the road and parked in the empty campsite beside the trailer.

Mike's eyes locked with Alonzo's as he lipped a cigarette from the pack in his shirt pocket and stepped out of the truck. "Hey, Alonzo."

Coming around the front fender, he bloused his untucked oversize shirt, tentatively pulling at the tail with his fingertips. That nervous action was a dead giveaway that the man wore a weapon hidden underneath. Alonzo's chest tightened. It took a moment to get his head in the game with the arrival of his third cousin from Gunn.

Mike stopped a few feet away, shirt flapping in the cooling wind. "Bet you didn't expect to see us, did you, but you know why I'm here."

"What'd they send you for?"

Mike cupped a cigarette in his hands and lit it with a disposable lighter. "Daddy Frank said for me to pick up your rig, and you to drive back in my truck."

The last of too many cups of coffee rose into Alonzo's throat, burning like battery acid. A Dodge dually came around the bend in the park road and stopped, the diesel growling in idle. Alonzo's attention flickered between Dillman and the stranger in a straw cowboy hat that emerged and circled the door to stop in front of the truck.

Who was this guy? Did Daddy Frank send one of Buck Henderson's contractors along with Dillman? If he did, then Alonzo wouldn't see the sunset.

A flicker from the corner of Alonzo's right eye caught his attention as something animal-like suddenly appeared from around the end of the camper.

Only one person moved like that.

Boone!

Chapter 26

Heavy clouds seemed to be within a tall man's reach when I turned off the highway into the Evening Star RV Park. The neat and well-maintained park shaped like a softened rectangle was larger than most, with mesquite trees blocking my view in several places. The wooden office building was just past the entrance shaded by huge live oak trees.

A few trailers were parked in two rows of pull-throughs in a center loop. I figured there were fifty or sixty in all, from what I could tell. Those on the outside edges were the kind of sites where RVers backed their rigs into the campsite.

Beyond the bobwire fence around the property, there was nothing but a pasture full of mesquite, cedars, and scattered live oak trees.

The truth was, I didn't know what I was looking for, but I figured I'd recognize it when I saw it. The coming rain drove most of the campers inside their rigs to wait out the storm. A couple of folks made of sturdier stuff were sitting outside, under the awnings attached to their trailers. They all waved.

I drove the loop, going clockwise, wondering if I was making a water haul when the peaceful appearance of the park changed. The action was at the far end at the last back-in.

A man with slightly graying hair was sitting in the doorway of his rig, sheltered by his awning. He looked peaceful, but the attitude of another man standing between the camper and an idling truck pulled onto the side of the little road spoke volumes. That guy was nervous or agitated.

They'd been having words before I showed up, and their discussion was amping up. I stopped the truck and stepped out without knowing what was going on or if the man sitting in the doorway was the feller I was looking for.

It didn't make any difference, because about the time I got around to the front of my truck one of the strangest-looking people I've ever laid eyes on seemed to pop up out of the ground with an open straight razor in his hand.

That's when all hell broke loose.

Chapter 27

Apparently startled by the readily identifiable Texas Ranger coming around the front of the idling Dodge, Boone froze in place at the end of the trailer, waiting to see what would happen next. Confused by the gnawing pain in his stomach and three men who were all looking at him, Alonzo tried to process what he was seeing.

They weren't sent to simply pick up the trailer and the cash. Boone's presence proved Mike's statement was a lie. The strange tattooed man's long, spiderlike fingers held a thin object that could only be a straight razor.

Alonzo was overwhelmed with a tidal wave of emotions and the pain in his gut. He paused, weighing his options and trying to clear his mind. Though the other men posed a threat, he couldn't take his eyes off the creature that brought death wherever he arrived.

Expressionless, Boone licked his lips. His tongue protruded far too long. "Alonzo!" Boone's high, gravelly voice surprised him. The odd man seldom spoke, and if he did at all, it was always the answer to a direct question. His eyes wide in tension and determination were the only thing that belied his anticipation. "Keep your hands where I can see them."

The damp air seemed to clear when fat raindrops landed with a splat on the hard ground.

Boone stepped forward, but none of them were ready for what happened next.

Alonzo snatched a Glock 19 from the floor next to his leg. The outcome might have been different if Mike hadn't been a smoker. Mike killed himself, in a sense. The cigarette stuck in the corner of his mouth certainly looked cool, and probably made the girls think he was tough back in Jasper on Saturday night, but he had to squint through the smoke.

That was all Alonzo needed, giving him plenty of time to shoot. Most people who practice on a range do well when they aim with care, but as most professionals will tell you, the majority of shots fired in a conflict miss their targets.

Alonzo drew on Mike, who suddenly found himself looking down the barrel of the pistol. "*Wait* a second!" The look on Dillman's face revealed that he wasn't ready for such a reaction. "Dammit!" He snatched a Colt Commander from under his oversize shirt.

The beavertail on the grip's safety caught in his shirttail, causing him to lose a precious half second.

The Hydra-Shoks did their job and expanded upon impact. Alonzo's first round blew out Mike's heart. He was the first person Alonzo had ever shot in a gunfight, and Mike Dillman fell straight down in a heap as the skies opened up in a torrent of water.

With his primary target down, Alonzo twisted back toward Boone, who had vanished as fast as the bolts fracturing the clouds overhead. One second he was standing in the open, and the next, he was gone.

The Ranger came into focus, holding a big .45 aimed at Alonzo. "Put the gun down, now!"

Alonzo fired again, missing. The Ranger shot once and the bullet bit Alonzo's side with the smack of a sledgehammer. His foot slipped off the wet step and he crashed into the aluminum doorframe with the force of a battering ram, hot and sharp, cutting his scalp to the bone. The world spun as the impact threw him out and onto the hard concrete pad.

His head slammed against the damp slab and the world spun.

Chapter 28

What at first looked like a standoff went to pieces when the guy in the trailer snatched up a pistol and went to shooting at the smoker. The bald, skinny guy vanished as quick as he'd appeared at the same time Trailer Guy pulled the trigger.

Smoker went down and I hollered at the shooter. "Put the gun down, now!"

Trailer Guy wasn't inclined to talk. He twisted in the doorway and fired. The bullet passed overhead with the buzz of a big, hot insect. My Colt came up, and when the front sight settled on him, I pulled the trigger two times.

The first shot missed, but the second caught him in the side, and he went down in a heap, bouncing off the doorframe. From the corner of my eye I saw the hairless man rush around the opposite end of the RV and charge through the hammering rain toward Smoker's still body.

With the initial threat down, I swung the .45 toward Baldy, but a sudden shout from my right stopped me in my tracks.

The high, scared voice of an elderly man cut through the ringing in my ears. "Put that gun down, cowboy. I done told you!"

My head jerked to the side. An elderly man stood by a picnic table in front of a bumper-pull trailer, aiming a big revolver at me from only twenty feet away.

"Easy! I'm a Texas Ranger!"

"I don't know that for sure. Keep still 'til I figure this out."

"Believe me! I'm a Texas Ranger. I'm the law! Get down!"

"Show me your badge!"

"The damned thing's on my shirt. Can't you see it?"

"Not without my glasses. 'Lonzo, you be still, too." The older guy's voice quavered, but he was game if nothing else. "None of this smells right."

Chapter 29

Lying on the wet ground beside the trailer steps, Alonzo found his actions suddenly came far too slow. The next thing he knew, Boone was standing beside Mike's body, holding a pistol he'd presumably picked up from the ground.

Alonzo rolled over, and the pain stabbed like a lance. Boone aimed the Colt at Jefferson, who swung his weapon back and forth between the Cowboy's big Dodge and Boone.

"'Lonzo, you be still, too," Jefferson said. "None of this smells right."

Alonzo really wanted to talk to the old feller about that, but he could barely draw a deep breath. Instead, he tried to buy some time and figure out exactly what was happening by tilting his head to see an already rain-soaked Jefferson in jeans and a thick Carhartt shirt, standing several feet away.

The muzzle of Jefferson's old-school .45 revolver swung back to Boone, who seemed content to wait and watch in the rain with the pistol hanging limp alongside his leg. He tilted his head like a puppy trying to figure out a strange, unfamiliar sound.

A sharp clap of thunder sounded like another shot and Jefferson flinched. That was all Boone needed. Jefferson jerked at the report and fired one shot that went wild as he tried to take cover behind a concrete picnic table. His feet tangled and the would-be Good Samaritan fell with a loud thump.

Boone did something that chilled even *Alonzo's* blood.

He shot Mike Dillman in the head.

The man's skull exploded from the impact as his arms and legs flexed and then stilled.

Alonzo shot at Boone over and over again, but his unbelievably heavy arm refused to cooperate. The bullets plowed the now-muddy ground five feet behind Boone. Alonzo's wrist flexed and the Glock's action froze as an empty shell stove-piped.

Alonzo closed his eyes, almost welcoming the coming bullet.

They opened at the roar of Dillman's engine. Instead of coming after Alonzo to finish the job, Boone jumped into the truck. The tires spun on the wet blacktop as he slammed the transmission into reverse. He spun the wheel, threw it into gear, and stomped the gas, almost losing control as he whipped the wheel and the pickup fishtailed. He let off to regain traction and in seconds the pickup shot out of sight in a spray of water.

The Ranger rose from behind his truck. "Don't shoot me!"

Jefferson kept the gun on him. "I won't if you stay

there. I bet the laws are on the way and they can sort this out."

"I am the law, dammit!"

Taking advantage of their standoff, Alonzo rose and stumbled to his truck, started the engine, and sped out of the park, leaving the two law-abiding men behind to work things out.

Chapter 30

Sheriff Buck Henderson steered his marked Chevy Tahoe along an oil road lined with tall pines. He was still steaming from their discussion back at Jimmy Don's house. The AC was on high to battle the sticky air. Willy rode shotgun.

Buck finally broke the silence. "Where'd you leave your truck?"

"At the house." Still quiet from his dressing down by Jimmy Don, Willy stared straight ahead. "Tanner came out and picked me up."

"You still live out there on Honey Road?"

Willy nodded. "Don't many call it that no more."

"That's a fact." Buck took a deep breath to calm himself. "These younger people and move-ins call 'em by road numbers now. You can't even tell 'em how to get somewhere like we used to, not that we do it much anymore now that everybody uses GPS. I still tell folks to turn by landmarks and about half the time they don't know where Art Stevens's barn is, or the Old Mill Road. Still livin' alone?"

"Yeah, cain't keep no woman out there in that piece-of-shit trailer."

Buck figured there were a lot of other reasons, too. The radio mounted on the floorboard crackled to life. "Sheriff?"

He plucked the microphone off the dash. "Go ahead."

"You in town?"

Buck flicked a glance toward Willy, and then back to the road that wound through the narrow slash through the loblolly and shortleaf pines.

"Naw, I'm following up on a report out here east. What's up?"

"Those feds say they'll be here in half an hour."

"I'll be a little late. It ain't my fault they're early. Have 'em wait."

"Yessir."

Buck hung the microphone back on the bracket at the same time they came upon a fresh scar on the land. One second they were surrounded by trees, and with startling suddenness, a clear-cut operation threw light into Willy's side of the car. The recently logged landscape studded with a few mid-story hardwoods that survived the chainsaws looked as if someone had called in an artillery strike.

Buck let out with a disgusted sigh. "I've lived here my whole life and I still can't get used to what this looks like after the Company gets finished."

The devastated land revealed all the terrain's dips and rises for a full five minutes before ending at the sharp edge of densely packed pines.

"It'll grow back." Willy kept his face turned toward the freshly logged lease.

A redheaded woodpecker flitted across the road as soon as they were once again surrounded by the forest. Willy turned his head to comment and stopped when he saw Buck's face.

Realizing he'd been projecting his mood, Buck forced the frown off his forehead.

"They're stripping my woods." He turned his attention back to the road to see a black youngster on the shoulder of the road, riding bareback toward them on a roan horse. The boy around twelve or thirteen grinned wide and threw up a hand to wave.

Willy instinctively waved back and they were past.

"Kid oughta be in school." Buck watched him recede in the rearview mirror. "I'll be draggin' his ass to jail before long. Little bastard won't graduate, and the next thing you know he'll be stealin' from his neighbors."

The road bent into an S-curve and when it straightened again, they came upon a black man walking in their direction through the short grass beyond the shoulder. There was twenty feet separating him from the woods and he carried a shotgun resting in the crook of his arm. Guns in that part of the country were as common as dead coons and possums on the side of the highway, but it was apparent the man was, or had been, hunting.

None of the lawmen in that part of the country paid much attention to those hunters who lived in the backwoods. Most of them, both black and white, barely scraped by and lived on food stamps and what game they could take. Venison was a staple, and most weren't trophy hunters, even in deer season. They were hunting to eat. Even the game warden looked the other way on many occasions, but not spring turkey season.

Buck saw the dismay on the man's face at the same time a beat-up station wagon slowed and the driver hung his arm out of the open window to speak to the hunter. The hunter was obviously uncomfortable about being seen. The asphalt road was so narrow Buck had to slow down to pass. Despite the look on his face, the hunter waved out of habit at the same time he opened the back door and slid the shotgun in, muzzle first. Both the driver and the hunter met Buck's gaze as he drove past.

Buck watched the car in his rearview mirror, memorizing the make and model. He was sure he'd read the backward license correctly and committed it to memory. "Was that Salvadore Williams with the shotgun?"

Willy had to completely turn his body to see with his good eye. "Yep." The car was still sitting there as Buck's Chevy went around another curve, and they disappeared from sight.

It was almost too much for the sheriff. His off-the-cuff plan looked to be going down the drain. He accelerated in frustration, and five minutes later came to an oil road that split off toward the Sabine. "This is it, right?"

"Yep."

A clearing appeared minutes later. Willy lived in a sagging trailer wedged on blocks in the trees. It had been there so long pines had grown in front and back, so close to the rusty trailer that the house's roof was covered with needles four inches thick.

Willy's wore-out old Chevrolet pickup was parked

in front. He opened the door, refusing to meet the sheriff's eyes. "Thanks for the lift, and Buck, I'm sorry for the problems I caused you."

"It don't matter none." Buck picked up the microphone. Willy was halfway to his truck when Buck opened his own door. "Willy, I changed my mind. Go inside and bring me that thirty-eight y'all used last night. I don't want to take the chance of you getting caught with it or that Colt. I'll take care of it."

"Yeah? You sure?" He paused in indecision, putting the Python into his pocket.

"Go get the other'n."

Willy shrugged. "Up to you." He dug out a set of keys and climbed the rickety wooden steps that looked as if a ten-year-old had hammered them together. Minutes later, he came back outside with the .38 and walked toward the Chevy.

Buck stepped around the open car door with his Glock in hand. Willy's eyes widened when the sheriff's Glock 19 came into view. Mouth moving in a silent plea, he raised the revolver, offering it to the sheriff.

Buck fired so fast the echoes through the trees sounded as one roll of thunder. All three bullets struck Willy in the chest. The .38 dropped into the sand and brown needles with a soft thud. Willy toppled like a felled pine and landed on his face.

Sheriff Buck Henderson listened for a moment and heard nothing but songbirds in the trees. A shadow passed over his car, and he looked upward. A buzzard drifted past. "How do you sonsabitches *know*?"

After checking over his shoulder, he holstered the Glock and walked over to Willy's body. He kicked the revolver to the side to keep the scene as realistic as possible, then bent over and rolled Willy onto his back. The dead man's eyes were full of sand. A pine needle stuck to the white scar.

Satisfied, Buck patted the front pocket of Willy's overalls, making sure the Colt Python that also contained the man's prints was still in there. He went back to his car and picked up the microphone. He keyed it once and stepped back to his original shooting position. "Dispatch."

"Go ahead, Sheriff."

"I just pulled up at Willy Henderson's house. Got a tip he might know something about last night's shooting . . . hey! You! Put that gun down! Put it down now! No, no, no!!!" He angled the Glock toward the sky and tilted it so the ejected brass would be easy to find. He pulled the trigger three times, sending the rounds over the house in the direction of the Sabine River. "Sonofabitch! Dispatch! Man down. I just shot an armed suspect. Get some people out here and an ambulance!"

The calm voice of the dispatcher came through. "They're on the way, Buck. You hurt?"

"No." He forced himself to breathe hard. "I . . ." He swallowed. "I'm fine. Y'all hurry. He might still be alive."

"Ain't Willy your cousin?"

"Ten-four. Looks like that don't mean nothin'. Hurry it up."

Satisfied with his performance, Buck replaced the mike on the bracket and located two of the hulls that had ejected from his pistol. The third was hard to find, and he was starting to get worried that someone would show up before he was ready. He finally found it inside one of his own shoeprints.

Sighing in relief, he dropped them into his pocket and leaned against the SUV to wait, trying to get his nerves back under control and decide whether he needed to do anything about the boy on the horse and the hunter he'd passed on the road.

Did they recognize Willy in the passenger seat, and if so, would they remember to tell any investigators about it? This was the kind of thing that might draw a Ranger in to investigate, but he doubted it. He'd make sure his number one deputy, the most well-paid and loyal, kept the focus on Willy's guilt in the DEA murders.

He lit a cigarette, noting his hands were calm and steady. Inhaling, he decided against dealing with them. Those people stayed to themselves, and none of his deputies would interview them about a white murderer's death.

Chapter 31

A massive thunderclap shook the courthouse with the force of an explosion, knocking the electricity out. Sheriff Gomez looked out the window to see another bolt of lightning bathe the town of Comanche in a cold, harsh light. Though it was impossible, Gomez would have bet money he could smell ozone in the office.

"Dammit! Daryl!"

His deputy appeared in the doorway with his flashlight in hand. "I bet everything that plugged in was fried."

"We don't need this right now." Gomez sighed in frustration. "Anyway, this building's supposed to be hardened against lightning strikes."

"Does low-bid mean anything to you? There's also supposed to be a backup generator, and *that* hasn't kicked in yet." The words were barely out of Daryl's mouth when the lights flickered, went out, and then came back on. "Well." He returned to the outer office.

Sheriff Gomez tapped the speaker button on his phone and was pleased to hear a dial tone. He punched in a number from the Rolodex on his desk for Ranger Enrique Elizondo, the Ranger assigned to Company A who he'd worked with in the past.

A clipped, no-nonsense male voice answered. "Elizondo here."

"Enrique, this is Sheriff Ed Gomez."

"I've been expecting to hear from you."

Surprised, the sheriff paused. "Why?"

"I'd be willing to bet you've met another Ranger named Sonny Hawke."

"Well, yeah, he was here a few minutes ago."

"Any trouble yet?"

"Trouble? No, why?"

"Well, it seems to follow that boy everywhere he goes." Enrique chuckled. "He's a helluva Ranger, but that boy's snakebit."

Gomez grinned at the expression. "How'd you know he was here?"

"My phone blew up yesterday when he tangled with some sex traffickers out in Dimmitt. He said he was heading in your direction."

"He just came in and told me what he was doing."

Another hard clap of thunder rattled the building. Ranger Elizondo heard it through the phone. "Sounds like that front's made it there."

"Yeah, hit just a little while ago."

"We got it here, too."

"Where you calling from?"

"Abilene, why?"

The sheriff explained the phone call he'd received. Elizondo listened without comment until he finished. "Was Hawke there when it came in?"

"Yeah, funny thing, he showed up not more'n five minutes before the call came through."

"That's what I was talking about, him and trouble."

"Well, he's chasing some vigilante that's going around taking out released felons. He was interested, but that's all." Gomez swiveled in his creaky wooden chair to see the café's lights through the gloom and falling rain. "He's eatin' breakfast across the street right now."

"You better hope he stays there. He was in Dimmitt, chasing that vigilante he was telling you about, and they're still mopping up the blood. Listen, I need to finish up here, and then I'll be out. By that time the kid might get back to you, or you'll know something else. Probably just a prank call."

Deputy Daryl blew into the office as if pushed by a giant hand. "Sheriff! Got a call from the Evening Star RV Park. They've had a shooting out there and the lady on the phone said there're dead people all over the place."

"Shit! Are they still on the line?"

"Yeah, I told 'em to get every'body away from the camper, if that's the one the call was about. Told 'em to get out of the park because if that camper blew up, it might leave a hole the size of this whole town. The fire department's on the way. I told them, too."

The deputy disappeared back through the open door and Gomez leaned into the phone. "Guess you heard all that?"

"I did." Ranger Elizondo snorted. "You sure Hawke's not in the middle of that? Knowing him, that's where he'd be."

"Pretty sure. He won't know anything about this."

"I'm on the way. I'll meet you out there, and Ed, don't you tell that sonofabitch what's going on. I don't want him involved."

"I won't." Shaking his head and grabbing his rain gear, Sheriff Gomez charged out the door, hoping to find the Evening Star still there when he arrived.

Chapter 32

A shaken Alonzo Wadler pulled onto the two-lane high-way. The green, limber mesquites in the pastures on both sides thrashed in the wind. Sheets of rain slashed across the road, bending cedars over bobwire fences.

The air inside the closed cab was thick with the scent of Betty's decomposing body and the various perfumes Alonzo had sprinkled on the sheet that covered her corpse. He cracked the window on the opposite side of the storm and opened the vents to admit as much fresh air as possible.

"Sorry, baby. It won't be long now."

He pressed the accelerator, punching a hole through the rain. A gray rooster tail of water blocked his view in the side mirrors. The red-hot wound in his side didn't hold a candle to what the badger had put him through, but he knew good and well he was bleeding internally. There was no telling how long he could stay conscious.

He used a bloody bandana to put pressure on the bullet hole. "I don't have the strength to stop."

The statement floated in the silence.

"I was gonna just pull up in Mundy's yard and knock on the door. It's worked before."

They passed the city limits sign.

"But they have a description of the truck." He paused as if listening to her answer. "It's all changed. It's all over, but we're not gonna do what Daddy Frank says anymore." He stopped talking for a moment when the badger woke up and scratched around, adding still another layer of suffering to the dying man. "It's his fault, what happened to you. I didn't want to haul all that coke out here. I told him that. I wanted out and by God, that's what'll happen when we get back home."

He took his eyes off the highway for a moment to make sure the simple detonator wired to the Semtex under his seat was riding safely in the nearest cup-holder. It wasn't hard to do. He learned how to set charges during his military service as a young man.

It was the perfect way to deal with Daddy Frank. The plastic explosive had arrived inside a shipment of Olomouc Cheese, a pungent, ripened soft cheese from the Czech Republic. The shippers used the cheese's strong scent and yellowish color to disguise the Sem-tex that had no identifiable odor.

The originators in Moravia packed the putty-like material in the same wrapping as real cheese and put it on a ship that eventually arrived at a dock on the north-east side of San Francisco Bay, where customs and im-porters checked the contents.

Their contact, an overworked, underpaid customs official named Jim Young, passed the shipment to a distributor who took his cut, separated the explosive from the real cheese, and offered it to Alonzo for a quarter of the money from the drug sale.

The badger slashed and Alonzo gasped, jerking the steering wheel. The truck rocked as the cancer tore his insides once again, sharp claws cutting deep, as if an animal were trying to claw its way out of his stomach. Alonzo's eyes watered and he folded into the steering wheel, releasing some of the pressure on the wound in his side. More blood leaked out and covered his fingers.

The fierce spasm of pain passed, and he took several deep breaths before his trembling fingers gripped the prescription bottle in his shirt pocket. He fought the child-proof cap for a moment, weaving on the highway even more. The stubborn cap finally turned and he shook two pills into his mouth, anticipating the coming relief.

Dry swallowing them, he pulled up to a stop sign at the outer edge of town and sat there a moment, gathering himself until another wave of agony washed over him. "Ohhhhh . . ." Teeth clenched against the pain, he was dimly aware of an approaching siren.

He closed his eyes until the tsunami passed. The siren grew closer, joined by more in the distance. A Comanche sheriff's car slowed at the intersection, lights flashing. Seeing the way was clear, it shot by and disappeared into the rain. Before Alonzo could press the gas, a fire truck appeared from his left. It slowed, turned, and passed in the same direction.

More sirens wailed in the distance. It was the perfect time to kill Mundy for all he'd done. Every first responder in the area would be headed for the campground, but it was impossible. Either the lightning-hot pain or the effects of the pills he was already feeling would prevent him from shooting Mundy.

He was also afraid he wouldn't be able to drive all the way to Gunn that day, either, but there was nothing to do but try. He turned right and headed southeast as more cars and trucks passed with their lights flashing in the storm.

Another deep burn joined the other two, red hot as a branding iron. It was time to end Daddy Frank's reign, and Alonzo had exactly what he needed to do it. The old man didn't know what was headed in his direction. Alonzo was driving directly to Daddy Frank's barn, and when he set eyes on that mean old bastard, they were all going to vaporize.

Chapter 33

"You have a description of the shooter and the truck? A name?" Sheriff Gomez looked about half amused, probably because I looked like a drowned rat and had been held at gunpoint by a creaky old guy with an antique hogleg pistol.

We were standing under umbrellas out on the blocked-off two-lane highway a quarter mile from the Evening Star RV Park. John Jefferson, the elderly man who'd drawn down on me, was sitting inside an ambulance, looking miserable as the paramedics checked him out. He and I both were soaked from the rain, and my general disposition wasn't exactly sparkling. Too much valuable time had been wasted while I stood behind my truck, talking fast to convince him that I really was the law.

He wasn't taking any chances, and we argued until blue and red lights came into the park. I was watching my coffee-drinking friend Deputy Daryl from Comanche who was changing the front tire on my Dodge. A stray bullet had caused the flat. Against everyone's wishes, I drove it out onto the highway when Sheriff

Gomez and his deputies ordered everyone out of the park.

I cut my eyes at Jefferson, both admiring the old coot for getting involved, and aggravated enough to pull his damned head off.

The description I gave Gomez was the kind that drove *me* nuts when I was interviewing victims or witnesses. "Graying white male, late fifties or so. Registered as Lon Wadler, but there's some discrepancy. Late-model Dodge. Folks can't agree on the color. I got white, light gray, and one guy says pale green."

I saw the same look of irritation I'd have felt at the description pass through Sheriff Gomez's eyes. "Anything else?"

"As far as the other two are concerned, all we know is two males pulled into the park in a truck. One suspect bald as a baby's butt, but tatted up, wearing shorts and a wife-beater-style shirt got out and made a circuit around the park. Cut through a couple of empty sites, like he was trying to decide where they might park a rig.

"Suspect Number Two got out of his truck, and Ward started shooting. Number Two drops, and while me and Mr. Jefferson are having our little disagreement, the suspect in shorts ran over and picked up a gun that Number Two dropped. Fired several times at Wadler, threw a couple in our direction, then anchored Number Two before jumping in the truck and leaving."

I saw the obvious answer. "So Suspect Two wouldn't talk."

"Yep, either that or he didn't like him one damned bit. Baldy won't be hard to ID with that big ol' spider and its web tattooed on his scalp."

"The others prison tats?"

"Didn't get that close enough to look."

"You have tags on both trucks?"

Even though I knew it was coming, I sighed. "No. Things happened so fast no one had a chance to get the assailant's tag. Wadler gave fake tags for both the truck and trailer on the registration."

Deputy Daryl's phone rang, and that wasn't unusual because it looked like everyone around me was on the phone at some point while I was there. He tapped Gomez's arm. "You need to take this, I think."

"Who is it?"

"The bomb guys. They're on the way."

Gomez was afraid there was Semtex wired up inside the trailer. They were in the process of escorting the rest of the campers into town for the time being. He took the phone and put the heel of his hand over the end. "I'm gonna need a statement."

"I know. I'm supposed to write one for my supervisor, too. How about I send it to you when it's finished."

"When will that be?"

"Once I catch this guy, I 'magine."

"You need anything else?"

"I don't believe so."

He started to put the phone to his ear and paused, still talking to me. "I talked to Ranger Elizondo. He wanted to know if you were here and when I told him, he *said* there'd be trouble because you're snakebit."

"He wasn't kidding. Hey, do me a favor, will you?"

"Do you a favor? What'n hell can that be?"

"I'm not going to take Mr. Jefferson in for holding me at gunpoint. He did what he thought he should do. I'd like for you to do the same."

Sheriff Gomez angled his body to see into the ambulance where Mr. Jefferson and his wife were sitting. "He cost us that guy."

"Maybe. Maybe they'd have shot me if he hadn't gotten involved. Everybody else ran and hid. He stood up. Let him go." My phone rang, and I answered. It was Yolanda and Perry Hale. "Where are y'all?"

Her voice came through first. "You're on Perry Hale's Bluetooth in the truck. We're on the way to East Texas."

"What for? Aren't y'all moving a little early?"

"We think that's where the plastic explosive could be headed, but I checked something else on your caller. You said his name's Wadler."

"Wadler is what the kid said." I told them about the shoot-out in the park. "One of the guys called a name, 'lonzo which I bet is Alonzo."

"So you got him?"

"Well, no." I explained what happened. "I have a pretty good idea I had the guy right here, but now he's gone."

"I think I know where." I heard Yolanda clacking on her iPad in the background.

"Where?"

"I ran the last name through the online white pages. Now what I did isn't exactly scientific or even thorough. It's more a sampling."

"Of what?"

"Of addresses or at least the ones that popped up. Most websites require you to pay for the information you're looking for, but there's a couple of half-assed pages that gave me most of what I want."

"What's that?"

"The Wadlers that popped up for the most part are here in Texas and Louisiana. For us, I concentrated on Texas, and the biggest cluster is in one place. *I* think it's where the plastic is headed, and maybe even *our* guy, if it's the same person. The kid who called didn't say gun when the phone was breaking up, he said Gunn, with two Ns. It's a little one-horse town about twenty or thirty miles from Jasper."

"Where those DEA agents were murdered."

Her voice was full of excitement. "Gunn, Texas, fits with this big 'ol target right there. I have the name of Alonzo Wadler who lives there."

We were quiet with our thoughts, but my pessimism reared its head once again, and I watched Deputy Daryl finish changing the flat. He threw the punctured tire in the bed. "He's in the Big Thicket. Sounds to me like the vigilante and the Semtex are headed in the same direction."

It all fit. Wadler drives out to California in an RV, picked up a load of plastic explosive, and then had some kind of meltdown on the way back and started killing *other* criminals. It made sense. A weak-minded man had some kind of revelation sitting there behind the wheel and decides his newfound cause is higher than the people he's working with.

"She's right." Perry Hale's voice was full of determination. "You've been tailing a guy who's killing people left and right at the same time hauling enough Semtex to start his own country. There're refineries all up and down the coast. Tankers use the Intracoastal Waterway to get in and out. They're scattered all the

way from Corpus Christie to Mobile, Alabama. He could
be a terrorist planning to hit a refinery."

It made sense. The FBI had dozens of cases in their
files of plots against refineries. They were batting a
thousand right then, but no streak goes on forever.

I shivered, suddenly chilled in my wet clothes.
"We've put out an APB on this guy, but it took so long
for me to do it that he could be anywhere. I'd be willing to bet he'll change rides before he gets there."

"Why'd you take so long to put out the APB?"
Yolanda asked.

I threw a glance at Jefferson, who looked like a
whipped dog. "I'll explain it later."

Chapter 34

Tanner lay on top of Shi'Ann LeBleu's chenille bedspread, but for the first time since he'd known her, it wasn't for pleasure. Wind pushed through the screens and caressed Tanner's damaged face. The humidity was high, but it was pleasant in the quiet house built to breathe in the swampland.

She half-sat on the side, leaning toward him with her hand lightly brushing his bruised and swollen face. Crusty blood still remained inside his nose. *"Je suis tellement desolé, mon amour."*

He took her hand. One eye was swollen shut, and he had to turn his head to see. "Speak English. You know I can't tell what you're saying in French. I barely understand any of those words you use."

She displayed bright teeth in her light brown face. Her Acadian accent was soft, her voice and tone mellowed by a short lifetime of sadness. "I said I'm sorry, my love."

He reached up with a forefinger and softly touched the deep dimple at the lower corner of her mouth. "You didn't have anything to do with it."

"But I'm truly sorry that you have such a family."

"Ain't we both. But you're married to that mean ol' bastard, so *we* have such a family."

"Only on paper. *Sha-bébé,* I'm yours."

He smiled at the Cajun-French slang most would spell and pronounce *chere-baby* as a term of endearment. Many people both young and old in that region of Louisiana that shared a common border with Texas used the common phrase in everyday conversation.

Tanner closed his eye, wondering how he'd gotten himself into such a mess. "Yeah, well, that ain't doin' us no good right now. I'm like, trapped with Donine and ever-body in the house wants her around but me."

Here he was with the woman he loved, girl actually, who was married to his grandfather of all people, while Tanner was living in a common-law relationship with a woman who'd gotten pregnant on their first date in the back of his truck parked down on the bank of the Sabine. She came to him two months later, after the one-night-stand that went bad.

By the time he fessed up to his dad out in the backyard, it was too late. Jimmy Don suggested an abortion, which neither Donine or Tanner would agree to, so Jimmy Don threw up his hands and was done with it.

Donine's mother threw her out of the house when she found out her daughter was pregnant, and the only thing Tanner could do was let her live with all of them in their old house that was getting dangerously crowded.

What he really wanted was Shi'Ann, who was with Daddy Frank at a street dance over in DeRidder, Louisiana, when he met her, about three days after he and Donine spent the night in his truck on the Sabine riverbank. He didn't know Shi'Ann's entire background, but she told him enough to know her sorry-ass daddy ran off when she was thirteen, after she finally told her mama what he'd been doing to her since she was ten. Her mama drank herself to death when Shi'Ann was fifteen, and the girl did whatever she could to stay alive until she met Daddy Frank, who offered protection and money, along with a glittering diamond ring that she suspected was glass.

"But you will leave her soon, no?" Shi'Ann tilted her head to look at Tanner the way he loved. Her hair fell long on one side, and every time it did, that dimple appeared.

"I'm gonna leave the whole damn family. I've had enough and cain't take no more."

"What about the *bébé*?"

"There's enough of them on her mama's side to raise it."

"Let's run away right now, then. You have the new car. We can go wherever we want."

He almost groaned at the thought. Leased cars were a sure way to get found, even he knew that, and it was in Shi'Ann's name from the money Daddy Frank deposited every month in her account. It was for the rent on the little house they were in, but the joke was on the old man. Shi'Ann paid it off a year earlier, from cash she got from other older men who liked the attention of young ladies. It was a lucrative business that she traded in whenever the old man was out of town.

Tanner opened his eye and blinked it clear. "Yeah, and the minute you stop paying the lease, they'll track it down. When they do that, Daddy Frank'll find out and we'll be done."

"Fine, we take a bus. I'm ready to get loose of this

place and this life. We can make it, just you and me. Let's go to Dallas, or better than that, San Diego! We can leave tomorrow. Himself is gone off with that *couyon* Boone." She never spoke Daddy Frank's name. "He gives me the *frissons*."

At the mention of crazy Boone, Tanner's one good eye roamed the room, as if he was hidden in the closet, or just outside the door. He checked the window, half expecting the strange man to be lurking beside the pier-and-beam house standing nearly four feet off the ground.

Outside, heavy dark clouds rested on the pine and cypress trees lining the nearby bayou. There wasn't as much Spanish moss draping the cypress limbs as most people expected in that part of the state, but it was enough to give the woods a distinct southern flavor. Crows called in the distance, anticipating the coming storm. The humidity was heavy, but the strong wind pushed through the screens, creating a cross-breeze inside the house that kept the temperature pleasant.

"He gives me the chills, too." Tanner gingerly touched his broken nose with the tip of a finger and winced. "We need to wait until tomorrow after the bank opens. By then I think it'll all be over. Uncle Alonzo put some money in my account this morning. As soon as it posts, we're gone." Tanner finally relaxed, enjoying the feel of her soft hand running up and down his arm.

"I still think we should leave right now, tonight."

"You don't know my family."

"I know dat old man and his ways."

"You do, that."

"But what are y'all doing? What is this thing he's so excited 'bout, that all y'all are working on?"

"They're trying to get rich and change the world. I'm just trying to get off."

Her soft accent became thicker with concern. "Look at you, down in the bed. What you gonna do?"

Tanner had an idea. He rolled toward Shi'Ann with a groan and reached for the pink Princess phone on the table beside the bed. Daddy Frank insisted on a landline and paid for it. She'd chosen the antique because her favorite color was pink.

"Who you gonna call on dat landline?"

He thumbed his cell phone alive, and swiped for a moment to find a phone number. "The sheriff of Comanche, Texas, where Uncle Alonzo is. I'm gonna call again and tell him everything else. He can pass the word to whoever can do something about it."

"You gotta tell him about Buck, so they don't get waylaid when they get here, but you can't call on my phone. They can trace it, you know."

He dropped back onto the pillow. "Dammit. I'll have to use the drop phone in the car again."

Shi'Ann stroked his arm. "Den what?"

"I don't know. I'll figure it out, and pretty quick, too, 'cause we're 'bout outta time."

Feeling slightly better, Tanner wanted to grin, because the longer he was with her, the more his speech patterns changed. His lips were split, and it hurt every time he moved them. He forced his facial muscles to relax and pushed at a loose tooth with the tip of his tongue. The hole from the knocked-out front tooth seeped, and he still tasted blood.

"*Va cooshay* for a little bit, then make your call."

"A nap sounds good. I could use one, *catin,* but don't let me sleep too long."

She kissed his forehead for calling her a pretty girl. "I won't, T-Tanner. That *cochon*'s gonna be here in a little while."

Tanner would have enjoyed the Cajun endearment she used when she put the T in front of his name, but he jerked upright when she pronounced *cochon*, calling Daddy Frank a pig. "No, then. We can't take the chance at getting caught. Boone's gone with Mike, so that old bastard might show up early."

Shi'Ann gave a start, her voice full of fear. "I didn't know dat he was *alone*." She rose and went to the window to make sure he wasn't coming down the dirt lane.

"See, this is how we get in trouble."

"We been in trouble since the first time you bed me, *sha-bebe*."

He groaned upright. "I gotta make that call. You pack a bag and hide it till we're ready. You got something to carry clothes in?"

She pointed toward the closet. "I gotta backpack over in dere."

"Good. Get it ready. I can't rest yet. Gotta go. I'll call you in a little while, and then we're gone."

She stood on her tiptoes and held him. He kissed her lightly with his split lips and left to make his call, but not to the Comanche sheriff.

He hit Daddy Frank's name on the scroll list as soon as he got in the car. Making a three-point turn, he counted the rings all the way up to a dozen before the old man answered. "What?"

You mean old bastard. You and Daddy're gonna pay for what y'all've done to us all.

"I just talked to Uncle Alonzo. He said he's getting

close and wants to meet all of us at the fertilizer barn tonight at six."

There was a three-beat pause. "Why'd he call you for?"

"Said he had a truckload a money, and it was a lot more'n what you expected. Said he wanted to divvy the extra up between us all."

"Then why didn't he call me?"

"Hell, I don't know. I didn't ask him."

"That boy don't make those kind of decisions, and neither do you. I do."

"I'm just tellin' you what he said."

"Why were *you* talking to him?"

Tanner's head spun. He hadn't thought that far enough ahead, not enough to make up why Alonzo wanted to speak with him. He passed a rural cemetery and it gave him an idea. "Because he was feeling down about Aunt Betty and wanted to talk. He knew I thought a lot of her."

Daddy Frank grunted. The deep sound reminded Tanner of a hog. "All right then. We'll all be there."

"Okay. See you then."

He drove down the pine-lined highway, remembering Shi'Ann's good-bye kiss because it was so light and soft, the sweetest one they'd ever shared.

Chapter 35

Boone drove with two hands on the wheel of Mike's truck, placed correctly at ten and two. He'd already left the mesquite-covered landscape of central Texas behind and now passed through the rolling hill country on back roads, and into the piney woods. Only highway sounds filled the cab. He despised music.

He'd failed once again. An occasional sob erupted from his chest as he looped over and over through the out-of-control scene back at the campground. Mike's plan went awry from the moment they pulled up. Boone didn't want to simply drive up and get out of the truck. He always expected the worst and, following his own experiences in life, convinced Mike to let him out as soon as they passed the office and camp store.

He expected Alonzo to be concentrating on the pickup and its driver as he circled the trailer. Neither of them had any idea the man would be ready to fight at the drop of a hat. Boone wiped a tear that leaked down his unlined cheek.

He'd failed again.

A car approached on the two-lane and he quickly replaced the hand at the ten-o'clock position, in case it was a highway patrol. The sedan passed with a little old lady with big knuckles at the wheel.

He caught up with the cold front, passing through the leading edge of rain that shook the truck like a terrier with a rat. Less than ten minutes later, he was back into a dreary world of dark clouds preceding the storm.

As speed forced rivulets of rain up the windshield, he was back where he belonged. East of I-45 was home, if he ever truly embraced that idea. Despite everything he could do not to look, he threw a glance toward Freestone County, far to the north and just west of Fairfield and the Boyd Unit, a Texas Correctional Institution where he'd spent five years as a G-5 prisoner.

It was a trail of teeth he'd collected during younger years that had been the prosecution's damning piece of evidence that put him there. One tiny self-administered tattoo was the only thing that he took from that place of Texas-authorized punishment for his crimes. A small, winking smiley face on his hairless pubic bone.

Ahead, two slow-moving eighteen-wheelers had traffic stacked behind them. There was no way to pass on the curved road, and he took the opportunity to calm himself by slipping one hand into the pocket of his baggy cargo shorts to withdraw his ever-present antique straight razor. The white bone handle fit comfortably in his fingers, and a great relief washed down his back. Boone shivered in ecstasy. His trembling eased and muscles relaxed.

It was the perfect device to release blood.

Boone loved blood, the sight of it, the feel of the warm, red liquid, both his and others, that sometimes seeped, sometimes pulsed, and often spurted in glorious, vivid fountains when his blade flashed. He especially liked how it felt as it dried, first tacky, then sticky and crusty. He enjoyed flaking it off his skin with the long finger-nails he maintained for just that purpose.

He also enjoyed collecting his victims' teeth and was saddened that he hadn't been able to take one of Mike's incisors to replace the pint jar full that the state had taken when he was twenty-one.

The line of cars following him ran bumper to bumper as they progressed another mile at thirty-five miles per hour, passing a speed-limit sign proclaiming that fifty-five miles per hour was the appropriate speed.

He rubbed his thumb against the bone handle. *Need to read. I need to sit in the shade and read.*

More socially acceptable, reading was his calming influence. He recalled the scene in the campground.

Need to practice with a handgun. Have to ask Daddy Frank for some ammunition so I can practice.

I promised I'd call Daddy Frank when I got close to Gunn. It's been too long. He knows I've been bad. He knows I failed. He's going to run me off. Say I'm use-less. Say he can find someone else to do the work.

His anxiety rose.

He should spank me hard with that big ol' belt he keeps hanging on the back of the bedroom door.

Daddy Frank had only used it on him once, when he'd caught Boone listening to him and Shi'Ann through the window of her house. Daddy Frank had ordered him to remain in the car with his book by the German-Swiss psychiatrist and philosopher Karl Jaspers. The book had been slow reading, and he'd grown bored with the doctor's theories as he sometimes did in the early afternoon.

Daddy Frank beat him like a dog after they got home, so much so that the last several lashes landed on the unfeeling flesh of his legs. When Daddy Frank finally tired of swinging the belt, he sat on the blue velvet sofa in his living room and called Boone to his side. Whimpering, Boone crawled across the floor and waited for permission to get on the couch. There, he laid his bare head on Daddy Frank's leg, and the old man caressed the tattooed web on his skull and forgave him.

Gripping the steering wheel with one hand, Boone returned the razor to his pocket. They were going so slow, it was finally safe to make the phone call.

Heart in his throat, he dialed Daddy Frank's number and prepared himself to admit failure, and to face the punishment that was sure to come. Then the shame would pass and it would be glorious when Daddy Frank unleashed him the next time on the next person who failed their cause. He was confident how it would happen, because he was like one of Daddy Frank's fighting dogs, and you never killed your champion.

Chapter 36

Late afternoon humidity compressed by thick clouds weighed like a wet wool blanket in the damp woods, drawing sweat on everyone. Even the blue jays were miserable in the still, breathless Sabine River bottoms. Only crows cawed from the treetops.

Daddy Frank and Brother Holmes, the Pentecostal preacher, were standing behind a chain-link fence that enclosed the dogfighting ring behind one of the old man's many barns. They'd been using it for the past several weeks and would continue until Buck told them the location was becoming common knowledge.

Daddy Frank had barns on properties he owned throughout the county. He alternated his dogfights with occasional bare-knuckle fights between younger Big Thicket citizens who didn't mind beating the holy shit out of each other for money.

One barn, though, would remain out of the rotation. It was the one built deep in the backwoods by men who wielded axes in the mid-1800s. Surrounded by a mix of ancient hardwoods and pines not far from the

Sabine River, the hand-riven barn was filled with more than ten thousand pounds of ammonium nitrate fertilizer he'd skimmed from his farming supplies and logging business, and what was stolen from other logging companies in the region. It was the same material Tim McVeigh used to bomb the Murrah Federal Building in Oklahoma City.

He'd purchased it in volume when he heard that a Canadian manufacturer had created a new fertilizer called ammonium sulfate nitrate that contained so much less sulfur it couldn't be used as an explosive.

The ingredients in his stockpile represented his first pass at creating a volatile substance that would become useful at some point. Once anything potentially dangerous was banned or phased out, its price dramatically rose. It was one more product in his diversified portfolio.

Two exhausted and bloody pit bulls snarled and twisted on the blood-soaked ground in a macabre dance that would end in death. The old man was bored and frustrated that his own dog was losing, but Brother Holmes's eyes were bright with the knowledge that the dog he'd bet on was winning.

Brother Holmes often used what he called "plate money" from his congregation to bet the dogs, but it was always when he put one of his own animals into the ring. Most of the spectators and gamblers trusted that a preacher wouldn't cheat, but he was human. Despite working closely with Brother Holmes, Daddy Frank didn't trust any man, or woman for that matter.

He wasn't paying much attention to the fight for once. Tanner's call only half an hour earlier had him confused, puzzled, and half mad. He couldn't for the life of him figure out what was going on and hated the feeling.

The ringing burner phone in Daddy Frank's pocket gave him an excuse to turn away and push through the crowd of shouting, sweating men reeking of beer, sweat, whiskey, and cigarettes, half of whom were losing. Absorbed by the dogfight, Brother Holmes never knew Daddy Frank had moved away.

"What?" He walked around the barn and put one finger in his ear to block the noise.

"Daddy. It's me, Boone."

The old man's wrinkled face widened in a smile. He hadn't shaved in days from nothing more than laziness, and the gray whiskers seemed to move of their own as the crevasses in his face deepened. "Howdy boy! D'y'all get it?"

Daddy Frank's smile disappeared as Boone hesitated. "No. Mike's dead."

"Who killed him?"

"Alonzo did."

"What'n hell happened?"

"Alonzo was waiting for us, like he knew we were coming. Mike was down before I realized what was happening and it wasn't him alone. Alonzo had another man working for him. I was under fire from both. Mike was possibly still alive, so I had no recourse but to finish him and escape. I knew you didn't want to risk him being arrested and questioned."

"You're mighty right about that." Daddy Frank stalked toward his truck with furious strides. Kinfolk were dying like flies. "And Alonzo?"

"I was forced to use a gun and wounded him, I think, but had to leave before the job was completed."

The old man's nose flared, and he saw red. "How could *two* men fail against *one*?"

"Again, he had help. Someone's joined him."

"And you left him alive after all that?"

Sheriff Buck Henderson's private truck turned into the drive and headed for the barn. Daddy Frank held up a hand to stop him and met Buck between the house and barn.

Boone continued. "Like I said, I think quite possibly he was ready for us. Someone must have tipped him off, because he had a handgun and was shooting before we knew it."

"He left with the cash and the cheese?" Veins throbbed in his forehead.

"Yes. I'm sorry."

Buck hung one arm out the open window and waited, knowing something was up.

"That means everything we planned is out the window."

Boone didn't answer, knowing from experience the old man was already thinking ahead.

"Tanner."

"Sir?"

"Only those of us in the Family had the number for Alonzo's drop phone. Jimmy Don whipped Tanner's ass yesterday for failing to make these damned agents disappear like I told him to. That boy's up to something. He's the only one who had a reason to call and warn Alonzo."

A beat.

"I don't understand all I know about this." Daddy Frank said, resting one hand on the open driver-side window of Buck's pickup. The sheriff lit a cigarette and blew smoke, watching the old man's lined face, waiting to hear what was wrong.

"He's traveling fast, then. I suspect he has another plan that we don't see." The old man mulled over the conversation between himself and Tanner, who'd already said Alonzo was on the way to Gunn with the cash.

Buck squinted, watching Daddy Frank's every move.

The old man nodded as if Boone stood beside him. "All right. Here's what I want you to do. You're not hurt, are you?"

"No."

"Where are you?" He listened. "You'll be back soon?"

"Yessir."

"Good. Go to Jimmy Don's and get Tanner. Wait for 'im if he ain't there. When he shows up, bring him out to my fertilizer barn. We're gonna have a little . . . gatherin' of the clan."

Buck's eyes widened at the mention of the barn. People only went out there for three reasons, and one of them wasn't to drop off or load fertilizer. More than one corpse had fed the gators in the Sabine, only a mile down a two-track lane behind the barn.

Daddy Frank nodded at Buck and reemphasized his order to Boone. "Yep, that's what I said. Take him to the fertilizer barn. That's where he wanted to meet us anyway, so he'll get what he wants."

"Yessir."

Daddy Frank hung up, wishing he'd thought to ask Tanner what time he'd talked to Alonzo. He dialed Alonzo's number. It rang until the automated voice told him there was no voicemail set up. He dropped the phone into the pocket of his khakis. "We got troubles." He told the sheriff what he'd just heard. "We're blowed up."

"You don't say, there's all kinds of trouble on my end, too. I got a call from a Texas Ranger named Sonny Hawke who's on the way to my office. Says he's chasing a vigilante by the name of Wadler who may be headed here to Gunn."

"Vigilante? What the hell does he mean, 'vigilante'?"

"He says Alonzo's been leaving a trail of dead people between California and here."

Daddy Frank took a long, deep breath to calm himself. "That makes sense now, why he's late. He snapped."

"Yep, snapped because Betty was killed by a released felon in California," Buck continued as Daddy Frank's eyebrows first rose, then met in a frown. "Look, I ran her name through my computer and found a news story and sure 'nough, she's dead. You know he was crazy about her. Somebody killed that gal, and he lost his damn mind. Sounds to me like it's a reckoning against anyone who beat the system."

Daddy Frank snorted as the years quickly rolled past like one of those old black-and-white movies counting off the months with paper calendars, recalling how he'd beaten the system in Newton County since he was big enough to shave.

Hell, even *he'd* been arrested in the past, and served two years for attempted murder. "He cain't be that way about it. Half these boys out here right now have records. Even *I'm* a felon when you get right down to it. This is such bullshit."

"Call it what you want. That Ranger said it, and I believe it."

"He's comin' here after me, too."

"What makes you say that?"

"I'm his last target." Daddy Frank calmed for a moment, then his eyes cleared as he came to a decision. "Fine then. If Alonzo's headed this way all hot and bothered, we'll be ready. Get a few of your contractors as you call them and stake out the roads for this Ranger. There's only three highways coming into town. Have them stop him before he gets to your office."

Once again Buck's eyes widened. "Really, a Ranger?"

"I don't want him snoopin' around."

"We can't keep trying to make people disappear."

"We've been doing it for years."

"Yeah, but they weren't feds or *Rangers*."

"We've put a few feds in shallow graves, one time or another. He's nothin' but one more lawman."

"Times are different."

"Are they?"

"You're damned right they are. You know killing a Texas Ranger right on the heels of them agents is gonna bring the whole world down on our heads. That's suicide. I just spent three hours dancin' with the DEA, allowing how I'm gonna work with them and the FBI to find out who shot their men, and I'm getting tired of walking this edge. Not even *you* pay me enough for all this."

The old man's eyes hardened. "This family is as powerful as the Sabine over yonder, and we're always gonna be here. Folks like us are the soul of this country. I ain't done by a long shot, and one day we'll be the foundation that the people will see when they think about who has turned this country around. I ain't changing a damn thing. We're gonna show them BranCo people who's boss, and then when that's done . . ."

Buck had heard it all before. "How about I let him talk and then send him on a wild goose chase over into Louisiana, just like I did with the feds? We can make up with the rest of that Thibideaux bunch and pay 'em what it's worth to sink the guy for gator bait if he starts to be a pest. Put it all on *them*."

"That would have been a good idea a month ago, but nope. I'm done with them coonasses for the time bein'." Daddy Frank pointed over the pines and toward his barn fifteen miles away. "How 'bout y'all bring this Ranger out to the fertilizer barn, too, when he gets here?"

"I'll call him back and give him directions."

"No. He'll call it in where he's going. We can't take that chance. Get aholt of 'im out on the highway somewhere and bring me what's left. I'll get the truth out of both him and Tanner before we decide what else to do."

"Tanner probably won't tell you nothin'."

"Yes, he will. I'll tell him I'll kill Shi'Ann if he don't. He's young and fool enough to do it to save her."

"Why would he do that?"

"'Cause he's in *loooove* with her." Daddy Frank drew it out so long it became obscene.

"How do you know that? He's with Donine, ain't he?"

The Old Man's eyes cut through the sheriff. "Because I know everything."

The sudden widening of Buck's eyes said that he understood. "I can't believe you'd keep her after that."

"There won't be nothin' to keep."

"I don't need to hear no more."

Daddy Frank looked almost sad. "Boone's gonna do it, and then it's past time for him to take the long sleep. He failed me, and nobody does that. You can shoot Boone and say he was working with Willy and it was him that killed Tanner and the Ranger. You'll be a hero and ever'thing'll go back to normal."

Buck chewed on that idea for a moment. "I won't miss that creepy little bastard, but I have to say that's a damn good idea."

"I have an idy I won't miss him much neither. He's done his do for me and he's like them dogs over yonder. When they can't fight no more, they ain't no good for nothin'. Besides, Boone died a long time ago."

Chapter 37

Pushing eastward through the cold front was like moving from one world to the next. Dark clouds filled my rearview mirror as I outraced the storm, looking much darker and more menacing than it really was. Gray skies ahead rested on the pines that were as still as telephone poles. Not a breath of air moved. It was that pause between three windy, humid days and the advance of enough rain to wash the world clean.

I was almost to Gunn, in deep East Texas, when I came up over a rise behind a ridiculously jacked-up Ford pickup driving ten miles under the speed limit. I followed it for several miles on the two-lane highway, looking upward at the beefed-up suspension full of mud, sticks, and grass. The big truck dwarfed my 3500 Dodge dually that looked huge up against regular-size pickups. The driver I couldn't see slowed down, sped up, and drifted from side to side.

These fools are texting.

Technology drives me nuts, seeming to fail at the worst times, and here was an idiot in a vehicle that looked like it belonged at a monster truck show endangering anyone coming in our direction on the winding road.

I don't understand why idiots will drive while looking down, not realizing how fast a wreck can happen. They're concerned with only themselves, and not the rest of the people on the road. In fact, they think they're the only ones in the world, and when someone yanks them back with a honk, they usually poke up that middle finger in a salute.

The kids and Kelly get aggravated at me when I honk people texting at lights. They say I should be more patient. I say people should pay attention to their driving.

The massive tires and much larger suspension filled the lane, making it hard to check for oncoming traffic. I let the Dodge drift toward the center stripe, hoping the driver would finally look up from his screen, see me in his side mirror, and realize he wasn't the only person on the highway. Maybe he'd put the phone down until I passed, and then he could kill himself if he wanted to drift off the road and hammer a tree. I'd feel more sorry for the tree.

He must've noticed me, and the tactic worked for a mile or so when the driver caught back up to the speed limit. I dropped back to give myself a cushion between us and set the cruise. We crossed a creek bottom, and he slowed again.

Frustrated, I waited until we finally reached an empty stretch of highway and hammered the accelerator. The Dodge's turbo roared, and I shot around the monster Ford, passing him like he was sitting still. I couldn't help but give the driver a once-over. The tinted power window went down to reveal slender guy with a Fu

Manchu mustache under a pair of white-rimmed sun-glasses. He shot me the finger in greeting.

I put the hammer down and passed him, giving a signal I was easing back into his lane. Seconds later I settled back in the seat, once again driving the speed limit. My phone rang, but I was a rock and ignored it.

A mile later the big Ford closed the distance and shot up almost against my back bumper like he really *was* in a monster show, intending to drive right over my own truck. The grille filled my rearview mirror. Though it was nearing dusk, the man's headlights were on bright, nearly blinding me. My eyes had long ago adjusted to the evening gloom.

I flipped my mirror to the night setting and accelerated. *Come on, buddy. I'm too old for kid games.*

Monster Ford shot around me on a solid yellow line that warned of an approaching curve.

What a moron!

I slowed to allow the truck to pass safely, terrified that some local farmer was going to come around the bend and find himself meeting the Ford head-on. In that case, the other driver *might* be able to dodge the oncoming truck, but at our speed, I doubted it. To make the situation worse, we were in logging country. I'd passed several clear-cuts and knew that pulpwood trucks could appear any time. Those loaded rigs don't stop on a dime.

All this loon needed was to come up on a loaded truck pulling out on the highway. It'd be all over but the cryin' for all of us. Grinding my teeth, I slowed to allow the Ford to gain some distance. It looked as if he were off the phone by the way he was driving, so I settled back to follow.

When I dropped back, Monster Truck slowed and I quickly drew uncomfortably close.

Don't do it. Don't do it.

The pit of my stomach fell out. I'd seen it happen before, a dangerous highway ballet between angry or testosterone-driven aggressive drivers. As a highway patrol officer, I'd worked a number of fatal accidents when similar dances went bad.

Grinding my teeth, I backed off even more and punched the Jake brake button on the dash. I'd no more than done that when the Ford's driver hit his brakes. I let off the gas, fearing the worst, and it came.

The Ford's brake lights flashed and I hit my own, decelerating fast enough for the seat belt to tighten. Tires squalled on the pavement and my auto-brake engaged, vibrating the truck with jackhammer pulses.

His head-high tailgate grew, and I swerved toward the narrow shoulder. Pine trunks swelled in size then retreated when I swerved back toward the center stripe, barely missing the raised bumper. Every muscle in my body tightened, expecting that harsh, metallic crunch I was sure would follow. It was the wide hips on my truck that helped me regain control, but I was about to lose control of something else.

My temper.

I could have pulled over and stopped to dial 911, but it would all be over by the time anyone showed up. I wish I had a nickel for every time I told a civilian that all responders to a 911 call could do was try and stop the bleeding, or do paperwork and reports on the aftermath, because the incident would be over by the time they arrived.

I had a good idea he wasn't alone, too. Guys like

that usually run in packs, and based on my experience, they were probably drinking. The badge on my shirt might make them back off if it came to getting out of the car, but with my luck the last few days, I could see the whole thing going sideways in a hurry.

Gaining control of a rising fury, I resisted the urge to jerk the wheel into the oncoming lane to pass again, but headlights appeared over the distant rise. I let off the gas and slowed even more to drift back in my lane. I was right. Four arms emerged from the Ford, shooting me the finger.

This crew was all class.

The oncoming car passed, and I slowed again. The Ford sped up, and I hoped it was over. They'd scared me, made their point, and now they could go home and lean back in their recliners to drink beer and laugh about how they'd scared that ol' boy in the Dodge. I took a deep breath to calm down just as they hit their brakes again.

Enough!

I whipped to the side in order to look ahead. There was a second rise past the first crest from the Trinity River bottoms. I changed my mind and was reaching for the phone to call in the altercation when a brief flash far ahead gave me an idea.

I hoped I was right. Stomach clenched, I punched the accelerator and shot around him one more time. Seconds later, the Monster Ford caught up and swerved into the oncoming lane, pacing me. We rocketed down the highway side by side. Two men in gimme caps leaned out of their windows, shouting curses that were lost in the slipstream as we crossed the muddy Trinity.

A beer bottle flew out of the front passenger window.

Whoever threw it wasn't a dove hunter. He didn't account for their speed and forgot to lead my Dodge. The bottle missed and I sped up, fully expecting the Ford to do the same.

They did, and I couldn't help but grin. Floor-boarding it, the big turbo under the Dodge's engine kicked in again and my truck pulled ahead by a hair. Again, the men on the passenger side leaned out, shooting me the finger.

Pacing me in such a dangerous situation, the driver juked toward my lane, trying to get me to brake or run off the road. Now it was getting serious. I didn't give an inch, expecting that he was just shooting for a reaction. He really didn't want to ding up his big ugly truck. That was his status symbol. It was his balls.

We crossed the bridge with me one car-length ahead and started up the rise. Heart hammering, I waited until what I figured was the last second before backing off on the gas and letting the Monster Truck gain the lead. Almost at the crest of the hill, I took my foot completely off the accelerator, letting the Jake brake gear the engine down.

The Ford shot past and was over the hill before he realized what I'd done. He disappeared over the crest and I followed at the posted speed limit, driving with my wrist hanging over the wheel.

When I topped the rise, a highway patrol car had already whipped around, lights flashing. He'd been in the perfect position, hidden from view until the last second, to catch any vehicle speeding down his highway. The Ford's brake lights flickered as he disappeared around a bend with the flashing blue and red lights following. By the time I made the curve, the Monster Ford was over on the much wider grassy shoulder with the highway patrol car turned in behind it.

I hit my blinker, as the law required, moved over, and passed well below the speed limit. I waved at the Ford and Mr. Sunglasses with a smile and dialed 911 with my thumb to tell Dispatch what had just occurred.

Welcome to the Big Thicket.

Chapter 38

Yolanda and Perry Hale were in their hotel room in Jasper when her cell phone rang with the *Uplift* ringtone she'd selected to identify Kelly Hawke. She swiped the screen. "Hey girl."

"Hey. What're y'all up to?"

She knew Kelly wasn't calling just to chat. They talked almost every day when she was at home, but out on the road, working for Sonny, the call meant much more. "I'm in East Texas with Perry Hale, waiting on your guy to get here. Wassup?"

"That's what I wanted to talk to you about." Kelly breathed into the mouthpiece. "He called me after he left Dimmitt and told me what happened."

"Yeah, that was a bad deal."

"We talked for a while and were into something pretty heavy when the call dropped. That happens pretty regular out here, so I didn't think much of it. We talked last night when he checked into that little motel, but he sounded really tired. I haven't heard from him today, and that's unusual. He should have called, and I've been worried sick. Everything all right?"

Yolanda knew better than to tell her what happened in Comanche. It wasn't her place to describe what they were dealing with. "As far as I know. He should have already checked in with us, too, but there's no telling where he is. Cell service isn't great here in the Thicket, but he could be out interviewing someone and hasn't had time to call."

Going through the items in his MOLLE pack, Perry Hale frowned in her direction and Yolanda raised her eyebrows in the question, "What else am I going to tell her?"

They'd developed their own way of communicating through expressions and head movements, much like twins who seemed to talk without using words.

Yolanda lowered her voice, not to keep Perry Hale from hearing, but because she felt something wasn't right. "You two all right?"

"Yeah."

Kelly was silent, probably thinking. The laugh track from a television in the background told Yolanda that the twins, Mary and Jerry, were probably nearby. Kelly came back, but her voice lacked confidence. "You're probably right. He'll call when he gets where he's going."

"Do we need to talk?" Yolanda's voice was full of concern. "It sounds like something else is going on."

"Yeah, but not right now. I shouldn't have said anything." Kelly stopped talking and Yolanda heard her move into another room. "You're getting some weather."

Knowing Kelly needed the break, Yolanda went with the shift in their conversation. "Yep, that cold front finally pushed through."

The idle talk was designed to fill the time while they

both considered where their conversation was going. They drifted into silence before Kelly picked up the loose thread. "Well, I know you guys'll watch out for him." Kelly's voice steadied. "I just always worry when I don't hear from my guy."

"You know how he is with phones. He probably let the battery run down." Yolanda had an idea what was bothering her friend. "He's been gone a lot, when he's not on desk duty. A lot has happened in the last few months."

"That's part of it. He's been—fragile in some ways. I think some of the people he's had to deal with has taken a toll."

"You mean the people he's killed."

The statement almost crackled. "In the line of duty, yeah."

"Death weighs on you." Yolanda thought for a moment. "There's something else."

"Yeah. My new vice principal here at the high school has been by the house a couple of times. Once he brought a pie."

"What's this man's name?"

"Juan Ricardo."

"He's interested in you."

"Maybe."

"Maybe nothing. That's why you're feeling so down. He's your immediate supervisor." Yolanda's face flushed with anger. "Sonny's been gone, and that guy's sniffing around."

"This is a small town. I can't say anything."

Yolanda's voice had a hard edge. "I can. I'll have a talk with that guy when we get back."

"It's not your place."

"It's my place as a friend."

"Maybe I can talk to him with you."

"You got it." Yolanda took a deep breath to cool down. "I'm with Perry Hale out here in Jasper. Sonny's trailing a guy out this way and called to have us meet him here. He's on the way, so he shouldn't have any trouble. We've already checked in a hotel and got Sonny a room, but under Perry Hale's name, if you call the hotel."

Kelly lightened. *"Girrrllll."*

Their mood lifted. "Yes, *mother*."

"Good lord, you sound like the twins." Kelly laughed. "How old are you?"

"Old enough to know better. Thanks, girl."

"Aren't we all? Talk to you later." Yolanda ended the call and looked across the room to Perry Hale, who was pulling on a fresh gray T-shirt. "You know, even with these phones in our hands all the time, we still don't stay connected all that well."

"What do you mean?"

She paused. "I don't really know."

Chapter 39

A light rain fell on the Big Thicket, and the sky was black through the living room window when Tanner punched his burner phone off and slipped it into his shirt pocket. He pushed back in the recliner and closed his eyes while his Uncle Marshall watched *Gunsmoke* on the television. The volume was so loud it was impossible to sleep, but he only wanted to rest his swollen and blackened eyes for a few minutes before he left.

As if she'd been watching and waiting for the second he leaned back, Donine called from the kitchen. "You want a beer?"

"No!"

"You hungry? Want me to make you a plate?"

"No!"

"Well, you don't have to be so nice about it."

Marshall maneuvered his wheelchair around and found himself trapped by the sofa and the leg rest on Tanner's recliner. "Hey boy, you need to get your lazy ass up and go to work."

The leg rest snapped down. Tanner launched himself up right. "Going outside!"

"You want to take that beer with you?"

"Hell no . . . yes!" He reconsidered and stomped into the kitchen to find Donine sitting at the table, licking peanut butter off a spoon. A cigarette burned in the ashtray. A sweating Schlitz tallboy made a wet ring on the worn Formica. "Y'ain't supposed to smoke or drink when you're pregnant."

"You ain't my doctor."

"You gonna get that beer for me?"

She pointed with the spoon. "You know where they are. I's gonna bring one to you in there, but you're up now. You wanna take me for a ride in the car?"

He suddenly realized he couldn't stand the sight of her mottled teeth and stringy blonde hair. He almost reeled when he realized he was destined to be with her for the rest of his life if he didn't do something.

"Not right now. Leave that beer in there. I'll come get it in a minute."

He left the kitchen and went down the hall to their room. Heart pounding with his sudden decision he opened the closet door, pulled down a large duffle-style camouflaged bag, and spent the next five minutes stuffing it with clothing. The last thing was his good Dan Post boots.

Taking a look around the room at their unmade bed, the secondhand chest of drawers, and piles of dirty clothes, he realized the only thing he owned and cared about was in the bag. He opened the window and lowered the bag to the ground, making sure it was against the house and protected by the eave.

He went back into the living room. Donine was curled on the couch with the remote control in her hand, lowering the volume far enough so her ears wouldn't bleed.

"Your beer's still in the icebox. Don't expect me to get up and get it for you now."

"I'm going over to Willy's house. I'll get one there."

"Well, come back before dark and bring me another pack of cigarettes. I'm going crazy waiting for this baby. Hey, can we go for a walk when you get back?"

"No. Go walk yourself if you want to."

"I don't like to do it alone."

"I'm going to Willy's, I said."

"Fine then. I'll just be by myself for a while. I don't need you." Her voice rose, hot and shrill. "I'll just follow that trail down to the creek and drown myself. How about that?"

He closed the door without answering and was halfway around the house to get his gear when Mike's truck came down the road and pulled up next to his car. Thinking it was him behind the wheel, Tanner started toward the pickup until he saw who was driving.

Hair rose on the back of his neck at the sight of Boone's pale face. He'd never heard of Boone driving *anyone's* car or truck.

He started for his car when Boone lowered the window and leaned out. "Daddy says for you to come with me."

Tanner grimaced at the name. "What for?" He tried not to look at the man's blank expression.

"Didn't say."

Tanner hesitated, torn between arguing, leaving, or going back into the house. "I'll follow you."

"No. Get in the truck."

Tanner took an unconscious step back. "I *said* I'm driving. Where's Daddy Frank?"

"At the fertilizer barn."

Tanner's neck prickled again. He checked his watch. "Uncle Alonzo already back?"

"Yes."

"Why're you driving Mike's truck?"

"Daddy Frank sent me."

"That don't make no sense. Where's Mike?"

Boone hesitated before answering. "Dead."

Shocked, Tanner couldn't decide what to do next. He swayed from side to side. "What happened?"

"You'll have to ask Daddy that question."

"He ain't your *daddy*. It's Daddy Frank."

"Talk to him about it when you see him, then."

"Fine." With no other recourse, Tanner went around to the pickup. "Let's go."

Chapter 40

I was feeling pretty good about myself after tricking the truck full of rednecks into getting pulled over by the highway patrol. Dispatch took my information, and I hung up to settle back and cruise. That's when I rounded a bend and another truck shot out of an intersecting dirt road angling into the highway from the left.

He appeared out of nowhere and was suddenly in my lane before I had time to think. The only way to miss him was to swerve onto that same dirt road that resumed on my right. It angled off at thirty degrees, and I could either take to the ditch and risk flipping over, or steer onto the dirt track.

He missed my front bumper by inches, and the truck seemed like a live animal under my hands as I left the road at seventy miles an hour. Enormous pines flashed past only feet away. The pine-needle-covered sand felt greasy under the tires. Grass and short bushes growing in the middle of the track hissed and slapped the undercarriage while the tires popped rotten branches that sounded like gunshots. The dually's big hips were dangerously close to the yaupons and pine saplings almost scraping my back fenders.

Mark Chesnutt came through my speakers with a sad, calm song about lost love as I braked, but not enough to skid on the sand. A washout bisected the road and dropped the front end with a sickening thump, followed by the rear tires.

Had it not been for the seat belt, the roof would have pushed my head down between my shoulders. Gaining my wits, I slowed even more with the intention to stop, back out, and chase down the idiot who'd shot out on the highway without looking.

A violent thump snapped my head back when that same pickup rear-ended my truck. The heavy brush guard on the front of the white Chevrolet filled my rearview mirror as I fought the wheel, and tapped my brakes. Before I could decide what to do next, a fallen pine across the road suddenly became the next fun aspect of that wild ride.

This time I showered down on the brake pedal. The sand and pine needles were slick as glass and there was no way I could stop in time. The auto-lock engaged for the second time in fifteen minutes, hammering the brakes with little taps, but the log grew larger.

The guy rear-ended me again and my tailgate folded inward. That was all it took. A slight gap appeared in the trees and I whipped the wheel to the right. The sickening crunch of a collapsing rear fender filled the cab when the Dodge fishtailed into a small, limber pine.

Another crunch filled my head and I fought the wheel. The air crackled with bangs and country music when I suddenly headed downhill into what I thought was a ravine. It turned out to be a creek and the next thing I knew, the big Dodge hit the water with a spray.

Running into the creek wouldn't have been so bad, except for a drift of logs extending into deep water. Hitting them at that speed wasn't pleasant at all. The airbag exploded with a bang into my face. It slammed my head back, crushing the brim of my hat against the headrest. I slapped the already deflating bag down.

The front end sank below the hood. There was no way to know how deep the water was, so I hit the seat belt release and yanked at the door handle. It creaked open with a metallic pop that was followed by half a dozen louder bangs of gunfire that punched through the inside of the door and shattered the glass. The rear window exploded. I flipped the drop-down console out of the way, threw myself across the seat, and pushed open the passenger door.

More gunfire erupted, and a second and maybe third weapon chimed in. The interior of the cab filled with glass. Only the front end was in the water, but the tangled logs shifted from the impact, allowing the front tires and grille to settle deeper.

I went out of the cab headfirst, tucking and rolling on my shoulder. The truck was between me and the shooters, and whoever was behind me had a bad angle, so most of the rounds impacted sheet metal.

My .45 came to hand and I caught a glimpse of the truck behind me, four doors standing side open and armed men spreading out. One guy slid to a stop behind a thick pine and cranked off several rounds in my direction. I sent three shots right back at him, two splintering white wood from the trunk.

A man fired from the shelter of a door. I squeezed

off another round in his direction and he ducked. A deep voice shouted that he was going around, and I appreciated the information. I hit the bank like an otter, losing my footing and slid down almost into the water, praying there weren't any broken bottles buried in the mud. My brother once slid down a clay bank back on Lake Tawakoni and wound up with thirty-three stitches in his leg from a broken beer bottle.

With the steep bank for cover, I crawled along just above the waterline for twenty yards. Shouts came from at least three different throats as I scrabbled even farther downstream, staying low. My thoughts weren't to shoot it out with those guys.

Run if you can. Fight if you have to.

The Old Man's wisdom served me well when I ducked under the trunk of a blowdown laying half in the creek. Three steps later I ran slap into a guy charging in my direction. We were both so surprised that neither of us had time to raise our weapons.

There were no calculations about what to do. The impact was enough for the gunman to stumble to the side. Our arms were tangled, and I had one hand on his rifle. One side of my brain was surprised to see that instead of an AR-type weapon, it was a lever-action Marlin. In a strange way, that was good, because even if he managed to get off one shot, he'd still have to cock the lever for a second.

Since I didn't know any of those fancy Chuck Norris spin kicks, I followed my instincts and grabbed him in a bear hug.

Keep the muzzle away!

It was a good thing. The rifle went off, and the muzzle blast was like a slap. He flinched, just like I did, but

I had the presence of mind to take advantage of his shock. Getting a leg behind his, I pushed hard and he fell back hard on the muddy bank.

The guy was probably a barroom brawler, because he was kicking with all he had to keep me off. I fell to the side and dug my heels in to push away from his thrashing boots. I'd have laughed, watching it on television. I kicked back, a move all guys have grown up with, and rolled quickly to my knees.

One sound is distinctive to anyone who has ever shot a lever-action rifle. It was the shucking sound as he cocked it again. There was nothing to do but shoot with the .45 that was still in my hand. The gunman jerked and twisted with the impact, but he still tried to swing the Marlin back toward me. Infuriated, I shot him again, and the rifle dropped.

Shouts came from over the bank and someone sent half a dozen rounds overhead.

They whizzed away as I rose and hauled ass.

Chapter 41

Misty rain dotted the windshield, running upward in long, clear rivulets as Alonzo Wadler took his eyes off the road to check the pickup's rearview mirror. The damp surface hissed under the tires and rose in a foggy rooster tail that quickly settled back onto the highway.

Under his stained shirt, dried blood acted like glue, holding the makeshift compression bandage against the wound in his side. He'd eaten one pain pill after another until they finally kicked in, and, to play it safe, he ate a couple more an hour later. "You know baby, they say these things are addictive."

A wet laugh rose and caught in his throat. He finally switched on the wipers that sluiced water off in a wave on the first pass. "I think the problem was them doctors all told me to only take two every four hours. Hell, a good dose is eight of the damn things, at least. If I'da know that, I'da been eatin' 'em like M&Ms since we left California."

He coughed again, blinking to clear his eyes. "It ain't like *they're* gonna kill me."

Another wet, phlegmy laugh filled the silence broken only by wind noise whistling around the truck, and the rhythmic beat of tires thumping on the highway's expansion joints. Still driving with only one hand, he sat a bit straighter. "I'm still weak as a kitten, but I have an idea that'll make me feel a little bit better. Since I couldn't kill that feller back in Comanche, I want one more to pay for you before we get to the cherry on top."

His crusty eyes stung as fresh tears welled. Words poured out, released by the medication, and he talked as if Betty's corpse in the back seat could hear. And maybe the dead could. He grunted. Who knows?

"I'm sorry I couldn't have stopped it, baby. It's my fault, and Daddy Frank's, too. If it wasn't for him making us go out there and deliver that load ourselves, you wouldn't be gone. I told him we didn't need to be involved in that part of the plan, but he was always mad at you 'cause you turned him down when we were younger and he couldn't take that.

"I knew he'd try, 'cause he tried to get to every woman that came into the family. It was his way, and once I heard him say it was the Warlord's right. Hell, I didn't even know what a warlord was when he said it. Had to go look it up. But you were one of the few who told him no and meant it, and he's had it in for you ever since.

"Shit. That hardheaded old bastard always wants things his way, and he wanted all he could get his hands on. He thinks he knows it all, too." Alonzo raised his hand from the wheel as if he were in church, instead of shooting down a two-lane highway, and mimicked Daddy Frank's high voice. "I don't want to hear any of what *y'all* have to say. I *said*, we're gonna deliver that shipment to prove to them people how easy it'll be and how much we can move. You'll do what *I* say."

Alonzo switched back to his own, phlegmy voice as his face reddened with anger. "He thinks he's a damned *god*!" His bloodstained hand slapped back down on the wheel as the truck drifted over the centerline. "And that *god*-damned preacher feedin' into some kind of vision that's gonna get the whole Family over-extended and tied in with folks that'd just as soon kill you for your hat. We were doing all right until he had that 'vision.' We had a kingdom in East Texas. A by-God *kingdom!* There ain't no one messed with us in years, 'cause they was afraid.

"But the minute we expand the operation, some-body's gonna get lazy or get caught and then every agency in the country's gonna be down there, rootin' around."

Squinting through the windshield, he thumbed the cap off the prescription bottle and dumped more pills into his mouth. Dry-swallowing them, he gagged for a second.

"Here's what we're gonna do before we get home, baby." A car passed on the left, and Alonzo realized that he'd unconsciously slowed down. He sped back up and engaged the cruise control, setting it exactly on seventy mph. "There's a drive-through up ahead there in Woodville where one last target's working. I read about it a week ago that one of two brothers got out of prison on a twenty-year-old plea deal. The youngest one rolled over on his own brother to get out."

His eyes flicked to the rearview mirror as if Betty was watching his reflection. "Yeah, that's right. Rolled over on his brother after *he* admitted to a murder back in the 1980s. This guy's name is Clem Gluck. How's that for a handle? Anyway, he confessed he knew his brother was a serial killer and covered for that bastard who raped and killed eight young gals while ol' Clem kept it all to hisself.

"Well, that sorry bastard finally saw he was gonna Ride the Needle down in Huntsville and decided family wasn't family no more. They got his brother all right and lit his ass up, and the good old American jury hung Mr. Clem with two life sentences, but the the government crawfished on the deal right after he fessed up and kept him in the brickyard ever since. But now some damned liberal judge just opened the cell door and said, 'Come on out there, sweetheart, we're sorry for what happened to you and don't care about them dead girls or their families, but you go on out in the free worl' and we're gonna cut you a check for all them years in there and give you a job to boot!' What kind of deal is *that*?"

His vision swam, and a deep warmth washed over Alonzo. For the first time since the shooting, his entire trunk relaxed. Both tight shoulders unknotted and leveled out. He leaned back with a sigh, almost forgetting to keep his left hand against the compress.

"Well, I got that sonofabitch! Found him a couple of days ago on that MyFace . . . no, wait, I'm feelin' a little fuzzy. That ain't right. Facebook, yeah, that's it. Read how ol' Clem Gluck is living with his sister who's so proud her sorry-assed baby brother's out and told ever'body on the news how she felt and that now he had a good job'n ever'body can sing Kume by Y'all together.

"See, people tell ever'thang these days, and when I went to what they call her Facebook page, she had pictures of them together in their house, all happy as little pigs in the sunshine. But the best thing is she told me where that bastard's working now."

He took his hand off the wheel once again to shake the half-full prescription bottle. Eyelids hooded, he peered at the label as if wondering how it had gotten there. "What the hell?" He shook two more into his mouth, and choked them down.

"So we're gonna pull up in the drive-through of that mom-and-pop burger joint there in good ol' Woodville, Texas, and order us up a burger so I can drive up to the window 'n blow that sonofabitch's head plumb off. That's close enough to home, and then we're gonna settle up with the old man and ever'body else for what they done to you."

Getting more swimmy-headed, he tapped the brake with one foot. Everything within view narrowed as if he were wearing blinders. The truck slowed until a sedan whooshed around him, startling Alonzo so much that his right-hand tires drifted off the pavement and onto the grassy shoulder. He jerked the truck back onto the highway and slapped his cheek to throw off the drug-induced blinders. The jolt of adrenaline cleared his vision. Alonzo took his eyes off the highway for a minute, studying the suddenly unfamiliar controls on the steering wheel. Punching at the buttons with his thumb, he finally engaged the cruise control again and steadied the pickup.

"Riddle me this, Betty. How can Daddy Frank be the way he is? Sent them boys out after us like he did.

I grew up with ol' Mike. We had some times together, but that's all done with now."

Alonzo quieted, withdrawing and contemplating what he could remember of the past few hours. "Daddy Frank and that Preacher's ideas are what got us here. Well, what I'm about to do is what Daddy Frank would have done if somebody messed with him, but you know what the . . ."

He drove in silence for a moment, searching for the word that was lost in the drug-shrouded closets of his mind.

". . . well hell . . . oh, the *irony*, that's it, the irony of all this is that I'm gonna blow that old man straight to hell. Daddy Frank don't realize I'm the same as he is. He made me what I am, and I'm gonna drive this son-ofabitch right up next to him and set the whole damn thing off. It'll look like one of them A-bombs, and me and you'll go straight to heaven with all our mol . . . moly . . . molecules mixed up together."

Steering with his knees, Alonzo searched with one hand along the seat, feeling through maps, pill bottles, a .357 handgun, and fast-food wrappers, until he found the burner phone Daddy Frank had ordered him to carry. Without looking down, he thumbed it alive and punched a button, ringing the only number loaded into the phone's memory.

He listened as it rang twice. A gruff voice answered on the third ring. "It's about goddamned time you called."

"I been busy. Daddy Frank, I'm almost home."

"What? I can't understand a damned thing you're saying. You drunk or something. You're slurring your words. Straighten up and answer me, boy!"

Frowning, Alonzo swallowed, wondering what the old man was talking about. "I said, I'm almost there."

"Shit! Can somebody listen to this drunk bastard and tell me what he's sayin'?"

There was a few seconds of silence before Sheriff Buck Henderson's familiar voice came through the receiver. "Alonzo?"

"Yeah."

"Where are you?"

"Uh, somewhere. Coming into Woodville."

"Say that again. I can barely understand you."

Alonzo focused. "I. Said. Woodville."

"Good. You're almost here."

"Going to the fertilizer barn."

"I think you said you're going to the fertilizer barn. That's good, we're here waitin' on you. Boy, you sound terrible. You drunk?"

"Shot. High as a kite."

"Shit."

There was silence on the other end as Alonzo steered. By the time the sheriff came back on, Alonzo had forgotten who was on the other end and why the phone was at his ear.

"You there, Alonzo?"

"Who's this?"

"Why, it's still Buck. Look, drive careful and try not to get pulled over. If you do, tell them to call me right then. You got that? We'll be looking for you."

"Yeah, and tell that sonofabitch I'm looking for *him*."

"Alonzo, I can't make out every word you're saying, but you're in trouble for sure and you're leading a whole damn conga line of lawmen straight for us. Put that phone down and drive with both hands. Stay just under the speed limit until you get to Newton County, and then I'll take it from there if you get into trouble, but drive careful. You hear me?"

The sheriff's tinny voice barely penetrated the fog clouding Alonzo's mind. Locking in on Buck's orders, he'd dropped the phone onto the floorboard and was concentrating on the fuzzy highway stretching into the distance.

He had a present for Daddy Frank, and the rest of them, if they were there.

Chapter 42

Perry Hale was standing beside the bed in their Jasper hotel room when his cell phone rang. He'd been searching through the television's guide for The Weather Channel. Yolanda sat at the desk by the window tapping on her iPad. It wasn't a number he recognized. "Hello?"

"Who is this?"

"Well, this is the guy who answered the phone. Identify yourself and we may continue this conversation. If you're trying to sell me a vacation, I'm all in. Since you have this number, you have my address. Just send me the cash or plane tickets, and thank you."

There was a long silence on the other end, followed by a grunt. "A Texas Ranger by name of Sonny Hawke gave me this number and said to call it if I couldn't get him to answer his phone."

Perry Hale laughed and settled on the end of the double bed covered in white hotel towels and weaponry. Two customized AR-15s shared space with the same number of Glock 19s, along with a pair of Beretta

M9 handguns. The bottom fell out of the sky and water hammered against the hotel room window.

"Well, you'll be talking to me all the time then. That old boy seldom answers when *I* try to call, and half the time he's where there ain't no service. I've been trying to call him for a while myself. My name's Perry Hale."

"Are you a Ranger, too?"

His radar immediately went up. He glanced across to Yolanda who tilted her head at his hesitation, or maybe it was the loud clap of thunder. He wasn't sure. Laying the phone on the desk, he punched the speaker icon so she could hear. "More like an answering service when folks can't get Sonny. How can I help you?"

Yolanda swiveled the chair to listen. There was silence again on the other end. Perry Hale could imagine the man trying to decide what to say.

"Well, I'm Sheriff Gomez from Comanche, Texas."

"Sonny told me he talked to you. I know why he was there."

"Well, I'm not sure I can tell you everything I know. I probably need to talk with Ranger Hawke."

"That might be tomorrow." Perry Hale had no intention of telling him they were getting worried about Sonny. He and Yolanda'd been calling for hours with the same results, and now a knot in his gut told something was wrong. "If it's about the vigilante he's chasing, I know it all. If it's about Semtex that's moving across the state, I know that, too."

Yolanda leaned forward, elbows on the knees of her 5.11 tactical pants.

A couple of small, wet crackles told Perry Hale the sheriff was likely weighing his thoughts, deciding what to say. The man on the other end sucked a tooth with a Bugs Bunny kissing sound before answering. "Fine then. So you know about the call I took in my office referring to explosives."

"Sure do. Came from a young man who told y'all it was headed to East Texas."

A deep sigh into the phone. "That's right. Tell Hawke the guy called back to say he thinks he's been made. His name is Tanner Wadler for sure, and he lives in Gunn. I called the sheriff of that county, Buck Henderson, and told him what we'd heard. He promised to look into it. I left a message on Sonny's voicemail with the sheriff's number. I've also talking to the DEA, ATF, and the FBI about the explosion and the shooting Hawke was involved in. Do you have anything to write on?"

Perry Hale raised an eyebrow at Yolanda, who swung back around and placed her fingers on the iPad's screen. She nodded she was ready.

Perry Hale unconsciously nodded at the question, as if Gomez could see. "Go ahead."

"Well, this is just to keep him up to speed. I done called a Ranger named Foster, and he said he was on the way, too." Sheriff Gomez gave them directions to Tanner's house off in the woods and told him about the war that was about to start in deep East Texas.

Chapter 43

Sheriff Buck Henderson met Daddy Frank just inside the fertilizer barn as rain hammered the rusty tin roof with a roar. He and Preacher Brother Holmes were watching the roiling sky through the open door. Daddy Frank's pit bull, Mud, was tied to a horse-chewed post. The dog didn't take his eyes off the old man.

Bare bulbs on ancient knob and tube wires dangled like dusty, glowing jewels from the long center beam over the great, open hallway running the length of the barn. Dark, hand-hewn timbers threw geometric shadows against the roof. Other bulbs lit old, unused stalls. Some were full of fertilizer, others contained barrels of diesel fuel stacked three high.

Lightning melted the seams between the clouds, fracturing them into individual streams of electricity. Like their daddies before them, they watched the sky when such a storm arose, looking for the telltale signs of an approaching twister.

Thunder cracked as Buck closed his car door and ducked through the rain. Stepping into the wide aisle, he didn't wait for either man to speak. "It's all going to hell, Frank." He took his hat off, flinging water onto the packed dirt floor. "This is all your fault."

The old man waited with both hands in the pockets of a brand-new pair of khakis. His voice was mild, conversational. "Watch your tone, Buck. Don't forget who you're talkin' to."

"Might as well. I'm having to watch everything else around here. We've got a mess on our hands, and I think you oughta clear out all your stock tonight and squat in a bush somewhere until everything blows over."

"We won't be doing that." Brother Holmes raised a hand toward the thrashing trees tormented by the wind. "For God says, in a favorable time I listened to you, and in a day of salvation I have helped you. Behold, now is the favorable time; behold, now is the day of salvation. Second Corinthians, Six, Two."

"He's right." Daddy Frank slipped both hands into his pockets. "We have to meet that delivery first thing in the morning, cash on the barrelhead and I intend to hit that damned oil pipeline at daylight."

Buck snorted. "You can come up with a verse for anything you want, Holmes, but the truth is we have a Texas Ranger on the run in the bottoms and I doubt my men can root him out before he realizes who's after him and calls it in. That means a whole company of Rangers might be here in the morning to tear our playhouse down. We can't take that chance."

"What do you mean you have a Ranger on the run?" Daddy Frank's voice was hard and sharp. "You were supposed to take him somewhere and bring the sonofabitch to me."

"I mean your idea of grabbing that guy was the

wrong decision, just like those two DEA agents. What-ever happened to just shooting the bastards and gettin' it over with?" Buck told him what had happened after the Ranger wrecked his truck and disappeared into the Big Thicket. "I have contractors beating the brush for him, and all we have is his truck. He's on the run in the bottoms and they ain't found hide nor hair of him and we don't have a snowball's chance in hell of chasing him down before it gets full dark. After that, people are gonna come looking for him."

Brother Holmes shrugged. "How much does he know?"

Buck pointed his finger. "I'm talking to Frank right now. You be quiet. Frank, I don't know how much of this I can hold back." Buck felt as if the rain symbol-ized how everything was falling in around them and there was Daddy Frank, cigarette dangling in his lips and as unconcerned as if he were at a picnic.

The old man inhaled and blew smoke from his nose. "You have ever'body in your pocket you need."

"I have people in my pocket just like you do when you spread the money around, but the Rangers are dif-ferent. Jesus Christ, this county's gonna be workin' alive with all kinds of feds, and once they talk to the right people in Jasper, folks who don't have sense enough to keep their mouths closed, they'll head this way as fast as they can, and it's all because of that damn-fool boy of yours. They never so much as turned an eye towards us all these years, and now we're like a magnet, draw-ing filings."

The Preacher pointed a finger, as if expecting blue electricity to shoot toward Buck's pounding heart. "Don't you *dare* blaspheme in my presence!"

"Shut the hell *up*, Holmes!" Buck's eyes flashed as bright as the lightning outside, and his lips quivered with fury. "I'm talking to Frank here and don't need to hear any half-assed preachin' from a man who's as crooked as a dog's hind leg!"

"You boys take it easy. We don't need that right now." Daddy Frank's voice was soft and low. "If they come down on us, only thing they'll find is this fertilizer what we use on our crops and nothin' else."

Buck shook his head in frustration. It was true that the Wadlers had diversified into row crops like strawberries, blueberries, pecans, and muscadines, as well as beef cattle, hay production, and hunting leases. He figured they had a fifty-fifty chance of convincing the feds that the surface business was legitimate, but there was millions in cocaine and marijuana squirreled away in the woods, buried deep in steel shipping containers, along with truckloads of prescription pills.

Daddy Frank's voice was calm as if they were watching the annual monarch butterfly migration that brought millions of the insects through the county each year. "Boone's bringing Tanner out. We're gonna get to the bottom of this and then ever'thing's gonna be all right. It's all been done, and there ain't no gettin' the genie back in the bottle."

"It'll let us know what we have to deal with. Anything we do'll increase our chances of getting caught for sure, putting all that stuff on the highway at the same time ain't no good idea." Buck sighed in frustration. "There's no reason to go *on* like this."

"There's every reason, and it's called money. Keep these people off us 'til tomorrow, then everything'll be all right."

The sound of an engine ended the discussion. The dog growled, straining against the chain holding him to the post. Buck wanted to continue the argument. Maybe Daddy Frank would listen if Holmes would keep his big mouth shut.

"Shut up, Mud! There's Boone and Tanner now."

The dog licked his lips and sat, still watching Daddy Frank. The truck stopped and the cab light came on when they opened the doors. Daddy Frank and Brother Holmes retreated into the barn and they watched Boone and Tanner trot through the rain.

Chapter 44

This kind of crap takes road rage to a whole new level.
I slipped as fast as possible through the trees.

Do all the bad guys have machine guns these days?

The only thing that saved me from getting chewed up and spit out by those automatic weapons was the sky that opened up with a vengeance. So much water fell at one time that fish could have spawned in the woods. Trees thrashed and thunder vibrated my stomach as the storm roared overhead.

And who the hell are they, anyway?

I couldn't imagine it was over a little highway altercation, so this was planned.

Dammit. Those guys back there in the Monster Ford were part of it, too. Hope I didn't get some highway patrol officer killed because of that little stunt I pulled.

My knees were already talking to me, and I vowed I'd get more exercise once I got back home. I had no idea which way to go, but at the moment any direction away from those who ran me off the highway was good.

Despite the storm, I heard shouting voices as I scrambled up the embankment and followed the creek for a ways, before angling upward, figuring the highway was at the top of the incline. Now I don't know if I had a particular thought as to what I needed to do once I got up there, because the last two trucks that passed were full of men who wanted to kill me, and I didn't doubt there'd be a third.

The only problem was that I didn't know who or why.

Oh, I had an idea. Somebody knew I was coming, and it was mostly likely that Tanner guy who called Comanche and set me up. How they knew my truck and me was another story, but I figured that with the Internet, anything was possible.

At least this time I had my cell phone that had somehow managed to stay in my pocket. It was probably because the kids had bought me a shockproof, waterproof protector after the last time I was in trouble.

I'd outrun my pursuers for the time being, and the heavy rain helped cover my escape.

Water funneled off the brim of my hat. I was soaked and hunted once again, but this time would be different. Help was just a phone call away. I finally found a hidey hole under a young pine tree growing against a larger, dead cousin. I crawled under the thick evergreen foliage and leaned over the phone to protect it from the rain.

I tried to swipe with my finger. Once again, technology defeated me because it wouldn't work. Frustrated, I swiped several more times until I remembered that the kids told me my finger needed to be reasonably dry. That was hard to do in a rainstorm, but I rubbed my thumb against my forehead under the Stetson until it didn't feel as damp.

I swiped again, and a blinding light took away my vision. The heavy clouds and driving rain made it feel like midnight, and the screen's intensity was like looking into a halogen bulb. To make matters worse, I figured some bad guy had me in his sights, thanking me for the assistance. I wished I'd listened to the twins when they wanted to turn down the display's intensity, but through the years, I needed more light to read, and the bright screen was best for my eyes.

I took my hat off and put the phone inside. It seemed to help some, but I kept imagining a circle of light five feet around where I crouched. My thumbprint wouldn't work to activate the stinkin' thing, but I punched in my code and it finally brought up the screen full of icons.

At least the waterproof cover was working.

No Service.

Either all the trees were blocking the signal, or I was out of tower range. My face flushed as I made myself turn the phone off and put it in my pocket instead of putting a .45-caliber hole in the infernal device.

Think, the Old Man would have said. They can't find you, it's almost dark, and you can't leave a trail in this rain. Either follow the creek to where it runs into a river, then follow it to a town, or work yourself back uphill to the highway.

Well, I wasn't in the remote Big Bend, where towns were few and far between. In most of Texas, towns are little more than twenty miles from each other, the distance a wagon could travel in a day, back before automobiles. Little communities like Gunn sprung up in those open spaces when the times were right.

All creeks and rivers eventually run to one of those towns or communities, so the thing to do was get to civilization and call the sheriff. I had Buck Henderson's number saved in my phone and I could call him . . .

Wait a damn minute. The only person who knew for certain that I was coming into Gunn *was* Buck Henderson. I'd called and said I'd meet him at his office, and he gave me directions down this exact highway.

I wasn't born yesterday. Not all lawmen are on the up-and-up.

There was only one thing to do and that was follow the pocket on my shirt out of those woods and get some help.

Chapter 45

Daddy Frank hadn't moved since the truck pulled up in front of the fertilizer barn. The storm had lessened, but wind still thrashed the pines and hardwoods outside. He lit a fresh cigarette from the butt and crushed it under his shoe.

Tanner was terrified and shriveled. He stopped just inside the barn door, like a rabbit needing to be close to safety in case he had to bolt. The truth was there was no real safety with Boone leaning against the wall, waiting for orders.

The air reeked of chemicals. One stall contained several bags of ammonium nitrate fuel oil, or AMFO, that would be used as the primary explosive agent when the fertilizer and diesel oil was mixed.

Sheriff Buck Henderson lipped a cigarette from the crumpled pack in his shirt pocket. He was about to snap the lighter alive when he glanced toward the sacks. He stuck the cigarette over his ear, leaned one arm over the top board of the nearest stall, and laced his fingers to watch.

After studying Tanner's swollen and bruised face for a moment in the harsh light of bare bulbs, Daddy Frank broke into a grin. He'd switched from smoking back to the chew of tobacco tucked into his cheek. "Somebody done wore your ass plumb *out*."

"Daddy."

"You probably deserved it, then."

"I don't think so." Sullen.

"I never did neither, when my daddy whipped my ass, but he was always right."

Tanner snorted a load from his broken nose and spat bloody mucus on the barn's packed dirt floor.

"I'magine you popped off one too many times." Daddy Frank turned to Buck. "Had the same failin's myself when I was a young man." He addressed Tanner again. "How's that new lease car of yours runnin'?"

"How'd you know I had a lease? You've been gone for a week."

"I know ever'thing, boy. There ain't a swingin' dick in this county that don't owe me in some way or turns their head when I pass. People give me information just to stay on my good side.

"I knew Jimmy Don ain't here where he should be, neither. My own damned son's out fartin' around when he should be here." Daddy Frank's eyes went flat. "I might need to call him." He held out a hand. "Give me your phone."

The young man produced a cell phone from the pocket of his loose jeans and offered it to him.

"No. The other'n I gave you. I want to see who you've been callin'."

He slipped it back into his pocket and kept his hand there. "It's in my car."

"Where's your car?"

"At the house."

He met Boone's eyes. The strange man nodded.

"You're supposed to have it on you at all times."

"Well, I ain't been thinking straight for the past few hours."

"Son, you ain't been thinkin' straight for the past few *weeks*." Daddy Frank spat a thick brown stream of tobacco. "You know what's wrong with you?"

Tanner raised his eyes. He sighed. "Looks like ever'body wants to tell me these days. What's *your* opinion?"

"You're a prissy smartass." Daddy Frank backhanded him, the slap hard and flat. Tanner's head snapped to the side, but he didn't go down. Nose pouring blood, he set his feet for the next blow, but Daddy Frank stepped back. "And you better watch that mouth. I ain't your daddy, boy."

Tears flowed but Tanner could no longer control his tears or tongue. "No, he hits harder."

Daddy Frank nearly punched through Tanner's diaphragm with a fist hard as iron, doubling the young man over in agony. He went down on both knees, gasping for breath that wouldn't come.

"Yeah, but I won't stop." Hands on his knees, Daddy Frank bent down as if getting a foot lower would help Tanner understand. "You ain't worth half of nothin' at all boy, watch your mouth."

It seemed like an eternity to Tanner before his diaphragm finally relaxed to allow a short breath. He sucked air in with a whoop at the same time Daddy Frank kicked him in the same place so fast he never saw the boot coming. His breath whooshed out.

"I'm mean as hell, and you're about on my last nerve. Looks like you forgot who runs this family. Hell, I run the whole goddamn *county*, boy."

Tanner writhed on the dirt floor, curled in a ball and fully expecting the next kick to be in the face. He covered his head with one hand while the other held his stomach.

The old man rubbed the gray stubble on his jaw. "Boone, get his keys and go get that phone. Leave Mike's truck there and bring his car back."

Boone pushed off from the wall and stepped forward. Tanner heard the order, but it look almost a full minute before he could dig the keys from his front pocket. He pitched them to Boone. They fell short. Boone picked them up without blinking and left.

Once the taillights receded down the dirt track into the woods, Daddy Frank watched Tanner struggle to breathe. "Buck, we're gonna have to sink Mike's truck. Don't need it sitting out there at the house."

"I'll get on it."

That piece of business finished, the old man checked his watch. "We're just gonna wait 'til I can check that phone, then I'll know for sure what to do. If he's lyin', I'm gonna be one grandboy short." Daddy Frank crossed the barn floor to watch the rain falling through the arc of yellow light pouring through the open barn doors.

Brother Holmes had been studying Tanner instead of the storm. "Frank, that boy's doing something in his pocket there."

Daddy Frank turned his attention back to Tanner still lying on his side with one hand in the pocket of his loose-fitting jeans. "Tanner, you *can't* be playing pocket pool at a time like this."

The young man twisted enough to see his grand-father. "Waiting for my stomach to settle before I get up."

"You're messin' with that phone in there."

"Thought I felt it vibrate. Alonzo might be calling."

Daddy Frank held out his hand again. "Give it here."

Realizing he'd made a mistake, Tanner struggled to his knees and passed it over. The old man studied the blank screen. "Unlock it."

"No."

Daddy Frank's eyes flicked over Tanner's shoulder at the arrival of Jimmy Don, Clifford Raye, and Sammy Saxon. "Boys. Glad you're here. You're just in time."

They came in out of the rain, one eye on the young man lying on the dirt floor, and the other on Daddy Frank. Clifford Ray's face went blank, immediately understanding what was going on.

The Old Man glared at Jimmy Don. "Remember what I told you?"

"But Dad . . ."

The old man interrupted. "Shut up. You didn't han-dle this boy like I told you. Now I got to do it."

Instead of answering, Jimmy Don slipped both

hands into the pockets of his jeans and stared at his own shoes, refusing to meet anyone's eyes.

The man with the rattail, Clifford Raye, didn't take time to make niceties. "We got troubles. What's going on here?"

Buck simply spread his hands in answer. No one answered for the old man when he was there.

"I keep hearing that." Daddy Frank scowled at Jimmy Don, daring him to say anything. "We have a little Mexican standoff going on right now, but one thing at a time. Boy, unlock this damned phone."

"I said I won't."

The Old Man studied Tanner as if he were a new life specimen. "Sammy, go back there in the tack room. There's a pair of hand pruners hanging on the wall. If this boy won't put his thumb on this damned thing and unlock it, then we'll cut it off and do it ourselves."

Jimmy Don turned his back on the scene as Saxon's face paled. "You sure you wanna do that? What's going on?"

Tanner's attention went directly to the stump of Clifford Raye's finger. The man's sad eyes spoke volumes. "That's gonna hurt like hell, boy. You better do what he says."

Trembling, Tanner struggled to his feet and pressed his thumb on the Home button. The screen flared to life. "Daddy, you ain't worth the dirt I'm standing on."

Jimmy Don's shoulders slumped and he spoke to the stacks of fertilizer. "I know it."

He passed it back to Daddy Frank, who looked at the screen and tapped the glass. "Now you're using some of that brain of yours. Looky here, somebody's been talking to my wife." He raised his head and gave Tanner a wolfish grin. "We gonna have to talk about that, ain't we?"

He went back to the screen and his face hardened. "You just sent a text."

Tanner squared his shoulders. "Yes."

Daddy Frank read the screen. "He just told some sheriff where we are."

Buck came off the stall in a rush. Daddy Frank turned his back to Tanner and offered it to the sheriff, who snatched the phone from his hand. "Gomez out in Comanche. God*damn* it!"

Behind him, Preacher Holmes shouted. "Don't use the Lord's name . . ."

"Shut *up*, Holmes!" Buck whirled, drew the Glock from the holster on his hip, and shot Preacher Holmes between the eyes from only three feet away.

The back of the man's head blew out, spraying the dog with blood and brain matter. Mud snarled at the smell and lunged at the body as it fell backward, yanked back only inches away from the body by the chain wrapped around a support post.

Every man in the barn froze in shock. Buck stuffed the pistol back into its holster. "I can't *stand* that sonofabitch."

Clifford Raye swallowed. "Well, you won't have to worry with him no more."

Daddy Frank snorted a harsh laugh. "How come you to do that?"

"Because I'm done with stupidity." The sheriff crossed his arms. "All right. Let's get back to business.

Daddy Frank pulled a compact handgun from his

pocket and turned back toward the barn doors and his grandson. "Boy, you done seen what happens . . ."

Every man in the barn froze at the sight of the empty dirt floor.

Tanner was gone.

Jimmy Don hid a relieved grin.

Chapter 46

Perry Hale and Yolanda slowed as they passed the turnoff leading to the Wadlers' house. The rain had come to a stop as the fast-moving storm pushed toward the Gulf, though lighting still flickered to the south. The humidity was gone for the time being. The croak of thousands of frogs chimed in with the tenor of crickets fiddling their legs.

Using information and directions Yolanda found online, Perry Hale pulled up to a farm gate a mile away. A padlock secured it in place, telling him this wasn't the driveway to a house. "I sure hope Sheriff Gomez was right about that text he got from the kid."

"You and me both." Yolanda put on a camouflage cap, pulling her long black hair through the adjustment hole. "He said it was full of typos. My nephew got in trouble for texting in class while the phone was in his pocket."

"You can get in trouble for texting in school?"

She grinned. "When you're texting the answers. This kid must have been too close to someone who cared."

She tapped her phone with a fingertip. "Look, here's the screenshot Gomez sent."

Granddad Frsnk has me. Fetlizer brn nr Gunn.

She turned the phone off. "I figured that was supposed to be Frank. The next word looks like fertilizer barn, whatever that is."

"I hope we find out from these folks."

"Do you think we're stepping out of bounds here?"

"Probably, but I don't like that we can't get hold of Sonny. If these people are part of the problem, it's justified."

"If they aren't?"

He killed the engine and they detrucked. "We'll cross that bridge when we come to it."

A whip-poor-will called, as if in celebration of the cooler weather.

Perry Hale locked the truck. Dressed in camo and carrying battle-slung ARs, the two experienced veterans geared up and disappeared into the dripping woods, moving fast and surefooted as cougars. Halfway toward their destination, Perry Hale paused and checked his GPS. "The Wadler place is about two hundred yards that way."

Yolanda adjusted her own ballistic vest and scanned the woods around them. She spoke in a whisper. She still couldn't shake the feeling of foreboding. "This feels a little weird for me to be creepy crawling up on a house in this country."

"Illegal as hell, too, but I'm worried sick about Sonny. There's no other reason for him not to call in by now other than he's in trouble. The only thing I know to do is work with what we have. If this guy has anything to do with it and Sonny's inside, we'll get him out."

"What if it's just a kid calling for grins?"

"It'll be the last time."

"We need to get in and out before the cavalry shows up." Yolanda used her elbow to point down the highway as they crawled over the pipe gate. "The county sheriff and his men might be here any minute."

"If anybody else shows up, or a pro team, split and meet at the truck. I left the keys on top of the passenger tire, in case I don't make it and you have to split."

Her white teeth flashed. "Let's keep positive thoughts."

They soon saw a glow through the dripping trees and worked their way toward the huge clearing. Lightning bugs sparkled across the yard. Crickets filled the air with their chirps. Night birds called. A television program blared through windows open to admit the cool night air.

Angling her rifle into the darkness, Yolanda mouthed the words in Perry Hale's ear. "I sure hope there's no dog." They were both soaked from the waist down from the wet underbrush.

"There's usually at least one to a house, but I doubt it could hear anything over that TV. If one pops up, I'll shoot it and we take the house as fast as we can."

She bit her bottom lip. "What if it's just a country family settled in for the evening?"

He heard the caution in her voice. "You know, we're way beyond bounds here."

"Then we duck out as fast as possible after saying we're sorry."

"You want to back out?"

She paused. "No. We need to find out what they know about Sonny. I just hope nobody pulls out a gun."

"Hell, I would if somebody came sneaking up to my house. I'll take this side where the cars are parked. The way the house sits with this end to the road, I 'magine these folks either go in through a carport door, or around back. The front door is mostly for show. You go in there."

"You country people are weird."

Perry Hale's voice was resigned. "I won't argue that."

They adjusted the earpieces that would allow them to communicate and separated. Despite his sense of urgency, Perry Hale crossed the dirt road and moved between the cars with glacial speed. Rifle to his shoulder, and muzzle down, he kept one eye on the ground and the other on the open windows.

Unlike his own people 250 miles away in North Texas, the Wadlers apparently didn't close their drapes until night. Every window was an opening into their world. Surprised that they didn't have a dog, Perry Hale circled around the corner, past a well-used fire-pit, and onto the back porch, staying below the level of the windows.

He pressed his back to the outside wall and peeked inside. A man in a wheelchair fidgeted in front of a large flat-panel television. A very pregnant woman was curled on the sofa beneath a cloud of cigarette smoke. She rose, startling him, and walked through the living room and into the kitchen.

Seeing the room was clear, he went to the next window and found her opening a beer that she sat on the table beside a bowl of ice cream. She drew deep on the cigarette and laid it on the edge of a Formica table, ignoring an orange ashtray only inches away.

The next windows opened into empty bedrooms. The only one he couldn't see into was a small fixed glass set high in the wall. Probably the bathroom. By the time he got to the corner of the house, he squatted and peeked around the edge.

He pushed the comm button on his chest. "At the corner."

"Me, too." Yolanda was in the same position. She waved when he stuck his head around the corner. She hadn't seen anything, either. Perry Hale spoke softly. "Clear except for a pregnant woman and an old man."

"We going in?"

"Yep." He jerked a thumb. "You see if the front door's open. I'm going in the back. I doubt that one's locked."

"If it is?"

"Kick yours open if you hear me do the same. Be careful. That girl in there's close to having a baby, and I don't want to scare her any more than we have to."

"Yes sir. Stay frosty."

Perry Hale returned to the back door. He tried the knob. It turned. Taking a deep breath, he stepped inside and found himself in a utility room containing a washer, dryer, and a chest-type deep freeze. Shelves against the back wall were full of canned food. A wooden pocket door was halfway open, spilling just enough light to see.

He peered through the crack to see the elderly man had turned his wheelchair away from the television that was booming the History Channel.

The TV covering the sound, he slid the door back and entered the living room, leaving muddy footprints on the linoleum. Wincing at the volume, but thankful for the covering noise, he crossed behind the man who never knew he was there. A quick glance around revealed the front door standing open. Yolanda was inside.

Perry Hale stepped into the kitchen with a finger to his lips. "Take it easy. We're not going to hurt you." The young woman standing beside the refrigerator started at the sight of the stocky man only feet away. He gave her a smile and held out a palm. "We're law enforcement."

She crushed out her cigarette in the half-full ashtray on the table. "I wondered when y'all'd finally show up." She drawled her words as if from a southern plantation movie.

Yolanda stepped through a door at the opposite end. "House is clear on this end."

The young woman's head spun at the sound of a female voice. "Y'all DEA? FBI?" Neither answered and she shrugged. "I'll tell you everything you want to know. I can even tell you how they're moving the drugs, if you'll just cut me a break."

Yolanda raised an eyebrow and gave her a smile. "We're here for information all right, but not about drugs right now. That can wait. You alone?"

"Yep, just like always, me taking care of that feeble-minded old man in there while ever'body else is out cattin' around."

"Do you know anything about a man being held here against his will?"

"I know of a *girl* held like that. Me."

Yolanda's eyes flicked to Perry Hale, then back. "Who're you?"

"Donine."

Perry Hale closed the kitchen blinds. "Last name?"

"*Was* Buckley, been a damned Wadler for the last six months."

"Well, at least we have the right house. You're being held hostage here?"

"Yeah." Donine lit another cigarette, ignoring Yolanda's frown. "Held by family and this damned baby inside me. Y'all ATF?"

"Nope." Perry Hale threw a glance back into the living room to see the confused old man was once again facing the television. "We're looking for someone named Tanner, and a Texas Ranger."

"Tanner's my husband, what he is of one, but like I said, ain't nobody here but me. Why would there be a baseball player here, anyway?"

Perry Hale leaned forward. "Not that kind of Ranger. A real Texas Ranger lawman. One who wears a badge and a gun."

"Oh. Naw, nothin' like that."

"Who's that in the living room?"

She snorted. "Marshall Wadler, what there is of *him*. The last man to cross Daddy Frank. Nobody in his right mind does that. He's the old man's *son*! Daddy

Frank beat him damn-near to death with a tire iron and left him in that chair, but anyway, he don't count." She twirled a finger around her ear. "Crazy as a bessybug now. Been that way for a couple of years."

"The Ranger we're looking for is named Sonny Hawke."

"That sounds like somebody on TV."

Perry Hale had to grit his teeth. "He's not. Tell me about Frank Wadler."

Her face hardened at the name. "Daddy Frank? I figured you'd know all about him since you're here."

Yolanda stepped forward. "Sit down if you need to."

"Don't mind if I do." Holding her protruding abdomen, Donine eased down into a chair. "You're awful pretty to be the law."

"Thanks. Is your husband with Frank?"

"*Daddy* Frank. That's what ever'body calls that mean old bastard. No, Tanner left a little while ago, and I've been waiting for him to get back."

"You know where he went?"

"I never know where that prick is."

Perry Hale closed the dusty Venetian blinds and backed against the kitchen counter to keep an eye on both doors. "What's the fertilizer barn?"

He saw Donine put two and two together. "You think Tanner's there or your Ranger? How'd you find out about that?"

"Tanner sent someone a text saying Frank took him there."

Donine's eyes filled. "If somebody gets took to the fertilizer barn, they're gone for good, vanish in the river out back for the gators 'n snappin' turtles as a washtub. You're tellin' me that's where Tanner is or maybe your Ranger friend, you're gonna need more people and a lot more bullets, and y'all need to hurry."

Yolanda took out her cell phone while Perry Hale spun his finger in frustration. "Get to talking."

Chapter 47

Unlike other parts of the country, Texas doesn't have huge expanses of wilderness, other than the Big Bend area southeast of El Paso. The vast majority of the East Texas landscape is chopped into a patchwork quilt by roads, highways, fences, pastures, and cropland. Greenbelt forests spread for hundreds of miles through this landscape like arteries, consisting of meandering courses of rivers, creeks, ravines, washes, and swamps linking farms to communities to towns to cities.

Lucky for me the part of the Big Thicket was close enough to the Texas/Louisiana border that the thickly wooded properties offered all the cover I needed as I put distance between myself and the guys who wanted to turn me into Swiss cheese. There was no safety in hiding in one spot for any length of time, and I needed to find Sheriff Buck Henderson. The goal was to keep moving until I could get cell service and call him, or have Perry Hale and Yolanda come pick me up, which was my first option.

I worked my way through the trees until I found what I was looking for. A game trail.

That gave me some relief, and I followed it along the path of the now-rushing creek. Animals take the easiest way through the woods. They move with a minimum of exertion, and the well-worn pathway allowed me to move as quickly as if I were following a highway.

Truthfully, animals do the same in our cities and urban neighborhoods, running streets and alleys at night when traffic is light and everyone's buttoned up tight in their homes. They follow those same greenbelts and parks and use the underground storm drains that city planners so thoughtfully provide.

Unfortunately, none of the trails I followed were as straight as a road. The distance "as a crow flies" is deceptive. Sometimes the trail veered toward the creek or back uphill, or away from cover and into open pastures, forcing me to move more cautiously. I stopped frequently to check my reception, but the words No Service were driving me nuts.

The rain slacked off and moved away. Trees and bushes dripped as thunder diminished and eventually stopped. It grew lighter as the clouds broke up to reveal a pale sky as fresh as a daisy.

Bobwire fences became my biggest frustration. I ran into three of them within half an hour, telling me that I wasn't truly in the wilderness, something I already knew, but far away from help. We grew up calling them bobwire, but by any name, they were a pain in the ass. Tight wires forced me to climb over, slowly, so I wouldn't slip and catch myself on the sharp barbs.

Old, loose wires were easy to slip through, but they had the frustrating tendency to catch the back of my shirt.

I ducked through a rusty bobwire fence that seemed only to separate trees. After that, my steady pace aided by the game trail ate up the distance. Again, the path turned and I crossed a shallow gully, spooking a deer that flashed its white rump and disappeared into the underbrush. I almost shot him before realizing what he was.

That same wet underbrush became thicker as the trail faded into an impenetrable mass of blackberry vines. Game trails sometimes merge and diverge, depending on the terrain. Bobwire fences won't impede a whitetail deer, they'll either jump it, or slide on their bellies under the bottom strand.

Half an hour later the path led toward even thicker tangles of blackberry vines and dense stands of understory brush. The brambles grabbed and tore at my exposed skin. I had to stop several times to extract myself from the thorns.

The trail intersected a muddy ravine and followed the sloping bank. The underbrush thickened even more and suddenly the dense woods abruptly opened up and I found myself beside a two-lane overpass. I checked to see how many bars I had on the phone.

Too low in the bottoms and still no service. Dammit!

A clear path led across the opening and alongside the sluggish river that churned with fresh runoff. I thought it might be the Sabine or the Trinity, but that was only a guess. It passed under the road suspended over the thick gruel of muddy water. I paused at the edge of the pines lining the highway, listening. My light-colored shirt and jeans were far from camouflage, and it wouldn't take much for one of the bad guys to see me skulking along the side of the highway.

Movement attracts attention.

Tires whining on pavement gave me enough warning to squat down in a thicket of yaupon hollies. I had an idea that I'd wait to see what kind of vehicle it was, then come out and wave them down, hoping they'd see me in their rearview mirror.

It's a good thing I didn't run out and wave my arms like an idiot, because as it came closer and passed, I recognized the jacked-up monster truck I'd tangled with earlier. It drove at school-zone speed as four armed men scanned the edge of the trees.

I took my hat off and settled down behind a vine-covered log with just my eyes peeking over the top and the Colt in my hand. There was too much vegetation between me and them, so they passed without slowing and I stayed still until the road was empty.

Slipping the automatic back into the holster, I listened for approaching cars. Sure the coast was clear, I sprinted down the bank and under the overpass, nearly plowing into a black man of indeterminate age dressed in faded coveralls. The pistol was back in my hand and pointed at his chest. "Don't you move. Who're you?"

I don't know if he'd been on the business end of a pistol before, but he did everything right. He stood stock still beside a concrete column without moving a muscle, a rifle cradled in his arm. He didn't move. "Hidy. You don't intend to shoot me, do ye?"

"I don't want to."

All his teeth on the left side were gone, making his speech mushy, but he was clear to me. "I ain't who you're runnin' from, that's for sure."

"Put them hands on top of your head."

"Can I lean my rifle against this here tree? I'd hate for it to get full of mud'n trash."

I relaxed, knowing he wasn't one of the men who were after me. "Slow. Then get your hands up."

"You gone shoot me, deputy?"

He'd seen the badge on my shirt, and I lowered the pistol. "I'm not a deputy and I don't believe so. What are you doing standing under here?"

"I's jus' squirrel huntin'."

"Bullshit." I made the pistol disappear.

"Well, I live over yonder a little piece," he nodded his head, "and heard a lot of shootin' out here. I figgered I'd wait here and see who came by. I got more sense than to stand in the rain. Who're you runnin' from?"

"Most ever-body for the moment 'til I figure out who's who."

A car hissed down the highway and slowed. We instinctively glanced up. An engine idled, and a door opened. Maybe they were back. I drew the .45 again and held it toward the sound. We relaxed at the hissing sound of water splashing on already wet ground as someone relieved themselves on the side of the road. The door slammed and they pulled away.

Back to my new friend. I liked the guy who seemed to be trying to live his life. "You're hunting out of season."

"I don't know persacktly when that is. I jus' try to

stay to m'self. Like I said, I live jus' right over yon-der."

"Umm humm. Most folks would hide in the house if they heard shooting outside the door."

"Well, my house ain't much, and I don't intend to get caught inside if somebody come in a-shootin'."

"You been in trouble with the law before?"

"Yessir. But I paid my debt, and now I try to mind m'own business. Can I ax you a question?"

"Why not? I don't have much else to do tonight but stand around under bridges and talk to folks."

"Mista Deputy, what 'choo doin' out here for them fellers to be huntin you?"

"I'm working a case, and somebody ran me off the road."

"You don't say. Mos' folks use the highway to get gone if they're being chased."

"Running the creeks is a good idy, sometimes, too." I realized I'd fallen into the speech patterns the Old Man grew up with and I'd heard up in Lamar County when I was a kid. "Some bad folks are after me. My truck's in a creek over yonder."

He nodded and grinned again. "Bullshit. The law don't run."

His statement embarrassed me, and I was glad it was dark so he couldn't see me redden up. "It does when we're outnumbered and outgunned. What do you know about the Wadler family? Guy named Daddy Frank."

The man's eyes widened at the name. "Shit. Man, if that's who's after you, you done messed with the devil hisself."

"That's what I'm learning. I believe it was some of

their men ran me off the road, and I'm trying to get some help. My cell phone don't work out in here."

"That's right. We're too deep in the bottoms and you know what, I've run from folks m'self a time or two. The way you're travelin', I'd thank you's tellin' me the truth."

I looked over my shoulder, not happy with standing around and talking like we were at a cocktail party. Crickets and frogs sang in the cool, damp air and I wondered if the sound was covering up footsteps creeping up on us.

He kept talking, comfortable now that he believed who I was. "Me and my people have lived in these woods since Heck was a pup, so we see what a lot most folks miss."

"I imagine you do. I need to get to where I can make a phone call to the local sheriff."

"Now look here, if I's you, I'd hold up a spell. The rest of the way behind me toward Gunn, you're liable to run into somebody, and you sho as hell don't want to call Sheriff Buck Henderson. He's crooked as a snake, and he's in cahoots with Daddy Frank. They's a lot folks drivin' this road right now, more'n usual, and if it's that Wadler bunch like you think it is, I reckon you need to go with me, Mr. Texas Ranger."

It took a second for that to sink in. He'd recognized my badge right off and was having a little fun at my expense. I reddened even more, embarrassed that I'd misread the man and mistook the depths of his understanding. "I think you're right."

"You come foller me a little ways to my shack and hole up there 'til my cousin comes by fer supper. He's been laying for a big catfish all day, and I 'magine we'll have a mess tonight. He has a pickup, and we'll carry you up to the edge of town and won't nobody say nothin' about it. We need to run up to the store for a few things anyway."

I studied on his idea for a few seconds.

"I's run to ground a time or two myself, and wished somebody would come along to lend a hand."

"There's cell service close by?"

He snorted and looked my shape up and down as if he could see in the darkness. "It's a long ways off, twenty mile or so."

I considered the risk his cousin would be taking with me in the car. "Won't people talk if they see me riding with y'all?"

"Naw, my cousin Sissy married a white feller, though God knows I don't know why. He's sorry as sand, but he's about your size. Jimmy Lee's rode with us a'fore, and they'll think you're him. Most of y'all look alike to us anyhow."

I matched his grin. "Well, you might have a good idea there."

"You're durn tootin'. My name's Salvadore Williams."

I started to answer, but he held up a hand. "Nope, don't need no name from you Mr. Smith. And I don't believe you're a Ranger, even though you got some kind of badge hangin' there on your shirt. They's a solid quarter apiece up at the store, though most say Sheriff on 'em. You jus' runnin' from the Wadlers and that makes you my frien'." He nudged at a 'toe sack beside his foot. "You can help me skin these squirrels I shot this evenin' and have supper with us to boot."

"Like I said, squirrel season's closed."

"Is you a Ranger or a game warden?"

"Ranger."

"So you want out of this or not?"

I considered my chances and didn't have any good argument, so I followed him even farther into the back-woods as he told me everything he knew about Daddy Frank and his family of criminals.

It was a lot.

Chapter 48

Tanner ran as fast as he could through the thick piney woods he'd played in and hunted in since he was a little kid, though they were dangerous as hell. He often rode with Jimmy Don when his dad came out to the old fertilizer barn to pick up a load of marijuana, or to load someone else's truck who was traveling through with the grace of Sheriff Buck Henderson.

Once he was safely away from the barn, he knelt in the soaked woods and pulled the drop phone that he'd sent Boone to fetch from his boot. Hitting the Home button, he cursed at the No Service icon. The trees were most likely blocking the signal, and the nearest clear spot was a mile away.

Still spitting blood, he jogged down a game trail that wound through what was left of the old-growth Big Thicket. Men had been lost forever in those woods, and he recalled stories from sixty years earlier of virtual skeletons crawling back to civilization after being gone for weeks. It was said that even people who grew up in those backwoods could step off a trail and get turned around if it was cloudy enough.

Right then anywhere was good as long as it was away from Daddy Frank. The longer he jogged, the happier he felt despite his throbbing nose and face, because now he knew exactly where the old sonofabitch was waiting.

He intended to call Alonzo and warn him. All he'd need was his car after that, and he'd get gone with Shi'Ann.

He finally broke out onto a blacktop road. He crouched in a dense thicket of small understory trees and checked the phone. Two bars were enough. He scrolled through names until he found Shi'Ann.

It rang three times before a male voice answered. "Who is this?"

Tanner's stomach fell. "Where's Shi'Ann? This is her number."

"I said who's this? My name's Sheriff Wayne Jennings."

"Acadiana Parish?"

"That's right."

"I'm Tanner. She's my girlfriend. What's wrong?"

The gruff voice softened. "Tanner Wadler."

"Yessir." The southern courtesy came without a thought.

"We found a letter with your name on it on her dresser."

"What does that mean?"

"Son, I hate to tell you, but she's dead."

Tanner stifled a sob. His knees went weak, and he dropped to the needle-covered ground.

"I'm sorry. Can you come out to my office?"

"She didn't kill herself. That ain't no suicide note. She's cut to pieces, ain't she?"

There was a long pause on the other end of the line. "How'd you know?"

"It was done by a freak named Boone."

"I've heard that name. Folks say he lives in the woods over in Gunn. I thought he was a booger made up to scare little kids."

Hysterical laughter bubbled up in Tanner's throat. "Shit, feller. He even scares Daddy Frank."

Chapter 49

Boone pulled Mike's truck to a stop beside Tanner's sedan. Though the skies had cleared and the sun hung low above the treetops, all the lights were on in the house, making it look like a party.

He stepped out and paused. The pregnant woman inside had fascinated him from the start. Skinny like him in some places, bulging and curvy in others, he wanted to run his hands over her body to feel the tiny life squirm inside her.

Instead, he settled for what he always did. He went to the living room window and peeked inside. The quick look inside told him Marshall was in front of the TV, as usual. Boone didn't see why they allowed the mindless man to live in his condition. He would have cut his throat and dropped the body in the Sabine River that seemed to absorb everything that went below its muddy surface.

His heart beating in anticipation, Boone picked at Shi'Ann's blood flaking from his fingernails and hoped Donine was in the bedroom. He hadn't been back from Comanche more than five minutes earlier that evening when Daddy Frank gave him a gift, sending Boone to eliminate his young wife.

Boone would have frowned, if he could. "Why?"

"Because a little birdie told me she's been tanglin' the sheets with my grandboy. Well, I'm splittin' 'em sheets, and then me'n that boy's gonna dance tonight."

The house was only two miles away, as the crow flies across the Sabine. With orders to not dawdle, he was in and out in minutes, but they were gloriously bloody minutes that tasted of copper and salt, punctuated by the popping, gristle-like sound of a pulled tooth.

Now, in the darkness outside of a house containing still another woman Tanner had bedded, Boone ached for even more release. It was spiraling, building like the storm that had just pushed through, and Boone felt the end of his peaceful time on the Sabine was coming to a close.

Watching Donine lying on the bed was everything he wanted right then. His impassive face flushed with heat that quickly died when he peered into the kitchen window to see the blinds closed.

No one ever closed the blinds in this family, not even at night. She was likely up to something.

His mind filled with possibilities. Could she have a male visitor? Wasn't she too close to delivery to be having any kind of relations? He allowed one corner of his mouth to twitch in a rare smile. He slipped one hand into his pocket and felt Shi'Ann's fresh molar and the bit of soft gum still attached. He closed his eyes in pleasure, using the tooth as a worry stone and picturing what Donine could be doing for a visitor.

A full minute later he moved like a shadow to check

the next window only to find the blinds open and the bedroom empty. Disappointed, he returned to the back door and stepped inside the utility room. The pocket door was completely recessed, giving him a clear view of Marshall, who'd rolled his wheelchair to the open window. He stared at the dark wire screen with the same intensity he watched television.

Muddy footprints led from the utility room into the kitchen.

Boone let go of the molar and slipped the straight razor from his pocket. Opening it with his thumb, he crept past the old man to the kitchen's entrance and found a melting bowl of ice cream beside a dead cigarette that had burned out on the table.

Disappointed, he searched the rest of the house to find it empty. He paused beside the table and spooned up the still-cool ice cream, tilting it into his slack mouth and rolling the sweetness over his tongue, wondering at Donine's taste.

Would it be like Shi'Ann's, cinnamon and unidentifiable spices? Vanilla and sugar maybe?

No, probably salty like her hot, pulsing blood. His eyes wandered the cluttered kitchen counter and he saw a folded note standing against a pitcher of tea. He plucked it up with two fingers and read the flowery script telling whoever found the note that she'd seen Tanner's car was still there and decided to drive it to her mama's house.

Disappointed that he'd missed her, he stepped into the living room. Marshall Wadler saw him pass. "Hey, it's over, you know."

Boone paused. "*What's* over?"

"Don't you make faces at me, boy. My show's over and the cat got out."

Boone remembered a pair of pliers in the kitchen drawer.

Why not? Maybe the old man was right. The way things were going the past couple of days, it probably *was* over. Besides, he could proudly finish what Daddy Frank left over.

Assaulted by the blaring television, the few minutes in the living room gave Boone a small bit of satisfaction when he choked Marshall Wadler to death and took another small memento. This time it was a *front* tooth.

He pulled away in Tanner's car as Marshall's dead eyes dried out. He was back at the fertilizer barn in no time.

Chapter 50

Sheriff Buck Henderson's drop phone rang. He stepped over the drying puddle of blood that was all that remained of Preacher Holmes and turned his back on the growing crowd of men assembling in the fertilizer barn. Holmes's body was already gator bait in the nearby Sabine, hauled there by the grim-faced men who wouldn't make eye contact.

He thumbed the phone awake. "Hello."

"Sheriff. This is Kenon."

Kenon Mills was one of Buck's most trusted deputies. "What's up?"

"I just pulled Alonzo over."

"Good."

"Well, it ain't that good. I guess you ain't heard, but a call went out a few minutes ago from Woodville. A man named Clem Gluck working at Ken's Burger was shot in the drive-though. Killed him dead, and the assailant's description matches the Dodge Alonzo's driving."

"Shit."

"That ain't the half of it. Everybody with a radio's

looking for him right now. He's shot, bloody from the waist down, stoned to the gills, and has a corpse in the back seat that's pretty ripe. I started to call an ambulance for him, but then I thought I needed to talk to you first, especially when he said tell you he has the. . . ."

"Don't say nothin' else." The sheriff interrupted, visualizing the scene. "Where are you?"

"Out on FM 1013, just east of Spurger."

"What's he doing *there*?" Though the road eventually wound back up to Gunn, the route was drastically longer.

"Said he wanted to get off 190, figured taking the back roads would be the best. He says he's headed out to see Mr. Frank where he keeps his fertilizer."

Buck watched another of Daddy Frank's kinfolk come into the barn. Every man was armed, and the sheriff had a bad feeling. "Does he have the cash in the truck?"

"He said it is, and something he calls cheese."

"Good. Tell Alonzo to let you put it all in your trunk, and then turn him loose."

"What?"

"I said turn him loose. Let somebody else pull him over. He won't get far."

"You know what else I still have in my trunk, don't you?"

Buck pictured several kilos of cocaine that was supposed to go to one of their distributors. Moving the drugs in a patrol car was the perfect cover. "You haven't delivered that yet?"

"I was on the way when I heard the call. I wanted to help get Alonzo taken care of first."

"Good man, but things have changed. Dump the product."

Deputy Mills's voice was full of surprise. "Where?"

"In the ditch for all I care. It's over. Take the cash and the cheese to the office parking lot and I'll meet you there."

"Yessir."

Buck hung up and waved a hand at Daddy Frank. "Something's come up. I'll be back in an hour."

The old man nodded and went back to his conversation with those around him.

On the way out, Buck passed Jimmy Don standing in the open barn doors. "Where you going, Buck?"

"Something came up. I'll be back directly."

"What's going on?"

"Just police work."

The man looked relieved. "Good. I thought something bad had happened."

Chapter 51

Red and blue lights reflected off every shiny surface on Alonzo's Dodge pulled onto the grassy shoulder. Not a car had passed on the lonesome highway the entire time.

Alonzo still had both hands on the wheel when Deputy Kenon Mills returned to his driver's door. All four windows on the truck were down.

Mills stopped with his palm on the butt of his holstered Glock. "Alonzo?"

The ghost-white man had to blink his eyes clear in order to focus on the deputy standing beside him. "Yeah?"

"Buck said tell you to let me have them boxes and bins."

"You know what's in 'em."

"I believe I do. He wants me to take them to the sheriff's office and let you go on to wherever it is you're headed."

Alonzo had to study on the demand, struggling to stay on track. Thinking, he stuck two fingers into his shirt pocket and plucked out the bottle of pills. As the deputy watched, he tilted it and dry-swallowed some of the contents.

"I got something for Daddy Frank."

"All Buck told me was to get what I told you."

Alonzo's hands tingled. His feet were ice cold. "I can't help you load 'em."

"I'll do it." The deputy went around to the other side and opened the passenger door. Alonzo watched as he peeked inside the container on top and nodded. He carried both back to his car and put them in the trunk. He returned for the heavy plastic bins in the back seat.

Alonzo didn't care. What he needed was packed under the driver's seat.

Deputy Mills returned to his window. "Buck says to go on and don't stop nowhere else until you get to him."

"Didn't intend to."

Chapter 52

After leaving the Wadler house, Perry Hale and Yolanda pulled onto the highway only seconds before her phone rang. She breathed a sigh of relief and held it up so Perry Hale could see Sonny's name on the screen.

She put the call on speaker. "We've been worried sick about you."

"For good reason. Where are y'all?"

"In Perry Hale's truck, heading for the Sabine River bottoms."

"How come?"

"Well, until the phone rang we were looking for you."

"I appreciate that. I'm east of Gunn. Got my truck wrecked and had to do a little cross-country jog that wasn't much fun. Just got a signal a little bit ago and made a few calls. Y'all are supposed to be waiting for me in Jasper."

She told him everything they'd done and heard since the storm blew in, including the fertilizer barn Donine had described. He traded that information for his own, and while he talked, she heard wind in the background. "I thought you said your truck was wrecked. Who're you with?"

"Some friends I met."

They heard him talking to a man with a deep voice before he came back on. "You have a map or something?"

She and Perry Hale exchanged grins. "I have a paper map, and we're using the map app on the phone."

"Don't you lose signal with that thing? I do all the time."

"Only in rare occasions with the app. Where are we going?"

"There's an old iron bridge on the Sabine. My friend here says meet us off CR1455 where it crosses the river. It's a hangout for fishermen and kids. See you there."

Chapter 53

Salvadore Williams rode shotgun while his bald, pointy-headed cousin named Kevin drove the pickup. The windows were down and cool late evening air blew through the cab. Salvadore rode with his arm hanging out the window.

I was in the middle of the rump-sprung bench seat, and it was a good thing the windows were down. I had to keep my head turned from Kevin's breath that was hard as kerosene.

I'd just hung up when Salvadore shook a Camel from the crumpled soft pack in his shirt pocket. "Here's what you do to get to the barn that gal of yours is talking about. Foller the river north from the bridge. You'll be halfway there when you see a bayou coming into the river on your right. Keep on a-goin' for a ways past where folks dump trash, and you'll come to a skinny dirt road cut through the trees. There's usually a couple of flat-bottom boats either tied up there or pulled up out of the water. The barn she's talkin' about is maybe a mile away."

"How do you know all that?"

Salvadore and Kevin snickered. "'Cause we've lived here all our lives and fish that river pretty regular. That bayou I was tellin' you about leads up to old man Wadler's girlfriend's . . ."

"Wife now," Kevin cut in.

"Right. Though she ain't hardly full growed. When he takes a notion, he uses them boats to run the river and bayou up to her house about three, maybe four miles into Loosiana as the crow flies."

"You sure about that?"

Salvadore cut his eyes at me. "I don't tell no tales."

Kevin slowed and turned onto a narrow ribbon of highway with crumbling shoulders.

"We're almost there now. It ain't far."

"Good. They're waiting there."

Kevin slowed again when we came to the iron bridge. He turned left off the road and onto a steep, well-used two-lane track winding downhill to the river. It was muddy and greasy from the recent rain, and he let gravity do most of the work. I was wondering if he'd be able to get back out since his tires looked about shot to me.

Salvadore pointed. "Somebody's already been down here since it rained. I hope it's your friends."

I squinted through the dirty windshield. "Me, too."

The sun was behind the tops of the trees when he steered around a rusting farm truck melting into the ground and onto a wide, level clearing full of beer cans and bottles and cold firepits.

Perry Hale's truck was parked facing us. Kevin gently slowed to a stop with several yards between us and the pickup. The cab was empty.

The pit of my stomach fell out for a moment, and I wondered if some of Daddy Frank's boys had intercepted my friends. I'd absorbed everything the Williams boys knew about the Wadlers, and knew they were kin to water moccasins.

Before any of us could speak, well-armed shapes appeared at each window. I recognized them right off, but poor Kevin and Salvadore nearly jumped out of their skins.

"Good to see you, boss. Sir, you better kill those headlights." Perry Hale waved toward the road. "We don't need to attract any attention to ourselves."

"Shit, man!" Kevin shut off the motor that ticked in the cool air. "Y'all scared the daylights out of me. I cain't turn the lights off. Wired 'em to come on any time the truck starts." He paused, considering their camouflage clothing. "Y'all army?"

They didn't answer, so I spoke for them. "Perry Hale, these are friends of ours, the Williams boys. They saved my bacon earlier today."

Neither Perry Hale or Yolanda looked too hard into the cab. Instead, they swiveled to keep an eye on our surroundings. Yolanda spoke for them both. "Good to meet y'all, but if I were you, I'd let this guy out of your truck and get gone."

Salvadore opened his door with a pop and slid out so I could scoot across the seat. "You're prob'ly right about that. Mr. Ranger, I believe you now. Y'all take care."

"I owe you one."

"You don't owe me nothin, Mr. Ranger. Here." He opened the door and rooted under the seat for a moment before passing me a worn pump shotgun with a barely legal barrel. "Ain't no plug in here, and it's loaded with double-ought buck. Here's five more shells. Stick 'em in your pocket."

"I'll get it back to you."

"Don't matter. It's probably hot anyways. Drop it in the river when you're done. Y'all take care. Kevin, get us outta here, we ain't got no business on this road no mo'."

Perry Hale and Yolanda were dressed for war. Each carried AR-15-style rifles and wore mid-size MOLLE packs. The tricked-out rifles hanging across their chests looked to be Colts, but I don't know much about them. I'm like a lot of other law-enforcement officers, I have the tools I work with, but not into all the specifics about weaponry I don't own.

"Lead off." I pointed upriver. "That way."

Perry Hale led the way, and I settled into what had become my position in the past, staying in the middle with Yolanda watching the rear. A pleasant breeze kept the skeeters away, and we passed the time in silence broken only by crickets and birds.

The bayou Salvadore mentioned came up right on schedule, a thick gruel of muddy water spilling into the already reddish Sabine and lined with overhanging trees.

A whipporwill called nearby.

I spoke low. "We're halfway there."

Yolanda's voice came over my shoulder. "I think you're right. This is what I saw on the satellite map." We walked another hundred yards before she spoke up again. "What do you want to do when we get there?"

"Find that boy before it's too late. Help'll be here soon, and if we're lucky, that vigilante we've been after'll show up, too." I didn't figure anyone had caught him. The guy seemed to be a charmed traveler, and with the luck he'd already shown, I expected him to come driving up at some point.

Dusk had arrived by the time we reached the boats tied up to a tree. The dirt lane was where Salvadore said it'd be.

I paused and pointed at a game trail that peeled off to the right. "All right, guys. This is where we separate. Salvadore said this winds around that barn up yonder and comes out up near where this lane comes in off the highway. I'm gonna take it and come in from the front. Y'all cover the rear."

"Then what?"

Yolanda's question was a good one. "I don't have any idea."

Chapter 54

Sheriff Buck Henderson pulled up in front of his office where a highway patrol car waited in the parking lot. He stopped next to it and stepped out at the same time Deputy Mills exited his own cruiser.

Buck scanned the lot, making sure they were alone. "You get rid of that product yet?"

Mills popped his trunk. "Not yet, but I'll dump it in a few minutes. Here's the bins you wanted."

Buck clicked a pocket-size flashlight to life and flipped the lid off the nearest box. Bundles of cash wrapped in clear plastic were packed inside. He grinned. "Looks like payday."

Deputy Mills reached in and picked one up. "I've never seen this many hundreds at one time. What's in the others?"

"Let's see." Buck lifted the lid and peered inside. "Why, this ain't nothing but canned goods. Leave it and get the rest."

"What do we do now?"

"We put the money in my car and then pretend you

never saw it. Go dump that product like I said. After tonight, this cash is gonna be ours."

"How so?"

"Because the feds are going to raid Daddy Frank's fertilizer barn tonight. I told them they'd all be there."

"They'll rat us out, too."

"No they won't. Not this family. Most of 'em won't be taken alive, and the others won't talk."

"They'll come after us after they get out of jail."

"Lots of people die in prison." Buck unlocked his trunk and picked up one of the boxes. "Let's get gone."

"Let me check this other bin."

Buck came back at the same time a cargo van appeared on the street and turned slowly on the opposite side of the parking lot. The driver rolled his window down and waved.

Deputy Mills set the blue plastic bin on the edge of his trunk and squinted at the stranger. "Who'n hell's that?"

While their attention was on the van, a loud voice split the silence. "Don't move! Don't move! Hands! Hands! Hands!" Armed men dressed in black and wearing body armor with the letters DEA poured out of the van, aiming shotguns and semiautomatic carbines while at the same time another van skidded to a stop, discharging even more agents.

Startled by the loud commands, Deputy Mills lost his grip on the plastic bin. The lid flipped off, pulling the lead of a friction fuse. The bin exploded, vaporizing Sheriff Buck Henderson, Deputy Mills, and most of the car and saving the good people of Newton, Texas, the cost of two trials.

Chapter 55

The clouds broke, brightening the dripping woods long enough for Tanner Wadler to use the lowering sun over his shoulder to push east. A thick line of brush ahead told him the anomaly in the woods identified a clearing on the other side. Heavy growth depended on sunlight, and he pushed through a tangle of briars and brambles anchored by still more yaupon bushes.

He stumbled through, onto the shoulder of a familiar highway. Recognizing the area, he followed the pavement northeast, not away from the gathering of men at Daddy Frank's fertilizer barn, but toward the turnoff leading right back to it.

One eye swelled shut, he followed the tree-lined ribbon of pavement, frequently checking over his shoulder. If a vehicle appeared, it would take only a couple of steps and he'd be invisible once again. The sun settled behind the pines. It was usually his favorite time of the day, when the light changed, signaling the coming dusk.

The whine of approaching tires ahead gave him time to duck into the pines. A pickup containing a young man with a girlfriend snuggled against his shoulder passed, intent on their conversation.

He stepped back into the clear and traveled a hundred yards before another vehicle approached, this time from behind. He was on a bend in the road and slipped back into the woods. A truck containing a man he recognized cruised well under the speed limit.

It was someone looking for him.

Tanner remained where he was until the truck passed from sight.

Aching, sick, and heartbroken, he continued down the road, stepping into the brush time after time to wait until there was nothing on the road but diminishing taillights. There was a lot of traffic for that time of the day, and he was sure the drivers were people he couldn't trust.

The one truck he wanted to see was driven by Alonzo, and Tanner hoped to be back at the turnoff to the fertilizer barn before he arrived.

Chapter 56

The intersecting lane leading up to the barn looked to be an easy, almost pleasant walk under any other circumstances. As they turned onto the pine needle–covered track, Perry Hale and Yolanda changed in a way I'd seen months earlier. One minute they were simply watchful, and the next they reverted to their military training. Guns came up, their knees slightly bent, and they advanced as if walking into a possible ambush.

We might have been, for all we knew.

Separating, they held close to the trees, in case they needed to duck in a hurry. The faint sound of a slamming car door stopped us. I stopped and spoke softly. "All right. I'm gone. I'm going to slip up on this place and take a look around. They'll act differently if somebody sees me and this badge, but they might go sideways at the sight of two people geared up like you. Y'all stay out of sight unless something happens. Find a place and watch my back, 'cause if I come a runnin', we're gonna have to bug out quick."

Yolanda pointed to the east and the dark woods.

"We'll stay in the trees. But I think you should let us do some looking, too."

Perry Hale slapped me lightly on the shoulder. "Try not to just walk in there like you want to do."

"You're getting to know me pretty well."

"Yeah, that's why we're here." He turned back to Yolanda. "You ready, babe?"

Eyes hidden under the cap pulled down almost to her eyebrows, she drew a deep breath. "Whenever you are."

Perry Hale's attention flicked between me and the far end of the lane, his carbine hanging muzzle down in the middle of his chest. "I'm swinging wide around to the front. You cover the rear." He pointed to one side, then the other and made some kind of motion with his fingers. They separated and disappeared into the woods, leaving me alone in the middle of the lane.

Wondering about their ability to communicate without speaking, I waited for five minutes to give my SRT team members plenty of time, then stepped onto the thin game trail through the woods. Blue jays argued in the trees, and I marveled at how peaceful it was right then but could go sideways in an instant.

I struck out with the twelve-gauge cradled in my left arm, though a lot slower. Understory brush raked my shoulders, and I had to duck several times. It became harder to see as the sun went down. Occasionally briars caught my pants, pulling loose with a soft ripping sound.

Noise from my left told me there was a lot of activity in the unseen barn. More doors slammed. It sounded like a parking lot, and I wondered just how many people were there.

One thing was for certain, we were outnumbered. I hoped my earlier phone calls had jump-started reinforcements.

Chapter 57

The atmosphere in the barn was alive with excitement and expectation. Armed men waited in small groups for Alonzo's arrival with the cash, sitting on bags of fertilizer and on buckets, talking softly.

Daddy Frank was anchored like a deeply rooted tree in the wide aisle running the length of the barn. He checked his watch and waved to Jimmy Don. "As soon as that Semtex gets here, you tell the boys get a package and one of them detonators over there that Alonzo fixed up before he left. There's fresh batteries there, but don't put the damned things in until they get the plastic set on those lines. I want all them to go up at six in the morning."

Four teams of two were assigned to place the explosives on the exposed oil pipeline valves. Standing up to sixteen feet above ground, the valves were much larger than the pipes themselves and weighed up to eight tons. Destroying them would be catastrophic to BranCo in monetary value, public relations, and to the environment as a river of crude oil could pour out for hours before the company managed to shut off the flow.

"Jimmy Don, you and Sammy have the most important job. Get that refinery offline."

Sammy Saxton licked his dry lips. "I have the perfect place to set the charge. It's right close to . . ."

"I don't care where you put it. Just blow the damned thing up." Daddy Frank cut him off. Already thinking of something else, he walked up to the double barn door and stopped just inside. "Where the hell's Buck?" He made eye contact with Boone, who'd found a place in a shadow outside the door so he could watch the lane.

"I tried to call him." Jimmy Don's voice full of concern came from behind. "He didn't answer."

"Well, call him again."

"Yessir."

"Sammy." The old man didn't take his eyes off the darkening woods.

He was farther inside the barn. "Right here."

"You and Clifford Raye take and carry some long guns outside. I don't like all of us being in here without having somebody keep an eye out." He stopped in the door. "Buck woulda already done that, if he was here."

Minutes later, Sammy and the others appeared in the doorway, loading magazines into AK-47 rifles.

"Good. Now you boys go on halfway up the road. No, stop just shy of the highway and wait for Alonzo. Give me a call when he gets here, then make sure nobody's following him in. I wouldn't put it past some of these feds to just let him drive on in big as Dallas and lead him right to us. The way he's been acting, he's liable to have a whole damn train of cars behind him."

Sammy, Clifford Raye, and two other men in jeans and T-shirts ambled down the road, angering the old man. "Goddamn it! I didn't say get there in the morning. Y'all get your asses where I told you."

Knowing the old man's temper, they broke into a jog and disappeared up the road.

A night bird peeped. Tree frogs that had been tuning up broke into a familiar chorus and filled the air with their high-pitched croaks. Daddy Frank remained where he was just inside the door, listening.

"Jimmy Don."

"Yessir."

"Something don't feel right. Get some more boys out here and keep a lookout."

Jimmy Don's eyes flicked to the dog. Mud lay on his stomach, watching all the activity around him. He didn't seem concerned. "What don't feel right?"

Daddy Frank met his son's eyes. "You questioning me don't feel right, for a start."

Chastised, Jimmy Don melted back into a teenage boy afraid of his daddy. "Yessir." He turned. "I need four of y'all out here till Alonzo pulls in. Boys, it's almost go time."

Chapter 58

After paralleling on either side of the lane in near silence for what seemed to be three hundred yards, Perry Hale slowed at the sight of a tired barn squatting in a small clearing in the old-growth forest. Reflecting light from bare bulbs spilled between the cracks of warped, vertical planks. Bright as day on the inside, dim beams escaped through holes in the roof. A pool of yellow spread out from the open back doors.

The air was filled with thousands of tree frogs' shrill songs. He pressed the comm button on his chest. "Got eyes on the barn, maybe fifty yards away."

Yolanda answered immediately. "Got it, too."

Catching glimpses of men moving around inside, Perry Hale angled himself to see down the length of the barn to more than a dozen trucks parked in front. Two armed guards walked into the open at the opposite end. It was dark enough that he couldn't see them clearly, just the outlines of their bodies and glinting reflections of their guns.

A faintly chemical smell competed with the odor of wet pines.

Taking shallow breaths, he crept through the dark woods, placing his feet carefully to avoid dead branches that littered the forest floor. Soon he rounded the barn and found the open lane leading to the highway. Perry Hale settled down beside a bush and pressed the button again, speaking softly. "Around front. I have many armed players."

"Sonny's not going to know where we are if things start happening." Her voice was soft in his ear.

"Knowing him, he's going to find that lane and walk straight up to the door. We just have to make sure no one sneaks up on him from behind."

He heard a crackle and spun just in time to duck a swing that would have taken his head off.

A guy dressed in full woodland camo made a serious mistake. Instead of shooting Perry Hale in the back, the man tried to sever his head with a large bowie knife. The absurdly long blade that looked like a machete sizzled overhead. Shocked that he'd missed the guard who'd been waiting still as a tree, Perry Hale used his rifle to deflect the backhand swipe that was just as hot and dangerous.

His right hand shot out and caught the assailant in the nose with the sound of an elastic snap. Blood exploded as the man's head snapped back and his knees went rubbery. Perry Hale pressed the advantage, grabbing the man's wrist and twisting backward in an acute angle that incapacitated the arm. The knife dropped onto the pine needles under their feet.

Suddenly the guy was yanked backward and Perry Hale saw Yolanda with her arm locked around the guard's neck.

The slender warrior was shorter than the man, and

she used her lower center of gravity to bend him backward. The guy wouldn't quit. He snatched a pistol from the holster on his hip and Perry Hale grabbed the gunman's hand. At the same time, he drew the Ontario Mark 3 knife from its sheath on his belt and buried the blade fast and furious into the man's chest until he dropped.

Yolanda let him go and the body dropped. She leaned in to whisper. "He'd been following you."

"I should have known."

"He was good. You think anyone heard?"

"Not with all these frogs singing. I've never heard them so loud."

"Good.

"You were supposed to be watching the other end of the barn."

She shrugged. "Yeah, well."

"You're out of breath. You gonna need more P.T. when we get back home?"

"I'm in better shape than you, big boy. It's 'cause you're so close."

"Charmer."

Neither looked at the body as they separated and took up positions to cover the barn.

Chapter 59

It was sundown when a glow on the highway told Tanner another vehicle was approaching. He again faded into the trees, only a hundred yards from the turnoff leading to the fertilizer barn until a loaded logging truck was past.

He resumed his walk and soon reached the fifteen-foot-wide cut through the woods. He found a small clear spot in a thick tangle of brush where he could keep an eye on the turnoff. He settled onto the ground with his back against a thick pine and closed his eyes, giving in to the pain still lingering from two beatings and the fear in his stomach.

Fighting the urge to weep, he finally calmed enough to drift into that gray world between sleep and wakefulness. The peace lasted only five minutes before tires slowing on the now-dry pavement brought him fully awake. It could have been those looking for him, but he hoped it was who he'd come to intercept, Uncle Alonzo.

Headlights cut through the gathering gloom, sweeping past his hiding place and nearly blinding him.

Blinking away the spots, he heard a truck stop, idling a few feet away. It took a few moments for his eyes to readjust to the muted light, and when they did, he recognized the model.

Tanner rose with a painful groan and pushed through the understory brush and out to the lane on the passenger side. All four windows were down, and the decaying odor of a rotting corpse made him step back. The dash lights illuminated his uncle slumped behind the wheel.

"Uncle Alonzo?"

White as a ghost, the man slowly raised his eyes and struggled to focus through the open window. "Tanner?" His voice was hoarse and weak.

He stepped to the door. "Yessir." The odor of death was stronger, and he glanced into the back seat to see an object wrapped in a blanket. The dash lights revealed a dark stain on Alonzo's shirt and pants. His eyes widened. "Good God. Your're hurt."

"Nope. Past that. Dyin'."

"That's not you I smell, is it?" The familiar odor of decaying animal corpses was something country people grew up with. Lit by the dash lights, the thing wrapped in the back seat was human shaped. He knew he'd scream if it rose up and started moving. "What's that?"

"Your Aunt Betty."

He recoiled from the window.

"Easy, son. I just brought her home."

"Uncle Alonzo, I can barely make out what you're sayin'. You're talking like you had a stroke."

"Doped up with pain pills."

"Look, you can't drive up there, especially not with

her like that. Daddy Frank's waitin' on you, and he's been looking for *me*."

Alonzo picked up a mini flashlight from the penholder in front of the console and flicked it on, directing it at Tanner's face. "Looks like he's already found you."

"Both him and Dad."

Alonzo pulled himself upright and squared his shoulders. The effort cleared his speech, at least for the moment. "I've looked in the mirror and seen the same presents from both of them bastards."

"You need to leave. Go somewhere else."

Instead of answering, Alonzo tilted his head back and emptied the contents of a plastic pill bottle into his mouth. He swallowed, gagging, then swallowed again. Obviously trying to retain the contents of his stomach, he pitched the empty container into the brush and waited before speaking. "No place else to go. I doubt I'll make it to the end of this lane."

"I've been waitin' on you to get here. Turn around and let's get gone." Tanner circled the hood and put his hand on the door handle. "Here, let me drive."

Alonzo held up a hand covered in dried blood. "No. You get out of here."

"Come go with me."

"I done told you. I'm dead already. I'm gonna drive this truck right inside that barn and set it off. When I'm done, you'll be the only one left. I put that money in the bank I told you about. Mailed you the key. You and Donine go start over somewheres else."

Tears rolled down Tanner's cheeks. "That's all over and done with."

Alonzo didn't seem to hear him. He reached into the penholder again and picked up a homemade detonator, keeping his thumb away from the simple silver toggle switch. "I'm gonna pull into the barn right up next to Daddy Frank and set it off. When I do, this whole damn riverbottom's gonna go up, so you get on outta here."

"My daddy's there. I don't want you to kill my daddy."

"You said he beat you."

"Yeah, but I don't want him dead. Come go with me."

Alonzo gave the young man's hand a pat. "You're a good boy, Tanner. Just born in the wrong family."

He slowly accelerated down the narrow road, leaving Tanner behind. The young man watched for a minute, then trudged back onto the two-lane, wondering if Donine had found the good-bye letter he'd left on their dresser.

Tanner took the phone from his pocket once again and saw that he had two full bars. Wracked with indecision, he finally dialed Jimmy Don's number to warn him about what was coming.

Chapter 60

From his vantage point in front of the barn, Perry Hale saw even more men walking around with trouble in their hands. Armed men took up positions behind the parked cars.

He pressed the comm button. "You copy?"

"Yep."

"I have eyes on a small army."

"Roger that. I see two who just came out the back."

"You see Sonny?"

"Not at the moment."

"You want to pull back?"

"Not yet. Let's see what he does." Perry Hale snugged the stock of his AR against his shoulder and waited. Sixty seconds later, gunshots echoed through the trees

Fifty yards away from the rear of the barn, Yolanda saw two armed men rise from the bushes at the pops of firearms and rush inside through the rear doors. From her angle, she could see inside the length of the barn.

Men took up weapons and sprinted toward the front, disappearing from sight.

Everyone was facing the opposite direction toward the lane leading in from the highway. That meant their backs were to her.

She smiled.

Chapter 61

Alonzo held the steering wheel in a death grip, barely capable of steering, though the truck was rolling along at idle speed.

"We're almost there, baby, and then we can both sleep. We need to sleep."

I sure am glad. I'm tired and you are, too. We need to rest.

His legs were cold, and both hands were almost numb. "Just a few more minutes."

Fifty yards down the lane, Alonzo groaned when his headlights picked out two men standing in the middle of the lane. Sammy and Clifford Raye waited, automatic rifles resting in the crook of their arms.

Clifford Raye held up a hand to stop. His face relaxed and he smiled, apparently recognizing Alonzo's truck. He approached the driver's side, and Sammy stepped up to the passenger door.

Think, boy.

I'm so tired.

You want to kill that old man in there, you gotta think. Study hard!

Alonzo shook his head to clear his vision. The agony boiling in his stomach had subsided for the moment, allowing him a few moments of relief.

What to do?

Back through the smeared, bug-splattered windshield, a massive shape the size of an elephant ambled across the road.

My imagination's playing tricks on me.

Maybe these guys ain't real, like that elephant. That wasn't real, was it?

Sammy spoke through the open window. "Alonzo. Glad you made it. What the hell's that smell?"

Men there with rifles. They're here to kill me.

That old sonofabitch's trying to ambush me.

"Betty, we're goin' home." He picked up the Glock that had been laying in his lap, expecting it to be heavy as a cinder block. Instead, it came up as if made of Styrofoam and centered on Sammy's chest.

Two muzzle flashes were blinding in the darkness. Strobe-like, they froze the startled look on the man's face as the 9mm rounds traveled only a few inches to blow out his heart. Sammy's finger involuntarily tightened on the trigger as he fell backward, sending a stream of 5.56 rounds through the truck's door, Alonzo's body, and Betty's corpse in the back seat.

In incredibly slow motion, Alonzo swung the pistol toward Clifford Raye, who stumbled backward, trying to swing the Russian-made rifle into position. He was too close, and the barrel rapped the side of the truck cab. "No no no, it's me . . ."

The Glock hammered a third time, then a fourth. The first caught Clifford Raye in the clavicle, shoving him backward. The second entered just under his left eye and blew out the back of his head.

Alonzo punched the accelerator and fired as he passed a man in a hat. He threw a shot at him and a shotgun boomed. A hot dagger plunged through both cheeks. His left shoulder went completely numb, and new fires arose in his side.

Feeling as if he were weightless, Alonzo laid the pistol on the padded console and focused on steering down the drive. The tires veered into brush, and the fender crunched against a tree. He overcompensated and rebounded across the shallow ruts to glance off another tree like a bumper car.

The shotgun boomed again, disintegrating the back glass. Lighter cracks of gunfire reached his ears, and his foot slipped off the accelerator. Quickly losing speed in the soft sand, the pickup rolled down the lane at school-zone speed.

Warm yellow light spilling from the open barn doors in the distance became his target.

His vision dimming, Alonzo's fingers searched for the detonator that wasn't where it was supposed to be.

Chapter 62

As I waited at the edge of the dark lane with the sawed-off twelve-gauge across my arm, my mind was going ninety-to-nothing. The smart thing would have been to wait for dawn and any support that might come from the feds, local law enforcement, or my Rangers.

On the other hand, the idea of plastic explosives scared the pee-waddlin' out of me, and the truth was, I wanted that vigilante. Sometimes I suffer from narrow focus and have to get away from everything in order to think things through.

After dragging around the state behind this guy, having people run me off the road and wrecking my truck, my blood was up.

This is why you're not home, dummy. Working during the day and spending the nights with your wife. You go off half-cocked and look where that gets you.

The Old Man's voice was as real as if he'd been standing beside me, and that showed how mad I was getting.

Headlights appeared in the distance and bounced up and down as the vehicle approached on the rough road.

They stopped a hundred yards away and I heard voices. Flitting through the trees, I made my way close enough to see two shadows materialize from the woods and stop a light-colored truck. The interior lights defined the weapons in their hands. A flashlight came on in the cab, giving me a great look at all three men.

The driver was white as a ghost.

It looked like the guy I'd shot in the RV park.

Is this my guy?

Excitement rose in my throat at the same time the peaceful evening ended with the pops and flashes of firearms that strobed the pickup.

Men fell, and the driver accelerated like he was in a school zone. He shot at me and I returned fire.

Chapter 63

A whip-thin man with steel gray hair stepped out of a black Expedition parked in the middle of the two-lane highway a quarter of a mile from the turnoff leading to the barn. ATF agent Gerald Marrs waited for his men to secure the area blocked off by a dozen similar vehicles.

More SUVs arrived, painting the dark trees with their headlights. Another Expedition crept through the blockade, discharging DEA agent Hart Lowell, who'd been cut from the same cloth as Marrs.

Surrounded by men in tactical gear and bristling with firearms, Marrs and Lowell met over several pages spread out over one of the SUVs. Since the primary information referred to plastic explosives, Marrs took charge.

"I'd rather not do this tonight, but the call I received from a Texas Ranger named Sonny Hawke suggested that these guys may try to use these explosives tonight or first thing in the morning. We can't wait."

Planting his feet, Lowell crossed his arms. "Like I told you on the phone, these guys are suspects in the shooting of my agents. Thanks for the call. Just between you and me, I don't care if we take these people in while they're still breathing."

"My thoughts exactly." Marrs held out a printed satellite map. "We drive to here." He pointed. "Then we form a skirmish line and move through the woods to the clearing. That will get us close enough to simply step out into the clearing around the barn and take them into custody."

"Sounds simple."

Marrs shook his head. "It won't be. Something always happens in the dark."

Everyone on the road ducked at the sound of gunfire. Realizing it was coming from farther down the wooded lane and no one was shooting at them, they straightened. Lowell's face hardened as he waved at his men. "Like you said, something always happens."

A line of vehicles turned down the lane as the men from both agencies melted into the wet pine forest.

Chapter 64

Daddy Frank and Jimmy Don tensed at the sound o gunshots echoing through the trees, which told on story. The string of automatic weapon fire after tha added punctuation. Deep shotgun booms added new chapters.

Jimmy Don weighed the pistol in his hand. "Look like the boys ran into something." Agitated, he pace back and forth. "What do you think happened?"

The old man snorted in disgust. "What makes yo think *I* know? Y'all get ready."

They listened to the night sounds that resumed afte several minutes. Daddy Frank's men waited behind several of the parked trucks like defenders behind embankments. Watching the darkness with the intensity of a wild animal, Boone unsnapped Mud's chain and led the pit bull to the door by his collar, then released the dog, who charged into the darkness with a roar.

Daddy Frank shouted. "Hey!"

Boone followed the dog into the woods.

"He turned my damned dog loose!" With no other

way to express his anger, Daddy Frank shoved his son. "Why'd he let my dog go?"

Jimmy Don snickered. "Your dog let your dog go. That's funny."

"Not one damned bit, it ain't!"

The growl of an approaching diesel truck reached their ears. A minute later a pair of headlights flickered around the slight curve leading to the barn. The white truck struck a parked pickup with a glancing blow, straightened, and plowed through an opening between two other vehicles that was too narrow for the truck's body width. Punching through, it headed for the barn doors as Daddy Frank's men opened up with everything they had.

Muzzle flashes from deep in the woods were followed by a shriek, and then a string of more rapid shots.

A faint shout came through the blasts. "Dogs!"

Seconds later, Boone charged back into the barn as men poured outside to join the others. The razor in his hand dripped blood, and his shirt was splashed red. "Daddy, we have to go!"

With the agility of a man thirty years his junior, Daddy Frank spun and charged halfway down the barn to a battered blue and white 1968 Ford pickup backed into a stall. Boone jumped behind the wheel and twisted the key.

The starter whirred on the old truck, refusing to catch.

Moving at barely a crawl, a battered pickup that looked like it had been through a car compressor knocked one of the barn doors off and plowed into the barn with Alonzo slumped behind the wheel.

Shouts and commands came from outside. "Federal agents! Put down your weapons!"

A fusillade from the barn drowned the orders. Heavily armed agents in battle gear flitted through the trees. Tactical lights snapped on in the woods, seeking out the armed men both inside the barn and taking cover behind the randomly parked vehicles.

"The feds are here!" A bearded man who was one of Daddy Frank's third cousins grabbed the handle on the Ford's passenger side.

Daddy Frank shouldered the man off balance. He crashed through a stall with the crack of snapping wood, striking his head on a support post and knocking him unconscious. The old man shouted at Boone through the open window. "Don't flood it, you idiot!"

The starter ground down again. With an expression of complete calm, Boone waited, staring at the darkness through the rear doors.

Jimmy Don and a second cousin named Scotty saw Daddy Frank yank the door open and slide into the seat. "Daddy! Wait!"

Carrying handguns, they charged down the long hall, intending to jump into the bed of the escaping truck.

Jimmy Don waved his arms, hoping to get their attention. "Daddy! Don't leave us!"

Furious, Scotty raised a Sig Sauer. "They're leaving anyway. I'm gonna shoot both them sonsabitches!"

"Not *my* Daddy!" Jimmy Don shot Scotty in the side with his Glock and ran. The man slammed face-first onto the ground.

* * *

Time slowed for Alonzo. There were men in tactical vests shouting from the woods for him to stop. Somehow the Glock was back in his hand, and he fired through the open passenger window. The woods rocked with return fire that punched even more holes in the truck's sheet-metal sides. Glass exploded, covering everything inside the cab with glittering shards.

Hot lances of pain in Alonzo's shoulder, neck, and side would have been debilitating if he hadn't been stoned from the drugs. Holding a gaping wound across his neck, Alonzo felt the gush of hot blood pulse through his fingertips and soak his shirt.

Randomly parked pickups and farm trucks blocked his way, but he pressed the foot feed and plowed through them as if he were driving a bulldozer. The hand holding the pistol was suddenly useless and it fell limp across the console as the truck finally reached the barn and punched through a dizzying swirl of scrambling men. Metal crunched as he sideswiped parked vehicles. His target in sight, he let go of his neck and steered through the open doors with a bloody left hand. Men danced out of the way as he drove halfway into the barn, crashing into the bed of a blue-and-white pickup stalled in the wide hallway.

The impact slammed the truck sideways into a support post that cracked like a falling timber. Hand-hewn rafters and support beams collapsed under the stresses of added weight. The entire side of the barn sagged, and a cloud of dust filled the air.

Half of the hayloft landed on the hood of Alonzo's truck in an explosion of ancient dust at the same time the light went from his eyes. His dead hand opened and the Glock slipped free to hang off his finger through the trigger guard. Directly underneath was the detonator's toggle switch.

On the lane leading to the barn, a line of headlights from a variety of vehicles snapped on, discharging a secondary swarm of men in combat gear. Tactical lights flickered in the woods, attached to rifles fitted against professional shoulders and finding targets behind the parked cars and inside the barn.

Stern voices barked commands. "Federal agents! Drop your weapons!"

The orders were swallowed by more gunfire from inside the barn.

Chapter 65

Damn, there was a lot going on all of a sudden. I instinctively knew the guy in the white truck was my vigilante. It might have been because he shot two people without blinking an eye, or maybe it was nothing more than instinct.

But all of a sudden the whole world blew up and I never expected to see so many men with guns in one place. I hollered at him to stop, but the guy swung a pistol and shot at me. The pump shotgun in my hands boomed and I was sure I'd hit him, but he kept driving like he was wearing body armor.

I threw another shell at him, and a voice in the distance hollered for me to put down my gun. I recognized the commands that came from law-enforcement officers. I think I heard someone say they were federal agents and maybe DEA, but before I could answer, drop the shotgun, or say kiss my ass, more than one gun opened up in my direction.

"Don't shoot! Texas Ranger!"

Flashes in the darkness told me they couldn't hear or weren't listening. Either way, I spun around and took off at a dead run to gain some distance until thos boys out there cooled down.

Return gunfire came from the barn, taking thei attention off of me. There was no use in trying to b quiet. Shoving fresh shells into the shotgun, I ducke into the edge of the trees for cover and sprinted bac where I came from, knowing Perry Hale and Yoland would be there for cover.

The idea was to disappear until the gun battle wa over, then come out when everyone had calmed dow enough to see my empty hands and badge. Vertica streaks of light coming from the barn's old planks gav me enough illumination to see my way. I kept one ey on the side, as I raced past a line of various-size closed doors lining the outside wall. Skinny trees an brush grew against the warped sides. The hammerin echoes of the firefight followed me like a physica cloud.

While one side of my brain concentrated on gettin me the hell out of there, the other worked on the puzzl that was the vigilante. He'd come back, but instead o making his delivery, he came shooting.

Good lord! That truck might have been full of Sem tex, just like the kid had said. Digging in my heels, came to a stop near the back corner of the barn. needed to warn the feds, even though it had been m who called them about the explosives.

A round took a white chunk out of a nearby tree. ducked. Everyone was shooting at everyone else.

Wait. Why was my vigilante shooting at *them wher he came in*? More pieces clicked into place. He'd bee traveling across the state, settling scores. What if thos

cores extended to his crazy-ass family? Was this one
ast issue, to go in a blast of glory?

Blast. Good God. Perry Hale had mentioned earlier
that if he had plastic explosives and wanted to take
people out, it would be clean and efficient. If I had a
truck full of plastic explosive, and was bent on suicide,
d drive straight into the hornet's nest before setting it
ff.

Brambles tangled my feet and I fell face-first, land-
ng hard enough to see stars. Desperate, I rose to my
ull height and pulled free of the thorns. "Perry Hale!
'olanda! Explosives! Run!"

If I was in there and people came driving in like
hat, I'd find the nearest exit, and that was only feet
way from where I tripped. The gunfire increased in
olume just as the world lit up with bright headlights
nd the roar of even more engines from the opposite
nd of the barn.

Great. They called in reinforcements.

Seconds later, an old 1968 Ford pickup shot outside
nd started down a two-track trail barely wide enough
or the two-tone body. The truck's back glass exploded.
t slewed for a moment and crunched into a pine tree,
hattering the left headlight.

Two men rushed out with pistols in their hands,
ooking as if they intended to roll into the bed. They
aw me and dug in their heels when I hollered and
aised the twelve-gauge to my shoulder. "Texas Ranger!
hrow up your hands!"

Another round from the engagement out front
lammed into a pine tree only a foot or so away. Splin-
ers flew, causing me to duck at the same time the run-
ing men brought weapons to bear.

The bores of their pistols looked huge, and I tangle in the briars again, which dropped me to my knees From a distance of only twenty feet, I saw my ow death in those muzzles. The weapon in the grip of prematurely gray-haired man spat fire an instant befor both men wilted from what sounded like two distinc streams of automatic-weapon fire that followed ther to the ground.

Only two people I knew would shoot like that unti the threat was neutralized. Perry Hale and Yolanda They'd saved my bacon again.

Pulling free of the thorny vines, I charged towar the pickup that shifted into reverse. "Get out of th truck!"

It backed up a couple of feet before the rear tire spun, filling my face with damp sand.

Chapter 66

Alonzo knocked the blue-and-white truck sideways, collapsing half of the barn. Boone stomped the gas, dragging the entire right side against a support beam, and further weakening the structure.

"Get us outta here, boy!" Daddy Frank's voice came through the open window, hoarse with fury.

Seconds later they shot out the door, followed by Jimmy Don and his high school buddy Spencer, who were running close behind, intent on jumping into the truck bed. They were within inches of escape when a man in a western hat appeared just outside the barn. He threw a shotgun to his shoulder.

"Texas Ranger! Throw up your hands!"

Gunfire splintered the bark of a tree only a couple of feet from the Ranger, staggering him.

Spencer dug in with his heels, bringing up a Smith and Wesson pistol The lawman holding the shotgun stumbled in the dim light.

From the darkness, an extremely accurate stream o
lead plucked at Spencer's shirt. He grunted and stum
bled sideways, still trying to raise the pistol. Bullet
followed him to the ground until he lay still.

Jimmy Don suddenly went completely numb from a
second river of lead, and the last thing he saw were in
credibly fast muzzle blasts coming from two position
in the dark woods. He died in the glow of warm yellow
light, wondering how it could have all gone so wrong.

Chapter 67

With the two threats down, Perry Hale pressed the comm button as soon as he lowered the rifle. "Good shootin'! You heard him! Go go go!"

Yolanda flitted through the trees like an oiled ghost, away from the barn at a dead run. They couldn't risk being caught by the federal agents who were intent on shooting at everyone they saw. Neither of the veterans intended to engage American law-enforcement officers. It was time to get gone.

Gunfire swelled behind them. Armed men loyal to Daddy Frank rushed out the front doors, doing their best to escape in any vehicle that could still run. They were met by intense gunfire from a swarm of federal agents who seemed to appear out of nowhere.

Tactical lights mounted on automatic weapons cut through the night.

"Drop your weapons! Drop 'em!"

"Federal agents!"

The commands came too late, and the barn's defenders ignored the instructions. Muzzle flashes from the woods revealed agents wearing glowing DEA and ATF insignia on their vests.

Daddy Frank's men had nothing to lose. They poured it on the agents, who hadn't expected such a ferocious response. Hearing the rising intensity of battle, Senior Agent Marrs issued orders over his VOX radio to pull back. He had no intention of fighting a frontal assault.

Like ghosts, the agents ceased firing and fell back with practiced precision.

Marrs had a better plan, and it would come from up above.

Staying low, Perry Hale dashed through the trees using his own dimmed flashlight. They'd taped the lenses, allowing only a slit of light through. He rushed past Yolanda, who fell in behind and matched his pace. The gunfire fell off as they gained distance.

She followed for more than two hundred yards before her voice came through his earpiece. "Sonny!"

Perry Hale didn't slow. "He's all right. I imagine he's hauling ass, too."

She caught up with him and grabbed the strap of his MOLLE pack. "Stop!"

He spun. "What!" They no longer needed the earpieces.

"He may be hurt."

"He's told us to run if the feds showed up. That's what we're doing. Those guys back there were so jacked up they'd've shot us before we told them who we are."

"We can't just *leave* him."

He saw the flash in her eyes and calmed. "Didn't you hear what he said? He told us to run, and my job is o protect you, too."

"It can't be like that."

"It is."

"Dammit!" She scanned the area. "But we just found im again."

His voice was flat. "So have they."

That was the moment lights appeared from their left nd they realized they'd stopped at the edge of the leared corridor through the pines.

She glanced down at the lane illuminated by the noon. "We're gonna have a talk about this, this situa- ion of ours when we get . . ." She quit talking when he headlights on a moving truck bounced up and lown, flickering in the trees.

Chapter 68

The truck that had punched out against the pine tree threw dirt in my face. I ducked my chin, using the hat brim to protect my face. Because of that, I didn't see Perry Hale or Yolanda at all, but that's what they were good at.

Just like them, I needed to get away from the chaos at the other end of the barn before I got shot. Those guys on my side were focused on one thing, targets. Even though I wore a badge, there was still the chance of getting shot.

Because the driver stomped the accelerator so hard it took several long moments for the worn tires to get a grip on the sand and pine needles. I don't know what possessed me to grab the tailgate as the truck accelerated through the darkness, but I did. I dropped the shotgun and grabbed onto the tailgate with both hands. The trailer hitch cracked my shin, and I stifled a scream.

There's not a farmer, rancher, or pickup driver who hasn't walked around the back of a truck and cracked his shin on the hitch sticking out like a scythe. We all know it's there, but we do it anyway and when we hit

he damn thing, it makes the rest of us laugh like lu-
atics every time, because we've all done it.

My eyes watered, and I barely had time to take two
unning steps before jumping onto the back bumper.
'he rear tires hit something, bucking the rear end into
he air and flipping me up and over into the bed full of
arm trash, beer cans, wire, and empty sacks that once
robably held feed or fertilizer. An empty plastic
ucket bounced up and over the back.

*There it is again. When am I gonna learn not to be
o damned impulsive?*

Right then, there were more pressing matters as I
ounced around in the trash.

A round ricocheted off the back of the cab, causing
he driver and passenger inside to duck. Another bullet
unched through the tailgate, hitting a spare lying in
he bed. It jumped, air escaping with a loud hiss. The
aillight reflector to my right exploded.

As the truck accelerated, I lay as still as possible,
vaiting to see what would come next.

That's when I realized I'd lost my hat, what there
vas left of it.

Chapter 69

Boone's eyes flicked to the Ford's shattered side mirror at the same time a white plastic bucket flipped up and over the tailgate. His bloody left hand slipped on the hard skinny steering wheel.

On the other side of the cab, Daddy Frank looked over his shoulder at the broken, frosted back glass. Unable to see outside, he squinted into the cracked side mirror at the barn disappearing in the trees. "Alonzo set us up?"

"Yes." Boone squinted through the glass. "It all fits."

"Good job." Daddy Frank pointed. "Let the feds have him. He never was worth a shit anyway. We take the river. The boat's still there. We take out at Shi'Ann's dock."

Boone knew exactly where he was talking about. He'd been there only a few hours earlier. "Why don't we take out at the iron bridge at the highway?"

"Don't question me. I have a plan."

"Where will we go?"

"Why, to Mexico, of course. There's nothing to stop me from simply driving across the border."

"Then what?"

"I have more money than God, son. I can live like a king anywhere I want in the years I have left."

Chapter 70

"Somebody's coming." They'd almost reached the river when Perry Hale dropped to a knee, Yolanda right with him.

A blue-and-white pickup rolled down the little clear track using nothing but its running lights. Perry Hale and Yolanda knelt behind the line of understory brush growing in the cleared edges of the trace.

The truck passed, only two feet away, and in the glow of the rising moon, Perry Hale saw an old man riding in the passenger seat. A bald apparition drove and he wondered if the man was wearing some kind of mask.

But it was the next sight that shocked him so badly he almost burst out in tension-fueled hysterical laughter.

From back against the tailgate, moonlight revealed Sonny Hawke's bare head rising above the bed to look around. He saw Yolanda start and gave them a tiny wave, then flicked his hand for them to run.

They ran, even harder.

Chapter 71

Glocks aren't that heavy, made from nylon-polymer called Polymer 2, but the dangling pistol was enough to stretch the tendon of Alonzo's nerveless finger until it slipped off the end.

The simple flick of the three-dollar toggle switch shot current down the wires and into the Semtex plastic explosive he'd packed under his seat, in two hidden storage bins under the back floor mat and in the cargo space under the back seat. The resulting explosion equaling nearly two hundred pounds of TNT atomized Alonzo, Betty, and the truck.

The old wooden barn itself was obliterated, and the Wadler crime family ceased to exist in a millisecond. Trees blown outward from the epicenter of the blast lay in ordered patterns, like iron filings aligned to a magnet.

The federal agents who'd pulled back to a prearranged point only minutes before were lucky, even though they weren't completely out of the woods.

The line of DEA, ATF, and FBI vehicles were protected from the blast itself, but falling pines knocked loose from their shallow root systems were as dangerous as grenades to the men retreating through the woods. Stronger hardwoods like hickory, oak, and pecan survived the energy from the blast radius. Surprisingly, only two agents in the somewhat protected line of SUVs were killed.

DEA agent Gerald Marrs kicked open the back door of his black Suburban and pulled himself out. Up and down the line, fallen pine trees looked like giant tiddly-winks scattered over the vehicles. "Son of a bitch!" He was relieved to see ATF Agent Hart Lowell appear from behind a downed tree laying square across the hood of his SUV. "Hart, that tip was right."

Five minutes later, stunned agents who'd been involved in the early skirmish against the barn's defenders staggered into the now-blocked lane lit by the bright clear stars and moon overhead.

Running as fast as possible through the dark woods, a massive detonation threw Yolanda and Perry Hale to their knees. The blast wave of supersonic pressure slammed the tall pines overhead, bending them to near impossible curves.

She landed hard, hands over her head as the wallop of compressed air felt like a sledgehammer. Perry Hale fell on top of her, almost knocking the breath from both of them. They didn't have time to lay there long. Even though they'd gained enough distance to get clear of the blast zone, seemingly random trees began crashing to the ground.

Perry Hale rolled off, scanning upward. "We gotta move!"

Yolanda rose to her knees and finally caught her breath. "I'd move faster if you hadn't fell on me."

A fifty-foot loblolly pine weighing almost a ton toppled with a crash only twenty yards away, vibrating the ground under their feet. Yolanda bolted to her feet and charged toward the dirt road. "We have to get out of these woods."

An unseen tree collapsed with a splintering roar. In the distance, still more trees cracked and went down, taking smaller, weaker vegetation with them.

They broke out onto the road just in time to see a pair of taillights wink out far ahead.

Chapter 72

At first I thought someone had detonated a nuclear device behind the pickup truck taking me down to the river. The enormous blast lit up the sky, only seconds before a tremendous shock wave pushed the truck like a giant hand. Trees crashed in the darkness on both sides. My head rang as if someone had whacked me with a baseball bat.

Taking advantage of the explosion, I flipped over the tailgate and dropped to the ground. The truck continued on for a short distance before it finally stopped with a squeal of worn-out brakes. The driver killed the engine and the gurgling sound of the Sabine took its place.

The air that had been filled with the croaks of a million frogs singing in the glory of the recent rain was silent. Beyond the blast zone, the shallow root systems of weak, diseased, or dead trees anchored in nothing but sand gave up their tenuous hold. In that vacuum, the splintering sounds of falling trees crashing to the ground made me worry about Yolanda and Perry Hale.

A low bellow punctuated the chorus, followed by a

loud splash. I didn't know for sure, but I imagined it to be an aggravated gator.

The men in the truck didn't waste any time in opening the doors. The dome light was bright as the sun and revealed that strange driver. He was the guy I'd seen back at the Evening Star RV Park, the one who'd shot his friend in the head. Something was strange about him. He had to have been wearing a mask, because I'd never seen anything like his rubber face that was smooth and slack.

An old man I took to be Daddy Frank stepped out and slammed the door. "The boat's right over there."

The other guy answered, but nothing moved but his jaw, his voice wet and mushy. "Careful here. The mud's slick."

The old man raised his voice. "You boys out here?"

"Don't move, or we'll blow you in half."

I froze at the order coming from behind me. Two voices rose from the darkness back there. "Here, Daddy Frank." I glanced over my shoulder to see a pair of armed men in camouflage clothing step from the trees and into the road. They both carried shotguns that couldn't miss at that range. "Look what *we* found."

The old man flicked on a flashlight, shining it directly in my eyes. "I told y'all somebody might come up from the river."

"He was in the back of your truck."

"Do tell."

I held out both hands to keep from being shot. Ignoring me, Baldy circled the front of the truck, heading toward the black ribbon of water. I had a clear line of sight to the old man, but there was nothing I could do with two guys behind me that I couldn't see.

"What do you want us to do with him?"

Daddy Frank Wadler lowered the flashlight and turned away as if dismissing a mouse caught in a trap. "Kill him and then foller me in the other boat."

He and Baldy disappeared toward the water. One of them slipped on the muddy bank, and the old man cursed. "I told you it was slick. The river's up with all that rain. It'll take you off if you fall in."

I used their conversation as cover and spoke over my shoulder. "Y'all don't want to shoot me."

One of the voices was raspy. "Why not?"

I held up both hands. "Because I have people out here who'll kill you if you do. Disappear, and they'll let you go."

"You're lyin'." Raspy Voice spoke again.

I heard the sound of a safety clicking off, and then two streams of reports that came from suppressed automatic rifles killed them deader'n nickel coffee.

Both men lay in heaps not ten yards away.

"Told you."

Perry Hale and Yolanda rose from crouched positions and stepped forward.

I kept my hands up. "Hey, it's me."

"We knew that." Perry Hale swung the muzzle of his rifle toward the river.

Breathing hard and keeping an eye out in the direction of the now-burning barn, Yolanda moved close. She reached out and touched my shoulder. "Are you all right?"

"I'm fine. Y'all hurt?"

Perry Hale's voice was gruff, full of testosterone and exertion. "We're fine. I don't know who those two out there on the river are, but I'd bet they were danger-ous as hell."

"I think the old man is Daddy Frank Wadler, the one who runs this whole sorry-assed clan, and he just dis-appeared down the bank over yonder with some other thing wearing a mask. I suppose it scares people and gives him an edge."

"Was that our target back there in what was the barn?"

That gal was like a dog with a bone. We had all the excitement around us that we could handle, but she wanted who we'd come after. "I got a good idea the one that set off the explosion was our guy."

"Who you think was doing all the shooting?"

"The feds I called in earlier. I say we lay low to see what happens back there, but I want this Daddy Frank guy."

A nearby tree crashed to the ground, making us all jump.

Perry Hale nodded once. "Let's take him." Without waiting for an answer, he brought his rifle to high ready. Yolanda paced him, and I followed them down to the river, looking back over my shoulder at the growing glow from the burning barn, and hoping all those men had survived the blast.

Chapter 73

Movement gives prey away and in some cases the predator.

His hand on the side of an aluminum johnboat sticking halfway into the current, Daddy Frank pointed back the way they came as multiple shots echoed over the bottoms. "Something. Check that out."

"I'll look." The moment his back was turned, Daddy Frank produced a short-barreled revolver from his pocket.

Dogs like you'll eventually turn on their owners.

"You had no right to turn my dog loose." He shot Boone. "Besides, it's every man for himself now."

Boone grunted and fell forward, slipping down the muddy bank toward the river.

Partially blinded by the muzzle flash, the old man fired again, the blast echoing across the water. Blinking away the spots, he shifted his focus, not looking directly at where Boone's body lay, but to the side, using his peripheral vision.

Boone was gone.

Maybe he slipped into the water.

Not believing his own deduction and frightened for the first time in decades, Daddy Frank wasted no time. He put one foot into the flat-bottom boat and pushed off. The current immediately caught the light watercraft and took it swiftly downriver.

Fearful that it would tip, he bent low and crawled to the back to sit on the rear seat in front of a small tenhorse outboard motor. He pumped the bulb on a rusty gas tank and flipped the engine's choke. He yanked the cord and twisted the handle to give it gas.

The engine coughed and died.

The current running high with runoff took the boat sideways. He yanked once again with the same result. Glancing back upstream, the old man braced his feet and jerked the starter cord with all his might. The engine coughed again and caught with a roar and a cloud of exhaust. Straddling the seat, he settled himself and twisted the throttle with his left hand.

The boat responded immediately and swung around, headed downstream.

Staying in the middle of the channel, he roared away to a dock he'd fished for years, the one jutting into the river only yards from Shi'Ann's quiet house.

The escape plan dissolved when two intense beams of light came around a bend in the river. Side-by-side cruisers running wide open meant one thing. The law.

Turning so sharp a spray of water sheeted the surface, he reversed direction and headed back the way he came.

Knowing the Thicket like the back of his hand, the old man had another idea.

If I can't get away on the water, I'll use the woods. You bastards don't have a snowball's chance in Hell of catching me.

Chapter 74

I instinctively ducked at the sound of a nearby gunshot. Beside me, Yolanda took a knee and brought her weapon to her shoulder. Perry Hale did the same, and we waited. The frog chorus paused. The bottoms held its breath.

Another bang in the darkness close by was absorbed by the trees. We waited some more.

Sensing it was over, a few frogs in the distance tuned up again, and Perry Hale rose. He pointed toward the river and moved out. I followed as Yolanda dropped in to cover the rear. We crept forward in single file along the edge of the woods, close enough to see the silvery, roiling Sabine, but deep enough for cover.

A familiar roar filled the air as an outboard caught.

"They're getting away." Perry Hale broke into a half-run, angling into the open lane, rifle to his shoulder.

A few more steps brought us to the edge of the woods and the riverbank. The low moon reflected off the river's surface, giving us a good sight picture of a long, flat boat motoring away.

Yolanda peeled a piece of tape off her tactical light and flicked it on. She swept the river with the softened beam that was half as bright as usual. "There were two. I see one."

The .45 held close to my chest, I edged sideways to see down the riverbank. "Could have been a little dispute about who was gonna drive."

"The winner's getting away." Perry Hale crept forward at the same time the sound of two heavy engines filled the air, followed by the high whine of the old man's outboard coming back in our direction.

All three engines were drowned by the roar of a helicopter coming from the direction of the barn. A searchlight bright as the sun lit up the world and probed the river.

Movement attracts attention. I froze. "Wait."

The light's glow lit up the surface of the water. I could see neither of my friends, and wondered how they'd disappeared so quickly. Moving nothing but my eyes, I found Yolanda on one knee again, partially under a yaupon. Standing, Perry Hale had become part of an oak tree growing over the bank.

The helicopter banked, first lighting up the truck, I imagined, then following the cleared lane to the riverbank. The light swept the bank, moving downstream. It banked again and steadied.

"The boat!" A loudspeaker blasted orders. "You in the boat. Beach now and don't move!"

Three loud bangs caused the helicopter to flit to the side like a dragonfly. It had to be the old man below, firing at the helicopter with a handgun. A long

ause was interrupted by automatic return fire. Muz-
le flashes told me someone in the chopper was light-
ng the boat up.

Perry Hale relaxed. "Sounds like . . ."

That's when a dripping, howling wraith appeared at
is side.

Chapter 75

I've never been so scared in my life. The soaking we
screaming booger that simply materialized and grabbe
Perry Hale was the thing of nightmares. I've fought me
up close and personal, and in those encounters, the
faces were always twisted in rage.

This terrifying attack from the guy in the mask wa
surreal. Perry Hale made a sound in his throat that I'v
only heard once, right then and there, and never war
to hear again. It was a sound of dread, of primordia
genetic fear of the unknown.

The thing howled long and loud through a mout
that simply opened when its jaw dropped. Yolanda an
I were a beat behind when Perry Hale responded wit
training I've never had.

I would have turned and run with my tail betwee
my legs, but he attacked, pressing forward and usin
the AR hanging over his chest to push the thing away
Yolanda's tactical light snapped, revealing the bald
tattooed man from behind the wheel of the truck.

I was close enough to see he wasn't wearing a mask
The man had no expression at all. Only his unnaturall

wide eyes revealed life in that terrifying head. His wife-beater shirt was wet, and dark rivulets ran bloody from a bullet hole on the left side of his chest and onto baggy cargo shorts.

Damn, things happened fast.

A blade flashed twice in Yolanda's light. Blood flew from Perry Hale's arm.

Digging in with his feet, Perry Hale pushed again with his rifle, gaining a few inches. His right hand dropped to the gunslinger-style holster on his thigh, drawing his Beretta M9. It rose at the same time I stepped forward. Using my arm and shoulder, I swept the man's arm up and back, trapping the blade.

Even though the odds were with us in that two-on-one dance, the straight razor in the man's hand produced a feeling of dread I'd never known before. The thought of getting cut, getting slashed deeply by that thin edge, made my skin crawl.

Odd things registered.

The helicopter clattered overhead.

Another tree toppled nearby with the sound of snapping wood, the impact rising up through our feet.

"Drop!" Yolanda's voice barely carried over the noise. "Drop!"

I wasn't sure who she was talking to.

Perry Hale's left arm also rose, fending off the razor. He grunted with a sound that could have been terror or pain. I plowed in, matching the Thing's movement. It was the three of us in a macabre dance.

The Thing's slack face turned toward me, still howling.

I almost fell into the depths of those eyes full of madness.

The Thing threw an elbow into my side. I gave with the blow that was followed an instant later by that same elbow against my jaw. Lights flashed in front of my eyes. With three people fighting, it was hard to know where to hit or grab.

A shot rang out and I realized it was my Colt pressed into the Thing's side.

I squeezed the trigger again at the same time another pistol opened up. Perry Hale's weapon matched mine in a roll of thunder.

Like one of the falling trees, the Thing toppled backward and his head snapped to the side as it exploded under Yolanda's 5.56 round.

The slack face didn't change as he collapsed, rolling down the steep bank and into the river.

Perry Hale staggered back, holding his wounded arm. His face splashed with blood, he holstered his pistol. "What the hell was *that*?"

The voice that answered didn't belong to any one of us.

"It was the son I never had. I knew that bastard would be hard to kill."

Chapter 76

he old man I assumed was Daddy Frank stood only a
few feet away, hidden from the knees down by the
iverbank. I don't see how the man was drawing air.
oaking wet with river water, blood ran from wounds
1 his chest, abdomen, and left arm.

Daddy Frank!

Time slowed.

Salvadore warned me about that old man who he
alled the Devil, and said to kill him more'n once
vhen we got the chance.

A flat-bottom boat drifted downriver behind him.
Who the hell *are* you sonsabitches?"

He fired and Perry Hale *oof*ed, stumbling sideways.

"Who the hell *are* you?" The old man fired a second
ime, then shifted his aim.

From the corner of my eye I saw Yolanda's rifle
wing up. I was between her and the old man and turned
way from the intense light mounted on the weapon,
ne thought going through my head. *She's gonna shoot
ne by accident.*

He beat her and fired again. The muzzle blast mad
me think I was shot, too. She went over backward.

Damn, this old man can shoot!

My .45 rose at the same time I heard Dad in m
head. *Gunfights aren't won by the fastest man. It's t*
guy who takes his time and aims. Sight picture. Li
up. Shoot.

Daddy Frank Wadler's silhouette against the glitte
ing river disappeared behind the front sight as the Co
leveled.

I squeezed the trigger and it bucked once. Hal
blinded by the muzzle flash, I saw the old man stumb
sideways from the impact.

The Colt roared again as the helicopter clattere
back overhead; the searchlight beam probed the woo
and passed directly over us.

The old man who refused to die shot still agai
Flinching at the pressure wave, I ducked. Tucking bot
elbows against my body and pulling the big .45 close
I squeezed the trigger, and it bucked again, adding t
the flashes. The old man grunted, folded sideways.

Taking a lesson from my two friends who wer
likely dead, I kept squeezing the trigger until the slid
locked back. Muscle memory awoke, my thumb auto
matically pushing the magazine release button an
dropping the empty. I slapped in a fresh mag as the o
man disappeared from sight down the riverbank.
splash followed in the sudden silence.

Blinking my eyes clear, I rushed to the edge to se
him half in and out of the river.

The helicopter swooped around, lighting the scen
in harsh, bluish glare.

Shot to hell, that guy was tough as rawhide. Strug

ling weakly to stay on the surface as the current pulled
t him, he raised the pistol in my direction and I emp-
ed the second magazine.

That's when still another horror arose that night when
omething huge swirled up from the black depths.

The jaws of an enormous gator that had to have
een sixteen feet long snapped on that old bastard's
un arm. Daddy Frank screamed as the gator rolled,
ragging him under. The shriek ended in a gurgle as
vater filled his mouth.

The searchlight beam moved from the river and
ound me.

It held steady. An amplified voice filled the night.
You! On the riverbank! Put down your weapon! Fed-
ral agents! Put down your weapon now!"

Movement attracts attention. I held up my left hand,
nelt, and gently laid the empty Colt on a mound of
rass, then dropped to my knees with both hands in the
ir, waving to show they were empty. The helicopter's
ight locked on me as Perry Hale and Yolanda flitted
hrough the trees.

"We're good!" His voice reached me through the
lattering machine overhead.

"Thank God!"

"You're on your own. We're gone."

And they were.

Chapter 77

Tac lights flitted through the trees like fireflies in ragged skirmish line.

Perry Hale once again led the way with Yolanda o his heels. Moving downriver, they cut through th woods at a ninety-degree angle to the unidentifie army headed their way. Soon they left the helicopte behind and, using a compass, made a wide sweep bac toward their truck parked by the bridge.

When he was sure they were clear, Perry Hal stopped to feel under his vest for an entry wound. H breathed a little easier when his hand came out dr "Hit me in the plates. You all right, Yoli?"

She patted herself. "I can't believe they missed me. She saw his bloody sleeve. "You're cut."

"Yeah, but I've had worse."

Yolanda produced a compression bandage an wrapped it around his arm. "We made it out all right.

"We did." He checked his compass once again, the his watch. He pointed. "That way'll get us out in a hour."

"Wish we didn't have to leave Sonny behind."

"He'll be fine. They'll sort it out soon. Catching us ould stir up an ants' nest. He'll check in soon enough."

She slapped him on the shoulder to show she was ady and cut him a look. "Oh, and if you ever call me oli again, you're gonna walk with a limp for the rest f your life."

His teeth flashed. "Roger that."

Chapter 78

Gerald Marrs was the DEA agent in charge. Har Lowell commanded the ATF agents. They'd pulle everyone back to the highway turnoff onto the land Two undamaged SUVs that were at the end of the col umn were parked across the highway, blocking th road and their impromptu Command Post.

Two AFT agents wearing face masks brought Tan ner Wadler into the headlights of a black Ford Expedi tion waiting with all four doors opened wide. Hands i the pockets of his windbreaker, Agent Marrs studie the young man.

"Somebody danced on your face, son."

Tanner stifled a sob and pointed with his chin in th general direction of the barn's ruins. "My daddy did. I he dead?"

Marrs jerked his chin in the direction of the fire "Was he in there?"

"Yes."

"Don't know yet."

Agent Lowell joined them, scratching his hooke

ose. "You the one told Sheriff Gomez about the explosives?"

The young man swallowed. "Well, Uncle Alonzo
old me he had some. I just figured that if I told the
sheriff there was four hundred pounds, y'all'd move
faster."

"This guy's name was Alonzo?"

Tanner went pale at the question. "Yeah. He dead,
oo?"

Lowell shrugged. "He is if he was in the barn."

"He said there was plastic explosives under his
seat."

"He probably wasn't lying."

"Sir!" One of the agents with a battle-slung rifle
pointed.

Lowell swung around when a group of men appeared at the turnout. They came into clear relief when
four armed agents stepped into the light, bracketing a
single individual who looked as if he'd been through a
thrasher.

The man set a hat on his head just right until it suited
him. "Glad I found it. I feel better when I have my hat."
He noticed a cuffed man with a Fu Manchu mustache
and a pair of white-rimmed sunglasses on a Croakies
strap around his neck. The man glared with recognition
as he was dragged roughly away.

The man under the hat watched as the prisoner was
stuffed into the back seat of an unmarked SUV. "Where'd
you find him?"

Agent Lowell ran fingers through his gray hair. "Got
pulled over coming out here. Driving a truck registered
to a Sonny Hawke. His name ain't Hawke, though."

The stranger in the straw hat gave Fu Manchu a tight grin. "I recognize, you, too. You're the guy who ran me off the road. We're gonna have a talk about your driving before this is all over."

The agents spread out and the stranger stepped forward. The badge on his shirt caught the light. "Sonny Hawke, Texas Ranger. I've been tracking a guy named Alonzo Wadler all across the state, and I imagine he's probably floating in the air around us right about now. I believe I have a lot to tell you boys."

ACKNOWLEDGMENTS

This novel didn't happen without help. Friends and life experiences seasoned this work and brought it to its full potential. I'd like to thank the good folks here in the Lone Star State for their support and stories.

Thanks to John Gilstrap, who has been instrumental in my success, along with C. J. Box, Jeffery Deaver, Craig Johnson, Joe Lansdale, and dozens of friends and fellow authors who have been there as my writing career progressed. Y'all are great.

Much obliged to my outstanding agent Anne Hawkins, who believed in me from the start and continues to provide guidance. And a special thanks to my editor Michaela Hamilton and the great team at Kensington Publishing.

And of course, the love of my life is Shana, my anchor in this world.

Don't miss the next exciting Sonny Hawke novel

HAWKE'S FURY

Coming soon from Kensington Publishing Corp.

Keep reading to enjoy a sample excerpt . . .

Chapter 1

My position overlooking a two-track pasture road cutting through the rough West Texas rangeland gave me a clear view of three late-model charcoal gray Expeditions speeding in my direction across the hot Chihuahuan desert. Thick rooster tails of dust boiled behind the dark vehicles. A dozen cattle grazing on protein pellets barely noticed the SUVs. The dusty vehicles shot past two horses standing nearby, heads drooping in the heat.

The late evening sun stretched across the sage and ocotillo-covered pasture fifty miles north of where we live in Ballard, Texas. Harsh and dry, the landscape was dotted with catclaw cactus, sage, and creosote that stretched to the distance.

Buzzards rode the thermals high above, winding above the landscape in endless spirals. It was wide-open country once home to the Jumano Indians, who were pushed out by the Apaches that held the area until they too were finally driven almost to extinction.

White thunderheads towered all around us, supported by dark gray foundations that seemed to rest on the thin ragged line of the blue Davis Mountains to the northwest. I was hoping the closest storm that looked to be 50,000 feet tall would collapse, pushing welcoming shock waves of blessedly cool air across the flat valley floor.

Beside me, my runnin' buddy Sheriff Ethan Armstrong adjusted his straw hat and used his thumb to wipe a trickle of sweat from his temple. "Those two behind the lead car can't be seeing a stinkin' thing."

We spoke barely above a whisper. "I'd be following a little farther behind, that's for sure."

Not far away, two dark Suburbans were parked in a wide clearing where the pasture road split in two directions to flow around the little ridge behind us. Eight men dressed in baggy clothes and white bandanas waited with automatic weapons. They were spread out in a skirmish line with their backs to us, watching the oncoming SUVs.

"I'd be standing closer to those cars." Ethan cut his eyes toward me and absently pulled at the tender gray leaves of a nearby West Texas sage in full bloom. "When the shooting starts, everybody hunts a hole and I doubt sage and cactus's gonna be much cover."

"*El Norte* there'll be the first to go. Why's he standing right out in front of the car? He'd just as well have a big red target painted on his shirt. *I'm* burning up, and the least he could do is take off that blazer and roll up his sleeves."

Ethan snorted. "*El Norte*. What kinda name is that for a cartel leader?"

"How do I know? I didn't name the guy."

The dark Suburbans split up and stopped, facing the

other vehicles like gunfighters spreading out in a dirt street. The men inside waited as the boil of dust caught up and billowed around the cars.

"Dumb move."

Ethan nodded. "I was thinking the same thing. I'd've turned parallel for more cover and to get away if things go bad."

"Bad guys aren't usually the sharpest crayons in the box."

The worst of the dust was gone when the doors flew open. The men waiting with their backs to us tensed as armed gangsters poured out onto the dry hardpan.

I watched the men face off. "I still think they should be using the SUVs for cover."

"Amateurs."

"Which one's Gabe?"

I pointed at one of the men looking in our general direction. All but Gabe wore white T-shirts covered by unbuttoned plaid shirts. "That's him in the black blazer that just got out of the Expedition, beside Guero."

"He's wearing a coat in this heat, too. What's with that?"

I shrugged.

"Which one's Guero?

"The only guy who doesn't have a gun in his hand."

"He looks like somebody's grandpa."

Hollywood's version of a Mexican bad guy, the squatty man with thick rolled shoulders wore a gray mustache, loose-fitting off-white *frontera guayabera* shirt, and baggy khakis.

Beside him was Gabe Nakai, my dad's ranch manager and a close friend. The hair rose on the back of my neck, watching my old buddy in the company of armed gangsters from Ojinaga, across the Rio Grande.

Ethan must have sensed how I felt. "It ain't right seeing him down there, is it?"

"That and the priest's collar around his neck."

"I'm still working on that one, too." He tilted his head like a dog, as if looking at the scene from a different angle would help evaluate the situation. "That's something else that doesn't make sense in all this."

"Ours is not to reason why." Even I was surprised at my quote.

"Tennyson."

"You *did* listen in Miss Adams's English class."

"Naw, just memorized those lines for the test and for some reason they stuck with me, too."

El Norte still had his back to us, but his voice came loud and clear, a trick of the acoustics from the horseshoe bowl surrounding our position. His hair was so black and slicked back that it looked to be oiled. The side of his whisker-stubbled face we could see looked to be chiseled granite. "*Guero!* Did you bring my money?"

The Mexican national standing beside Gabe spread his hands. "My coke?"

El Norte flicked a command with his fingers. A gangster holding an AK-47 reached inside the open door of his SUV and withdrew a leather briefcase. He flipped the latches and dumped a pile of wrapped and taped packets onto the hood. The cartel leader waved his hand toward the drugs. "As promised."

"Who uses brand-new English leather briefcases

ese days? It's backpacks, mostly, from what I've seen."

than sighed. "This is making my head hurt."

I pointed at three more dark SUVs roaring down the
irt track, directly toward the scenario unfolding at an
chingly slow pace. "Who're *those* guys?"

"Don't know."

El Guero snapped his fingers and one of his men ap-
eared with a briefcase. Holding it awkwardly in one
and, he clicked the latches and it opened, revealing
he interior packed with hundred-dollar bills.

"They must have gotten a deal on briefcases at
Costco." Ethan cut his eyes to see if I'd take the bait
nd continue our evaluation, but I wanted to hear what
he gangsters were saying, so I concentrated on their
onversation.

"*Bueno,*" El Norte waved. "Make the deal."

Trouble started when the gangster tried to close the
riefcase. Losing his grip, it flipped out of his hand,
lumping the contents onto the ground. White paper cut
n the shape of U.S. currency exploded in a cloud, flut-
ering to the ground and revealing that the authentic
ills were only a thin layer on top.

El Norte shouted and retreated for cover behind an
pen car door. "*Mátalos!*"

Kill them!

The clear crack of a single gunshot opened the ball.
To a man, the cartel soldiers on both sides raised their
weapons and the world was filled with automatic gunfire. I found myself looking down the muzzle of a rifle
pointed at one of the gangsters standing in front of me.
My skin crawled at the flashes.

Reacting to the exchange of gunfire, Gabe grabbed

Guero by his collar and threw him into the back seat of their Suburban.

The gangster who fumbled the briefcase struggle with the rifle slung over his shoulder, fighting to brin it to bear on the men who had opened fire. Half a doze bloody explosions erupted from his light gray and blu paisley shirt. He wilted to the ground, face contorted i agony.

Men on both sides dropped like falling leaves whil those who survived the initial exchange scrambled fo cover. The hammering sounds of battle filled the ai echoing off the low rocky ridgeline behind our posi tion.

The approaching vehicles rolled into the scene onl seconds later, sliding to a stop in a thick cloud of dus The lead car angled toward Guero's parked SUV an sheared off the open driver's door, crushing a gangste who'd taken cover there.

His yelp of terror and pain was high and shrill butting through the air like a knife.

"Shit!" Ethan charged toward the car, waving hi arms. "Stop! Everybody stop!"

I followed, rushing past one of several movie cam eras filming the scene.

"Cut!" The director James Madigan rose from unde the umbrella beside his canvas chair. "Cut!" He turne to a woman holding a sheaf of papers. "Who the hel *are* these guys?"

Hard-looking men rolled from the newly arrived ve hicles. Dressed in everything from torn jeans, te shirts, track pants, and even an Adidas pullover, eac one had the rigid look of those who killed for a living obviously a hit team from a Chihuahuan cartel. Faces covered from their eyes down by a tangles of tattoos, they all carried automatic rifles.

An individual in a wife-beater shirt and torn jeans stepped out of the lead car's front passenger seat and pointed at the director. The only one without a bandana, his face was a web of tattoos. The year 1518 was etched into his forehead. "*Ese es Madigan. Mátalos!*"

Those words sent an icy knife through my stomach. "Ethan! No! This is real!" The smooth Sweetheart Grips of my 1911 Colt .45 filled my hand. I waved at the confused movie production team and the uncertain actors. "Down! Down! Everyone down!"

You've heard of that old saw where in times of stress time slows down. People say it seems they're moving through molasses, and they're right. Even more frustrating, the people I was warning simply looked at me without understanding. It wasn't their fault. Civilians hopefully go through life without experiencing trauma, and aren't trained to deal with life threatening situations. Unfortunately for me, they also go through life expecting nothing bad to happen.

Most law-enforcement officers are on the other end of that spectrum. They're always evaluating the world around them, thinking, "what if?" and planning for any and every event that might occur. But there was no training for what was unfolding on that hot desert floor.

Even Gabe, who'd been in more than his share of fights and gunfights, was startled at the sudden change from make-believe to reality. It took a couple of seconds before he could make sense of what was happening around us and shifted from a guy trying to make a few bucks as a movie extra, to a potential victim. Even *he* paused beside the open door to take in the scene.

I waved him back. "Gabe, get down! It's real!"

A gangster, this time a *real* gangster, leveled an AK-47 and held the trigger down, shredding the surprised director who went backwards, to land in the dust. The *cuerno de chivo,* or goat's horn, as they nicknamed the rifle because of the distinctive curved magazine, sprayed a stream of hot lead that also punched holes in anything and everyone around the shooter.

The thing we were there for was happening. Ethan and I were acting as security on the set of *The Mexican Pipeline*, a controversial movie that the Hidalgo Cartel in northern Chihuahua had targeted. They threatened to kill everyone involved if they continued filming the story depicting a fictionalized version of their cartel activities.

They were also known as 1518, the numbers signifying the year before Cortez landed on the shores of Mexico to conquer the Aztecs. The last year of their power before the destruction of an entire civilization.

A hard-looking tattooed gangster squeezed the trigger of what I took to be a Bushmaster spraying indiscriminate .223 rounds left and right. More men than I could have imagined streamed from the dusty SUVs and strolled casually through the movie set, firing on the terrified actors who scattered like quail. The guns in their hands belched fire and the assistant director tangled his feet and went down as rounds blew out his chest.

The chaos was complete. Actors and crew members screamed, scrambling for cover. Guns were everywhere, half in the hands of actors armed with blanks, and each one registered as threats to me and Ethan.

He and I charged into the melee, not by design, but because the only cover in the area was behind all the equipment used to film the movie. He jumped behind a stack of thick cases, using the only concealment he could find.

The words "thank God, thank God" repeated over and over in my mind, a chant of relief that my wife Kelly and our teenage twins Mary and Jerry weren't on the set. They'd been pestering me for weeks to come out and watch one day's shoot and I'd almost relented that morning.

My .45 came up and a guy holding a Bushmaster disappeared behind the front sight. I squeezed the trigger and he went straight down.

Before I could swing the muzzle to a second guy crouched not far away, he dropped from a round fired by Ethan. We weren't the only ones fighting back. My dad, Herman Hawke, was thirty feet away. He was also making a few extra bucks acting as the set's wrangler of two dozen head of cattle and horses used as backdrop stock.

A retired Texas Ranger, he was always armed. The Old Man took cover behind his pickup parked just off camera and drew his Colt. Sighting across the hood, the .45 barked. He shifted and fired again. His presence and demeanor in the suddenly real shoot-out was as calming to me as a Xanax.

I squeezed the trigger and my pistol barked again, heeling a gangster when the bullet's impact knocked one foot out from under him. I never said I was a good shot. A firm believer in the anchor shot, the Old Man drilled the wounded gangster twice more to keep him down.

Cameras exploded, bodies fell, and the roar of gun fire filled my ears. The cartel members continued to hose the area, spraying at random. Everything snapped back into real time as I juked behind a large metal box full of electronics and used the shoulder-high container as cover.

One of the only things on the law-enforcement side was that in all the gunfire, most of the bad guys weren't certain who was sending in return gunfire. Terrified movie people ran for cover in all directions and incongruously, I saw two of the actors return fire with their weapons loaded with blanks. Purely instinctive, their actions caused some of the cartel gangsters to take cover behind their own vehicles, but others returned fire murdering the terrified extras.

A hard-looking young man swung his *cuerno de chivo* in my direction. He was standing in the open, probably the way he'd seen it done on television or in movies. I shot him twice and he crumpled. Ethan emptied his Glock and dropped the magazine.

A string of explosions stitched the dirt around me. The guy who popped up slightly behind me would've had us both had his own mag not run dry. He was close enough to see the surprise in his eyes as he fumbled to reload. Ethan and I both put him down.

As three others sprayed the area with gunfire to keep our heads down, their tattooed leader struck a pose beside the car, fists on his hips, and shouted above the gunfire. "*La mujer del diablo de Chihuahua, la reina del Chihuahua,* the Devil Woman Queen of Chihuahua says that this movie will not be completed.

Next time we will kill everyone here!" He waved. "Vamos, chicos!"

Doors slammed seconds later and the three SUVs filled with their surviving gangsters spun in tight circles, speeding away back down the same dry pasture road. I rose and punched holes in the windows and sheet metal until they were out of range.

As soon as they were gone, the air was filled with dust, cries, and screams. I sensed the crew members rushing around as I kicked the weapons away from the real cartel members on the ground.

Ethan joined me beside the first young man I'd shot. "I think I'm gonna go back to smoking again."

Before I could answer, the wounded man's arm rose, beckoned, then fell.

"This guy's still alive." I knelt beside him, patting the kid down to make sure he didn't have any other weapons. Finding none, I pulled the bandana with a skeleton's face down to reveal a smooth, unlined face.

Someone joined me and I saw it was Gabe. He ripped the boy's shirt open to reveal a dark puckered hole in his upper chest and covered the wound with the palm of his hand.

"This looks bad."

The Old Man's voice came from behind me. "It is. There's two more holes down lower."

Blood welled from between Gabe's fingers. His eyes were filled with sadness. "He's not much older than Angie."

I understood how he felt. Angie was his high school-age daughter, and I had a set of twins the same age. "He's older than he looks, and he also tried to kill us."

The boy's eyes flicked open and he whispered.

"Padre." It took a second to realize he was looking at Gabe's priest collar. "*Quiero confesion.*"

Gabe shook his head and answered in Spanish. "*No soy un sacerdote.*"

I'm not a priest.

"*Confesion.*" The boy turned his pleading gaze to me. He must have recognized the cinco peso badge on my shirt. "*Guardebosque, to lo ruego. Pidele que me confesion.*"

Guardebosque is what some Mexicans call us Texas Rangers.

"It won't hurt to hear him, Gabe." The Old Man's voice was soft.

My eyes burned, because I was watching a boy die from my gunshots. I know, he'd been trying to kill me, but I also saw my son Jerry lying there.

The dying man groaned and switched to English. "I need to say something." The statement was a shock, because he spoke with little accent. "I need to tell you something."

The back of my neck prickled.

Gabe met my eyes, then leaned down to better hear. "*Adelante.*"

The dying man held Gabe's hand and whispered in his ear for a moment, as the ranch hand cum actor cum priest, listened intently as his voice weakened, then stopped. The gangster's eyes lost focus and drifted off to the side as he gasped, convulsed, and went limp.

His death brought me completely back into the real world of panicked victims, crying men and women, and unheard orders issued to people who simply wandered among the bloody carnage with vacant expressions.

Licking his dry lips, Gabe straightened. "Oh my God."

I saw fear in his eyes and leaned in. "What'd he say?"

"He's a federal agent, undercover, and there was another agent with these guys, too."

My head reeled at the thought of shooting a brother in arms. The attack unreeled in my mind. He was firing his weapon, but I hadn't seen anyone fall. Was he shooting over everyone's heads?

No. I'd looked directly down the muzzle of his weapon when it was aimed at me and remembered seeing muzzle flashes. My stomach clenched. "Is that what he confessed?"

"No. Worse."

When he told me what the dying boy said, my blood went cold.

"He says the 1518, the Mujer Malvada cartel is sending more hit teams between here and Van Horn. They have a plan to clear a path through the Border Patrol for the drugs and people coming across the river. More people are going to die."

My blood chilled. An organized hit team targeting the Border Patrol was in my country, and I wasn't going to stand for it.

Connect with Us

Visit us online at
KensingtonBooks.com
to read more from your favorite authors, see books
by series, view reading group guides, and more.

for sneak peeks, chances to win books and prize packs,
and to share your thoughts with other readers.

facebook.com/kensingtonpublishing
twitter.com/kensingtonbooks

Tell us what you think!

To share your thoughts, submit a review,
or sign up for our eNewsletters, please visit:
KensingtonBooks.com/TellUs.